The
BREAK-UP
AGENCY

The BREAK-UP AGENCY

SHEILA McCLURE

LAKE UNION
PUBLISHING

Text copyright © 2022 by Sheila McClure
All rights reserved.

Published by Lake Union Publishing, Seattle

www.apub.com

Amazon, the Amazon logo, and Lake Union Publishing are trademarks of Amazon.com, Inc., or its affiliates.

ISBN-13: 9781662505331
ISBN-10: 1662505337

Cover design by The Brewster Project

Printed in the United States of America

For Chantal. You are wondrous for surviving Beige Tony, The Boyfraud, Sleazy Jet, GI James, Surf's-up Sam, The Dog Stalker and Phil McCavity — none of them deserved you. But someone does, and I can't wait until they find you.

Chapter One

It was, to be fair, a perfect night to dump someone. An exquisite bouquet of misery. Pouring rain. A bitterly cold wind. A restaurant soon-to-be-single Dave couldn't bear. Oh look! There was even a leak in the ceiling. Tremendous. Ellie called the waiter over and ordered some salt and pepper squid. If she'd timed things right (and she usually did), the dish would arrive shortly after Dave did. Dave hated salt and pepper squid. And Ellie hated unnecessary emotional pain. Which was why they would end things tonight.

After the waiter left, Ellie pulled a few strands of hair free from either side of her topknot so that they lightly covered her ears, then shared a complicit smile with the woman sitting at the table opposite her. She was offered a half-smile in return, but no lasting eye contact as she too was tweaking her hair. Unnecessary, of course – it was perfect as it was – but Ellie wasn't surprised. The fidgets were inevitable when sitting on your own in a restaurant. Worse if you were waiting to smash someone's heart into bits. Never mind. They'd both leave with smiles on their faces. She was sure of it.

The waiter reappeared to replace the red plastic mop bucket that sat beneath the leak with an empty metal one. A surprisingly loud plopping sound pulled Ellie to attention. Not. Ideal. Then again, if this was an ideal world, Ellie wouldn't be preparing to crack poor, unsuspecting Dave's heart in two.

She'd tape it back together again. *Obviously.* But first came the pain.

A rush of gratitude that she'd done this a few times swept through her. A year ago she'd have been vainly attempting to wring her hands free of the shakes or running to the loo with the dry heaves. These days, when it came to nipping things in the bud, she was far more disciplined. Able to curb her more visceral responses to the privacy of her flat. A bit of a weep. A cuddle with her dog. But right now? She had to be clear-eyed with only one goal in sight: singledom. Even now, it was still a revelation. What the world looked like without rose-tinted glasses. Her solitary concession of gratitude to Sebastian was that he'd enabled her to see the world, very, *very* clearly. Discovering that he hadn't loved her after all had torn something open in her. Rather than bleeding out and dying of a broken heart as she thought she might, the wound had unearthed a character trait she hadn't known she'd possessed. Resilience. She hadn't realised it straight away, of course. Didn't witness it in a heavenly ray of sunshine or a message burnt into her morning toast. No. It had come later. The initial wounds from the demise of her long-term relationship had cut so deep her body had gone into shock. She'd been unable to feel the pain. The second bombshell had been that she'd *wanted* to feel it. So she'd dug as deep into her pulped emotional foundation as she could, then shapeshifted the anguish into something positive and proactive. Empowering.

All of which meant, these days, she could break up with some-one with the same emotional ease with which she selected a loaf of bread. It was her superpower.

Present the relationship and its fault lines clearly, then – *fwiiip!* Pull the plug. It rarely took long for the penny to drop, was far more effective than faffing about with *I'm not really in the right place* platitudes, and actively took the sting out of an *I'm just not that into you* ending. Whoever said you had to be cruel to be kind was full of it.

She glanced at her phone when a text pinged in. Dave. He'd emerged from the Underground. Good. They were a two-minute-and-ten-second walk from the tube station. More likely ninety seconds in the rain. Dave had long legs. She set the timer on her phone and gave the woman across from her – aka her client Cassie Booth – a quick *this is it* smile before thumbing through her notes one last time.

Next, a moment of stillness before the storm. She closed her eyes, slowed her breath, and conjured up an image of Dave. Her heart softened. He'd chosen his profile picture well. Smiley, lanky, and with a full mop of curly brown hair in adorable need of a comb. He looked kind. Almost to a fault. Well, in this case, definitely to a fault, but that was by the by. She could see why Cassie had swiped right. He was good-looking in the kind of way that you wouldn't necessarily want to rip his clothes off and have wanton sex but you might fancy undoing a button or two if he gave you his umbrella in a sudden downpour.

Generous too. As much as his teacher's salary and London prices would allow. But Ellie would've been the first to remind people that generosity didn't mean opening up your wallet. It meant opening up your heart. For weeks now, Dave's heart had been open like the front doors of Selfridges on sales day. Tonight, it was her job to ensure that the remains of his soft-hearted wares were left unpillaged. Refortified would be even better. And luckily for Dave, that was the plan. Over the next few minutes he'd experience a swift ripping off of the Band-Aid. The quick, deft press of a hand to dull the pain would come later. Her own experiences in pain management had taught her that it wasn't yet a perfect system.

She'd get there eventually, but, like any novice superhero, she was still navigating the best way to recover from throwing herself in front of the rejection bullets and absorbing the pain herself so the rejectee didn't have to. If she could, Ellie would gladly rip her own heart from her chest and lay it next to Dave's for comfort while he got used to the fact that his and Cassie's would no longer beat as one. But some pain, sadly, was inevitable.

That's what happened when the love mist became a thick, impenetrable fog. To be fair, Dave's poor brain was being held hostage by an all-consuming love buzz. Life was still sunshine and roses for him. Unicorns and butterfly kisses. His ability to see things clearly was completely disabled by an oxytocin takeover. In contrast, Cassie's frontal cortex had kicked back into action just over a week ago. At which point, she'd seen some very clear writing on the wall: the party was over. So she'd called Ellie at Softer Landings.

As predicted, timing at precisely ninety seconds, the storm blew in Dave and his dismembered umbrella. Ellie's heart swooped round her chest and lodged in her throat. Beneath his drenched winter duffel, Dave was dressed head to toe as Thor.

Synthetic, shoulder-length, blond wig. Faux-six pack covered by an all-in-one body suit with detachable red cape. Plastic hammer.

Poor Dave. He didn't deserve this. Nor, Ellie reminded herself, did he deserve to be in a relationship that was doomed. If she'd known the same thing about herself seven years earlier, who knew where she'd be now? Still doing the break-ups for her sister's endless stream of suitors – for free – no doubt. Heaven knew how she'd come up with so many ways to make them think another path would be the route best to take. Attention to detail, she supposed. Everyone had a dream. And on an island as small as Jersey it wasn't difficult to tap into it, tweak a few things and then, hey presto! Suddenly the world was seen through a brand-new filter and Aurora was free to run off and break someone else's heart.

Anyhoodle. That was then and this was London. She crammed her personal feelings back into their Ziploc bag, pinched it shut and got to work. She tapped a finger to her ear, made eye contact with Cassie and whispered, 'Ready?'

'Maybe?' Cassie winced, her back stiffening against the breeze as Dave, still at the door, shook the raindrops off his inside-out umbrella.

'Well, get ready,' Ellie spoke into the microphone on her wrist, priming herself as much as Cassie. 'He's here.'

This wasn't meddling, she reminded herself through the loud buzz of nerves that always kicked in about now. It was *helping*. Because of her, Dave would regain weeks, if not months, of his life that would otherwise be lost to a relationship that could crush his belief that he was a man worthy of someone's love. And just like that her focus snapped to twenty-twenty.

'Alright, team,' Ellie whispered. 'Operation Adios Dave is live.'

Fifteen seconds later

Dave spied Cassie, smiled as if he'd just been washed in sunshine, then wove his way through the restaurant to her table. Ellie was in her element. A director creating a highly choreographed break-up designed to hurt no more than a tumble into a pit full of fluffy marshmallows.

It took precision. Focus. And every ounce of empathy she possessed. For both parties, obviously, but mostly for Dave.

As directed, her colleague Simon swept through the front door of the sparsely populated restaurant with classic Scene Stealing 101 panache and bellowed, 'Darling! Soz about the time. It's *horrendous* out there.' Though he was headed straight for Ellie, arms outstretched and smile cranked up to full dazzle, she caught his energy briefly divert to Cassie and Dave, who were going through the *awful weather, isn't it* phase of sorting out his coat, figuring out where to put his wind-mangled brolly and getting him settled at their table. Cassie, Ellie noted, had yet to comment on the Thor ensemble.

'Oooh! What's this?' Simon narrowly avoided tripping over the bucket collecting awkwardly timed raindrops. 'The newest accoutrement for Swimming Pool Barbie?'

Ellie gave an appreciative smirk but said nothing. Cassie was nervous-tugging on the sleeves of her jumper, which created a rustling noise against the miniature microphone pinned inside the cuff. It made hearing Dave's side of their conversation just that little bit trickier. Nevertheless, Simon's breezy arrival had done precisely what it was meant to: take the immediate edge off Cassie's nerves while getting Dave in place, which, after a bit of a wrestling match with the zipper of his saturated duffel, finally happened.

From her table, Ellie could see both Dave and Cassie's faces. Simon, who claimed to have been cruelly overlooked by an MI5 recruiter when he was at St Andrews, had a sixth sense for knowing exactly how to angle his chair so that Ellie could keep a continuous eye on the clients throughout the break-up experience while looking as if she was utterly engaged in conversation with him. He leant in for a left-then-right cheek kiss, using the proximity to whisper the news that Thea was ready and waiting under the awning of a nearby newsagent's but had forgotten an umbrella so wanted things to move along sharpish. The Princess Leia costume wasn't much of a buffer against the elements.

'Not a problem,' Ellie murmured. And then more brightly. 'Shall we order?'

It was Cassie's first cue. The easiest. All she needed to do was ask Dave how his day had been. Through a series of trial-and-error

6

break-ups in both her personal (thank you, Aurora) and professional capacities, Ellie had learnt that the *how was your day, dear* manoeuvre was the most efficient way to gauge how the tone of a break-up should proceed. If Dave had had a rotten day, it was best to dive right in with a rueful, 'I'm afraid I'm about to make it worse.' If this was the case, Ellie would cancel the squid. No additional squirts of lemon juice in the wound required.

If Dave had had a good day and presumed it was only going to get better, experience dictated it was best to ease into the bad news. Not for long, of course, but the squid would definitely give the downward spiral a twist in the right direction.

Ellie nodded encouragingly as Cassie asked him how his day had been. An excellent sta— No! *No, no, no!* Instead of listening to Dave's answer – he'd had a *GREAT* day, couldn't *WAIT* to see her – Cassie was craning round towards Ellie for her next line. A classic school nativity mistake.

Eye contact with anyone but Dave could instantly expose the fact that she'd hired Ellie and her team at Softer Landings to help end things. She had, but the entire point of hiring them was for the dumpee to leave the Softer Landings experience oblivious to the fact that it had been a set-up. (A snip at £109.99 plus expenses. Packages may vary depending upon the nature of the break-up. Terms and conditions apply.) Instead of returning the imploring look, Ellie signalled to the waiter hovering at the kitchen door. He lurched into action and, as requested, slid the slate of artfully piled salt and pepper squid on to the table between Cassie and Dave.

The effect was instantaneous.

Dave lurched back with a weird guttural noise, then painstakingly forced himself to scooch back in, regroup, and apologise through some astonishingly fulsome gagging sounds. Gosh. He really did hate squid.

'Sorry,' he finally managed. 'It's the – *urp* . . . I told you I have a thing about that smell, right?'

He had. Which was why Cassie had listed it in the *Things Your Future Ex Hates* section of their information sheet. Apparently, Dave's prankster brother had been inspired by a string of drying squid during a long-ago family trip to Corsica and had pelted his younger brother with them until he'd given up the 'good' snorkelling mask for his brother's 'inferior' one. Ellie felt Dave's pain. Her little sister also had that myopic ability to zero in on what she wanted and grab it, regardless of anyone else's feelings. Sebastian had been the only thing she'd never touched.

'Do you think we should've brought an epi pen?' Simon asked, more repulsed by the noises than concerned about Dave's imminent demise.

'Not allergic,' Ellie said in a way that made it clear to Simon that he should know by now she always did her homework. 'PTSD. Bad holiday.'

'*Erp*,' blurped Dave. 'Sorry. Corsica.'

'Should've gone to Sardinia,' Simon sniffed. 'Much better seafood.'

Dave patted his plastic Thor tummy and grimaced. 'I'm a sensitive little bear sometimes. *Uumph*. Sorry.'

Cassie impaled a squid ring with her fork then aeroplaned it towards him. 'Are you sure? These look really good.'

'No!' he screeched. 'I mean, please, you go ahead. They're all yours. Enjoy.' Urp. 'Sorry.' His reaction was much more painful to witness than Ellie had thought it would be. She made a silent note to herself not to do food aversions any more. Dave gave his throat a scratch and blew out a weird snort, then rubbed his hands together as if it had suddenly gone really, really cold inside. 'So! Are you looking forward to tonight?' He looked around the table and then under it. 'Where's your costume?'

Ellie sat up straight. *Here we go, Cassie. It's break-up time.*

'Yeah . . . ummm—' Cassie gave the squid a squeeze of lemon juice as Ellie cued her with her next line.

'I wanted to talk to you about that.'

'I wanted to talk to you about that,' Cassie echoed, then speared another forkful of squid, dunked it in the garlic sauce and ate it in a oner.

'Well done. Just stick to the script and this'll be over in no time.'

'Ahhh, Comic Con.' Dave sighed, a genuine smile blooming on his sweet, about-to-be-single face. 'What do you want to know? I've been going pretty much every year since I was born. My dad and I—'

'I know,' Cassie cut him off, clearly having heard the story multiple times. 'He brought you in a baby carrier dressed as an Ewok.' Cassie said *Ewok* the way a carnivore might say *vegan*.

Dave finished the story anyway, and with a hint of cruelty that reinforced Ellie's commitment to giving Dave the very best of break-ups, Cassie began waving a piece of squid in front of Dave's increasingly pale face. The waiter appeared at their table and pointedly began listing the specials.

'Dial it back, Cassie,' Ellie whispered as the waiter talked the not-so-happy couple through a winter squash risotto, a beef cheek stew and a twice-grilled pork chop. 'We want him to leave feeling happy to be him, not ashamed.'

Cassie put down her fork, unfolded her serviette, covered her mouth with it and whispered, 'This is *painful.*'

'I know, but you hired me to make it less so. For *both* of you. Trust in the process.'

Cassie shot her a look. Ellie gave her an encouraging smile then signalled that she really should be paying attention to Dave now that the waiter had gone.

Cassie lowered her serviette, snapping it out to lay on to her lap, inadvertently sending a proper cloud of squid scent straight into Dave's face. As if trying to escape the fabled cephalopod assault of his childhood, Dave jerked up and out of his chair, accidentally knocking over the metal bucket and slipping on the now wet floor. Rather than help him, the waiter stomped over, handed poor Dave the mop, then flounced off to find the *Caution: Wet Floor* sign that should have been there in the first place. After cleaning the floor and handing the mop back to the waiter, a decidedly more frazzled Dave collapsed back on to his seat, managing to sit on his cape and choke himself in the process. Compassion, or, more likely, the gagging noise, finally pushed Cassie into action. Face reading like a sleep-deprived mother of an exhausting toddler, she unsnapped his cape, tugged his wig back into place, then sat down in her chair with a decidedly grim, 'So. Comic Con.'

Dave gave an intense little nod, actively narrowing his field of focus so that it didn't include the squid. 'I can answer any questions you have.'

This was the point where Ellie truly felt herself come into her own. The moment in which she would briefly take the reins of Dave's life and steer him towards a new destiny.

Cassie gave her head a sorrowful shake. 'That's the thing,' she said, almost speaking the words in tandem with Ellie as she spoke quietly into her wrist. 'I don't have any questions because . . . I don't think I should go.'

Ellie's heart squeezed tight as Dave's mouth began to open and close like a goldfish, as if the right response might silently float in then come back out again as actual words. 'But . . .' he finally managed, 'this is my three-month anniversary present to you.' Cassie ignored Ellie's suggested *And that's very kind of you, but*, opting for a much more pointed 'I think it's more like your three-month anniversary present to you.'

'What?' Dave gave a half-pained, half-perplexed look over his shoulder, not because he suspected his girlfriend was being fed lines, but because he couldn't entirely understand what he was hearing.

Cassie sighed heavily. 'It's just that – Comic Con is what *you* love. Not what I love.'

Dave's dismay escalated, along with the pitch of his voice. 'But I thought the whole point of a relationship was to share the things we loved with one another.'

'I love salt and pepper squid,' Cassie parried.

Dave's hand flew to his mouth.

Ellie growled into her wrist, 'You want him to leave here *happy*, not vomiting. Tell him something you like about him.' Inspiration struck. 'The dimple on his cheek!'

As if Ellie had spoken actual magic words, Cassie's body language suddenly changed. She signalled to the waiter to take the squid away and took Dave's hands in hers. 'Do you know the first time I realised you had a dimple in your cheek?'

Dave shook his head, his expression reading like someone desperately trying to catch up with the plot of a Shostakovich opera when their grasp of Russian peaked at *borscht*.

As Ellie whispered, Cassie continued, 'The first time I knew you had a dimple was on our third date.'

Dave frowned then raised his forehead as the memory arrived. 'Oh yeah! We saw that Polish movie.'

'Czech,' Cassie corrected.

'Total downer,' Dave said at the same time Cassie sighed, 'Exquisite film.'

Dave cocked his head to the side. 'Didn't we go to that restaurant after? The one where they brought little bits round on trolleys and we had to go to Five Guys?'

Cassie nodded. 'Dim sum with a cheese-burger chaser, yes.'

'Back to the dimple, Cassie,' whispered Ellie.

'Anyway.' Cassie waved off the foreign film and dim sum fail. 'We were talking about *Hamlet* and you told me how one of your proudest moments as a teacher was when you'd used Spider-Man's origin story as a means of explaining Hamlet's angst.'

Dave's face lit up and then . . . *ping!* . . . the dimple appeared. 'Yes!' He laughed with pure delight. 'The Peter Parker Parent Problem!' His features turned soft and wistful as he cradled the plastic hammer to his artificial six-pack. 'It's an imperfect theory, of course. Peter's parents were killed in a plane crash and it was actually his uncle who died a violent death, but it really showed how the loss of a loved one combined with guilt and an all-consuming desire for revenge can define the man you become . . .' He gave a contented, deep-dimpled sigh. 'That was a beautiful classroom moment.'

Awwww. He looked so, so happy. Ellie sniffed.

Simon gave her an eye roll.

As a rule, she didn't tend to get emotional during the break-ups. Feeding the lines required her full attention, but sometimes, like right now, it got to her. Like saving a kitten.

Ellie whispered, 'You deserve a life filled with beautiful moments.'

Cassie repeated the line as if she were in a Latin telenovela, cupping Dave's face in her hands, then abruptly pulling them back into her lap as if reminding herself he was now forbidden fruit. It was a nice touch. Ellie would remember that one.

Dave's brow furrowed. 'I do?'

'You do,' confirmed Ellie.

Cassie nodded and swiped at a crocodile tear as Ellie fed her another line. 'You deserve someone who is fuelled by your passions. Who understands where you're coming from. Your very own Pepper Potts.'

Dave pulled back, his face creased in an involuntary grimace. 'Pepper Potts was with Tony Stark. Peter Parker's girlfriend was Mary Jane Watson.'

'Oh, Dave,' Ellie said, 'how do you even put up with me?'

Cassie repeated the line in the same hapless but adorable way in which Meg Ryan gently informs her buttoned-up fiancé that their destinies would never be intertwined. Undeterred, Dave began a detailed soliloquy on the Marvel couplings. He was so swept away he failed to notice Cassie clearly didn't give a monkey's until, when he hit secondary character couplings, she openly yawned. 'There's a lot to take on,' he conceded.

Cassie covered her face with her hands. When she dropped them away, a solitary tear snaked its way down her cheek. 'You deserve someone who knows all of this, Dave. Someone who can feed off your love for all things Marvin.'

'Marvel.'

'Whatever.'

'You can learn,' he pleaded. 'I have spreadsheets!'

Ellie thought her heart might break. This was one of those pivotal moments when Dave would either see the writing on the wall, or need it spelt out letter by painful letter. This relationship wouldn't make him happy no matter how many spreadsheets he had.

Ellie saw a change in Cassie's demeanour. She looked taller. Liberated. She'd crossed that emotional bridge to freedom and was not turning back. 'Softer now,' Ellie instructed. 'Gently. As if you were easing your granny into her favourite chair.'

'I don't want to learn, Dave,' Cassie consoled. 'Or wear costumes. Or spend hours analysing the differences between the comic and the film.'

'Wait.' Everything about him stilled and then, finally, the horrific truth hit him between the eyes. '*What?*

Ha! Got him. Ellie smiled as he continued, his emotional investment in the relationship held taut like a slingshot about to fire a crucial missile.

'You said on your profile you were a Wonder Woman fan. I know that's DC Comics, but how can you not—' He stopped himself then asked, 'What *do* you like?'

Cassie rattled through an impressive list of things she loved she knew Dave didn't, wrapping up with a not entirely apologetic 'I want to watch films with subtitles.'

Dave barked a loud laugh. 'You obviously haven't seen *Guardians of the Galaxy*. No one in it speaks English. They all have these two-way translator chips—'

'That's great,' Cassie cut in, in a tone generally reserved for six-year-olds. 'And, in the spirit of honesty, I think at this point, you should know that I don't actually care.'

Ellie winced. Dave froze, the pronouncement hovering between them like one of Cupid's poison-tipped arrows.

'But it's a defining—'

Cassie placed a single finger on his lips. 'Shhh.'

Dave sat back in his chair, distractedly bonking his Thor hammer on the table. He considered Cassie in the way one might squint at a complicated mathematical equation on a chalkboard.

'What *have* you enjoyed doing with me?' he eventually asked.

Cassie gave a sheepish shrug as her cheeks pinked up. 'Sex.'

He gave a *fair enough* nod and Ellie's shoulders dropped an inch. Being told he was a stud had definitely softened the blow. According to her *Ending It With Ease Enquiry* on the Softer Landings website, Cassie had had a bit of a dry spell in the sex department. Dave had been the first in a relatively long line of dates who'd finally met most of her requirements: a tidy flat, fresh milk in the fridge, regularly changed sheets and the added bonus that he was a bit of a Clark Kent in the sex department. After a couple of months of not bothering with the getting-to-know-you part of things, Dave had insisted that they try out some traditional courting. Dinner. Movies. That sort of thing. Getting to know one another had been their kryptonite.

Now it was Dave's turn to use the gentle *there, there* tone. He made an *it pains me to say this, but I'm going to say it anyway* face. 'I want to be loved for more than my body.'

Cassie valiantly kept a straight face as Dave continued. 'Do you think maybe we should call it a day? I mean – I think you're great and everything, and if you want to stay friends, that's cool, but . . .' He gave his heart a bonk with his hammer. 'I'm looking for something a bit more meaningful on the relationship front. Something genuine. This might be time to . . . to take different paths.'

Cassie gave a forlorn little shaggy-bobbed shake, her eyes sparkling with unspilt tears. 'I think two separate paths might be a good idea.'

Ellie beamed and into her wrist whispered, 'Well done, Cassie. You are officially single.'

Chapter Two

Ellie inserted her key into the lock of her minuscule studio flat and a flurry of motion ensued. She could hear books being swiped off the bedside table, a step stool clatter across the strip of linoleum in the 'kitchen' and the *bang, bang, bang* of a tail on the wall. Gus, a 'failed' guide dog, was, quite simply, the best flatmate in the world. He was a picture of pure elation when she opened the door, tail wagging as if they'd been separated for months.

If Cassie hadn't been allergic, he probably would've joined them tonight. As an active service dog, he was allowed into restaurants and was a frequent participant in the Softer Landings jobs, ably providing any number of services. Mournful, yet sympathetic looks. A head to pat. Ears to stroke. And, in the case of one briefly heartbroken soul, an instant babe magnet. Ellie shut the door behind her, sank to the floor and, because it was pretty much the law, booped Gus's brown nose. He perched up on his haunches and wrapped his golden, furry paws around her neck while she had her requisite post-break-up sob. It never lasted more than a couple of minutes, but it felt necessary. A purging of all of the highly charged emotions. Thea and Simon usually did shots. After her tears abated, she gave him a watery smile. 'You ready for your walk?'

He wagged his tail until his entire body wiggled along with it. She hugged him again, ever grateful for the undiluted joy he exuded. She dreaded the day when they would have to part ways. She stuffed that particular horror back into her pocket along with a couple of poo bags, pulled on her well-worn sou'wester and together they headed out to the canal.

After their walk, she and Gus shook off as much of the rain as they could before entering the Flower & Tun, a canal-side pub where she, Simon, and Thea held their post-break-up debriefs. After greeting the owner, Jasper, Gus pootled over to the open fire to steam himself dry. 'Tough one tonight?' Jasper asked.

Ellie tipped her head side to side. 'Not too bad. Well, happy in the end. Unless Thea has something earth-shattering to report.'

'Well done, buttercup.' He held up his hand for a high-five, a move incongruous with his hipster Santa Claus aesthetic. 'The regular?'

She patted her palm to his and grinned. 'Yes, please.' Anonymity in London was easy. Having someone who knew you liked your hot chocolate with seven mini-marshmallows? A triumph. To be fair, Ellie and her team had adroitly extracted Jasper from a year-long relationship a few months back so she knew him a bit better than some of the other regulars. Jasper was an alpha teddy bear. A man as capable of pulling apart a pair of brawling drunks as listening to a weeping twenty-something pour out her heart. Which was probably why his girlfriend had adored him. But her day job, dominatrix, had filled his head with one too many images he'd been unable to shake and, with genuine sorrow, he'd asked Ellie for help. His ex was now happily in love with an accountant called Marcus Plinth, who had recently proposed. Jasper had yet to dip his toes back into the dating pool, preferring to 'watch and learn' for the time being. At his age, he said, he wanted to find The One and see the relationship through to heaven's gate.

'You go on over to your office, love.' He nodded towards a corner booth near the fireplace with a reserved sign on it. 'I'll bring it over.' Though she, Simon and Thea had devised the concept of Softer Landings at the recruitment agency where they'd met and still had day jobs, they'd decided early on that water-cooler debriefs wouldn't go down well with their boss, Vee. Vee actively encouraged an entrepreneurial spirit among her staff at Media Angels and was always on the lookout for innovative enterprises – but not if the side hustle infringed on their work hours. Times, she regularly reminded them, were tough. The two vacant offices that had housed Vee's ex-partners were daily reminders of this. Simon had it on good authority that Vee had remortgaged her house and cashed in her ISAs to buy them out when they'd pushed to sell to their main competitor after Covid lockdowns had virtually disembowelled the business. The partners escaped to the country to flesh out their cottagecore lifestyles while Vee proactively pursued urban renewal. Lockdown had made the world ravenous for content, and Media Angels had the staff to make it happen. And now it was . . . on her terms.

Simon arrived at the pub a couple of minutes later and ordered a bottle of Pinot Noir and three packets of crisps – most likely the only food he'd eaten that day.

'How's Diego?' Ellie asked.

He pointedly kept his eyes on her as he poured himself a goblet of wine more suited to a giant.

'Ah.' She gave his hand a pat but knew not to press. While she, Simon and Thea spent countless hours together, their private lives were just that. Well, Ellie's was separate from the long-term besties, anyway. They'd never spoken about it, or set boundaries. They'd pre-existed in the same way Ellie had always known she would never be one of the popular girls at school. She hadn't had the hair for it, for starters.

'Her Highness has arrived.' Simon nodded towards the pub door, where Thea was dramatically revealing her Princess Leia ensemble, then fake lightsabering everyone who stood between her and their booth. She hung her saturated, ankle-length puffa jacket on the corner of their booth and, after checking he was dry, commanded Gus to climb up beside her to act as a hot-water bottle.

'How'd it go?' Ellie asked.

Thea's phone pinged. She snatched it up from the table, her frown turning into a wicked grin as she read.

'Looks like Dave wasn't the only one to score at Comic Con,' Simon intoned.

'Don't be jelly, Simone.'

Ellie winced. A year on, you'd think she'd be used to Thea calling Simon Simone, excepting the rare moments when she was very, very cross with him. Somehow it didn't seem entirely PC, but Simon never batted an eye.

Thea took a glug of Simon's drink then purred, 'Not my fault you're in a relationship and can't enjoy the perks of the job.'

'Umm . . . oh . . . so . . . Does that mean you hooked up with Thor?' Ellie had been aiming for a super-casual tone, but Thea's annoyed huff made it clear she'd failed. After a few Softer Landings snafus in the early days, Thea 'problem solved' by dating the newly dumped boyfriends, only to have to call on Ellie to break *them* up. After that, they'd made a strict no-picking-up-the-dumpee rule for staff. Staff, meaning Thea.

'Puh-lease.' Thea flicked the notion of having it off with Dave into the ether. 'What do you take me for?'

'A strumpet,' said Simon as he topped up his drink.

'A sexy Stormtrooper's strumpet.' Thea beamed, turning her phone round to show a picture of her being held up like a 1940s film star by four Stormtroopers.

Simon peered at the picture. 'Which one are you shagging?'

Thea shrugged. 'Dunno yet.' She began to hum the theme song to *Jaws*.

'Wrong film, stoopid.'

'Not if I plan on taking *all* of them under my control,' Thea countered, trying and failing to make her lightsaber snap out to its full length, but managing to knock Simon's rapidly emptied wine bottle to the floor.

Being the deeply mature thirty-somethings that they were, Thea and Simon began to play-fight. Ellie moved their glasses of wine out of the way as the lightsaber fell to the ground and they launched into a vibrant round of slappety hands. Ellie tried and failed to cover up a yawn.

'Awww, look, Thea.' Simon sat back against the wooden bench, winded by the exertion. 'Our widdle biddle Ellikins is about to turn into a pumpkin. Is it sleepy time for our little country mouse?'

Thea made clucking noises.

Their *Big City Mummy and Daddy* act no longer threw her hackles up as it once had. It wasn't as if she'd put in a pre-birth request to be born and raised on a sparsely populated island only to discover she had absolutely no clue about so-called 'real life'. Or, more accurately, London.

To be fair, their paths had crossed when Ellie had all but literally just got off the boat from Jersey (she'd flown). But that was where her finesse with big-city living had peaked. That afternoon – her first in London – she'd discovered she no longer had a boyfriend. Or a place to live. And that the last seven years of her life had been a complete and utter waste of time. A fantasy. Unless having a boyfriend who dated other people and lied about it was the endgame. In which case, it had been a roaring success.

Ellie decided she was far too angry about having wasted her twenties on a romantic folly to let grief swallow her whole and, contrarily, was far too ashamed to return home. After aimlessly wandering through London's maze of streets with her suitcase in tow, she'd found herself in Fitzrovia, standing outside Media Angels Recruitment Ltd, had walked in and asked for a job. Thea, who was in charge of secretarial/office-manager-type posts, had said if Ellie could wait, they'd have a bit of a chat and see if there was anything suitable, but first she had a staff meeting. She'd got up from her desk, knocked a massive pile of CVs on to the floor, sworn, then disappeared into the meeting for two hours. When she'd come back and discovered the CVs tidily fanned out in alphabetical order next to a precise row of unearthed pens and screamed, 'Oh my god! I have a paperclip tray!' she'd disappeared again to have a chat with Vee. Ellie was hired as Media Angels' office manager that day. The next, she'd become Thea and Simon's pet project. The Ellie Doolittle to their Henry and Henrietta Higgins. Now, here they were, a motley crew of mismatched colleagues who created successful working relationships during the day and ended personal ones at night.

She stifled another yawn by making a big show of pulling out her trusty notebook. 'Alright then, team.' She clapped her hands. Simon, Thea and Gus all sat to attention. 'Okay. Couple number sixty-one! Dave and Cassie parted on friendly terms at the bistro, so all good on that front. How did phase two pan out, Thea?'

Thea pulled her enormous brown ear coils off, twirled them in front of her boobs with a triumphant 'Princess Leia strikes again!', then launched into a minutely detailed account of her role in the evening. As planned, she'd been standing outside the restaurant armed with nothing more than her lightsaber and a damsel-in-distress story. When Dave had appeared, she'd tearfully told him about her 'lost' ticket to the sold-out event. She had girlfriends waiting for her, she'd wailed. A dead phone. No way to get in touch with the lucky few who were inside. She re-enacted her fake-lashed, doe-eyed, *how will I ever be happy again* expression. It was a winner of a look.

Unsurprisingly, Dave had been unable to resist. He valiantly stepped in to save Princess Leia's bacon with his spare ticket, only to be adopted for the night by Thea and her 'friends' (a group of resting actresses they'd costumed up as Marvel heroines and 'paid' with tickets to Comic Con and some unsubtle mentions of the film producers and directors who would be on site). Dave's post-break-up blues, admittedly fairly minimal, were completely obliterated. Attractive Comic Con fans lavishing him with affection and assuring him that he wasn't at all nerdy? What wasn't to like?

After explaining that they were lesbians (they were pansexual, so not entirely a lie), they hooked him up with two women they'd found on a location-based dating app now downloaded on to his phone (he'd only ever heard of Tinder). Thea flicked through her photos again and, with a triumphant grin, revealed a gorgeously Rubenesque Harley Quinn and a petite Gamora sandwiching a beaming Dave.

'Good job.' Ellie made a couple of short notes then thumbed through her texts. She double-tapped a photo of Cassie on her way into an arthouse cinema with a takeaway bento box in hand. Ellie raised her mug in toast. 'Well done for another happy ending.'

Thea spat some of her wine out.

Simon patted Ellie's hand. 'Don't say that, dear.'

'Why? It is. I love giving a client a happy ending.'

Wine came out of Thea's nose and she began to choke. As Simon thumped her on the back, he explained to Ellie why she shouldn't say 'happy endings' in this context any more. When he'd finished, Ellie felt fifty fewer shades of naive.

Simon drained his wine glass and, though he was pulling on his jacket, asked, 'Any new enquiries?'

'A few.' More than a few, actually. Ellie was surprised at how many there had been since the New Year. 'I think the build-up to Valentine's Day is sending a lot of people into a panic. I'll go through them tonight and we can prioritise tomorrow.'

'Oh!' Thea tapped Ellie's notebook. 'One of the actresses we hired wants us to dump her girlfriend next week if we can. I think she needs it done by Wednesday.'

'Oh, that's a shame but . . . good?' She still hadn't quite figured out the peculiar balance of commiserations that a relationship was on the outs and satisfaction that they'd come to Softer Landings to help ease their partner's pain. She flipped to a different part of her notebook, pen poised. 'Why does she want to end it?'

Thea took a slurp of wine and gave a melodramatic *how was I supposed to get actual details when I was busy saving Dave* shoulder shrug. 'She's just been cast in some soap opera and her agent thinks that for PR she'd be better off single and, well, straight. Straightish and single,' she corrected. 'She's fine with that, but she's been with her girlfriend for a while—'

'How long's a while?' Simon cut in.

'Two years? Maybe one. Dunno.' Thea waved her hand. 'She doesn't want to be the one doing the dumping in case the tabloids get hold of it.'

'Would they?' Ellie asked. 'Is her girlfriend the vengeful type?'

Thea pulled a face. 'Worse. She's a TNTD.'

Ellie winced. Simon stuck his hands over Gus's ears and did a high-pitched '*La, la, la! Not in front of the baby!*'

Softer Landings had begun because of a TNTD. Too Nice To Dump. A relationship status that still seared the more heavily frayed edges of Ellie's nerve endings. 'How soon did you say she needs to be single?' Ellie asked.

'By Wednesday.'

Ellie grimaced. Five days wasn't much notice. Especially for a TNTD. Then again, she'd done it with zero minutes' notice the first time.

Thea picked up her phone and pinged a contact over to Ellie. 'I said you'd call her tomorrow to get the details.'

'Thanks.' She opened the contact. Flicka Bright. It sounded like the brand name of a long-reach fire starter. Appropriate.

She started bundling her things into her tote. More work was good, but a complicated split like this took time to execute properly. And time wasn't exactly her friend right now. She hadn't told Simon and Thea yet, but right before she'd left the office, she'd received a tersely worded email from Vee about a 'long overdue performance review'. It had appeared in her calendar without the normal *are you free* call. Eleven a.m. tomorrow. She was tempted to ask Simon and Thea for advice, but they were thumbing through the pictorial evidence of the evening's triumph and when Simon launched into a gleeful re-enactment of Cassie's reaction to Dave's Thor outfit, it was virtually impossible to get a word in edgeways. Thea howled with delight and they lavished one another with praise. If Gus hadn't been sandwiched between them, Ellie would've left and, no doubt, they wouldn't have noticed. Even now that they were officially a trio of colleagues, she knew where she stood. On the outside.

She'd felt so beige compared to them when they'd first met. So basic. The first time they'd all gone out for drinks, she'd virtually disappeared into the wallpaper of the ultra-chic cocktail bar they'd chosen. She was still the vanilla to their raspberry ripple, but at least now it had a purpose. The stage manager to their spot-lit role playing. The mysterious woman behind the curtain. And she liked it that way.

Stories exhausted, they finally said their farewells and, after the shortish walk, she and Gus were home.

With the performance review now foremost in her mind, she struggled to get to sleep. When she eventually managed to drift off, her brain yanked her from one panic dream to the next. The printer ran out of toner. Highlighters drained dry. Thea decorated the office in penis-shaped Post-its. And, the one that never failed to make Ellie break out in a cold sweat, the American Dan dream. She'd had this one too often to ignore. He appeared, just as he first had, in the doorway to Media Angels, with a halo of light around him. Tall, a little bow-legged and a lot broad-shouldered. His smile was bright, but not without a hint of world-weariness. Leash in one hand, dog bowl in the other, American Dan looked her in the eye and asked the unthinkable. 'Can I have my dog back?'

Chapter Three

At precisely the moment Ellie determined enough calm reigned in the office to call the afternoon meeting, Thea shrieked, dropped her mobile on to her desk and flew out of her chair so dramatically it appeared as if she'd been ejected from it.

'Oh no he didn't!' She stared at the text message accusingly.

Ellie pulled herself up short to avoid colliding with her, unable to stop the slosh of tea out of mugs on to the plate of delicate Italian pastries destined for the meeting. *Sugar.* Corner-shop generics bought by her predecessor would have to do. Her boss, Vee, was many things. Kind. Generous. Egalitarian. So long as she was fed and watered at regular intervals. Which was fine. Ellie had grown up with 'one of those' – her little sister, Aurora. She too was kind, open-hearted and gifted with the same engaging joie de vivre that made people want to please her. But if her sugar levels weren't kept on a more or less even keel, things had a tendency to spiral out of control. As such, Ellie had easily taken to the role of discreetly offering snacks at well-timed intervals to maintain her boss's serene recruitment guru aura.

As a counterbalance, Thea was like an electricity wire flailing free of a grounding pole in a hurricane. You never knew when and where she'd touch down and send sparks flying. Because she was clinging to this job like the two-week-old life raft it was, Ellie made a U-turn back to the kitchen, remembering she had some easy-peel mandarins she could also pop on the tray. Thea began singing a very loud and remarkably off-key rendition of 'You Ain't Nothing But a Hound Dog'.

Several pairs of hands clamped over ears as the hushed tones of work calls grew louder.

'Volume!' Simon, the only one brave enough to point out the obvious, arrowed a finger at his headset, making it clear to Thea that he was on an *important* work call versus the *pedestrian* calls everyone else was on. In fairness, his jobs did garner the biggest commissions – something the entire team, but mostly Thea, both admired and envied. But everyone also knew that Simon's partner had multiple, degenerative health problems. His salary went straight to carers, private healthcare insurance and an endless stream of pharmaceuticals. So, while his quarterly bumps in pay allegedly had one more digit than anyone else's, no one begrudged him the income or his odd foray into the nearby advanced skincare and medical enhancement clinic. In his words, dying inside didn't mean having to look like shit.

'I need you *now*, Simone!'

Simon pressed his perfectly plumped lips forward into an irritated moue, then did a melodramatic *cool your jets, I'm almost done* gesture that succeeded in sweeping a stack of CVs on to the floor. The concept of a paperless office hadn't yet reached Media Angels.

Ellie instinctively moved in to pick them up then remembered the tray she was holding. She looked down. Tea and *sfogliatelle* soup.

She glanced at the clock. The staff meeting was in eight min-utes. Vee liked her biscuits crispy and her meetings timely.

'I can't . . . *even* . . .' Thea was pointing at her phone as if slob-bery aliens were crawling out of it. She glared pointedly at Simon. When he finally took off his headset and gave her his *now you can speak* look, she pronounced, 'Simone! He's done it again.'

Simon was Thea's work wife. The moniker was one in a long list of eccentricities that bound him and Thea to one another's hips. *Love at first sight,* one of her colleagues had explained when she'd first joined. *Apart from the gay thing, obvs.*

Whatever you do, she'd been cautioned, *don't pit one against the other. That's one nasty can of* mm-mm don't go there *that you never want to open.*

Ellie had never heard of a work spouse until she'd moved to London. Then again, there were quite a few things Ellie had never heard of, let alone believed possible, before arriving here. Getting dumped by her long-term boyfriend in front of his girlfriend was one of them. Being bone-deep grateful to secure a job as a trumped-up tea lady was another. How quickly the goalposts had changed.

It was laughable really.

Sebastian, one of London's shiniest up-and-coming divorce lawyers, dumping his long-term girlfriend, whose only dream had been to become a relationship counsellor. In a matter of seconds, she'd watched her entire future morph into something about as impressive as the biscuit soup slopping round her tea tray.

'Simone! Come bear witness. Instantly.'

Ellie bridled on Simon's behalf. Thea ordered him about as if she were his drill sergeant rather than his peer. And, also, even though he was openly gay, did that mean she had a free card to call him the feminised version of his name? 'Do you think it's right to call him that?' Ellie asked in a low voice.

Thea bridled, bellowing, 'What? Simone?'

'Yeah.' Ellie was beginning to think she may have opened the can of *mm mm don't go there*.

'He's like, literally, my best friend.' Thea shouted across the office to him, 'Aren't you, Simone? My BFF?'

He pretended to consider the question. Thea began to turn puce, at which point Simon drew an air heart then clutched his hands to his chest as he choked out the words, 'You . . . complete . . . me.'

Thea smirked then threw Ellie a *see* look that made her feel almost more lost and alone than being dumped had. Thea's phone beeped again, relieving Ellie of being caught with the sting of tears blooming in her eyes.

Sharp, funny, stylish, urban and urbane. Thea was the poster girl for a cool thirty-something living her best life as her most authentic self and yet . . . something about all of that verve never entirely penetrated through to her eyes. Ellie couldn't help but think that there were elements of Thea's 'most authentic self' that were entirely for show. Armour protecting her from a vulnerability she daren't show the world for fear of appearing mortal like every-one else. Or worse, ordinary.

'Simone!' Thea bellowed.

'Ohmigawd, *whaaaaat*?' Simon scuttled over to her desk then pulled himself to a sharp, teetering, stop. He followed the direction of Thea's pointing finger, his torso drawn back from the lower half of his gamine frame, as if expecting something to pop out of the phone and grab him.

Given the importance of the afternoon team meeting, Ellie should've been heading back to the kitchen and redoing the tea and biscuits. But this particular Thea-atrical, as she'd come to call the daily outbursts, was on a different level.

'American Dan?' Simon guessed.

Thea nodded. Her expression sober. 'American Dan.'

Ellie shook her head. Why Thea's boyfriend wasn't just Dan had never been made clear. It wasn't as if there were flocks of Dans running amok in her life. When pressed, Thea waved off the query with an airy, 'He's American. Need I say more?'

According to Simon, American Dan was different from the rest of Thea's conquests. For starters, Thea hadn't dispensed with him after the usual handful of dates it took to determine his shagability rating. She'd been seeing him for a good three months now. According to her, he was utterly smitten. Grounds, apparently, for being vilified and, of course, dumped. When Simon pressed each morning as to whether or not she'd done the deed, she'd give a filly-like shake of her head and pronounce, 'Too much like kicking a puppy.'

In other words, he was Too Nice To Dump.

Thea brandished an invisible sword and struck a pose. 'His behaviour is beyond the pale. Once more unto the breach, dear friends!' She was Joan of Arc prepared to sacrifice herself at the altar of Gotta Go Boyfs. Chunky fringe and kick-ass leopard-skin ankle boots were her uniform, sheer moxie her weapon.

Simon reached out to pick up Thea's phone then yanked his hand back as if it were emitting toxic waste. 'I want to look, but I don't. I'm so scared!'

'Do it, Simone,' Thea instructed. 'You must see what he's done to me. I swear to god this is the final straw.'

He drew in a quivery breath, gave a solemn nod, reached out again – then just as his fingers grazed the surface, squealed in horror. The pair of them dissolved into hysterical giggles that surrounded them in that warm, cosy, bestie bubble that made Ellie ache to be included. Not so much for the squealing and being ridiculous part, that wasn't really her. More . . . to be known. She'd not been a somebody in Jersey, but she hadn't been a nobody. Invisible. Come to think of it, she'd been many someones. *That poor Hannah*

Shaw's daughter. Or, *that lovely blonde-haired girl's sister – no . . . not the attractive one – the mousey one. Aurora! That's it. No, not her, the sister.* Or, *the reliable one on reception at the little hotel down by the quay. The one with the blue awnings on it? With the weather-worn bits, yes. That's her. She's a girl you can count on. Dependable.*

She'd thought Sebastian had known her better than the rest. Had seen in her what everyone else had proactively ignored. She'd been wrong. Ha ha. Hee hee. Nope. Still not funny.

Thea and Simon were at fever pitch now, all of their energies engaged in an approach and retreat, approach and retreat dance towards the phone, daring one another to pick it up.

Ellie glanced at the clock again. Tick tock. Two minutes to go. Honestly. She'd never met two less sensible people in her life. How they survived in the modern world . . .

She dialled back the judgement. With an empty bank account, a broken heart and not even close to the job she thought she'd have by now, she couldn't hold a flame to their clearly superior London survival skills. Even the poor romantically doomed American Dan had a better grip on life in the big city than she did.

Obviously, it was all hearsay, but Ellie felt she knew him better than anyone here. Courtesy of his position as forerunner in the office gossip talking points, she knew his faults, his foibles and all about his 'persistent Americanness' – whatever that was. How he was constantly inviting Thea out for morning runs when *obviously* she was not a morning person. How he actually, *genuinely*, bought a hotdog from the creepy vendor near Buckingham Palace even though she'd assured him dysentery would follow. Why on earth Thea hadn't freed the poor lovestruck Yankee after their first date and gone out with someone she actually liked was beyond Ellie. Power? A cruel streak? Ellie didn't like to think so, because beneath all of the bravura, she was pretty sure Thea had a sensitive side, but even so . . . it was no reason to pick on someone quite so much.

Another glance at the clock and Ellie decided to hustle the two of them along. Vee hated to be kept waiting. She marched across to Thea's desk, picked up her phone, stabbed the black screen with her finger and watched the offending image bloom into life. Her heart flipped then melted.

A dog. An adorable golden retriever with chocolate-brown *love me forever* eyes and a nose straight out of the Most Boopable Hooters in the World catalogue.

Thea wheeled on her. 'Did you just sigh?'

Ellie reflexively looked over her shoulder, and then, because there was no one there – there never was – said, 'Yes. It's a dog.'

Thea shuddered. 'Precisely.'

'What's wrong with a picture of a dog?' Ellie asked.

Thea opened her green eyes wide for effect and, as if she were explaining something very, very simple to a toddler, said, 'Because it's not just a picture of any old dog. It's a picture of *American Dan's* dog.'

Still not understanding, Ellie persisted. 'Why can't American Dan get a dog?'

Thea rolled her eyes and shot a *Bless – our little bitty country bumpkin still has so much to learn about the big bad world* look at Simon. Realising there was no quick fix to the *American Dan got a dog* problem, she handed the phone to Thea, picked up the tray and headed back to the kitchen. 'Vee wants us in her office at the top of the hour.'

As if on cue, Vee appeared at the glass wall of her office and knocked on it with an expectant *I'm waiting* look. A couple of minutes later, when Ellie arrived in the doorway with a fresh tray of tea and biscuits, her boss's violet eyes met hers, dropped to the tray, then lifted back up to meet Ellie's. There was no need to verbalise her disappointment. Nor was there any point in explaining about the American-Dan-boopy-nose-dog-phone incident so Ellie merely smiled and said, 'I thought I'd try the new boulangerie on Charlotte Street tomorrow.'

Vee's brows lifted in approval and, at long last, the warm smile that could light up a room appeared. She took a biscuit, welcomed the team in, waited until everyone had dropped or folded into their regular positions on the pair of sofas across from her desk, then leant back in her made-to-order ergonomic chair and said, 'Right then, what's all this hoo-hah about American Dan?'

Chapter Four

Simon and Thea were leaving Vee's office as Ellie approached. Thea looked pumped. Simon's expression was more difficult to read, and not just because his forehead didn't move any more.

'You've got this, lil' tiger.' Thea made a muted roaring noise.

'Keep an open mind, punkin'.' Simon's toothpaste-advert smile shone encouragingly.

Barely managing to hold the shakes at bay, Ellie entered the office. Vee's back was to her. 'Just finishing off this email, dollface.'

Ellie slid a half-caff, barista's choice almond-milk cappuccino and a plate with twelve organic almonds and three biodynamically grown figs on to Vee's desk. Nearly twelve months of experimenting had led to this as the perfect elevenses boost. Her early phase of exotic bakery purchases had proved to be 'too thrilling' for Vee's waistline. That, and a *Huffington Post* article on Britain's Fibre Crisis, had led to the change.

'Thanks, love.' Vee pushed her keyboard to the side, took a thoughtful sip of her cappuccino, then weighted her Elizabeth Taylor look-a-like eyes on Ellie as she took another. 'All ready for our little chat?'

Ellie gave a shaky nod, actively confused as to how a 'long overdue performance review' had turned into a little chat. And why were Thea and Simon doing cheerleading moves outside Vee's office window?

She picked a chair, uncertain what pose to adopt. Was she meant to look relaxed, only to be banjaxed with the news she was going to be fired? Maybe she was meant to sit up to attention. A soldier prepared to go to battle where no recruitment office manager had gone before. Perhaps it was all an elaborate set-up for something else entirely. The post-New Year's break-up rush had meant she'd been devoting a lot of out-of-hours time to Softer Landings. But so had Thea and Simon. Neither of them had had performance reviews. (She'd checked Vee's diary. One of the perks of her job was access to everyone's email.) She'd ensured the break-ups hadn't impacted on her role as office manager/PA/general dogs-body, but . . . maybe she'd missed something. This 'spontaneous' meeting seemed an awful lot like Vee was priming the pump for A Change. Vee loved A Change.

Ellie forced on a smile. 'I'm ready if you are.'

Vee raised an eyebrow. 'Did you want anything for yourself? We've got some new green tea.' She tapped her index finger on a clay tea beaker that looked as if it had been made by a toddler or a highly sought-after craftsman (it was difficult to tell the difference sometimes). 'It's got ashwaganda in it.' Vee's lips shifted into a soft smile. 'Topaz brought it in.'

Topaz was Vee's newest addition to the team. A computer games recruiter. She looked about twelve, dressed like a sponsored skateboarder and effortlessly catered to Vee's on-trend tendencies. Every time they crossed paths, Ellie felt her own monochromatic canvas crave a few residual splashes of Topaz's multicoloured one. Topaz also brought in huge commissions.

'I'm not sure I know what that is.' Ellie tucked her fist under her chin and leant forward, hoping she looked fascinated at this new discovery. *Ashwaganda.*

Vee didn't respect people who played the *fake it till you make it* game. As one of London's premiere recruitment consultants, she honoured bald honesty. If she was going to stake her reputation on someone for a client, she wanted to be crystal clear about exactly who it was she was championing. Ellie hadn't come to this realisation tactically. She'd simply been too naive to be anything other than honest when she'd first arrived at Media Angels. A tiny victory in a sea of embarrassing snafus.

'Ashwaganda,' Vee enunciated as if she were writing it out on a chalkboard for a lecture hall full of keen-to-please, aspiring recruitment consultants. 'It's Ayurvedic. Good for anxiety and is purported to help with performance. Although the vote's still out on that one.' She gave Ellie a look suggesting she'd like an opinion.

'I'm good, thanks.' Ellie fought a strange, nervy tickle in her throat. She really could have done with some boring old water. But when she was nervous – and she was nervous – she always needed to wee. She leant back in her chair to assume a relaxed posture, only to discover someone had completely undone the tension on it.

'Hmmmm,' said Vee. She gave each almond a tap with the tip of one of her beautifully manicured nails, as if syncing them with bullet points she hoped to hit over the course of their meeting. 'Do you like that chair, Ellie?'

Errr . . . 'Yes?'

'What was it that made you choose that particular chair?' Vee leant forward and perched her elbows on the desk. In her ultra-modern silk top and casually immaculate tangle of ghetto/not ghetto necklaces, Vee looked like the love child of Nefertiti and RuPaul. Her entire demeanour screamed, *Dazzle me.* It was freaking Ellie out. Vee knew Ellie wasn't an in-the-spotlight kind of woman. Usually, their chats were sofa based and entailed Ellie taking copious notes while Vee brain-dumped thousands of ideas cached as 'blue-sky thinking'. Ellie had gradually come to learn that this meant *make these things happen and if they don't work we'll pretend this talk never happened.*

'Tell me, Ellz . . .' Vee slipped off her statement glasses and *really* looked at Ellie. 'Is choosing this particular chair your way of telling me you want more from your job?'

Panic gripped her. This was one of those trick questions, wasn't it? Surely it required a quick and impassioned 'Yes'. But Vee wasn't so straightforward as that. By definition, a 'yes' would indicate she was perfectly happy and couldn't imagine living the rest of her life any more joyously than now, ensuring her boss's blood sugar levels were kept topped up with an array of organic nuts and berries, fixing the office printer whenever Simon attempted a multi-page, double-sided colour document, and, of course, pulling out the wet vac at least once a week when Thea inadvertently (but predictably) whacked one of her coffees off her desk on to the cream carpet while in the throes of a *you have got to meet this woman* discussion with a client.

So, telling Vee she was perfectly contented when the company's entire ethos was built on personal and professional ambition would be stupid.

Which would, of course, mean that the real answer was 'no'. Employees were meant to want more from their jobs, right? To strive harder and aim higher. But that, presumably, was the double bluff. Her brain began to short-circuit.

She would never be invited to a monthly achievers' lunch. Arrive at work to discover someone else had laid out the early-bird breakfast. Her salary would remain unchanged no matter how superlative her wet-vac performance. And then she remembered, none of these were things she actually wanted from life. She wanted to be a relationship counsellor. More pressingly, she also wanted to pay her rent and keep Gus in kibble. Therein lay her dilemma.

She began to scavenge her mind for a word that sat somewhere between yes and no. One that rang with ambition but honoured the pragmatism of a reliable salary. *Maybe?*

Vee leant back, templed her hands beneath her chin and said, 'Tell me, Ellie. How many piano tuners do you think there are in London?'

Wait. What? How had they gone from her professional ambitions to piano tuners? Her silence had clearly answered the question for her. To make up for it, Ellie made a quick calculation of the population, the number of people she thought might play piano, taking into account the numerous symphonies and music colleges in London and the fact that pianos didn't require tuning all that often. 'I would say between one hundred and twenty-five and one hundred and fifty.'

Vee clapped her hands, delighted. 'There are one hundred and forty-two.' She sighed and gazed at Ellie as one might smile at a beloved child in the wake of a flawless recital. 'Excellent. Now, Ellie. I'd like to talk to you about this little side hustle of yours.'

'Oh?' Ellie squeaked. This was the first time Vee had openly acknowledged Softer Landings.

'Yes. I'm curious. Is it something you want to see through to some sort of meaningful fruition?'

Wow. Talk about a loaded question. In terms of goals, it wasn't like it was Ellie's master plan to break up every relationship in London, but . . . 'I like to help people if I can.'

'Yes. You do.' Vee nodded with a concentrated intensity, then opened up her palms. 'Which is why I was wondering if you'd like to push the boat out on that.' She gave the invisible boat a nudge.

'Sorry. I'm not following.'

Vee looked disappointed and then, just as quickly, was all business. 'As you know, we're having to take the new global economic stage into consideration as we move forward. Inflation. Downsizing. The climate.'

Ellie froze. Should she have recycled more? It was those containers with film on top that always threw her for a loop.

'As such,' Vee continued, 'I've thrown a few balls up in the air.'

'Oh, okay,' Ellie said, bewildered, then added, 'Great.'

Vee nodded. 'And when they came back down there was no longer room for an office manager role.' Her shoulders did a teensy shrug. 'I'm going to repurpose the position.'

Ellie's heart flew into her throat. 'In what way?'

'I'm giving some of your responsibilities to Fern.'

Fern? Fern the airhead receptionist?

'Okay.' Still not entirely understanding what was happening, Ellie said, 'Did you want me to talk her through anything in particular?'

'Well, it's not really your job to talk through any more, is it?' Vee reminded her. 'It's been repurposed.'

'Into what?'

'Office Enhancement Actioneer.'

Ummm . . .

And then Vee's words registered. She was being fired.

Vee sat back and watched the blood rush to Ellie's cheeks. After a bit of awkward staring, it became clear Vee wasn't going to give her any more information unless Ellie asked for it. 'Is there any particular reason you weren't happy with my performance?'

'Oh, darling. No one's done it better. I'm sure you could've done it in your sleep if necessary.'

Ellie managed a small smile, not entirely sure if this was a compliment. She pressed her hands on to the armrests of her chair. 'I'm guessing I should get my things and go.'

'No. Well. That's up to you, isn't it?' Vee looked put out.

'Vee, can you please tell me in actual, precise words, what is going on?'

Vee clapped her hands and hooted. 'Ellie Shaw. You're like an Excel sheet. No room for poetry. Fair enough, then. I want you to trial-run Softer Landings on a bigger scale. Full time. Use one of the spare offices. I'll give you two hours a day of Thea and Simon's time. You may have access to some but not all of the office resources. Printers. Phones. Stationery cupboard. We'll reassess in three months' time.'

Heart still lodged in her throat, Ellie choked out, 'I'm sorry. I'm not really understanding.'

'Recruitment is an ever-changing world. I'm having to trim corners in some areas, expand in others.'

'But . . . Softer Landings doesn't really recruit people.'

'Not yet, it doesn't.' Vee tipped her head towards the main office, where Thea and Simon were now sitting on Simon's desk, sharing a bowl of popcorn and openly watching them. 'I understand there is ample room for growth. You've hit a potential gold mine, darling. The dating market is huge. And cluttered. The break-up market is entirely untapped, unless you count ice cream, and you know how I feel about dairy.'

Ellie's head was spinning. It was true. Vee preferred nut milk to dairy. But what did that have to do with taking Softer Landings to a different level?

Vee started bullet-pointing ideas about franchising. The UK first, then branching out to EU countries – Brexit bylaws pending – and America. Then she began rattling off things like passive income, revenue streams and a whole bunch of other terminology that made no sense. 'Of course, there wouldn't be a salary to start.'

'I'm sorry, what?'

'Just like when I started out, your role will be commission-based to start with.'

Ellie's heart actually stopped beating. She wasn't going to get paid any more?

Vee continued. 'It's not very *Dragon's Den* of me, I know, but no one bankrolled me when I started out and, let me tell you, impending poverty was quite the motivator.' She let the comment sit for a moment. 'I didn't bankroll Nita either.'

'Sorry, who?' asked Ellie.

'Nita's Carnitas?'

Ellie frowned and then, because she was a walker, remembered seeing a small DIY burrito bar pop up all over London during the past few months. 'You're an investor in Nita's Carnitas?'

Vee shook her head. 'Not an investor. A believer. Here.' She pushed across a piece of paper full of logos. A cupcake decorating business. A mobile hairdresser for seniors. A pre-party on-site make-up service.

'How did you meet all of these people?'

Vee laughed. 'Darling. Who do you think had the office manager job before you?'

Ellie couldn't help it. She laughed. 'Are you the patron saint of office managers?'

Vee frowned, clearly unhappy with Ellie's inability to understand what she was really saying. 'I encourage entrepreneurial people like yourself to move out of dead-end jobs.'

She tried not to let the comment sting. She'd worked at her family's hotel in a job pretty much like this one since she'd been able to staple an invoice to a compliment slip. Which meant . . . maybe Vee was right? Sure, she'd moved from Jersey to London, but was she anywhere nearer to being a counsellor than she'd been a year ago?

Just to make sure she'd got the right end of the stick, Ellie asked, 'So . . . you encourage them by taking their salary away?'

'By offering them a different lens through which they can envision their future.'

'And you think my future is . . .'

'. . . a bright one if you're brave enough to reach out and grab it.'

Ellie glanced out to the main office, where Simon and Thea were giving her hopeful thumbs-up. Was she brave enough to take a risk? Could she risk homelessness and discount doggie kibble on a once-in-a-lifetime opportunity to push Softer Landings to the next level? The alternative wasn't very nice. Spending the rest of her life wondering . . . what if?

Vee swept a tiny spoon along the foamy remains of her cappuccino. Her tone was reflective when she spoke, her look far away. 'It's difficult to find people who believe in you in a place like this. London,' she clarified, before continuing. 'I began my life here as a temp. Fresh out of uni, head full of dreams, I applied for job after job, struggling to even get into a temp agency, work was so hard to come by. I finally landed a position at a production company. My boss needed someone to retype some poorly photocopied *Judge Judy* teleplays for a German broadcaster. The job paid minimum wage but it was all I had. Over the next few weeks I typed hundreds of scripts and ate a lot of instant noodles.'

Ellie was shocked. It was difficult to imagine a time and place when Vee had knowingly eaten MSG. Before she could ask why the Germans wanted immaculately typed teleplays for *Judge Judy*, Vee changed tack. 'Do you know how I got my first client?'

Ellie shook her head.

'She was the woman who fired me from the typing job.'

'What? *Why?*

'I would put in addendums. Notes in the scripts when I disagreed with Judge Judy.'

'Why didn't she just ask you to stop doing it?'

'Because she did something better instead.' She gave Ellie a pointed look, indicating that Ellie, too, could be the benefactor of something better. 'She told me my temp agency didn't have a clue what they were doing. They wanted someone who was happy typing, not thinking. And that's when it hit me: I wanted to recruit thinkers. Put the right people in the right job until it was time for them to do something else. So I shook her hand, went to the train station, printed out some business cards for Media Angels, then went back to the production company and signed them as my first client.'

Then, as if she'd had enough philosophising for one day, Vee clapped her hands together and turned to her computer. 'By my cal-cuuuu-laaaa-tions . . .' She did a little tippity-tap on the numbers section of her keyboard. '. . . working full-time on Softer Landings should earn you a proper salary in three months' time. Rent for the office space will kick in then as well. As will the costs associated with Simon and Thea. I'll take a profit share once the franchises begin, but we can worry about that later. For now? I'm really excited to see you run with this. You won't just be changing your life, Ellie, you'll be changing Thea and Simon's as well. Not to mention all of those couples facing horrendous heartache. There's so much low-hanging fruit out there, dollface. Reach out and grab it.' She crossed her palms over her sternum. 'Making relationship endings less toxic? Genius. You could single-handedly make the world a nicer place, Ellie Shaw.'

Pretending terror wasn't motivating her next question, Ellie asked, 'What happens if I don't accept your offer?'

Vee's forehead raised. Bemused. 'Then, I wish you well in your future endeavours.'

'So, I *am* fired?'

'Well, that's your choice, isn't it, sugar bean?' Vee gave her a kindly but businesslike smile. 'I prefer to see this as a chance for you to leap from a job you're clearly overqualified for to other, higher planes of professional self-discovery.'

Blimey. That was roughly how she put it when she counselled the recently dumped. It wasn't being rejected, it was being offered an opportunity to find someone new – someone better suited to them – that could lead to long-term happiness.

She had to give it to Vee. As someone who prided herself on predicting her boss's moves before Vee herself knew them, she hadn't seen this coming. She was being forced to step up or step out. Going back to Jersey wasn't an option. Dumped for being boring and then fired because she lacked aspiration? No chance. 'How did you—? Did Thea and Simon give you our pricing structure?'

'Mmhmm.' Vee opened one of her desk drawers, pulled out a piece of paper and pushed it across the desk. 'This first column here shows you what I think you could make over the next month.'

It matched her current salary.

'This one here is next month.'

It was the same again plus fifty per cent.

'And this is what I see for month . . . number . . . three . . .'

It was double her current salary.

Ellie swallowed. She could get a flat with a garden for Gus.

'Longer term, of course, those figures could become limitless. The world, as they say, is your oyster. Minus twenty per cent for Media Angels, of course, for start-up fees and ancillary administrative support. We'll hammer out the details once you can afford a lawyer.'

She looked out of Vee's office towards Simon and Thea. They both looked so hopeful. So . . . trusting. They believed in her. They were also the ones who had supplied her with her very first paying clients. Without them, she never would have given Dave his freedom. Or Naomi before him. Or Ken, Jilly, Diana, Lakay, Tandy, Mike, Aaron or Jason. And, of course, American Dan, without whom there would never have been a Softer Landings. Or a Gus.

She closed her eyes and pictured a beaming Dave in his Thor costume, surrounded by women who genuinely saw him as a catch, his heart almost instantly healed after a break-up that could have easily carved away large slices of his self-confidence.

A fire lit in her gut. If she quit Softer Landings now, who would give those poor, unloved, destined-for-a-heinous-dumping Londoners a new beginning? And not just Londoners. What about the future dumpees of Manchester, Birmingham, Edinburgh, Inverness even. Blackpool? Skegness. All of those people out there who deserved better. Deserved more. Deserved love.

Vee began tapping her nails on the desk. Her version of *the clock is ticking, my little chickadee.*

'Would you like to take the weekend to think about it?'

Yes. Absolutely, she would.

Taptaptap.

'No.'

Vee's energy shifted from holistic spa relaxation artist to corporate mogul. 'What's your decision?'

Ellie's lips parted. Whatever she said next would change her life forever.

She was meant to be a relationship counsellor by now. On Jersey. Pregnant with her and Sebastian's first child, on the brink of taking maternity leave. Time in which she would have pre-planned months of wholesome meals for her family. Spring was on the way, so she'd take up gardening. Flowers and veg to start. The flowers, of course, would be for the foyer at Sebastian's law firm (except in hay fever season, obviously – she was sensitive to things like that). She looked at Thea again. All chip-choppy bob, sparkly cropped

45

jumper atop a pair of mint velvet leggings sprouting from a pair of leopard-print old-school Vans. Simon in his trademark skinny jeans and black Samuel Beckett turtleneck. They were looks she'd never in a million years be able to pull off. Not that she'd tried.

Maybe that was the solution. Walk the walk, talk the talk and eventually everything would fall into place. She'd spent her entire life helping other people shine. This was a chance to not only help people, but to see if what she felt burning inside her had legs. Discover if she could make something of herself to the point that she could buy a ticket to Jersey, fly home, stride into the hotel and say to her sister, *See? I* do *have what it takes. And I did it with my eyes wide open.*

'I'll do it.'

'Wonderful.' Vee rose. 'Shall we shake on it?'

Ellie stood and stretched her arm out, but at the moment their hands were meant to connect Vee's dropped away, her features widening in surprise. Her gaze had moved to the front door where, bathed in a midday glow of wintry sunlight, stood American Dan.

Chapter Five

Three Hundred and Forty-Nine Days Earlier

'Whatever you do, don't let him in!'

Ellie looked to the security cameras, then the front door, then to the key Thea had just pressed in her hand. 'Thea, we can't lock him out.'

'Why not?' she demanded.

Apart from the human decency factor? 'Fire laws?'

'*I* will catch on fire if you let him in!'

Ellie was thrown back to one of the many times Aurora had come screaming into the hotel lobby, eyes wide with terror, hiss-whispering to her sister as she flew past, 'Whatever happens, I'm not here!'

'He's a man, not a firestorm,' Ellie said to Thea.

'That's what *you* think! You haven't met him yet!' Thea stabbed at the air between them, then, hearing the *whomph* of the lift heading down to the foyer, screamed.

Simon, who'd been absorbing the entire thing while insouciantly sucking on a lolly, scrunched up his nose and said to Ellie, 'Just lie, little mouse. Tell him Thea's gone out.'

'No.'

Both Ellie and Simon did double-takes. 'What?' they said as one.

'Thea.' Ellie looked her new colleague straight in the eye and, knowing she might be putting her job at risk, said what she was thinking anyway. 'You have to break up with him.'

Thea recoiled like an injured animal. 'You're taking the piss, right?'

No. Ellie wasn't. She was sick to death of kind-hearted people being treated like poop. Good people. People who, by all accounts, sounded like her. Nice.

When she didn't answer, Thea blinked some Bambi eyes at her. 'You do it.'

'Okay,' Ellie said.

'Wait. What?'

'I'll do it.' She wasn't going to put American Dan through one more minute of this nonsense.

Thea's features strobed through a myriad responses. Gratitude, disbelief, wonder. 'Seriously?'

'Seriously. But if I do this? You can't go back. What's done is done.' She trotted out the conditions Aurora received from the age of six onwards: no taunting, flaunting or reigniting.

Thea wove her fingers together in prayer position. 'I promise you with every fibre of my being I will never go out with American Dan again as long as I live.'

Ping! went the lift doors.

'Game on!' trilled Simon, pulling a bag of caramel popcorn out of his desk drawer.

'Go get 'em, tiger,' Thea said, a bit too jauntily for someone who'd just had tears of gratitude in her eyes. Then promptly hid under her desk.

Ellie closed her eyes to gather herself together. Then, upon hearing the front door open, raised her head, only to realise she was wholly unprepared for the battle she'd just agreed to go into.

Thea was right. Life had changed as Ellie knew it. And all because of the arrival of one man, in a doorway, to which she held the key.

Though she couldn't physically move, she was sparking and tingling in parts of her body she'd never known existed. Everything around her blurred. Noises were muted by the roar of blood surging to her brain as her entire nervous system tried not to implode. Here he was in flesh and blood. American Dan.

Tall, sandy-brown hair, blue-eyed and all-American-looking in the way only someone who had actually been prom king could be. He had presence. Not showy or brash, more . . . the type of man who could suddenly appear in the eye of a storm and assure you that everything would be alright. And you could believe him. Because he wasn't a liar. Or a cheat. He didn't date other women while he was engaged to someone else. He was kind, modest, self-less, brave. He was a Disney hero with a real-life heartbeat.

She knew this, of course, through Thea. Though her take on Dan's attributes leant more in the direction of ennui than marry me. *He's just so . . . nice,* she had complained. Over and over as if being nice was the worst possible attribute a human could possess. For Ellie, it was the very best of attributes. A synonym for kind. The type of guy who was confident enough to cry at *The Notebook*, unembarrassed to buy tampons for his girlfriend and aware enough to know that the woman behind him at the supermarket with the screaming child wasn't vile, she was just having a very, very bad day. He'd get the kid to smile. He was the type of man who, one day, might appear at his true love's workplace dressed as a knight in shining armour months after she'd idly mentioned she'd love for it to happen – only to go down on bended knee and ask her to marry him. And already Ellie knew she loved him with her entire being.

It felt like being cracked in two. The most exhilarating and painful two-pronged epiphany she'd ever had. Well, apart from finding out her fiancé didn't love her. That had been big too, but . . . The world as she knew it had literally changed.

There really was such a thing as love at first sight. Her mum hadn't been lying. But, heartbreakingly, it turned out that pure, unfiltered, instant love could and sometimes had to be unrequited. Dan Buchanan wasn't and never could be hers. He was Thea's. And Ellie had just promised to break up with him for her. The unwritten Girl Code was very clear on this point: Though Shalt Not Go Out With Thy Friend's Ex Even If He Sets Your Lady Garden on Fire.

'Hi,' he said. 'I'm Dan.'

'Yes,' she said, like an idiot.

'This is Gus.'

Her eyes dropped to Dan's thigh, then dog – and she fell in love all over again. Gus was even more gorgeous in real life. Fluffy, golden, big *love me forever* eyes.

'Is Thea here?' Dan asked, his smile slightly uncertain, as if he was already aware that taking ownership of a dog to prove his love for someone who wouldn't commit was, quite possibly, a step too far.

Ellie waited for the nerves to kick in the way they had with Aurora's fleet of beaux. But they didn't. Because she wasn't doing this for Thea. Or her naughty sister. She was doing this for Dan. 'She's had to pop out, I'm afraid. Umm . . .' She twisted round and, seeing that the former partner offices weren't being used for meetings said, 'Can I make you a cup of tea and have a wee chat while we wait?'

His expression changed then. Still open. Still honest. But far more intelligent than Thea had ever given him credit for. He said no thanks to the tea, he hadn't quite caught 'the bug', but he and Gus would be delighted to have the chat.

'Great! Well . . . why don't we go in here?' She all but ran into the office and threw herself in the desk chair to stop him seeing

Thea crawling across the floor to Simon's desk while mouthing to Ellie, *Put the phone on speaker!*

'So!' Dan said once he'd sat down in the only chair that faced the desk and Gus had parked his chin on Dan's knee. 'It looks like you're going to fire me.'

'Ah ha ha ha ha!' said Ellie, awkwardly aiming her elbow at the phone's speaker option.

He crossed then recrossed his arms, the pair of them pretending he hadn't just foreshadowed exactly what was coming. He looked to Gus, then to Ellie. 'Is this the part where I find out Thea's deadly allergic to dogs?'

Her heart bashed against her chest. Poor, semi-aware-he'd-done-the-wrong-thing American Dan. 'No,' she said, already certain little white lies weren't the tack she had to take. She caught Thea making a *keep it rolling* gesture with her finger. Ellie stabbed the button that took the phone off speaker. Her role here was to comfort Dan, not provide Thea with entertainment. She looked across at him and said simply, 'This is the part where you find out Thea's version of her future doesn't quite meld with your version of it.'

'Huh,' he said, blue eyes glued to hers. 'Okay.' He cupped one of his rather lovely hands over Gus's head, his thumb idly stroking the longer fur behind Gus's ear. It felt wrong to wonder what it would feel like if he did the same to her, but she did it anyway.

The silence, amazingly enough, wasn't uncomfortable. He was giving himself time to absorb the blow. He didn't shout. Cause a scene. Blame her. Blame Gus. Or kick an inanimate object. He took it stoically. Head on. Like an adult.

'I'm guessing the dog was a step too far?'

'Not for someone who loves dogs,' she said, willing her arm not to involuntarily pop into the air as she shouted, *Me! Me! I love dogs!*

He looked over his shoulder towards the office. Simon threw his bag of popcorn over his shoulder, grabbed his phone and took a fake call as subtly as if he was in a Broadway musical.

Dan looked back at her. 'She's really not here, huh?'

Again, a crossroads moment. Carry the lie with her the rest of her life or treat American Dan the way she'd wished Sebastian had treated her.

'She's crawling out from under Simon's desk towards the ladies.'

Dan cracked a smile. His two front teeth slightly overlapped. It was gorgeous. Gus received some scritches behind the ear. 'She's a nutburger, that girl.'

That was one way to describe her, Ellie thought, and then, because it felt mean-spirited said on behalf of both of them, 'It's hard to hurt someone you care about.' Thea, like her sister, wasn't all bad. Her intent was commendable, if not cowardly.

'What does she care about?' Dan asked.

Herself. Simon. Animal-print athleisurewear. Ellie wasn't really sure beyond that. Surprisingly, that added to her compassion for Thea. Of all the things she'd learnt about her in the past fortnight, of this she was suddenly, absolutely sure: Thea Stephanopolis had no idea what she wanted from life. She was as lost as Ellie was. 'I think she's kind of focussed on her career right now.'

'Really?'

Ellie gave a confessional *maybe* shrug. 'I've only worked here a fortnight.' She thought for a moment then added, 'I know what she *doesn't* want, if that helps.'

'Good. Cool.' He pulled a finger gun out of an invisible hip holster and said, 'Shoot.'

'No dogs, no marriage, no kids, but definitely a shit tonne of shoes.'

He gave his head a scrub and made a couple of sounds that indicated he was digesting the information. 'That's a fairly clear list.'

'Yes, it is.'

'She wants a shit tonne of shoes more than going out with me, huh?'

They had been Thea's exact words, and Ellie their messenger. She silently pled with him to understand she wouldn't have ever said *shit tonne* of her own accord. Even so, giving hope when there was none was cruel.

With daggers lacerating her heart, she said the one thing she knew to be true. 'I know there is someone out there who will love you as perfectly as you deserved to be loved.'

He snorted and laughed. It was rich and heartfelt and sad. He drew his finger between them. 'The fact we are sitting here having this chat is not a particularly good indicator that what you say is true.'

Oh, it is true. So very, very true.

'Honestly,' she said. 'Just think. She's actually expedited that happening.'

'Love's right around the corner, is it?' Astonishingly, his eyes actually twinkled.

Ellie persisted. 'What if Thea kept you hanging on for years? Think of all that time you could've been living the life you wanted, rather than trying to insert yourself into the life Thea did.'

He looked at her, then. Properly looked at her. Her heart began to flutter as if his gaze alone had the power to fill it with a million butterflies. 'Sounds like the voice of experience.'

She cleared the lump in her throat. 'Just trying to put some good karma back into the universe.'

'You've done that alright.' He tipped his head to the side and gave his beautiful, cowboy-esque jawline a scrub. His gaze dropped to his brand-new dog and in that lovely, low drawl of his said, 'You know? You've just given me an idea.'

'Oh?'

'I don't know how much Thea's told you about me.'

She offered him a neutral smile, hoping it didn't say, *Thea's told us alllll about you.* How he couldn't pronounce Leicester Square properly. How he talked to everyone who accidentally made eye contact with him – on the Underground, no less. How all he ever wanted to do was 'tourist shit': go on the London Eye, see that Agatha Christie play that would never end or, worst of all, visit the Tower of London and get a selfie with a Beefeater. Mercifully, Dan took Ellie's silence as a cue that Thea hadn't said much. He explained how, in case she hadn't known, he'd come over here for a year's residency at Moorfield's Eye Hospital. He was an ophthalmologist. An eye surgeon.

She grinned and, in an unfiltered moment, blurted, 'How many souls have you seen?'

He beamed back, their eyes meeting and holding for a few seconds too long. 'You're the first person to ever ask that.'

'Really?'

'Mmmnn,' he said, his teeth grazing his bottom lip as he considered her for a moment longer before drawing in a sharp breath, sitting up straight and launching into a very detailed explanation about how, for the first nine months here, his life had been all work, work, work, until he'd reminded himself that he was in London. One of the most interesting cities in the world. He'd signed himself up for a bunch of walking tours so that when he went back to North Carolina, his home state, and took up a residency at a hospital in Raleigh and got married and had kids, he wouldn't have any regrets about not making the most of his time here when he'd had the chance. 'And that's how I met Thea.'

'On a tour?'

'Yeah, you know . . . she gives those little personalised tours of Camden Town?'

No. Ellie hadn't.

'Anyway, from the moment I met her, all of those life plans I had went – *poof* – up in smoke.'

Ellie gave a faint smile. 'Yes, well, Thea has a knack for throwing hand grenades into best-laid plans.'

Dan frowned, his blue eyes latching on to hers with an intensity that gripped her vital organs and squeezed. He was searching for a deeper meaning in the comment. There wasn't any. She didn't know Thea well enough to have any true insight into what made her tick. She didn't know anyone in London well enough to know anything. Just as she was about to confess as much, Dan sighed, gave Gus's head a good ol' scrub then said, 'I'd built this little script in my head about how my life would play out, you know?'

Oh god. She felt seen. Dan ticked his fingers off with his thumb. 'Sort myself out professionally. Meet a girl. Fall in love. Two point two kids, the picket fence. Maybe a pony?' He grinned at her as if to show what an 'out there' dreamer he was. Wanting a pony for his kids. Ellie couldn't imagine anything more perfect. She knew exactly which rugs she would unfurl when she and her future family had teddy-bear picnics. The wicker basket. The daisy chains she'd crown her children with. A pony would've been a lovely addition.

'I think I got stuck to it,' Dan said. 'The plan. I could see it so perfectly.'

Snap.

His frown shifted into a wistful smile. 'I suppose getting this guy here' – he pointed at Gus – 'was me trying to prove I was spontaneous, but it was actually superimposing my plan on to Thea without listening to what she wanted. It's a guy flaw, isn't it? Not listening.' He was genuinely asking.

Ellie looked out to the office, where Thea was pretending to be grabbed and strangled by a stranger behind the wall leading to the loos. 'I don't think that's exclusively a guy thing.'

He laughed and, shaking his head, ran his fingers through his hair. Her fingers twitched as if she too had been given the privilege. When her eyes dropped to his, he was looking at her with that crooked smile of his. 'I guess it looks like I'll have to tear up the plans and start over.'

Good. This was definitely a good sign that she'd done the right thing. 'You said you had an idea?'

His eyes shadowed from blue to grey as he glanced down at Gus then back at her. 'Aww . . . this may be trying to lasso the moon, but . . .'

'. . . but?' Ellie prompted.

'It's something I was toying around with before I met Thea.' He waved his hand between them. 'You'll probably think it's stupid.'

'I don't think anything about you is stupid.'

His eyes snapped to hers.

A glitter bomb detonated in her chest. He was going to tell her he loved her too.

'Have you heard of a charity called Unite for Sight?'

She hadn't.

'They've got a project in Africa. There's one in particular in Ethiopia I was looking at. Really exciting grassroots stuff.'

'Oh?' For the second time in her life, she felt her heart shatter into a million pieces.

'There's a problem, though.'

'Oh?'

Too hopeful! She'd definitely sounded too hopeful.

'Gus,' Dan said, just as Ellie guessed, 'No visas?'

'What was that?'

'Nothing – I – uh – you were saying?'

'Gus here can't come. Which is nuts, right? I mean, he did all of his training to become a guide dog and failed his final exam for—'

Dan cut himself off, pride nearly bursting the buttons of his shirt. 'Guess why he failed.'

'Poor eyesight?'

'No!' Dan slapped his thigh as if that too would've been a corker of a reason. 'He failed . . . wait for it . . . for being "too friendly". Imagine that.' Dan shook his head in disbelief. 'Getting fired for being too friendly.'

They both winced.

'Birds of a feather,' he said with a rueful laugh as he gave the dog's head another scrub, and then added, 'What're we going to do with you now, big fella?'

'I'll take him,' Ellie heard herself say.

'No.' Dan drew the word out so that it synced with a slow shake of his head. A thick lock of his hair fell across his forehead as if he'd just freed it from a cowboy hat. And then his sky-blue eyes connected with hers. 'I couldn't ask you to do that.'

He could've asked her to do anything. Walk on hot coals. Climb Everest. Run away with him forever. But she bit her tongue, because there were rules.

'Really?' he asked.

She assured him she meant it. It would be nice to have a friendly face to come home to every night. But he should take the night to think about it. Two! As long as he wanted. The more she talked the more she wanted him to say yes. After all, since the Girl Code dictated she couldn't have Dan, what would be the next best thing? Dan's best friend!

She grabbed a notepad and wrote down her work number, her mobile and her email. They exchanged a few more *Are you sure?*s and *Yes, absolutely*s until, finally, Dan had been convinced to think about it.

'Wow!' Dan's voice had a proper lift to it. 'I don't know what to say.'

That you wish you'd met me first?

'You should break up with people all the time.'

'Ah ha ha ha ha,' she fake-laughed. 'Not really a skill base I like to put to work that often.'

'Right then!' Dan rose from his chair as if that was that. 'Well, Ellie. Thank you very much. You're a good woman. Now I guess I've got me some work to do.'

After being absorbed into a thank-you hug that her body would remember at a cellular level, he left the office with a smile on his face and a charge to his stride.

Thea emerged from the staff kitchen after a stage-whispered, 'Is it safe?' Then, when she was assured it was, screamed, '*La Liberación!*' She'd done Spanish at uni. 'Here you are, *chica*.' She jiggled a bottle of tequila in front of her. Ellie stared at it, confused. Why on earth would she need tequila when her entire insides felt as if they were one hundred proof?

The next few days passed in a dreamlike haze. Being lovesick and heartbroken all at the same time did that to a girl. Dan found a position with the charity of his choice pretty much straight away. Ellie assured him she really had meant it when she'd said she'd take Gus.

After a handover of leads, some kibble and a promise that he'd email every day and be back in a year, American Dan walked out of her life. One she no longer recognised. In the space of three weeks she'd left her home, been dumped by her fiancé, found a job, a flat, the unrequited love of her life and a dog called Gus. Wasn't life funny?

Thea moved on to Canadian Mike, Kiwi Karl and Scandinavian Styr. Ellie broke up with all of them for her until, eventually, she joked that she should start charging. Simon said that was genius and Thea said she alone would make Ellie rich. And so it was that, between the three of them, her services became a commodity.

Chapter Six

Right Now

American Dan, Thea, Simon and Ellie were all staring at one another – the same cast of a different play. A thriller. Each of them wondering what on earth was going to happen next. And not just with Gus. With one another. The dynamics of the moment hummed between them like electricity. The only thing they all knew for certain was that everything was about to change. It was at this moment that Ellie noticed some movement behind him. A woman. A very pretty woman holding American Dan's hand.

'Hey, everyone,' Dan said. 'I'd like you all to meet Sadie.'

Chapter Seven

Ten Minutes Later

Safely locked in the staff bathroom, Ellie pulled an Edvard Munch face in the mirror. When it became abundantly clear that not even a silent scream could help, she let it hang there. Saggy and blue. Mere moments ago, she'd foolishly thought life had thrown her sufficient curveballs. But no. Not only was she out of a humdrum but reliably paid job, she was about to go out for drinks with American Dan and the whole posse. And by 'posse' she meant Thea, Simon, herself, American Dan and . . . drumroll, please . . . Dan's new girlfriend: Dr Sadie Goodwin.

Now, Ellie had always considered herself a generous soul. Someone who didn't judge by first impressions. Even Kanye helped the poor. But as instantly as Ellie had loved American Dan, she'd disliked Dr Sadie Goodwin.

Sadie was a smiley, tousle-haired blonde who made not wearing make-up look like a good thing. She was dee-lightful. The Kate Humble of the medical world. Smart, funny, worldly in a down-to-earth kind of way and, from the looks of things, on track to spend the rest of her life with American Dan. Which, if history was going to repeat itself – and it definitely leant that way:

#SpiceGirlsReunionTour – it meant that the precisely stacked dominos of Ellie's London life were well and truly tumbling down. Dan would want Gus back. Simon and Thea would turn on her when Ellie inevitably discovered that the entire population of the United Kingdom was, in fact, in blissful relationships they'd never dream of ending. Once again, Ellie would be penniless, dogless and totally alone.

Not that she was catastrophising. Much. Her eyes hit the mirror again. Her scream face sagged further. Freaking out about the rest of her entire life while applying blusher had been an unwise choice. She looked like a Nineties glam rocker. She batted around in her tote and unearthed a packet of make-up wipes. (Organic *and* recyclable, if anyone was asking.)

She scrubbed at her face while simultaneously trying to deal with the emotional squall reaching storm-force levels in her chest. Getting pretty for someone who was clearly never going to love her back was pointless. He'd all but disappeared off the face of the earth for the last nine months. Totally ghosted her, as if she hadn't meant a thing. Proof, as if she'd needed it, of the undercurrent of fear that he had only been nice to her those first few months he was away because of Gus and not because he had fallen madly in love with her too. She thought of the paroxysms of fear and care that had gone into deciding whether or not to put a lower case *x* beside her name when she signed off and wanted to stuff her own head in the toilet and flush it for being such an idiot. And then, just as quickly, she was in a rage. How very dare Dan show up like this? Out of the blue and with a girlfriend. She wasn't going to let him run roughshod over her instinctively kind and generous nature this time. And no way was she letting him anywhere near Gus. He was hers and that was that. Just like Dan was Sadie's and that was that.

Her fleetingly cheered reflection wilted in despair. She'd worked herself into enough of a state that she wouldn't be needing the blusher. Her eyes looked like a mortician had stuck two out-of-date chocolate buttons on either side of her nose, and her hair was a lost cause. It got stuffed into a topknot.

She pulled out her mascara wand and brandished it at the mirror. She wasn't showing up tonight for herself. She was doing it for Gus.

Far too easily, she pictured Gus's adorable gold face and soulful brown eyes retreating in the back window of a Land Rover destined for Ulan Bator, where Dan and Sadie would single-handedly restore eyesight to an entire tribe of ancient peoples struck blind by some evil laboratory disease. Dan and Sadie would be sitting in the front seat, their little fingers hooked together where Dan's hand rested on the gearstick, the pair of them laughing joyously about how terrific they both were. Better, now that they were a threesome. Ellie's throat thickened with the threat of tears.

And then Thea pounded on the door demanding to know why the country mouse was holding everyone up.

◆　◆　◆

Three margaritas, a thousand shards of glass in her heart and one mumbled *excusemeIneedtheLadies* later, Ellie left the cocktail bar's basement loo, unsure if she could bear another round of the full-frontal assaults of shame and humiliation waiting for her upstairs. Not that anyone noticed, of course. This was a very private, excruciatingly painful perfect storm. What on earth had possessed her to believe that when American Dan reappeared in her life he'd fall in love with her? Thea and Simon were right. She was as naive as they came. Only a class-A numpty would've translated a few friendly texts and emails into flirtation. Brief missives in which Dan had asked about Gus and, because he was a polite human being, herself. She hadn't even told him! Well, of course she'd told him Gus was alive and well, but like a lovestruck school-girl she'd saved 'the big stuff', the really *good* parts, for when they were reunited. But then the emails had stopped as abruptly as he'd come into her life and somehow she'd convinced herself that that was okay. But now that there was living, breathing proof she *had* misread things it hurt a thousand times more. So she did the only thing she could think of. She began banging her head against the wall. *Thunk. Thunk. Thunk.*

'Ellie? Everything okay?'

American Dan. Of *course* it was. Who else would appear in this humiliating moment of self-flagellation?

'Hey! Hi. Yes. Definitely. I'm just—' She pointed at the wall. 'It's a little post-tequila ritual I have.' Ah ha ha ha. '*Olé.*'

He frowned, tipping his head one way and then the other as if slipping the information into place. 'Not seen that one before.'

'Yeah, well . . .' She gave a shrug she hoped said, *It's not my fault I'm this interesting*, then, cheeks burning, stared at her shoes. Even making eye contact with him was mortifying. As if her feelings for him were tattooed on her face. When she looked up he was still staring at her. Like a zoo exhibit. 'Gents is upstairs.'

'Oh, I – I wasn't here for the gents.' His blue eyes met hers and by the way her body responded she may as well have been swirling a knife around in a toaster. She looked deep into those eyes of his, praying they might tell her something. She saw something alright, but it wasn't what she had expected. Vulnerability. They both looked away.

'Sorry for appearing like this. Out of the blue.' She followed his fingers as he gave his hair a scrub and envied them instantly. More so when they slid down to his neck. He lifted his eyes to hers. Annoyingly she felt another electric jolt of connection. 'It's been quite a year.'

Humph. Well.

'Sounds like it.' She gave a few tequila-elasticated nods.

'Can we talk?' Dan asked. This didn't sound at all like he was going to confess his undying love for her so, pretty much, she didn't need to talk to him. Whatever salt he was planning on sprinkling in her wounds he could keep. For life seasoning. Or the next round of shots they ordered.

Ellie forced some crushed ice into her veins and took a step forward, hoping to squeeze past him, only to trip over one of his feet. He caught her by the elbow and righted her in a way that landed her in a kind of leg-straddling flamenco position. Goodness, he smelt nice. And felt nice. Nice enough to break every rule in the rulebook for . . .

No. Most assuredly not. Why, oh why, hadn't she stuck to the stay-sober plan?

Sadie was so damn lovely Ellie's will-power had instantly been stripped away. So she'd ordered a pitcher of margarita. Then Thea had ordered another. And Simon a third as Dan's gorgeous, South African-born, destined-to-win-a-peace-prize girlfriend bewitched them all. All of which would've been perfectly grand if Ellie wasn't tipsy and trying really hard not to grind against Dan's awfully lovely thigh. In a failed bid to remove herself, she accidentally leant into him. He winced and stiffened, grabbed her arms and practically lifted her off him, then abruptly stuffed his hands in his pockets as if touching her had giving him germs. 'Ellie, I—' he began.

She cut him off with a tight 'What is it you need to talk about?'

A woman about her age swept down the stairs and half aggressively, half apologetically pushed between them with a 'Sorry, I'm bursting.'

Ellie watched her disappear, desperately wishing she could follow her.

Dan dipped his head, trying to catch her eye. 'I owe you an apology, Ellie Shaw.'

She'd forgotten how his voice made her knees all melty. And that he had an adorable little spray of freckles across his nose. She considered them for slightly too long. One, two, three, four . . . twelve. She would've noticed freckles on the bridge of her unrequited love's nose before, wouldn't she? Perhaps they were new. Something he'd picked up in Africa. Like giardia. Or Sadie. She sucked in a breath. That was mean, and of all the things she knew about herself, being a vindictive meanie pants wasn't one of them. She closed her eyes, forced herself to remember that Dan Buchanan owed her absolutely nothing, then opened them only to feel her heart break afresh.

'You were saying?' she managed, taking a step back and leaning against the wall, trying to adopt an aura of nonchalance she definitely wasn't feeling.

Dan held his hands up and said, 'I know this is a little awkward and there are a lot of things I need to explain, but . . . I wanted to talk to you about Gus.' He spread his hand flat out on his heart as if he knew saying this exact collection of words would smash her heart into smithereens.

It did.

And in the space between those cracked bits of her cardio-vascular system, fear and panic and outrage poured in. Gus was her best friend. He knew her better than anyone. Better than her mum. Her sister. Her co-workers. He knew her scent, her whistle, the way she had to boop his nose before she hugged him goodbye every morning. He knew all of her secrets. Dark. Light. Silly. Anguished. And he didn't judge her for them. The same way she didn't judge him for drooling whenever she ate a Nando's. Fair was fair.

One year ago she couldn't have imagined life with him and now there was no way she could live without him. So she gave Dan a perky smile and said, 'No. I don't think so.'

He looked gutted rather than annoyed. 'I know I have a lot of explaining to do, Ellie, but . . . it's been a bit complicated.'

'Oh?' She continued in her bright *I'm pissed off but I'm going to sound cheery because I'm the better person here* voice. 'Complicated enough to make it impossible for you to contact me via Facebook or Twitter or Instagram or the email you used for two months before falling off the face of the earth?' She would've added something about the bank deposits stopping as well, but she didn't want to give him even a hint of an impression that she couldn't afford Gus, which, she had to admit, was tough, but if things progressed in sync with Vee's projection sheets, Gussy's kibble could be upgraded to premium-grade in a few months' time. When Dan failed to answer she said, 'I thought not,' and once again tried to move past him. He grabbed her arm. Not hard, but firmly enough so that she jolted to a stop millimetres from his face. This felt far less flamenco and much more face-off. She shook her arm free. 'Please don't do that.'

'Sorry. That wasn't how I—' He gave the back of his neck a frustrated scrub and tried again. 'Ellie, I . . .'

She looked at him, then. Really looked at him. He was different. And not just the freckles. There was something slightly less carefree about Dan Buchanan than there had been a year ago. Something guarded. And it didn't sit right. One of the things that had instantly pulled her into his orbit was his open honesty. The man seemed utterly incapable of keeping a secret unless it was a surprise party and even then, she suspected 'Don't tell Dan' had been a common childhood refrain.

'What happened out there?' she heard herself asking. 'In Ethiopia?'

He took a couple of jerky steps back, putting more space between them than felt natural. 'I just . . . I'd like to see Gus. Is that something we can set up? Like . . . a play-date kind of thing?'

Ellie's innards were savaged with indecision. Something had clearly happened out there. Something bad enough not to want to blurt it out or make something up like a normal person. *I got hit on the head by a huge bunch of bananas and had amnesia for nine months. Forgive me.* That sort of thing. But no. Dan just stood there and waited.

'Of course.' What else could she say? 'But . . .' She bit down on her lip. 'Can it just be you? You know. Too many people might be overwhelming for Gus.' And by Gus, she completely meant herself. Too late she realised that meant being alone with Dan.

Before she could retract the condition he agreed. Enthusiastically. 'Absolutely. Yes. Definitely. Whatever's best for Gus. And you. Obviously.' Dan was knocking out a series of rapid nods. The type a person did when a huge weight was lifted off their shoulders, only to realise the boulder that had just been moved made room for a thousand other problems they hadn't considered. 'Maybe we should meet after you've walked him? End of the day sort of thing? Where does he go during the day? Are your walks local to where you live? Is there a café near you?'

Ellie held up her hands with an emphatic 'Woah!' and increased the space between them. Dan's questions felt like hands grabbing at her. Wanting access to parts of her she wasn't ready to share. Even if they were gorgeous surgeon hands. She considered the situation. She had a break-up on Saturday and the last thing she wanted Dan to know was that she'd set up a business on the back of his split with Thea. 'How about Sunday morning? South Bank.' She was about to add, *Because walks are in public, where*

I can scream, 'That man's trying to steal my dog!', in a joking/not joking voice, when she noticed a few beads of sweat appear on his brow. Even though she didn't know him well, nervous sweat did not seem very Dan Buchanan.

'Okay. That's cool.' He shifted his weight back and forth, as if he was warming up for a sprint. 'I'm pretty flexible on the time front, so . . . whenever suits.'

Her heart felt as if it was being squashed in a vice it hurt so much. 'We'll walk along the South Bank,' she improvised. 'From the London Eye to London Bridge.'

His eyes lit up. 'The London Eye?'

'Well, not on it because . . .' She made a doggie noise.

'Aw, shoot.' He gave a rueful smile. 'I tried to get Thea to go on it with me I don't know how many times, and Sadie's been, like, half a dozen times already on previous trips, so . . .' He let the rest of the sentence falter and splutter between them as his eyes went wide and mournful, just like Gus's did when he really, really wanted a second doggie treat.

Oh, Dan Buchanan. You're making this so difficult.

Technically, Gus was an assistance dog. He helped little kids with their reading at the primary school across the street from her flat as his 'day job'. If he wore his working-dog vest, he could go on the London Eye. Telling Dan would be the nice thing to do. The generous thing to do. But he was here to take her dog back, so she said nothing. He had his secrets and she had hers. They exchanged phone numbers. She managed not to point out it was the same one she'd given him a year ago. Then they picked a spot to meet on the South Bank. When they'd finished, an awkward silence hung between them. He looked up towards the bar, then at her. 'We'd better get up there. But, thanks, Ellie. I really appreciate this.'

She broke the eye contact before he did. Staring into eyes that weren't hers to get lost in was a bad idea. 'No problem.'

He stood back and, gentleman that he was, held out a hand for her to lead the way.

When she got home she didn't even bother trying to get Gus to sleep in his own bed. She opened her arms for a cuddle, hoping like hell he didn't know she was bracing herself to say goodbye.

Chapter Eight

Name:

Amanda Brookes

How Did You Meet?

Hinge

How Long Have You Been Together?

Three dates

Reason There Was More Than One Date If There Was No Chemistry On First Date:

He's really awesome. I totally like him, but I'm pretty sure it's not going to work out.

Reason for Softer Landing:

I totally lied in my profile and said I liked rock climbing and dancing until dawn and a whole load of other stuff I would never do. I'm more of a boxset-in-my-onesie kind of girl. He wants to take me rock climbing this weekend and I said YES even though I am petrified of heights. (I know. Stupid.) PLEASE HELP!!!

Break-up Style (Please Tick Preferred Option):

☐ Text
☐ Email
☐ Scripted Phone Call
☐ One-to-one tutorial (Skype/Zoom/In-person session, price gradient applies)
☑ Bespoke Split (POA)

Please don't judge me, but if he and I ever meet again I'd love for him not to remember me as the girl who ugly cried on the first step of the rock climbing wall.

NOTES:

PS – He's a really cool guy so if there's any way to preserve my dignity but have him set his sights elsewhere (*sob!*), let's do that.

NB: Softer Landings requires a telephone or in-person interview prior to agreeing to Break-Up Style and reserves the right to refuse a split and/or to recommend an alternative method to that chosen by the client.

Thea bounced up to Ellie like Tigger after an afternoon at trampoline camp. 'Who am I?'

'Someone who just got the number of the sexy rock-climbing instructor?'

Thea held up an invisible microphone and dropped it. 'Boom!' She gave Ellie a hopeful smile. 'Help me out of it when I discover he's vegan?'

Ellie rolled her eyes then returned to her checklist. This break-up was trickier than most because Amanda didn't actually want to end things with Matt. They'd been out for coffee, then dinner, and, last weekend, held hands during a walk around Borough Market after taking a How To Make Doughnuts class. Each date had been better than the last, but when, after they'd had their first proper snog, he'd suggested they try one of their 'shared' interests – rock climbing – she knew her luck had run out. He was amazing, she'd enthused during their evaluation meeting, but she felt obliged to end things for his future happiness – a sentiment that really touched Ellie. On paper, Amanda's own parents had been polar opposites – her mum's homebody to her father's more adventurous spirit – but somehow it had worked. Yings to yangs. But Amanda was terrified it wouldn't be the case if she were to come clean. Not only did Matt's profile actively enthuse about a passion for rock climbing (with pictorial evidence), he also liked kite boarding (swimming in the sea made Amanda motion sick), kayaking (ditto) and, rather mysteriously, making sushi on rainy nights (which Amanda said she was all over but worried that her shellfish allergy might be the final nail in the coffin). She wanted to leave the relationship with her dignity and heart intact, and needed Softer Landings to help her achieve it.

Ellie gestured for Amanda and Simon to join them. 'One more quick run-through before Matt arrives?'

Amanda did some rapid nodding and, for the fifth time, wiped her sweaty palms on her workout leggings. Ellie clipped the chalk bag she'd just got at reception to Amanda's waist harness. Ellie's mind reeled with calming techniques she'd read about online. Her poor client didn't have an ordinary case of the pre-break-up jitters, she was entering proper panic-attack territory. 'You can do this,' Ellie assured her.

'No. I can't.'

Ellie put her hands on Amanda's shoulders. 'You've already been up to the second level of rocks. That's amazing.'

'I literally peed my pants doing it.' She pointed at her fresh leggings. 'This is my last pair of spares.' Panic suddenly consumed her. 'Oh god. He'll want to have a race or something, won't he? First one to the top!' she said maniacally, then hugged her arms around herself and shivered as she took in the towering wall at the far end of the cavernous hall.

Ellie reassured her. 'We've got this, remember? It's why we're going to start with you up the top of the abseiling wall with Thea.'

Amanda started shaking her head. 'No. I can't do it. I can't even walk up the stairs to get there because you can see down.'

'I can walk beside you – block the view. I know you don't believe it, but you are so much stronger than you think you are.'

Tears sprung to Amanda's eyes. 'That's so nice, but I can't do it.' The tears began to fall. 'We should just cancel this. Maybe you could meet him outside. Tell him I couldn't make it or something. Skip the part where I abseil and fake break my leg, and cut straight to the part where I have to move back to Sheffield. Maybe I should move back, anyway. I don't know if I'm cut out for this.' She spread her arms wide as if signifying the whole of London, and let out a solitary, heart-rending sob.

Ellie knew what she meant. London could be hardcore. It could also be one of the best places on earth. A place where you could meet the love of your life. She regrouped. This was one of her more inspired plans and she'd really been looking forward to watching it play out, but it didn't take an online psychology undergraduate degree to figure out Amanda's fear was real. Pushing her into doing it at this point would not only be mean but had the potential to be genuinely dangerous. She gave Simon and Thea a quick glance. Simon grimaced. Over-emotive clients were not his department.

Thea stepped in. 'I promise it'll be safe as houses up there. The ropes are strong. They, like, totally never break.' Thea gave the coiled rope clipped to her hip a tug. 'See? Solid as.'

Amanda squawked. 'I didn't even think of that! Oh god.' She grabbed Ellie's arms in a vice grip. 'Ohgodohgodohgod. Please don't make me do this.'

Amanda was entering full-on panic attack now. Ellie tried to get her to slow her breathing, to no effect. They'd have to change plans.

Just as she was digging out some tissues, Amanda's tearful whimpers turned into *no, no, no, this isn't happening* moans. Ellie looked up. Her heart sank. Matt was fifteen minutes early. He looked alarmed but not in the way she might have expected for an adventure guy encountering his new girlfriend in full-on crisis mode. Nor did he look like your average outdoor fitness buff – earth-toned clothes, wafts of patchouli and an obvious disdain for shampoo. No. Matt was more your cuddly bear variety of big and strong versus self-disciplined foraging for edible bugs and medicinal herbs lean. His stomach looked as if it had some give. His clothes were city-guy clothes. In fact, now that she thought about it, why had he shown up for rock climbing in a woollen winter coat, immaculate chinos and a blue button-up shirt?

Ellie whispered to Thea, 'He looks like he's going to brunch with his mother.'

'Amanda? Jesus. Are you okay?' He opened his arms and, to Ellie's surprise, Amanda ran into them.

Though her voice was muted by Matt's chest, most of what she said was audible. He could dump her right now if he wanted to. She was a lying liar pants from Liarsville. She hadn't been getting any dates she liked and a friend suggested she make stuff up on her profile to see if she could snag some different kind of guys, and then she'd met Matt who was perfect in every way, except for the outdoor stuff, which, she might as well admit it now, she hated. She was a bunny-rabbit-slippers kind of girl. She didn't like long walks and wasn't particularly good with people except for the three perfect dates she'd had with him and she knew she'd ruined it all now, but if they could remember the doughnut-making class with fondness, she'd be happy. And the little-finger holding. That had been one of the highlights of her entire four years in London.

He pulled a crisply ironed, polka-dotted cloth handkerchief out of his coat pocket and handed it to her. 'I owe you an apology.'

'What for?' Amanda sniffled. 'I'm the one who lied to you. About everything. All of it. Climbing, walking. I *hate* swimming in the sea. It makes me itchy.'

'It does?' Matt soothed, rubbing his gentle meat-cleaver hands over her shoulders, again and again, like he was petting a cat.

She looked up at him and nodded. 'It's all of that . . . *salt*.'

Matt considered her for a moment and then said, 'Well, that's a fucking relief.'

Amanda quirked her head to the side. 'What?'

'I hate it too.'

'You do?'

Matt nodded, a smile twitching at the corners of his mouth. 'I lied about everything as well. My mates set up my profile. Told me no one would want to date a guy who likes cooking classes and bottomless brunches so they Photoshopped me into some pictures from an adventure-wear catalogue.'

She sniffle-laughed. 'You like bottomless brunch?'

'I do.' Matt swept a few strands of Amanda's hair off her tear-stained face. 'And you know what else?'

'What?'

'I am terrified of heights.'

Amanda began to giggle. 'No, you're not. You're just saying that.'

'I'm not! Seriously.' He took a step back from her. 'Why do you think I'm dressed like this?'

She shook her head.

'I was going to tell you I forgot I had to meet my mum for brunch and that you'd have to do the session without me.'

Bingo. Thea elbowed Ellie in the ribs. Explaining away Ellie, Simon and Thea's presence as people who were meant to be in their session, Amanda gave them a grateful smile as Matt collected her things from reception so they could go for a meal and tell each other what they actually liked to do.

'I don't think we really earnt that one,' Ellie said when Amanda discreetly asked how much she needed to transfer.

Amanda went wide-eyed. 'Are you kidding? I wouldn't have even set foot in this place if it hadn't been for you guys. Who knows? Maybe we will try it one day.'

They all looked up to the abseiling 'cliff' where a woman was lowering herself with a high-pitched squeal.

Amanda paled. 'No. Forget that. It will never happen. But thank you. Seriously.'

They waved her off, then, once they were on their own, Thea turned her coiled rope into a lasso, swung it around and said, 'Right. It's time for me to go catch my instructor!'

Chapter Nine

As arranged, Dan was waiting by the carousel, his eyes glued to the morning joggers zooming along the Thames Path. As she walked towards him, her pulse punching out Morse code danger signals in her throat, Ellie noticed that, instead of his usual relaxed demeanour, Dan looked self-conscious. He kept shifting his body weight from one hip to the other. Readjusting his baseball cap and plucking at the sleeves of his winter coat. A navy-blue ski jacket that, if he hadn't looked so nervy, would've transformed him into a classic Netflix festive film hero. The kind who'd stayed at home in Montana working on the family Christmas tree farm instead of pursuing his dreams of becoming an architect, only to have built a fantasy house on the side of a mountain. But Dan definitely wasn't embodying that vibe today.

One of the things that had driven Thea nuts about him – in a bad way – was his complete lack of self-awareness. She'd endlessly complained that he had no clue how American he sounded. How white his trainers were. How easily he was awed by how old things were, and a myriad other annoyances that made it a complete mystery as to why she'd dated him at all let alone for three months. Apart from the fact he looked like Superman. But Ellie hadn't known about his looks back then. She'd not seen his beautiful blue eyes. His carved-from-marble bone structure. His tousled sandy brown hair that all but begged a girl to run her fingers through it.

She'd become aware of Dan complaint by complaint, slowly putting together a portrait of the man by the sum of his allegedly faulty parts. Simon had been dutifully horrified by each revelation. (*He wants to go to the London Dungeon by choice? He eats pizza with his hands? He spoke to someone on the tube?*) Whereas, the more Ellie had heard about him, the more she'd been convinced that if she'd met Dan first, she would've met a kindred spirit. What was wrong with wanting to go to tourist hot spots when you were, basically, a tourist? Why not see the Crown Jewels, queue for half-price *Phantom* tickets or watch the Changing of the Guard? It wasn't like the cool police would arrest them and release mug shots on Twitter. Maybe strawberry daiquiris and nachos at TGIF in Piccadilly was his version of being homesick. Sure, it wasn't exactly cutting-edge cuisine, but who cared? It was endearing. And who didn't like nachos?

The truth was, she'd probably fallen in love with Dan before she'd even laid eyes on him because she loved his approach to life in London. Where her version was to go to work then return straight home to Gus for cosy cuddles, he treated the city and its many treasures as one might a celebrity friend: with complete and utter awe. And he was right to. London was amazing. Everything was bigger, faster and brighter in the capital. Modern and overwhelming. Historic and strangely familiar. The first time she'd seen Buckingham Palace she'd actually burst into tears. It had been unbelievably comforting to see something so completely familiar that she'd felt as if she could walk up to the gates and be granted entry. And yet she'd got lost on her way back to the tube. Then ridden the wrong way round on the Circle Line. One of countless moments highlighting just how little she knew about the place after all. Her cheeks still burnt when she recalled the time she'd explained her transport route from work to one of their client's places on Piccadilly (bus to Tottenham Court Road, tube to Leicester Square, then tube to Piccadilly Circus) only to discover she could walk it from the office in about five minutes. Thea had literally wept with laughter.

That sort of thoughtless derision was one of the many reasons Ellie had stepped in to release Dan. Her sister was exactly the same way. Flippant with her word choice. Unaware that her disdain could not only sting, but poison. Just because Ellie had a degree from the Open University didn't mean it didn't count! And yet, somehow, Aurora had always been the centre of attention. The most lovable. The prettiest. The most fun. Unlike Ellie. Whose solid choices and steady ways had only made her discardable in the end. She looked down at Gus.

'Well, bud?' she said. 'This is it.'

◆ ◆ ◆

Still a couple of metres away, Dan's face lit up when he saw them. His eyes dropped from hers almost instantly down to Gus. Every nerve ending in her body prickled with anxiety. Would Gus remember Dan? Bound into his arms the way they did in the YouTube videos where dogs and owners were reunited?

Gus's tail was wagging with his trademark enthusiasm. Dan knelt down so that they were on the same eye level. Gus tugged on his lead, clearly wanting to saying hello. To stop herself from screaming *No! You can't have him!* and running away, Ellie tersely reminded herself that this was Gus's normal modus operandi. He'd never met a human he didn't like. No matter the human, the tail was wagging. The bum swing keen. But . . . it wasn't what you'd describe as exuberant. There was no special *I remember you! You're American Dan!* about it. Which, unexpectedly, made her sad. Her entire nervous system had short-circuited when Dan had reappeared. Why wasn't Gus's?

Maybe she was giving off vibes. Vibes that extended to Dan because even he seemed hesitant. Rather than pull Gus into his arms and bury his head in his golden ruff as she would've expected, Dan held out a hand as if she'd just introduced him to a new colleague. Because Gus was an obliging pooch, he sat down and held out his paw. Dan shook it. Gus tilted his head, trying to figure out if he was meant to do anything else and, clearly deciding that his work here was done, lay down. Dan looked up at her, his smile unsure. 'Do you think he remembers me?'

Ellie didn't have a clue. 'Sure. Of course. He . . .' She scrunched her shoulders up round her ears. 'He always lies down in front of people when he feels really comfortable.'

The lie twisted in her gut. How weird that she'd *wanted* Gus to remember him. Had wanted Dan to have that moment where his faithful hound recognised him from two hundred metres away, tugged himself free of his lead and bounded across the esplanade, leaping up into Dan's arms, licking his face and wriggling with undiluted joy that his master had, at long last, come back to claim him. She would've liked to follow suit, but was pretty sure Sadie's existence and the fact they'd already met would make leaping into Dan's arms and licking him a little weird.

Dan pushed himself back up to standing with a small *oof* and gave Ellie a forlorn smile. 'Two weeks probably wasn't enough time to make a proper impression.'

Ellie begged to differ. Dan's existence had been burnt into her soul from the moment she'd laid eyes on him. Maybe this was Gus's way of showing loyalty. An *I'm with her now* kind of thing. At least someone wanted her.

'So!' Dan clapped his hands together. 'Are you ready for this walk?'

'Sure thing,' she said, looking up to the sky as she did. 'It's not looking very promising, is it?'

Dan laughed. 'Sadie says anyone who expects British weather to do anything obliging in February is living in a fool's paradise.'

Oh, did she now? Ellie bit back a snippy comment stinging the end of her tongue. A grey English winter affected anyone who'd grown up in a sun-soaked paradise. And just like that, she suddenly missed Jersey's sprawl of fields filled with daffodils. And her family. Which came as a surprise. There were a thousand things she thought about her mum and sister, but longing for them hadn't been among them.

'Don't you think?' she heard Dan ask.

'Sorry.' She pulled a face. 'What were you saying?'

'Lordy!' Dan scrubbed a hand over his face. 'Sadie was right.'

'About what?'

He shook his head and shifted his hand to his neck. 'Nothing.'

Desperation clawed at her. Had he been baring his soul to her and she'd missed it? 'Please,' Ellie practically begged. 'I'm interested.'

He looked away. 'It was nothing, really. Should we give this guy his walk? He seems rarin' to go.'

Gus was still lying on the pavement, looking pretty relaxed. She glanced back at Dan. He was proactively not meeting her eye. That niggling feeling that something awful had happened out in Ethiopia wormed its way back into her brain. As self-appointed Queen of Dodging Personal Issues, Ellie opted to let whatever it was gnaw away at her rather than torture Dan into repeating himself. Another moment lost she would have to live with. She pointed them in the direction of London Bridge and, steering clear of the steady stream of joggers, they began to head east.

After a few minutes of not entirely companionable silence Dan said, 'You were going to tell me what Gus gets up to during the day. Do you bring him into work?'

Again, her emotions clashed in response to the question. This was meant to be her big reveal. The moment when Dan realised he'd not only got the perfect dog, but the perfect girl. 'No. He got his own job pretty much straight away.'

'A job?' Dan sounded dismayed.

Ellie held up her hands. 'Gus helps little kids with reading.'

His features softened, then morphed into a proud papa expression. He reached out and gave Gus's head a big old hand scrub. 'Do you, Gussy, ol' boy? You help the kiddos, do you?'

Ellie nodded, her annoyance slipping away. 'He does. Monday to Friday at the primary school across the street from my flat.'

'How did you know to bring him there?'

'I didn't,' she admitted. 'I was taking him out for a walk on the first night I had him and this woman came out of the school.'

'A teacher?'

'Librarian,' Ellie corrected. 'Mallory Post.'

'Ha!' Dan hooted. 'Great name.'

Ellie smiled. 'Great woman.' She explained how Mallory had come out of the school and had spotted Ellie trying to get into their playground. Mallory had stopped her with a 'Sorry, it's private property and we can't really have dogs pooping on it because of the children.'

Ellie had been mortified, fell over herself apologising and explaining how she was brand-new to dog ownership and didn't know the rules.

'Sweet dog,' Mallory had said. 'There's a small park over this way. Shall I show you?'

They'd got chatting. Ellie explained how she'd come into possession of a too-friendly failed guide dog. Mallory had perked up at this. 'You mean, they didn't try to place him with another charity?'

All she'd known was that he had been American Dan's one day and now he was hers so, by extension, she and Dan would be linked forever. She left that part out in the retelling. Obviously.

'I got him through the hospital,' Dan explained.

'Oh! I can't believe I'd never asked.' She totally could. She'd been too busy trying not to throw herself into his arms and beg him to make them a family of three to ask sensible things like *What's your dog's origin story?*

Dan stopped walking and gave the side of Gus's face a stroke with his knuckle. 'Yeah. They have these great volunteers who work with the Guide Dogs charity. They bring trainee hounds into the hospital sometimes. You know, to see how they do in the environment and to have trial runs with some of our patients who are either partially sighted or blind.'

Ellie nodded, too embarrassed to ask why a person who was already blind would need an ophthalmologist. 'Anyway. This furry guy was having a session with one of my patients – cutest little kid.' His expression went all dopey as he described an eight-year-old patient who he clearly had a soft spot for. 'Gus here was good as gold when it was just the two of them, but the second you put them in a room with a bunch of other little kids?' He laughed and gave Gus another little knuckle stroke. 'You loved everyone. Didn't you, bud?' His voice faded as he spoke, his expression shifting to somewhere far away.

Ellie blinked up at the sky, grateful for a sudden increase in the drizzle that had descended upon them. No way was she going to let Dan see her tear up because of his awesomeness.

Dan cleared his throat and waved a gloved hand between them. 'I'm sorry. I keep interrupting you. You were saying?'

Ellie gave him an abbreviated version of explaining to Mallory that she was trying to figure out the best way to ask her boss if she could bring him to work because she couldn't find a doggie day care that was in her budget, only for Mallory to volunteer to train him up to be a reading assistance dog.

Ellie had never heard of such a thing. Mallory explained that kids who struggled with reading were frequently found to be much better at it, or more relaxed about trying, if they read with a PAT dog.

Ellie had leapt at the opportunity. Her sister was dyslexic and trying to get her to read had been one of the many banes of their mother's existence. All Gus had needed to do was pass a test with a certified Pets As Therapy group. 'Which he did with flying colours,' Ellie said proudly.

'Course he did.' Dan shared her pride.

'He's a bit of a champ, isn't he?' Her eyes swept up to his.

'Total dude,' Dan agreed. Their eyes caught and cinched over Gus's golden head, and for a minute the world stopped spinning and Ellie had exactly what she'd dreamt of. A perfect family of three. And then, because this was real life, Dan said, 'I wish Sadie could meet him.'

Ellie kept her smile pasted in place and concluded brightly, 'So that's what he does during the day.'

'And at night?' Dan asked.

'He hangs out with Mallory until I get home or sometimes she pops him in the flat if she knows I'm not going to be late.'

'Oh?' Dan's forehead crinkled. 'Do you work late nights often?'

Not for Media Angels, she didn't. But for Softer Landings? Yeah. 'I've got a pretty regular schedule,' she lied.

'That's great. I— You've been amazing, Ellie. Seriously.'

Dan's phone beeped. He pulled it out of his pocket and frowned at it. By now they'd reached the arch under the Millennium Bridge just outside the Tate Modern. It was raining so hard Ellie was going to suggest they put Gus's service vest on and get a coffee inside the monolithic museum.

'It's Sadie,' he said apologetically. 'I'm real sorry, but I've got to scoot. Do you – I don't suppose you know where the nearest tube is?'

Ellie pulled out her phone. 'I think there's one just across the bridge. It's perhaps a fifteen-minute walk?'

Dan frowned. 'Maybe I'll just get an Uber.'

'Might be tough in the rain.'

He tapped on his phone and held it up for her to see. 'There's one two minutes away.'

'They're always a good half an hour away whenever I'm desperate for one.' Ellie waved an invisible magic wand. 'You must have the lucky touch.'

'Lucky in some respects,' Dan said in a tone she couldn't put a finger on. 'Lucky in some.'

As they said their goodbyes, Dan asked if he could reach out again for another play date. Ellie said fine but only waved rather than walked with him when his Uber came. Then, only a little guiltily, she put Gus's assistance dog vest on and went inside for a coffee. And possibly a very large pastry. She turned off her phone, too nervous she'd receive a text from Dan remembering to ask for custody. 'We can live without the phone for a bit, can't we, pal?' she asked Gus.

He nodded soberly. *Yes,* his expression read. *We can live without a lot of things. But not without each other.*

◆ ◆ ◆

Back in her flat, Ellie towelled Gus dry, wrapped her own hair in another towel and popped the kettle on. She turned on her phone, surprised to see that she'd missed not one but three calls. The first two were from Thea.

'What the actual hell, Ellz? Is there a plan for this lesbian split or what? She's really counting on us before they announce her role in the TV thingie.'

The second an even less subtle 'Deets. Now. Otherwise I dump the lesbian by text.'

This, of course, wouldn't do.

The third message was from her mum. 'Hello, darling. I hope you're well. I just thought I'd let you know, in case Aurora hasn't . . . I think she's feeling a little sensitive about it . . .'

Ellie huffed out a sigh. She loved her sister, but what wasn't Aurora sensitive about?

'Anyway,' her mother continued, as if knowing Ellie would be suppressing a sigh, 'your sister's getting married. To Chris.'

What? Was this a joke? Chris Le Brun. The one man whose heart Aurora had crushed over and over and over ever since they'd first met in the sandpit at nursery. She'd never known how Chris had the stomach for it. Going back to Aurora after she'd dabbled elsewhere in the boyfriend playground then, as ever, returning to Chris, contrite for a while, happy for a spell, and then, inevitably, utterly miserable and demanding yet another break-up.

She made herself tap out a text to her mum.

Wow! So happy! True love triumphs in the end! I can't wait to hear all of the details. Ellz xx

It was a lot of exclamation points for something that made her stomach churn. She massaged her temples in time with an oft-repeated mantra that Aurora wasn't evil. Or cruel. In fact, she'd always reminded Ellie of Kate Winslet's character in *Sense and Sensibility* – the artless but completely magnificent Marianne, who lived with her heart on her sleeve as if each day would be her last. Ellie, of course, played the far more sensible Emma Thompson role, a woman who knew that unrequited love was painful but safe. Or maybe it was just painful. With her sister getting married and Dan showing no signs of dumping Sadie and declaring his love for her, Ellie was the cheese who stood alone.

She balled her hands into fists, knowing there was no one to punish but herself. She knew it would hurt to spend time with him and should have exercised her right to say no. Her heart crumpled at the thought of never seeing him again, then seared with pain at the thought of doing precisely that. How could she be so good at other people's romances and utterly horrendous with her own?

She dialled Thea's number, her body all but twitching with undirected energy. When she picked up, Ellie didn't mince words. 'Pub. Now. Let's break up some clients.'

Chapter Ten

To: Metro Advertising Department
From: Softer Landings Relationship Co.
RE: Ad copy

Dear Advertising Department (sorry – there
wasn't a name on the email),

I'd love to put in an advertorial puff for my
company, Softer Landings. Copy below, with
attached graphic. Please do let me know if you
have any questions.

Best wishes – Ellie Shaw
MD Softer Landings

♥ Would your Valentine's Day be better if you were single? ♥
Softer Landings can make that happen for you and your partner
with *both* of your best interests at heart.
Please contact us at query@softerlandings.co.uk
For more information visit our website at www.softerlandings.
co.uk

Or follow us @SofterLandings and be sure to spread the word: breaking up *isn't* hard to do, if you're doing it with heart. Don't prolong the inevitable – give your partner a softer landing.

◆ ◆ ◆

Flicka the actress, Simon, Thea and Ellie had been in deep discussion for a good hour when Thea abruptly slapped both of her hands on the table.

'I'm thirsty. Shall I get another round in on the business account?'

Before Ellie could protest, Thea was up and signalling Jasper at the bar.

'I guess that was rhetorical,' Simon laughed, then asked Flicka, 'Another red?'

She shook her head. 'Vodka tonic. Slimming.'

'Ellz?'

'Lime and soda, please,' Ellie said pointedly. They were here for work. Now that Softer Landings was a proper business that had to pay her rent, low-priced beverages and a head that was screwed on straight were essential. With Valentine's Day on fast approach, their client list was growing. Which was a relief, as the date when she would be paying Vee rent was careering towards her at a terrifying rate of knots. Her phone buzzed. She peeked at it. It wasn't a number she recognised. She flipped it back over with a silent reminder that she needed to change the answerphone message. Or maybe get a whole new number. It would be a class-A disaster if her mum, sister or, worse, Dan, rang her, only to hear about Softer Landings' £29.99 Valentine's Split Special.

Gus nudged her foot under the table as he adjusted his snoozing position, a subtle reminder that humans weren't the only couples that might not be together on Valentine's. She pushed the thought away. Dan had already had two chances to ask for Gus back and hadn't, so she was considering that a good thing. She started to ask Flicka a question about her intended ex when Flicka bounced out of the booth to join Thea at the bar.

Seriously? This was *her* break-up. Getting sozzled on bison grass vodka and lite tonic was not the point of this exercise.

Simon gave Ellie a knowing smile. 'She's annoying you, isn't she?'

Ellie opened her mouth to protest and then couldn't be bothered. She held up the questionnaire Flicka had barely filled in and wriggled the list of one and two-word responses between them. 'Beyond knowing that her future ex helped create the crowd scenes in *World War Z* and did some freelance work on *Shaun the Sheep: Adventures From Mossy Bottom*, you would think they'd been together for two weeks, not an entire year.'

Simon shrugged. 'Maybe they've both been really busy?'

Ellie blew a raspberry. 'The first year you're in love with someone? You want to know *everything* about them. The need is voracious. The same way you need ice cream when you've got PMT.'

'Not really my area of expertise.' Simon toyed with the stem of his wine glass for a moment then said, 'She probably doesn't want to acknowledge that she's dumping her girlfriend to preserve an image she doesn't even have yet.'

'Insightful.'

'I know, right?'

She smiled. All of his *ewww, don't even!* fussiness masked a wondrous, empathetic heart. Simon was proper off-the-charts perceptive. She did find it curious that he only pulled out his laser-sharp insights when Thea wasn't within witty repartee distance. 'You're so wise,' she said with a little bow.

He nodded and made a gesture inviting her to repeat after him. 'And beautiful.'

'And beautiful,' she dutifully added, knowing his recent trip to the microdermabrasionologist to unearth a fresh, dewy layer of skin meant he'd need a bit more positive affirmation than normal. The fact he'd come out at all was a testament to his belief in Softer Landings. She raised her glass to him. 'I wanted to thank you.'

'For what?'

'Helping me go legit.'

'Whatever keeps Vee happy keeps us all happy, and she *loves* a project.'

Before Ellie had a chance to let the comment fully register, Simon leant forward and whispered, 'I heard Flicka's contract is only for three months with the option to kill off her character if the producers don't feel it's working.'

Simon knew things like this. His job at Media Angels was to place freelance producers with production companies. He not only read all of the industry insider mags, he knew the people who wrote them. As such, he was a font of *Heat* magazine-worthy nuggets.

'Interesting.'

'Isn't it just?' Simon said in the way Poirot would give a *this just might be a clue* wink and nod to the camera.

She gave the questionnaire a tap. 'Maybe Flicka genuinely doesn't have a clue what her girlfriend wants from life.'

Simon made a buzzer sound. 'That would mean she doesn't care. In which case, she would've chucked Jessie the minute she got the role and thrown her to the wolves, tabloids be damned. You know what they say. All publicity is good publicity. The fact she's called us? It means she cares.'

'Aww. You're a secret romantic at heart, aren't you, Simon?'

He pulled a face then winced, still a bit sore from the morning's treatment.

She just smiled at him. Anyone who had the home life he did definitely believed in the power of love. Even more than Celine. Which did beg the question . . .

'Simon? Why are you here instead of home?'

He rapid-blinked at her for a couple of beats then said, 'Apart from the fact you demanded my presence?'

'Yes. Apart from that.' They both knew she didn't wield that sort of power over him.

He looked her in the eye. 'I think doing this is important.'

'Really?' She thought she was the only one who had an emotional investment in Softer Landings.

'Absolutely.' Simon's voice went unexpectedly scratchy. 'Life's too short to spend it in a horrible relationship.'

She raised her lime and soda to him. Then, after she drank, asked, 'Do you ever think we're enablers rather than genuinely helping?'

'In what way?'

'Letting spineless, cowardly people unable to be honest with their partners off the hook by doing their "dirty work" for them?'

Simon laughed. 'So much for "compassion for one and all"!'

She pulled a face. *Compassion for one and all* had been the tagline for the speech she'd given them when they'd first decided to do this. It was, she'd insisted, a stance that ensured what they were doing was on the right side of morally justifiable actions.

She scrubbed her fingers through her hair. 'You know what I mean. Is our remit capitalising on other people's misery?'

'Of course it is,' Simon said with a careless flick of his hand. 'But like I said, life's too short to be miserable, Ellz. We offer a salve to the misery. We don't stick the knife in. We're like . . . chemotherapy.'

She gave him the side eye. 'Yeah, I'm not following that one.'

Simon explained. 'Chemo's shit, right?'

Ellie nodded. She hadn't had it herself, but she knew enough to know it wasn't a holiday in the Maldives.

Simon continued, 'Anyone who knew going through chemo would give them many happy, healthy years to live would do it, right?'

She was about to say having a disease that could end in death was a million times harder than breaking up with someone they'd met on a dating app, but knew Simon's boyfriend, Diego, didn't have chemo as an option. So from his perspective? Torture by chemicals was very much a silver-lining scenario.

'What you have to remember, my little Ellzy Bellzy, is that, excepting *moi*, your good self and Diego, obvs, all human beings are vile. Including My Little Pony up at the bar.' They both turned to look at Thea. Her ponytail was swinging into the face of a poor vertically challenged man trying and failing to wrangle Jasper's attention. Completely serious now, Simon took Ellie's hands in his and said, 'Softer Landings is a company people come to if they're having a crisis of conscience. If they were genuinely horrid people, they'd just dump their other half. Ghost them. Whatever. What we do allows clients to believe that they are kind and that the course of action they've chosen is the right one.'

Ellie shook her head. 'I don't know. It's a bit like adopting a sanctuary donkey and never following up, isn't it?'

'No! Not even close,' protested Simon. 'The person who gets dumped *is* the donkey, Ellz. We love the donkey. We comb the donkey. We feed the donkey. We make sure that donkey is kicking up its heels when we send it out to pasture. We are donkey lovers, Ellz.'

She frowned. 'So what does that make Flicka?'

'The person who should never have had a donkey in the first place,' Simon said matter-of-factly.

They looked back up at the bar. Flicka was one of those beautiful people who could command the attention of any room she walked into. She exuded confidence the way a peacock possessed poise. *I am beautiful*, her aura read. *Deal with it*. And yet, Ellie didn't buy it. Actors were actors for a reason. They were good at pretending. When she turned back, Simon was staring at her.

'What?'

'Is your crisis of conscience actually about Flicka?'

Of course it wasn't. 'Yes, and you've cured me. Thank you, Simon.' She blew him a kiss then flipped her notebook to a new, blank page. 'Now. I've got an idea. Flicka said Jessie worked as a digital special effects artist, right?'

◆ ◆ ◆

Two hours later, Flicka and Jessie were holding hands across the table from one another, tears pouring down their faces. Also nestled in the booth were Ellie, Thea, Simon, and Gus – each of them, by turns, sombre-faced, sympathetic and, as and when necessary, doling out tissues. 'Are you sure you're good with this?' Jessie asked Flicka. 'It's a bitch of a way to end a relationship.'

'I'm sure,' Flicka said a bit too quickly. 'I mean, obviously, it hurts, but . . . I can't hold you back professionally.' Flicka looked up, a few tears poised on her fake lashes as if they'd been balanced there by one of Hollywood's premier make-up artists. Ellie hid a smile. Her character definitely wouldn't be killed off on the soap.

'We could try the long-distance thing . . .' Jessie began half-heartedly.

With a sorrowful sigh of resignation, Flicka dipped her gaze then raised it with a fawn-like innocence. 'We both know how hard that would be.'

This appeared to be all the confirmation her now ex-girlfriend needed.

Jessie broke into a goofy smile. 'I can't believe Peter Jackson's production team want me!' She clapped her hands and shook her head in disbelief. 'Sorry. I shouldn't be grinning like a lunatic when . . . well . . . when we're splitting up.'

Flicka was quick to protest. 'No. You deserve this. You've wanted to be a fur groomer for ages and you'd be completely stupid to turn this down.'

Thea guffawed. 'I totally thought you were grooming actual dogs.'

Ellie glared at her while, mercifully, Jessie launched into a detailed explanation of how you animated dog hair.

Thea, annoyed, mouthed at Ellie, *What?*

Duh! They were the ones who were supposed to be the experts in this. The film aficionados Flicka had just *happened* to run into at the pub she'd *spontaneously* sought shelter in when an unexpected downpour drove her indoors and into the booth of this particular group of recruitment specialists. Oh, the coincidences.

Honestly. Sometimes Ellie couldn't believe people fell for their set-ups. Then again, she'd believed Sebastian each time he'd asked for 'just one more year' of knuckling down on his own to get that junior partner position he had his eye on. Anyone could have the wool pulled over their eyes if they were desperate enough for the lies to be true. Ellie tuned back into the conversation in time to hear Flicka saying to Jessie, 'I think it was fate speaking to us. I mean . . . of all the pubs in all of London . . . I walked into this one.'

Ellie hid her face. Seriously? *Casablanca?* Did she *want* Jessie to know this was a set-up?

Oblivious, or too happy to care, Jessie shot grateful looks around the booth. 'I will tell everyone I know to use your company. You are genuine Media Angels.'

'Just doing our job!' Simon quipped, making a little halo out of his fingers and placing them above his perfectly coiffed head.

Simon had properly pulled one out of the bag tonight. On the back of Ellie's idea to find Jessie an all-consuming job she couldn't turn down, Simon had called in a couple of favours. When one of them came up trumps, Simon rang Lara, the special effects recruiter on the Media Angels team. Lara had demanded an explanation as to why he couldn't wait until Monday like a normal person, but after a lot of artful blustering about 'creative types like herself', pinging through of CVs and the promise of a chunky commission, the questions had abated and their story was taken as read.

So now, here they were, chinking glasses in a farewell toast. Farewell to a year-long relationship and farewell to Jessie, who was going home to pack her bags for a contract at Peter Jackson's Wellington film studios, where she would move animated dog fur from one side of a dog's forehead to another for an indeterminate number of years. It was a gold-dust job offer. It always surprised Ellie that those types of jobs required recruitment agencies at all. Mind you, it also surprised her that girls like Thea could date men like American Dan and not want them, so . . . wasn't the world just full of mystery?

A few hugs and many cheek kisses later, Flicka and Jessie left the pub to paint the town red. It was such a satisfying ending, Ellie decided now was the perfect time to properly toast the official beginnings of Softer Landings.

When she suggested they get another drink, Thea, most unusually, cried off, saying she had to get home. Returning to the garden flat that she shared with her sister was something Thea rarely opted for, which meant she was probably going on a date with someone either Ellie or Simon wouldn't approve of. After she'd left, Simon's newly refreshed face suddenly looked very, very tired.

'Are you okay, Si?'

'Diego's got three months left,' he said plainly.

Ellie gasped, the news hitting her like a free-swinging wrecking ball. Simon's boyfriend had received his diagnosis a year before Ellie had joined the team at Media Angels. Motor neurone disease. 'I'm so sorry. I thought he had ages yet.'

If Simon could have frowned, he would have. 'What gave you that impression?'

She pulled a face, embarrassed. 'I watched *The Theory of Everything* when I found out what he had. I thought maybe – well – Eddie Redmayne lived for years.'

'You mean Stephen Hawking.'

Ellie considered punching herself in the face and not stopping until it had gone completely concave. Instead she started to cry. Which, all things considered, was probably worse.

Gus gave her a nuzzle and then she cried harder, because if life threw these kinds of curve balls at couples who truly deserved a happy ending, who knew how much longer she'd have with Gus.

Simon handed her a tissue. 'Some say it's kinder this way.' Her heart ached for him. She'd only met Diego a few times. The first time, she, Thea and Simon had been sitting out in the sunshine in the pub's canal-side garden discussing a Softer Landings client when all of a sudden Simon had shot out of his seat and said, 'Diego would love this,' and disappeared. While he was gone, Thea filled her in. Diego was originally from small-town Spain, where being the flamboyantly homosexual son of a bull-fighting saddle maker wasn't *bueno*. He was desperately gorgeous and, having grown up helping his father in the saddlery, was a dab hand with a needle and thread. After being pummelled in dark alleys one too many times, he'd run away to London and secured himself a job at the National Theatre Costume department, where he'd worked for years, right up until he'd designed an iconic handbag that now swung on the forearms of supermodels and film stars alike. He and Simon had met at some crossover event – a play that was to become a film that needed costumes and, of course, a producer. And that had been that. Love at first red carpet. When he'd received his diagnosis, he had begged Simon to leave him. It was time wasted, he'd insisted. Time Simon could use to find someone else.

'But he wouldn't do it,' Thea had said in a reverent tone. 'He's always said Diego was his first true love, and his last.'

Simon had wheeled Diego into the pub garden and it was as if the whole world went a brighter shade of summer. Diego was funny, smart and very clearly the love of Simon's life. When the two of them left, Thea had downed the trayful of shots she'd bought but that no one had taken and drunkenly informed Ellie that if she were ever to fall in love she wanted to do it properly, the way those two had. And then she'd left with a man she picked up between their picnic table and the gate to the canal path. Thea's absence now spoke volumes. She knew Simon's news. And she didn't want to know.

'Can I do anything?' Ellie asked.

'No.' Simon began to pull on his jacket. 'I kind of wish I hadn't told you.'

'I won't tell anyone, I promise.'

'No, it's not that,' Simon assured her. 'I know you're discreet. It's more . . . this particular problem shared isn't really a problem halved, is it?'

Ellie shook her head. No. It wasn't. If anything, it magnified it. 'If it helps,' she added lamely, 'it puts everything I've been worrying about in perspective.'

Simon hooted and gave her hand a pat. 'Thrilled to be of help, darling.'

It struck Ellie that Softer Landings was the last thing Simon needed crowding up his calendar. Surely he'd want to spend all of his time with Diego now that there was an actual clock ticking. She was just about to say as much when he closed his hand around hers and gave it a squeeze. 'I should be the one thanking you, actually.'

'What for?'

He gestured round their booth. 'This. Softer Landings. It's the only thing keeping my head above water.'

'Really? I always feel like I'm taking more than I'm giving. Your time. Your contacts. Your—'

'Not even,' Simon insisted. 'Diego's always trying to get me out of the house, desperate for me to prove to him I'll have a life after – you know.'

. . . after his world fell apart. It had never occurred to her that Simon might be using Softer Landings as a life raft.

He took both of her hands in his. 'Doing this gives me something to look forward to. And though she'd never say, it means the world to Thea as well.'

'Really?' Ellie found that hard to believe.

'Deffo,' Simon assured her. 'She might seem all hard edges and snappy comebacks, but our little whippersnapper struggles with the whole human relations thing. Working with you has changed her. In a good way.'

Wow. That was news. Simon gave her a jaunty little chuck under the chin. 'It's us who owe you, Ellie Shaw. You're a real life-saver.' He pulled up the zip on his coat then dropped her a sad little wink. 'Besides, I might need a staff discount in a year's time. Who knows what sorts of bad decisions await me.'

Chapter Eleven

Ellie curled up in the corner of the sofa, waiting for Gus to climb up beside her and rest his head on her thigh before she thumbed through to the number she needed and pressed it. Seconds later, as if she'd been sitting at the kitchen table and staring at it, her mum picked up the phone. 'Hello, darling.'

'Hey, Mum.'

'How are you, love? London still keeping you busy?'

'As ever,' she chirped.

'And Seb?' her mum asked through the clatter of a spoon rattling round a teacup.

'He's good.'

'Working tonight?'

Ellie gave one of those dry but loving girlfriend laughs. 'When isn't he?'

'Oh, darling. The both of you work ever so hard. You must be close to having a deposit for a house by now. You know, your father and I—'

Ellie cut her off. When her mum hit memory lane it was next to impossible to reel her back in. 'Shouldn't we be talking about Aurora?' Ellie asked as brightly as she could muster.

'Yes, well. That.'

'Yes,' Ellie mimicked the tone. 'That.'

'Now, Ellz, I know you think Aurora might not have treated Chris all that well, but I've seen a real change in her over the past year.'

Ah. Her mother was in protective mode. Surprise, surprise.

'Mmmhmmm,' she managed as neutrally as she could.

Her mother tutted. 'Ellie Shaw. Cynicism doesn't become you. Just because you and Seb have been together forever and haven't endured the bumps in the road Chris and Aurora have doesn't mean things won't work out.'

Ellie would reserve judgement on that, but pushing things to the extent that her non-existent boyfriend was being lauded for his ability to commit was a bitter pill to swallow.

Her mum took a slurp of tea then said, 'You know, I actually think it was you leaving the island that changed her.'

'What? No.' She doubted that. The two of them had had a massive row after Ellie had given Chris the bad news that Aurora just wasn't that into him, for the fourth time. Ellie had unleashed a *this is the last time* lecture on her and, for the first time ever, Aurora had come back fighting. Aurora, it turned out, was well aware of her faults, but Ellie? Ellie just liked to stick her head in the sand about hers. Fixing everyone else's life instead of her own. She'd literally forced Ellie to look in the mirror and demanded to know how she could act so superior when she had spent seven entire years waiting for Sebastian to give her a date when either he'd move to Jersey or she'd move to London.

'You're pathetic,' Aurora had screamed at her. 'Can't you see he's lying? Everyone knows he's lying except for you.'

Ellie had barely managed to stop herself from slapping her sister.

'You know what your problem is?' Aurora's face had gone puce by this point. 'You're too scared to live your own life so you just preach to other people about how to live theirs.' Before Aurora had even slammed out of the house, Ellie had packed two bags and bought a ticket to London.

When she'd landed, she'd gone straight to Sebastian's law firm, caught him kissing an associate in front of a statue of Sir Thomas Moore, and that had pretty much been that. It had been more humiliating than that, of course. She'd stood staring to the point that the woman had noticed and asked Seb, 'Who even is that?'

His response had carried to her on the wind. 'Dunno. Nobody. Weirdo.'

He'd sent a text later saying he'd moved on, probably should've let her know earlier, but she was just so nice he'd never found the right time. No hard feelings? She could keep the ring.

Her mother's voice brought her back. 'I think Aurora was so used to leaning on you for support your departure came as a bit of a shock to the system. You know . . .' Her mother's voice grew cautious. 'It's been a year now, and with the wedding to plan . . . maybe you could convince that boss of yours to give you some time off.'

Ellie fuzzed her lips. 'I don't know, Mum.' She hated this topic. Of course she wanted to go home, but how could she, with the lies she'd told? Christmas had been the toughest. They'd never had one apart until now, but shame was a powerful motivator. Maybe in a few months. She chewed on the inside of her cheek. In a few months' time Aurora would already be married. Like it or not, she was going to have to go. She was also going to have to tell her mother that she was a complete and total liar. 'I'll talk to Vee,' she said.

'Wonderful!' The phone clattered to the table. 'Oops! Sorry, darling. I was clapping my hands and forgot I was holding the phone.' The bell at the front desk sounded. Ellie heaved a sigh of relief. The number of times that bell had saved her from having to tell her mother the truth.

'I'd better go get that, my love, but keep me posted. Tell your boss it's to see your ageing mother.'

'Ha ha. You're hardly ageing.'

'Well, I'm not getting any younger.' She briskly continued, 'Your sister wouldn't ask, but I know she'd love some input for the wedding.' Her mother's voice was already taking on that *How can I help you?* quality she used with the hotel clients. 'Sorry, love. Must dash. Bye, love, bye.'

Even though her mum had hung up the phone, Ellie held hers to her ear a while longer. There had been a time she never would've believed she'd go so much as a few hours without speaking to her mother, let alone an entire week. She gave Gus a scratch on the head, preening his eyebrows for him. 'What do you think, Gussy? Is it time I practised what I preached? Faced my fears head on?'

He lifted his head and gave her cheek a lick. *I'll love you either way*, it said. *Just so long as you promise to never leave me.*

◆ ◆ ◆

Despite a night of dreams involving Ellie standing up in the middle of a packed church screaming, 'You want reasons? I'll give you reasons!' when the vicar asked if there was any reason why Aurora shouldn't marry Chris, Ellie was feeling good. This was her first official workday as MD of Softer Landings.

The weather was bright and full of promise. The kind of crispy winter's day when Londoners actually smiled at one another. After an invigorating walk during which Gus made friends with a cockapoo named Farfle, Ellie skipped her regular caffeine hit at Starbucks, opting for a ginger shot instead. Today was a day of change. She had heels in her tote instead of her customary ballet flats. Hair down instead of up. And a decided bounce to her winter-booted step. She arrived at the office early, hoping to build on the fizz tickling her entrepreneurial spirit into action. Fern had clearly been fizzed up as well. The newly promoted receptionist had spent the entire weekend rearranging the stylishly functional open-plan office into something more 'in keeping with the spirit of Scandinavian comfort and Japanese clarity'.

'Oh. My. Fucking. God!' Thea screeched from the main door when she came in. 'What hygge god threw up all over this place?'

'Fern's making a mark with her new role,' Ellie said protectively. She was standing in the 'creation circle' – an area, Fern had informed her, to be seen as a central but welcoming space where staff could feel they were part of a community rather than a hierarchical construct designed to create linear power structures only benefitting those highest in the food chain (in other words: Vee).

Thea looked set to launch into a monologue detailing precisely what she thought of Fern's mark on things when Vee appeared with Simon and Lara following in her wake. Everyone went silent as Vee took in her 'reimagined' office space. After a few heavily weighted seconds, Vee popped on a smile and said, 'How nice,' then swished into her office, beckoning to Fern to come in as well and to be sure to bring a notebook. After exchanging a few *that was weird* looks, Thea gave the new layout a scan, said, 'I bagsy the pink beanbag,' and then they all got to work.

◆ ◆ ◆

After putting her new office into a semblance of order, Ellie's day passed in a surprisingly productive blur. The looming arrival of Valentine's Day was seriously tightening the screws on a lot of relationships and, as such, her inbox was overflowing. A smattering of long-term relationships began to appear among the *get me out of this Tinder hell* submission pile. Their presence pulled her up short.

She wasn't going to end a seventeen-year marriage for £149.99 plus expenses. She wasn't going to end a seventeen-year marriage at all. That was for the professionals.

Okay, sure, she had her Open University Psychology with Counselling BSc (Honours, thank you very much), but she'd never actually sat down with someone in an official capacity to . . . you know . . . counsel. That came with the masters course she was meant to have taken over this past year while setting up house with Sebastian. Hey ho. She drew up a set of new, clearer guidelines and sent them to Thea and Simon so that they were all on the same page.

By the end of the week, Ellie was priding herself on elevating Softer Landings' presence in the world. Sure, she would only be eating tomato soup and pasta for the next month, but a few tactically placed ads next to the lonely hearts pages in the broadsheets and the freebie commuter papers were already proving to be game changers.

When her mobile rang, Thea was doing a hip-hop dance in the creation circle, distracting enough that Ellie didn't even look at the screen to see who it was before offering a bright, 'Hello, Media Angels.'

Whoops. She should've said Softer Landings. She'd have to work on that.

'Ellie?'

Her arm skin shivered with a rush of goosebumps. It was Dan. 'Hey! Hi,' she said in a super-high-pitched voice she never would've used with a client, let alone someone she'd love to dazzle.

'This is Dan. Dan Buchanan?'

'Hello,' she repeated in a lower, more sultry tone. 'I know who you are.'

'Are you okay?' Dan asked. 'You sound a bit— Do you have a cold?'

'No, ah-ha-ha-ha.' *Mortifying!* 'Healthy as a horse!' She neighed. Idiot. She tried again. 'It's my work voice. Work, work, work! That's what I do during the day.'

'Cool. Glad you're not sick.' He cleared his throat, then, in a not entirely casual voice said, 'Say, I was wondering what you thought about me coming to meet you after your work. We could pick up Gus together and maybe take a walk? I have something I wanted to talk to you about.'

Her stomach clenched tight. A week had passed since she'd seen him and she'd heard not so much as a whisper. There was only one thing Dan could want to talk to her about. Taking Gus.

'Ellie?' Dan prompted. 'We could meet somewhere else if you prefer. Or another day?'

Her heart was in her throat but she made herself chirp, 'Today's good.' She always told clients it was best to rip off the Band-Aid. This was no different. Prolonging the inevitable would only be torture. 'Wear your crampons,' she gabbled. 'If it's as icy as it was this morning, you'll want both of your feet stuck solidly to the ground.'

The line went quiet.

'Dan?' She pulled the receiver away from her ear and looked at it. 'Hello? Dan?'

The call ended and a few seconds later she received a text.

Sorry. Bad connection. I'll pick you up at six.

Chapter Twelve

Dan met her outside the office at six o'clock sharp, but his mood was decidedly quieter than the bright-eyed, bushy-tailed Yankee Doodle Dandy Ellie had in her mind's eye. He still smelt great, though. Courtesy of a packed rush-hour bus, Ellie's face was squashed against his chest, which, if this had been a normal commuting day and Dan a stranger, would've been gross, but because it was Dan? The proximity added a not unwelcome element of commuter erotica. Until the bus changed drivers.

The new driver was doing that painful stop-start lurching thing that meant she kept head butting his chest as she tried to stay upright without clinging to his gorgeously athletic body. After one particularly vibrant lurch, he wrapped an arm around her waist and held her to him. He looked pained. She felt horrified. Her body was desperate to dry hump him. It took all of the power she possessed not to unzip his jacket, bury her face in his chest and inhale. Rather than succumb to the bliss of proximity, she did what any British person in an entirely awkward embrace with someone they secretly loved would do. She talked about the weather. Once they'd both agreed that the weather wasn't very nice but that a cold snap was typical for the time of year, she really pushed the boat out. 'How was your day?'

'Pretty quiet.'

'Your new flat?'

'Nice. Good.'

'And Sadie?' *Not jealous at all!* 'How's she getting on?'

'Busy.'

None of the answers were surly or laced with animosity, but . . . he really wasn't acting like American Dan. More like . . . mid-Atlantic Dan or, worse, Stereotypical-British-Northern-Male-Who'd-Had-a-Bad-Day-And-Didn't-Like-To-Talk-About-Feelings Dan.

She tried to figure out what on earth she might've said on the call that would've upset him but couldn't come up with anything. She peeked up at him. The eye crinkles were definitely not from a smile. Not today, anyway. Could he and Sadie have had a fight? Perhaps Sadie didn't approve of this possibly clandestine meeting. Was she jealous of their 'love child', Gus? Had she given him an ultimatum: this lady or the tramp!

Mercifully, traffic cleared, and Ellie found an actual handhold on the bus, and thoughts of Sadie disappeared as soon as the bus deposited them outside Mallory's. After she'd made introductions and Dan had bent to greet Gus, Mallory made an *Ai carumba! He's a looker* face at Ellie, followed by a double thumbs-up. Ellie gave a pained *I know, right* smile in return.

'Hey, bud!' Dan was down on one knee, his big old hands giving Gus that kind of scrubby-wrestle-cuddle-thing dogs love. 'What do you say we take you for a walk?' He pushed up to standing, using Mallory's doorframe as ballast and, once Mallory had wished them both a good night, he finally looked at Ellie with something approaching the easy, open-faced kindness she'd originally seen in him. 'Where to, boss?'

She pointed down the road. 'We usually go along the canal at night. It's better lit. It can be a bit slippy this time of year, but I feel safer walking there at night than the park. How's your footwear? Grippy?'

They looked down at his feet, which were poised in sort of wonky third position. He was wearing Timberlands. Dan didn't say anything.

'Those definitely look like they could handle a bit of frost.' Ellie gave him a cheesy thumbs-up. He gave her one of those earnest nods of his. The type where he tucked his lips in and his eyebrows dove together. His perfect blue eyes met hers.

'Good. And I'm glad you're thinking about your safety at night. It's important.'

Her heart melted against her ribcage. What she wouldn't give to have the kind of guy who genuinely cared if the people in his life were safe. Dan was also, it turned out, the kind of guy who put his hand on the small of a woman's back when they were waiting at a crowded level crossing to prevent her from being jostled on to the road. She tried to spark up some conversation to cover the fact that she had never found a simple gesture of courtesy so damn sexy, but her brain was too busy trying to fight off the endorphin rush to say anything. She'd loved and lost. Seeing him as a friend was her only option.

After the light had changed and they'd crossed, Dan gave her a sheepish look. 'Sorry. I'm acting like a real weirdo, aren't I?'

'Not at all,' she protested and then, a minute later, 'Maybe a little?'

He didn't offer an explanation, but she could see something was definitely playing on his mind. He reached out and gave her shoulder a squeeze. 'You're a good friend, you know that?'

Ooookay. They barely knew each other and she was in love with a fictional version of him she'd fostered with far too much attention to detail over the past year, but other than that, bang on.

'Thanks, Dan. You're not so bad yourself.'

He gave her arm a nudge with his elbow, which, she guessed made the friend-zoning official. *Hoorayyyyy! *Sob!**

After a few minutes of walking, Dan volunteered, 'So . . . Sadie's got this locum posting at UCL.'

'Oh! Wow. Didn't she need to do any extra training or anything? You know, being international and all?'

He shook his head. 'She did her training here. Her family's got a flat in' – he pointed towards Regent's Park – 'Marylebone.' He pronounced it Mary-le-bone. 'It's where we're staying, actually. At the Mary-le-bone flat.'

Her lips twitched. She knew she should helpfully correct his pronunciation, but really, she hoped he said it that way until the end of time. Adorable! And not at all attractive because friends didn't find friends' mispronunciations adorable.

'I was hoping to do my masters there one day. UCL,' she volunteered.

He perked up. 'Really? In what?'

'Counselling. I've done a psychology undergraduate degree.'

'Oh. Cool. So, why are you at Media Angels?'

'Saving up.' She laughed. 'At this rate I'll probably be a hundred and twelve by the time I can afford it.' Or just a year older, if Vee's projections were anything to go by.

Dan was nodding. 'London's so expensive. I can't even imagine how much it costs to raise a family here.'

Ellie's heart cracked in two. He was going to ask Sadie to marry him, then move thousands of miles away, where they would have children and a huge colonial house and ponies and . . . Gus.

She pulled Gus's lead a little closer in as they walked on, arms occasionally brushing as and when the path narrowed or a cyclist passed. The contact didn't feel as sexy now. It felt like a build-up to an epic betrayal. *After all I've done for you!* she shouted in her inside voice as her outside voice asked, 'Is Sadie's shift over soon?'

'Yup. Well, seven, I think, but they always run over. She's been pulling a lot of doubles, but she's booked supper at a restaurant across the park from us at nine.' He laughed softly, as if dining at the twenty-first hour of the day was the most endearing thing he'd ever heard of.

'Cool.' Ellie's tummy rumbled. She pulled an apology face. 'I can never eat that late.'

'I thought that's what you Londoners did? Work hard. Eat late. Party till dawn.'

She pulled an affronted face. 'Thea, maybe. She's an actual Londoner. I'm from Jersey.'

'Huh.' Dan looked confused. 'I thought you were local, but now that you mention it, your accent's a bit . . .' He tipped his head to the side, eyes narrowing as he inspected her. 'It's kind of like Sadie's, actually.'

Ellie choked. ''Fraid not! Plain ol' Jersey speak for me. The island, obvs. Not the new one.'

He gave her a sly grin. 'You sure? I thought I might've seen you on *Real Housewives*.'

She pushed her lips forward to make them look collagen-injected then lifted her eyebrows as high as she could. '"Haters are going to hate. But I just love, love, love."'

Dan guffawed. 'Oh my god, you've actually watched it?'

She raised an eyebrow. 'The fact you know this means you have too.'

He popped on a nonchalant air. 'I saw some trailers.'

'Same. You know, before watching a series of really powerful documentaries about cleaning the oceans. That's the kind of thing I usually watch. If I watch TV at all.'

He reached out and gave her forearm a squeeze. 'Hey, I was messing with you. Everyone's seen *Housewives*.' He tucked his hand back into his pocket. 'Besides, you're way too beautiful to be one of them. They're all so fake.'

'I hate fake,' she said, possibly too passionately.

Dan sighed. 'It's hard to find someone who's truly genuine these days, you know? Like you are. Come to think of it, you're probably the most real person I've met here in London.'

The atmosphere between them thickened, cocooning her in a warm, sugar-scented bubble that was tugging her body towards his. An organic magnetism crystallising just how much the two of them had in common. Hopes. Dreams. A shared moral code. And then she remembered she took money from people to end their relationships.

'Oh look! A duck.' She pointed at the duck-free canal then quickly resumed walking.

When he caught up with her, she briskly asked, 'So, what was it you wanted to ask me about?'

'Oh yeah.' Dan's features lightened then clouded. 'Sorry. I didn't mean to cloak it in mystery. With Sadie working so much and my work only being part time, I've got a lot of alone time and, well . . .'

She made a spinning sign with her index finger.

He sucked in a breath and put it out there. 'I was wondering if you'd mind letting me hang out with Gus a bit more.'

'Of course,' she forced herself to say with a smile. It'd be torture, but . . . Madame Bovary wasn't famous because life was one rapturous moment after another. 'We go on two walks every day. Morning and evening. Long ones on the weekend. You're more than welcome to join us.'

'No, sorry.' He stopped walking and put a hand on her arm. 'I meant just him and me. I could pick him up from school. He could stay—'

She threw her hands up. 'Woah, there, cowboy!' Gus was *hers*. Dan had lost ownership when he'd dropped off the face of the earth nine months back, so if he thought he could just smile his gorgeous smile and touch her on the small of her back with his beautiful man hands then take back the one actual friend she had in this blasted city before going out for his fancy nine o'clock candlelit supper with his perfect girlfriend whose hair alone was worth dying for, he had another think coming. 'Wow!' she said instead. 'Ummm . . .'

Such a smooth talker.

He put up his hands. 'Only if you're cool with it. I've signed up for this charity run – a half marathon round the London parks – and thought maybe he could be my pacer.'

She stuffed her hands into her pockets and looked at Gus, who had taken their pause in walking as a cue to lie down and grab a quick snooze. Total hero. 'Gus is more of a sedentary chap than a runner.'

Dan gave a few of those *yeah, yeah, I hear you* nods of his but obviously didn't really, because he kept on talking.

'I've actually done a lot of research on it. I called the retriever breeding club and a couple of running clubs. Goldens are good for up to about six miles.'

'A half marathon is longer than six miles.' There was no pulling the wool over her eyes.

Dan held out his hands between them, his voice slow and gentle, like he was trying to talk a gunman down from shooting a group of innocent children. 'Hey. I'm not trying to take him from you.'

'It sounds a lot like it,' she snapped.

He opened his mouth, his expression reading like someone about to tell her he was on the brink of solving global warming with a canine locomotion device and Gus was the only dog in the whole world who could enable him to do that. Instead he pressed his hand to his chest, covering that big, wonderfully kind heart of his, and said, 'I'm just not that great at running these days and with Sadie gone so much at work I thought, in the beginning, anyway, it'd be nice to have him along.'

Ellie suddenly realised that this wasn't about running. Or stealing Gus. This was about being alone in a huge city that, sometimes, had an agonising capacity to make you feel bone-achingly lonely. Especially if your girlfriend preferred double shifts to date nights.

Her heart squeezed tight for him. Her first couple of months in London had been the most excruciatingly painful period of her life. Apart from losing her dad. That had definitely been worse. But London loneliness in the wake of epic heartbreak had a lot to answer for. It was why she'd pounced on the chance to adopt Gus even though it had seemed completely insane. She'd been flailing. Totally at sea. She'd thought she was moving to London to live one life and, pretty much straight off the bat, had found herself living an entirely different one. Just like Dan was now.

Oh, Dan Buchanan. The poor man had just spent a year in Ethiopian tent hospitals out in the middle of nowhere. He'd very likely seen some pretty awful things. Which could lie behind the reason he still hadn't given for why he'd fallen off the face of the earth for nine months. Whatever had happened must've been bad. And now, having moved to London expressly to be with his girlfriend, it sounded as if he was being left to his own devices more often than not. If she were in his shoes? She would be wondering what the universe was trying to tell her, not trying to rebuild connections with dogs that belonged to women who were secretly in love with them but had the moral fortitude to know they could only ever be friends.

'I'm sure we can work something out,' she finally said.

'Really?' Without waiting for an answer, he pulled her into a warm, all-consuming bear hug. She smelt cinnamon and lemons and maybe leather, but she might've imagined that part because he was wearing his ski jacket. Too soon, he held her out at arm's length, his grin so bright she couldn't help but smile as well. 'Ellie, you don't even— This means the world to me. I can't begin to thank you enough. I know I owe you a lot of explanations—'

For a nanosecond she considered putting her finger to his lips like Cassie had done to poor old Marvel Dave, with a sexy, *Shhhh. You don't owe me anything.* She owed him for bringing Gus into her life. The golden furball who'd been her salvation during her darkest days. Besides, if he told her something unbelievably heart-breaking she'd have to give Gus back, so, no. He didn't owe her an explanation. And doing the sexy finger thing would just be weird, so instead she said, 'Listen.' She pointed at her ear then up beyond the banks of the canal.

Dan stared at her for a second then cocked his head to the side. 'What am I listening for?'

'Lions.' She grinned. 'And tigers.'

'And bears?' He paused and when the sound Ellie had heard happened again they both shouted, 'Oh my!'

Gus got up and looked around, startled.

'Unless I've really lost touch with the animal kingdom, I don't think that was any of the aforementioned animals,' Dan said.

'They're pygmy hippos.' Not that she'd seen them. She hadn't been to this zoo yet. Zoos and Ellie had a complicated history. And yet, here she was, pointing one out to Dan. Who knew what she'd be telling him next? About her dad's premature death? Her mum's dark and lengthy spell of depression? Her sister's inability to ever treat anything seriously?

Ellie watched him as he tilted his chin up, actively listening, smiling as the odd snort or snuffle drifted across on the wind. All too easily, she could picture unzipping her chest and letting all of her hopes and fears pour out at his feet. She knew he wouldn't step on them. Or make her feel small. But she also knew better than to say a word. She'd already given far too much of her heart to the imaginary him. Giving it to the real thing would just be dangerous.

Dan got that faraway look of his again and said, 'I'd invited Thea to come here once. To the zoo.'

Pipped to the post again. 'So you've been?'

'Nah. Remember?' At the same time they said, 'She doesn't do "tourist shit".'

Ellie laughed then said, 'Ironic, considering you met when she was doing tours of Camden.'

'She stopped doing them when the Urban Outfitters opened. Said Camden had lost its edge.'

She stopped doing them when she met Dan, Ellie silently corrected. She'd only done them to widen her dating pool.

'Plus,' Dan said fondly, as if he and Thea had split amicably rather than Ellie having done it for her, 'she hates queuing. Not a girl who likes to stand in line.'

Thea had either been insane or blind. This man's smile alone was worth the queuing time. Not to mention the fact that a long queue gave you extra cuddling time. Kissing time. Murmuring sweet nothings time. 'We should go,' she heard herself saying. 'To the zoo. The London Eye. Tower of London. The cheesier the better.'

'Really?'

Ellie beamed right back at Dan's happy face and, caught in its infectious glow, went all in. 'We could make it a weekly thing. When Sadie's at work, obviously. You know, two dorky tourists, living their best lives.'

He tipped his head to the side, trying to read something into the description and then, finding none said, 'Result!' He held up his hand for a fist bump. 'To dorky tourist buddies.'

They bumped knuckles and then, tactile man that he was, he gave her arm a butterfly-inducing squeeze. He turned to Gus with a 'What about you, buddy? You up for being a dork with your mummy and daddy?' Dan missed her double-take.

He was running his finger along Gus's cheek the way Ellie had once allowed herself to imagine him skimming his knuckle along her jawline before he kissed her. She swallowed her heart back down into her chest cavity and turned away.

When they got back to hers, she didn't have it in her to invite him in for a cup of tea. He wished her goodnight then pulled her into a hug. God, he smelt delicious. Like a lemony gingerbread man. When he spoke again, she could feel his voice vibrate through to her ribcage. 'It's good to have a friend here, Ellie. I don't know what I've done to deserve a pal like you, but it's nice knowing there's someone here batting for me.'

'Pleasure,' she squeaked. If only he knew.

Chapter Thirteen

Wednesday

To: Ellie, Thea
From: <u>Simon@mediaangels.co.uk</u>

Hey Ellz

What plans do you have for this week? Diego's carers are having to come more frequently and he is in hellacious mood, so need some DISTRACTION!!!! Maybe a working lunch is in order? Like, in ten minutes?

◆ ◆ ◆

To: Simon, Thea
From: <u>Ellie@softerlandings.co.uk</u>

Hi Simon! Hi Thea!

So sorry to hear about Diego. Maybe you could get Thea to do one of her sock puppet shows for him tonight? You said he loved those. Deffo on for a working lunch. Can we make it in half an hour? I don't want to take advantage of the time allocation Vee has given me for you both. Saying that, there are *a lot* of Striving To Be Singletons out there.

◆ ◆ ◆

To: Ellie, Simon
From: Thea@mediaangels.co.uk

TAKE ALL OF THE FUCKING ADVANTAGE YOU DESIRE! I'm sooooooo bored at Media Angels. Who gives a shit how fast anyone can type these days? The whippersnappers can only type with their thumbs, anyway. I want to smash relationships, become Cupid's full-time evil twin – Lady Cuntificent. Let's max the cash flow during the Valentine's rush and get me a full-time job!

◆ ◆ ◆

'Thea Stephanopolis, Media Angels, howcanIhelp?'

'It's Ellie. Did you know Fern has access to all of the staff emails?'

'What?'

'She can read everything you type.'

'Seriously? How do you know that?'

'Because I could when I had her job.'

'Why?'

'Because the office manager sends emails on behalf of Vee and somehow the system gives you access to everyone.'

'That's some fucked-up Big Brother shit.'

'Yes, well, if you want to poop on Media Angels? Maybe don't do it in an email. Or, alternately, make use of the Softer Landings email we set up for you last week.'

'Roger that, lil' tiger.'

'Check your email. I've just sent you a new one.'

SOFTER LANDINGS CLIENT QUESTIONNAIRE

How Did You Meet?

Mother's best friend's sister's daughter. Long story. They're in the Midlands. She's just moved to London. We both like musicals.

How Long Have You Been Together?

Almost two months. Well, since the new year. It feels longer.

Reason There Was More Than One Date If There Was No Chemistry On First Date:

I'm gay.

Reason for Softer Landing:

Nice enough girl. Obviously not the one for me. I can't ghost her or text dump her because my mum helps pay my rent and, owing to her recent alliance with UKIP, I am fairly certain telling her that her son likes a quickie down the sauna won't go down a storm.

Break-up Style (Please Tick Preferred Option*):

☐ Text
☐ Email
☐ Scripted Phone Call
☑ One-to-one tutorial (Skype/Zoom/In-person session, price gradient applies)
☑ Bespoke Split (POA)

NOTES:

Will pay or do anything to get this girl to like someone else. My mother will kill me if I hurt her feelings and I've got to get out before Valentine's Day.

NB: Softer Landings requires a telephone or in-person interview prior to agreeing to Break-Up Style and reserves the right to refuse a split and/or to recommend an alternative method to that chosen by the client.

◆ ◆ ◆

To: Ellie, Thea
From: Simon@mediaangels.co.uk

Maybe she's a fag hag and already knows.

◆ ◆ ◆

To: Simon, Thea
From: Ellie@softerlandings.co.uk

Thanks, Simon, I'll pop that idea in the hat.

◆ ◆ ◆

To: Ellie, Simon
From: Thea@mediaangels.co.uk

Have him take her to *Everyone's Talking About
Jamie*. She'll be confused at first, but then
get it. After? He should endlessly tell her how
pretty she is, bring her out for fancy cocktails
somewhere super hetero so she can drown her
sorrows then find someone to snog on the tube
ride home. Worked for me. They'll probably
become besties and laugh about this. Later.
Unless she's in UKIP too, in which case . . . Plan
B: she must never know the truth.

◆ ◆ ◆

To: Thea, Simon
From: Ellie@Softerlandings.co.uk

Another good option. I'll certainly discuss it
with him when we Skype today. Was also going
to suggest that if they haven't done anything
intimate yet (and I'm guessing no), he play

innocent and accidentally on purpose set her up with one of his straight friends for a date and/or offer to help with her dating app profile.

To: Ellie, Simon
From: Thea@mediaangels.co.uk

Gosh, Ellz. It's like you should do this for a living. Oh wait! You do. Now get me a full-time job!! (Soz, Vee. Love you!).

Chapter Fourteen

The tube ride from Kentish Town to the West End was the perfect amount of time for Ellie to work herself into a proper tizz. Proposing to hit London's tourist hot spots with Dan was one thing. Actually doing it? Torture. Without having even caught the slightest whiff of his delicious man scent, she was already feeling the slow, poisonous drip of forbidden attraction. Or maybe it was the croissant that woman was eating further down the carriage. Maybe she'd get a crush on a Beefeater.

Not today, you won't. They were going to Westminster Cathedral so her chances of finding love with a guardian of the Crown Jewels was relatively minimal. Perhaps there was a hot, naughty vicar lying in wait in the Cloisters. It was all she could do not to tip her head back and cry like a Disney character – big, fat tears water-cannoning everywhere. Why couldn't she fall in love like a normal person? *With* a normal person.

A sultry voice inside her head, also very like a Disney character, whispered, *American Dan is as normal as they come.*

He's forbidden territory! she primly shouted back at herself and then, for the next three stops, composed a very stern lecture on *boundaries* and the value of *friendship* and *feminism*. She also tried to imagine Dan as an overweight, beardy weirdy sitting on his porch in a rocking chair with a shotgun on his lap, but somehow, against the odds, her pulse still quickened.

Outside Leicester Square station she saw him straight away. As ever, he stood out from the crowd, but this time for more than the usual reasons. Clearly a fan of their Dorky Tourists theme, he had gone to town. Bright white trainers, a 'fanny pack' slung low on his hips, khaki chinos, a glaringly obscene Hawaiian shirt over what she hoped was an extra warm ski jersey because it was freezing. Topping it all was an immaculate white trucker cap that read I ♥ BBQ. Her breath caught in her throat when she saw that behind his tourist map, he was holding a solitary red rose.

And just like that, everything she'd been worrying about drifted away in the wind. She felt complete again. As if his presence rendered her whole. He stood tall and steady among the crowd. A mix of real tourists – eyes flicking between maps and landmarks – and Londoners, heads down, shoulders hunched against the weather, gaits brisk and officious. Her heart began pounding out huge, juicy beats of pure happiness as she guiltily savoured the unguarded moment: a tiny fraction of time when his sole purpose was to find her. Oblivious to the barely disguised derision of the Brits shouldering past him, his eyes scanned the crowds, his expression hopeful, excited, in the way someone would be at the airport as they waited for a loved one to appear after a long absence. It was a perfect moment and she wasn't even physically part of it. A sharp reminder that Kelly Clarkson had been right all along. What didn't kill you did actually make you stronger.

She sucked in a lungful of wintry air and wove through the crowd towards him. 'Excuse me.' She approached him with an innocent expression. 'You look a bit lost. Can I help you with directions?'

He beamed, then boomed out in a hillbilly voice, 'Why, yes, ma'am. That'd be mighty kind of you. I was hoping to see that big church of yours. West-mine-ster Abbey?'

'Oh, Westminster, you say? Well, wouldn't you know it, I just happen to be walking that way.'

He feigned shock at their mutual good fortune. 'Of all the coincidences. You wouldn't mind if I tagged along with you, wouldja?'

Ellie laughed and stood back from him so that she could give his outfit a proper appraisal. 'I like,' she said. 'Although . . . I must say I'm a tiny bit surprised that after a year in Ethiopia you have all of this in your wardrobe.'

He laughed good-naturedly, but his eyes left hers, as if acknowledging the comment would be allowing her access to a part of him he wasn't prepared to share. He looked down at his hands and then, cued by the rose, handed it to her. 'A thank you for spending your Saturday with me and my shirt.' His held out the hem of the garish top, blindingly bright with sunsets, pineapples and neon-coloured coconuts. His smile turned a shade forlorn. 'Sadie hates it.'

'Well, then, aren't you lucky to have a friend who loves it to bits?'

He frowned at her.

Too much?

He gave his chest a pat. 'Sadie wanted me to donate it to charity, but I thought I'd give it a whizz round London Town with my bud first!' A thread of concern cut through the brightness of his eyes. 'You don't mind, do you?'

Ellie wouldn't have minded if he painted himself silver and walked like a robot. She took a sniff of the rose, then pushed her lower lip out, pretending to consider her options, before giving him a toothy smile. 'I think I'll survive.' She looked down at her own, completely innocuous ensemble of blue corduroy skirt, cream jumper and the wild addition of brown biker boots, and then reminded herself she wasn't supposed to be dressing to impress. Dan offered her his elbow. 'Shall we take a turn round Lei-chester Square, milady?'

She laughed and, only a little guiltily, slid her hand into the crook of his proffered arm. If she was in *Bridgerton*, the possibilities such a gesture promised would have been endless. Perhaps she shouldn't be thinking of *Bridgerton*.

'How's Gus?' Dan asked as they walked. 'He's not on his own, is he?'

'No. He sends his regards, but announced he had far more important things to do than see a bunch of old stuff in central London.'

'Oh?'

Ellie explained. 'He sometimes works with special needs kids on a Saturday at the local library. Today is one of those days.'

Dan clutched his heart. 'What a dude.'

'Indeed,' Ellie replied with matching respect. 'That he is.'

As they made their way from Leicester Square, down past the National Portrait Gallery and into Trafalgar Square, where Dan insisted they admire the various street performers and *ooo* and *ahh* at the chalk drawings, before heading down Whitehall to the green outside Westminster Abbey, Ellie began to wonder what on earth she was even doing here. This was time she should be spending on Softer Landings. There were scores of potential clients, and Simon and Thea had all but begged her to let them start doing the splits on their own, which really didn't sit well with her. Thea was such a loose cannon and Simon had a tendency to be *too* clear. As such, she'd insisted she supervise all of the break-ups.

Thea had been enraged and threatened to quit, then had sent a series of drunken texts well into the night ensuring Ellie knew she was available this weekend should she need her.

Simon had said he was impressed. He hadn't realised Ellie had it in her to be a control freak. The backhanded compliment stung more than he knew. It was a variation on a nickname Aurora used to call her: Little Miss My Way or the Highway. Sebastian had thought it was hilarious but only because that wasn't the version of Ellie he knew at all.

The first time he'd come to Jersey, she'd been awestruck by him. He was a level of exotic she'd rarely encountered. Worldly, ridiculously cool, and available. A Jersey unicorn if ever there was one. He was also a bad boy. Truant. Sexually mature beyond his years. And fond of pranks that involved laughing at another person's expense, followed up by a half-hearted *sorry, just kidding*. He was someone who should have repulsed Ellie, but numerous conversations held in hushed tones between her mum and his grandparents assured her the behaviour was all for show. A response to his parents' acrimonious divorce. He was a good young man with kind intentions, they'd insisted. Which was why her mum had agreed to hire him as summer help at the hotel. Ellie, she'd told them, was such a good example. Her behaviour was bound to rub off on him.

On his first day, she stapled her finger to a guest's bill because she'd been too busy staring at him. He'd turned when she'd yelped, taken her hand in his, inspected the solitary drop of blood, put her finger in his mouth and sucked it. She'd thought it the single most erotic thing that had ever happened to her. And that, as they say, had been that. She should've known he was a vampire. A man who sucked the lifeblood from innocent girls, always on the hunt for new sources of eternal life.

'You look thoughtful.' Dan nudged her with his elbow and handed her a ticket. She considered telling him the truth. That she'd been thinking about her ex, who had not only ripped her heart out and broken it, but stomped on it too. That's what friends did, right?

Shared stuff. She turned and looked up at him, his blue eyes clear, the divot between them concerned, and she knew in an instant she would tell him anything if only he would ask. Which, technically, he had literally just done. But, because she was a repressed ex-office manager forging a new, bold, empowered identity for herself, she pointed up and said, 'Look!'

They both looked up at the epic majesty that was Westminster Abbey. Golden, gothic slabs of stone soaring up to the winter's sky. She looked down at the flagstones beneath her feet, imagining all of the different types of shoes that had worn them smooth through the centuries. Hand-cobbled leather boots to silk slippers to the future queen of England's. 'Can you believe Prince William and Kate were actually married here?' She sighed, remembering. 'You couldn't tear me away from the telly that day.'

He grinned at her. 'Is that what you want one day? A big, showy wedding?' His eyes caught with hers. The way the light was shining made them look like bright blue kaleidoscopes full of endless possibility.

'No,' she managed. 'I'd always imagined something more . . .' She flushed as her mouth voiced what she'd foolishly daydreamed about sharing with him. '. . . intimate.'

'Same,' Dan said, his eyes linked to hers until it became awkward. Ellie took a sudden, avid interest in the tourists joining the queue while Dan began flipping through the booklet he'd bought at the ticket desk. After a couple of minutes, Dan showily thunked himself on the forehead. 'I'm such a bad friend. I never even asked you if you had a boyfriend that I'm stealing you away from.'

Kill me now! Ellie made a silly boo-hoo face. 'No boyfriend.'

'Seriously?' Dan looked baffled. 'But not always, right? Back when we first met—?'

Now this was awkward. *It doesn't have to be.* She brightly explained, 'Back when we first met, I'd just been dumped like a hot potato.'

'Whaaaaaaat? No. You're lying.'

'Nope!' She gave him a cheesy grin, her chest unexpectedly flooding with relief at having told someone apart from Thea and Simon. And they only knew the bare bones of it. Boyfriend one day. Gone the next. 'Impossible to believe, right? That someone wouldn't want all this.' She fanned her hands down along her sides and struck a pose.

'Hey!' He took hold of her shoulders, forcing her to look at him, his tone almost sharp. 'Don't you do that. Don't put yourself down because of some peanut-brained goofball who couldn't see that he had a diamond when he had you.'

She swallowed, unable to think of a witty response. It was actually really nice to think of Sebastian as a peanut-brained goofball rather than a superior being who'd found her wanting.

'And there's been no one else since then?' he asked.

She barked out a little laugh. 'No. It's just me and Gus these days.'

Guilt shadowed Dan's smile and then, to her disappointment, it completely dropped away.

'Ellie, I feel like I owe you some honesty.' Again, his signature hand over the heart gesture stole the oxygen from her lungs and then, as he began to speak, her blood ran cold. 'Look, the thing is—'

She cut him off. 'We need to draw a line in the sand about Gus. I've had him a *year*. I think you can take that as a fairly big sign that I want to keep him. If I'd wanted to get rid of him? I probably would've done it when you stopped writing to me.'

A flash of anguish creased his features. He opened his mouth but said nothing. Whatever words were lodged in his throat looked almost impossible to bear.

Desperate to fix whatever pain it was she'd caused, Ellie leapt in, 'Look. Even though I might not have known it at the time, you did me a favour by bringing Gus into my life. I honestly can't imagine my life without him. Besides,' she gave him a desperate grin, 'I just bulk bought some hair-removal rollers, so . . . those'll take me a while to work through. You wouldn't want to deprive me of the pleasure of removing Gus's golden locks from my work skirts, would you?'

Dan looked up at Big Ben as if it might know the answer, then back at her. 'I don't know. You weren't expecting it to be forever. What I did verges on the unforgivable. To be honest, I'm surprised you're even talking to me.'

She would talk to him until the cows came home. And then some.

'Dan,' she began, trying to ignore the scratchiness in her throat. 'Gus is . . . Gus is the best thing that's ever happened to me and you brought him into my life, so . . . by proxy . . . that makes you the second best thing that's ever happened to me.'

He looked doubtful. 'Number one jackass, maybe.'

She laughed. 'No. That spot definitely goes to my ex. You will never prise that accolade away from him.'

A hint of a smile began to soften the creases fanning out from his eyes. 'I get to be number two?'

She elbowed his arm. 'Absolutely.'

'Cross your heart and hope to die?'

She sombrely crossed her heart and put her fingers up in the *I promise* gesture.

'Damn, Ellie,' he whispered under his breath, his eyes catching with hers. 'You really are one of the nicest people in the world.'

She scrunched her nose and tried to look pleased.

Dan became a bustle of activity. 'Look. This is a bit crass, but I keep meaning to do this.' He dug into his back pocket and pulled out his wallet. He pinched out a wodge of fifty-pound notes and handed them to her. 'For looking after Gus.'

She held her hands up, refusing to touch them. 'No! I'm not going to take that.'

'Yes.' He held the money out. 'You will.'

She pushed it away. It felt like blood money. 'No. I love Gus.'

'And I love you for taking care of him.'

They both stopped, tripped up by the intimacy of his word choice. Finally, after a staring contest offered no winner, Dan took one of her hands in his and pressed the money into it, folding her fingers one by one over the notes. 'Set up a trust fund for him if you don't want to spend it now. He might need it for college. Or his dotage.'

She couldn't help it. She giggled. 'His dotage?'

'Yeah.' Dan laughed too. 'You know. Wicker wheelchair. A smoking jacket. He'll need a pipe.'

'Obviously.' Ellie was properly giggling now. 'And a subscription to the *Times*.'

'Not the *Telegraph*?'

She fuzzed her lips. 'No. Gus is totally anti-fox hunting and voted against Brexit. He's more . . . Green Party. He insists upon me using biodegradable poo bags.'

Dan smiled at her. A proper smile this time. Sunlit with affection. 'You really do love him, don't you?'

Emotion clogged her throat. Even if she could speak she didn't think she could put into words just how much she adored Gus. So she nodded.

'Well, then,' Dan said. 'As long as you're happy, it looks to me like he ended up with his rightful owner.'

'Happy?' She put on her own variation of an America twang. 'I'm over the moon, good buddy!' She threw her arms around him and hugged him so hard he stumbled backwards into a family of Italians, who cheerfully righted him again with a flurry of *va bene*s.

They stood there grinning at one another, neither of them entirely sure what to say any more now that the Gus matter had been settled and, as if the energy of the universe sensed their need for distraction, the queue began to move and they were finally permitted entry into the abbey.

Chapter Fifteen

They'd barely made it through the massive wooden doors before Dan boomed, 'This place is so freaking *old*!'

Ellie grinned. He really was a dork. There was no containing his enthusiasm. He loved it all. The enormous nave. The chapel where the coronation throne sat proud of looped velvet ropes. The Winston Churchill memorial. An elderly couple glared at them and muttered something about respect, but another couple gave them a double thumbs-up and said, 'Nothing like this at home, is there, big guy?'

'Not even,' Dan said, turning to them. They were middle-aged, had cameras slung round their necks, matching fanny packs and a pair of army vet caps peeking out the back of the guy's backpack. The woman was unzipping her jacket to reveal a sweatshirt featuring a prosthetic leg decorated with the colours of the American flag.

Dan's smile faltered for just a fraction of a second before he gestured to a nearby seat and asked, 'Should we grab a pew?'

They laughed about the 'pews' actually being chairs, sat opposite one another and exchanged information in a cheerful, open way. Ellie learnt that Dan had actually been born in New York, but that his parents had moved to North Carolina once their children had been born. The couple was from Iowa. Well, military, so they'd moved round a fair bit, then they'd settled in Iowa, where they now served as a homing beacon for their three grown kids, who'd all joined the army, like the little troopers they were. Travellers. The lot of them. Pete and Alice had been taking one long trip a year ever since they'd retired. Took themselves on a road trip the entire length of the Mississippi last year.

'Barbecue,' said Pete, stretching his leg out into the aisle to give his knee a rub as he pointed at Dan's hat. 'That was what we ended up discovering.'

'Our lives were changed by it,' agreed Alice. 'We will never deep fry a turkey again. It's B-B-Q all-the-way for the Blumenhoffs!' She leant in and conspiratorially said, 'I have a hat just like yours in hot pink.'

A tweedy couple made a great show of trying to get past the husband's leg. Dan shot them a look.

Oblivious, Pete kept on rubbing his knee as he embarked on a story about the great battle currently being waged among their children over the merits of dry rub over sauced brisket. He and Alice roared with laughter over the hullabaloo that had been Thanksgiving.

A docent asked them to keep it down.

Ellie flushed scarlet at being told off, but the other three just made oopsy faces and carried on chatting. It looked so relaxing to be American. To be Dan.

She bet he could make friends with anyone anywhere. She'd never really had that gift. Hers had been shyness. A shyness that had morphed into a fastidious need to be useful once her dad—

'And what about you two?' Alice asked. 'What brings you both to London?'

'Oh, we're not—' Ellie began.

Dan overlapped her. 'I came for work originally.'

135

'Stayed for love?' Alice asked, her eyes bright with delight. Without waiting for an answer she grabbed her husband's hand and made a happy *ooooo*. 'Isn't that just the business, Pete? He came all the way over here and found his Princess Charming. It's just like a fairytale, isn't it?'

'Just like it,' Dan agreed and then, to Ellie's complete surprise, he wrapped an arm around her shoulders and gave her a look so tender it melted her knees into a gooey fondue. 'Love at first sight wasn't it, honeybuns?'

'Yes,' she whispered.

'In fact,' Dan continued, his eyes dancing between hers and the Iowa couple's, 'we came here today to see the vicar about getting married.'

They what now?

Ellie's inside voices began waging a volatile *I thought we were just friends* Q&A, as Dan continued, 'Ellie here said she always wanted to feel like a princess, so I thought what better day to feel like a princess than on your wedding day, right?'

Ellie stared at him. This was a joke, right? Because they were friends. And friends played pranks on one another like Thea and Simon always did. But friends didn't let friends joke about weddings when one of them secretly had the deep-down hots for the other one. Did they? Maybe they did it differently in North Carolina. Whatever the international definition of friendship might be, she suddenly didn't care, because for the first time ever, Dan Buchanan was looking at her as though he'd never seen anyone more beautiful. More perfect. As if he, like she was now, had finally been made whole. She wanted to crystallise the moment and put it in a snow globe. The brightness of his eyes. The slight flush in his cheeks. The way his crooked front tooth snagged his lower lip as if he still didn't quite believe he was the lucky man who had won Ellie's affections.

'Oh, I do love a love story,' Alice sighed. 'Tell us everything.'

She was looking at Ellie, who suddenly realised it was her turn to play along. Improv was not her strong point. 'Erm . . .' She fluttered her eyelashes at Dan. 'You tell it, snookums. I always muddle up the details.'

'You do, don't you, buttercup?' He booped her on the nose the way she booped Gus. She felt stupidly pleased by it.

'That's me! A little cup of butter!'

Everyone stared at her. Maybe best to leave the improv to her fake fiancé. Dan, it turned out, could weave quite the tale. They'd met at London Zoo. By the penguins. She'd been rescuing a butterfly. 'Well . . .' He gave a little laugh then gazed at her as if he was basking in the glow of an angel. 'It wasn't a butterfly yet, though, was it honey?'

'Noooo.' She shook her head. Were they going to the realms of fantasy with this one?

'What do you call it now?' Dan prompted. 'The thing before a butterfly. Listen to this. So cute.'

Delighted to have a cue she could run with, Ellie shouted, 'It was a caterpillar!'

Dan laughed, completely unfazed by the sharp looks of the tourists around them, slapped his thigh and gave her a look so tender it was impossible to believe it wasn't real. 'Isn't that adorable? The way she says "caterpillar"?'

The Blumenhoffs agreed it was adorable. Dan gave a happy sigh. 'And now I get to hear her say it for the rest of my life. Luckiest man in the world, me.'

The Blumenhoffs pronounced them the cutest couple they'd ever met, apart from their own children and spouses, obviously, and then Pete's enormous watch beeped, reminding them that it was time for Alice's medication and to head off for a matinee performance of *The Mousetrap*. They bid one another a farewell so fond you would've thought they'd survived the sinking of the *Titanic* together rather than a chance meeting in the nave of Westminster Abbey, but maybe this was what life was like with Dan Buchanan. Brief encounters that blossomed into something much, much better. No wonder Sadie had fallen for him. An ice cream cone in the middle of the Sahara. After they'd gone, Ellie gave him a playful side eye. 'Do you always tell strangers porky pies?'

'What now?' He looked bewildered.

'Lies,' she explained. 'It's Cockney rhyming slang. Porky pies, lies.'

'What? Oh! Yeah, sorry about that. I hope you didn't mind me playing around with them, I just—' He scrubbed the back of his neck and threw her a bashful look. 'They really seemed to want to hear a love story and – you don't mind, do you? It's not my most admirable trait, but sometimes if I think a little white lie can make someone happy I just run with it. Drives Sadie insane. She can never figure out what I'm doing and always kiboshes it right at the good part. Not like you. Caterpillar.' He laughed with an appreciative grin. 'You're good. Throw me some low bones, lil' buddy!'

'Hells to the yeah!' she said, entirely awkwardly, as her knuckles skidded off his and almost hit his crotch.

'Woah!' Dan comedically cupped his manhood. 'We don't want to make me a choirboy just yet. Sadie would be very, very cross with you.'

'Ha! Ah ha ha ha ha!' *Dear god, kill me now.*

They walked on and, to her complete surprise, she realised she was still smiling. And not even in an evil, joyous way for nearly making his penis a no-go zone for his girlfriend. Being Dan Buchanan's fake fiancée for ten minutes had felt like living life in Technicolor. As if she actually, genuinely, was part of a twosome. Or, in other words, a friendship.

She looked at Dan, whose head was bowed, his expression sombre as he read about the Tomb of the Unknown Warrior. It killed her to know this friendship, or whatever it was, was temporary. His relationship with Sadie would inevitably evolve into something more committed. They'd realise London wasn't the place for them and move to America or Cape Town. Ellie would carry on ending romances for cash. And that would be that. With that cheery thought clonking round her head, they walked around the abbey, occasionally pointing things out to one another, but mostly dipping into long, reflective silences. After a while, Dan sank down on to a chair with a big old sigh and patted the one next to him so that she'd join him. 'My mom would love this place.'

Ellie had no idea what her mum would think of it. Her life had pretty much always been confined to Jersey. The furthest she'd been was Southampton, which she claimed hadn't been to her taste – too busy for her liking. Ellie sometimes wondered if it was fear that kept her glued to Jersey. Or grief. Either way, she knew she'd never get a surprise phone call announcing a trip to London. Which in many ways was a relief. Sometimes, though, she had to admit, she would've loved the gesture.

Ellie looked around the small chapel where a couple of people, kneeling, looked to be lost in prayer. If she knelt down, would she pray for her mother to come and release her from her web of lies? She shook the thought away and, in a low voice, said to Dan, 'It must've been ages since you've seen them.'

'Actually, they're coming over in a couple of months' time. We had a bunch of stuff planned – you know, touristy stuff to do with Sadie – but . . .' He made an explosion sound, which Ellie presumed meant Sadie's busy schedule had blown up his well-laid plans, and then grinned. 'Hey!' His eyes lit up. 'You could come. They'd love you.'

Ellie crinkled her nose, terrified at the idea of fake-friending in front of his parents. 'Don't you want to have some alone time with them?'

'Absolutely not.' He gave her leg a pat. 'They're mostly coming for my run. You know, to be my cheer squad, seeing as Sadie's unlikely to make it.'

Ellie frowned. The run sounded really important to him. Like, *becoming a doctor* important. She pulled a yeesh face. 'There's no way Sadie can take the time off?'

'Not sure. I don't want to get attached to the idea in case it doesn't happen.' He stopped, his expression turning hopeful. 'Maybe you could lead the cheer squad. You and Gus,' he added, as if asking her to come without Gus was crossing some sort of line that pretending you were getting married in front of strangers didn't.

'Of course!' She waved some invisible pompoms in the air. 'We'd love to. Gus would look completely amazing in one of those little skirts. We get outfits, right?'

'You can have whatever makes your heart sing.'

Oh, her heart was singing alright. The blues!

Rather than get lost in his eyes and tell him she would very much like the key to his heart, she looked away, staring intensely at Thomas Hardy's tombstone, reminding herself that the only reason she was here was because she was a second choice. Third if you counted Thea.

'Hey. You okay there?' Dan began unzipping the gilet he wore over his Hawaiian shirt. 'You're shivering.'

'No. I'm good, thanks.' No way was she going to get all snuggled into his gilet. That was one hundred per cent not in the *How To Be a Gal Pal* handbook. Which, now that she thought of it, could be an offshoot of the break-up business . . . *How to be Mates with the Man You'd Rather Date.*

Dan leant towards her, his eyes seeking answers in hers. 'You sure?' She could feel his breath whisper across her lips. They were close enough to kiss. 'Look at you.' His lips were tugging into a soft smile.

Oh, sugar. This was it. He was going to tell her that he loved her. That everything he'd known to be true before this moment in time was a falsehood apart from the one solitary burning reality that she was the love of his life.

'What?' she asked in a voice way too breathy for a Church of England chapel.

'You're filthy,' Dan said with a smirk. And then, just as she was about to show him just how filthy she could be right here in the House of the Lord, he made a beckoning gesture for her to take off her glasses. 'Come on, you. Give 'em here.'

Mortified, she handed him her glasses. He took a soft cloth out of his bum bag and polished them clean for her. He looked studious as he settled them back on to her ears, his eyes once again moving between hers. She closed them, knowing if he looked hard enough he'd see all the things she was too frightened to tell him. When she opened them, she saw what she should have seen all along. A nice guy who thought he'd found someone to pal around London with. Nothing more. Nothing less. He held out a hand and placed it on the small of her back, steering her towards the exit. 'C'mon, lil' caterpillar. That's enough tourist action for today. Let's find you a cocoa or something. Get you cosy and warm. We can't have you catching cold when you've got a Gus to look after.'

Before they left, they stopped to light candles at one of the altars. The mood between them shifted once again. Having Dan there, a reminder of both what she did and didn't have, unexpectedly compounded the weight of losing her father. Her fingers shook as she took one of the little candles from the box. How was she going to let go of it once it was lit? Leave him here, all on his own?

Dan lit his candle and tipped the flame to her unlit one. 'Here,' he said. 'I think it's nice to light one life with another.'

She looked at him in awe, her heart straining at the seams with gratitude. How did he even do that? Know exactly what she needed before she did.

She let her gaze drop to their candles. The flame on his flickered for a moment, then doubled in size as the wick on hers began to burn bright. They placed the candles in holders near, but not adjacent to, the other, then stood in silence, neither of them offering an explanation as to who they'd lost or the chasm of emptiness that had been left in their wake.

'Right then!' Dan said, giving his hands a brisk rub. 'Are you a marshmallows-on-top kind of girl? I bet you are.'

Chapter Sixteen

Gus came bounding down Mallory's short garden path with his usual verve, crashed into Ellie's knees, then sat on her feet, very clearly expecting a cuddle.

'Gus! Sorry I'm late.' Ellie shot Mallory an apologetic smile as she dropped down and submitted to the obligatory face wash. Mallory ducked back into her tidy little two-up two-down Victorian and handed her Gus's lead, vest and, to her surprise, a small bouquet of rainbow-coloured tulips.

Ellie frowned at the flowers. 'What are these for?'

'Sorry, love. They're not for you.' Mallory tipped her head to the side and, with a mischievous smile, said, 'They're for Gus.'

Ellie grinned. 'Really?' She gave Gus's head a little scrub. 'You've got an admirer, have you, Gussy?'

'He sure does.' Mallory's smile was pure affection.

At least one of them was getting flowers for Valentine's. Seb had sent her bouquets back in the day. Like clockwork. One dozen roses with a speckling of baby's breath. They were beautiful, but they usually died within the week and, more to the point, they weren't her favourite flowers. Even though she'd dropped multiple hints that she preferred tulips to roses, it was always roses. About four years into their relationship, he'd admitted to setting up an annual direct debit, one that would apparently be a hassle to change, and roses were more traditional, so couldn't she just accept the gesture for what it was? She buried her face in the bouquet, wishing yet again that she'd been brave enough to get on a plane years earlier and discovered that the romance she thought she'd been pursuing had been entirely fictional. As opposed to the wholly authentic friendship she was now sharing with Dan.

'They're from a little girl called Keisha,' Mallory explained. 'Half-term's over Valentine's Day this year and she was panicked she wouldn't see him, so she wanted to make sure Gus knew how she felt before anyone got in there first.' The older woman closed her eyes, her smile faltering, eyelids flickering as if she were watching a film of memories. 'If all love affairs could be this sweet.'

'Mmm,' Ellie managed as her heart bashed out a few painful beats. Even though, intellectually, she knew that today had been nothing more than a mate's date, every other part of her was convinced otherwise. They just . . . clicked. They clicked like Lego and, despite her best efforts to convince herself Dan was a friend and nothing more, every single pore in her body wished things were different, wished they could find out what it was that fizzed between them whenever they were together, but, painful as it was, she had to face facts: Dan Buchanan had chosen someone else to love.

Anyway. When Mallory opened her eyes she looked lost for a moment, as if she had literally been transported elsewhere. It took her a moment to refocus on Ellie. 'Oh!' She clapped her hands together. 'I forgot. There's a card as well. Let me run and—' She stopped herself and turned back to Ellie, her expression changing yet again. 'Would you like to come in for a cup of tea?'

Ellie almost instinctively said no – they had somehow never moved beyond the Gus handovers into cups of tea and personal chats – but something in Mallory's eyes hinted at a need to talk. To connect. And maybe Mallory had seen the same in her, so she said yes. She led Ellie into the small house (inherited from her grandmother and not changed much since, not on her salary and definitely not on her mother's). They passed a small, cosy-looking lounge where a worn but clean blanket had been spread on one corner of the sofa. Judging by the gold hairs, Ellie guessed this was Gus's corner. Mallory bustled ahead into the kitchen, a brightly lit room that had French doors leading out to a small fenced-in garden. The kitchen smelt of spices Ellie had never used and it all felt very much like a home.

'Here we are!' She handed Ellie a bright pink store-bought envelope, but when she opened it, the card inside was home-made. On the front was a crayon drawing of Gus with a huge heart around him. There was a skew-whiff crown on his head and an enormous bowl of dog bones beside him. A little girl with pigtails stood off to the side outside of the heart with a book under her arm and about a dozen hearts were coming out of her chest, as if they were all of the beats pounding just for Gus.

Inside was a message written in red crayon, penned, Ellie presumed, by an adult, as it was very tidy.

> Dear Gus, I love you. You have beautiful brown eyes and also you don't laugh at me. Out of everyone I know you have the best smile in the world and the longest tongue. Love you forever and see you in two weeks. Please don't forget me and also we are on page 37 of *The Secret Garden*.

Below it, written in raggedy purple letters was a huge *KEISAHHA*. Ellie couldn't help it. She burst into tears.

Without batting an eye, Mallory handed her a tissue, glanced at the card and teared up herself. 'I know.' She tugged another tissue out of the little packet she'd just tucked back in her pocket. 'These kids. These kids.'

It was such a heartfelt response it made Ellie wonder why Mallory didn't have children of her own. She didn't ask because . . . well . . . she was British. There were a thousand reasons people didn't have children and in her limited experience she guessed someone who had wanted them but didn't get them probably wouldn't have chosen to be a primary school librarian. It would've been a form of torture she didn't think many could bear. A bit like trying to win the unrequited love of your life's heart while wearing filthy specs.

Once tea had been poured and some lovely home-made ginger biscuits had been fanned out on a plate that looked like it had also been inherited from her grandmother, the two of them offered shy smiles to one another.

'So . . .' Ellie started. 'Do you think it's serious? Between Keisha and Gus?'

Mallory smiled. 'It's looking that way. Flowers. A card. That's how all of the best romances start, right?'

Ellie smiled. She was pretty sure they didn't start by breaking up with someone else's boyfriend for them. 'I presume they met at the library?'

Mallory gave the plate of biscuits a nudge in Ellie's direction then, with a fond look at Gus, began the tale. Keisha was eight, had pigtails cute as can be, suffered from a horrendous stutter and was also slightly dyspraxic. Her favourite thing in the world was escaping into a good book. To add insult to injury, she had a whopping problem with dyslexia.

'But with Gus?' Mallory's eyes drifted to the furry beast who was plopping himself on the floor between them. He looked up, saw their eyes on him and rolled upside down so Ellie could rub his tummy with her foot. 'With Gus she is like a child transformed.'

146

As they talked and asked one another questions and Ellie heard tales about Gus and the children he worked with, she had another, all-consuming longing to go home. Jersey was small. A place where everyone knew everything about everyone else. The big stuff. The little stuff. Details about one another's lives people weren't afraid to ask because, faults and all, Jersey was a place where people looked after each other. The proper locals, anyway. There wasn't a casserole dish she hadn't known the home for after her dad had died. They hadn't had to cook for weeks, which was just as well, seeing as they had still had to run the hotel, but . . . the kindness. It had been off the charts. Not a single person had wondered whether or not they should reach out and help because the only answer to that question was YES.

It occurred to Ellie that London life provided a sort of invisibility cloak. One she'd happily disappeared into when her life had imploded. Fear and shame had kept her from going home, where that cloak would disappear. Sure, it wasn't her fault her ex was a duplicitous swine, but . . . it kind of was. Not to have noticed for seven actual years that he'd been stringing her along? She'd been every bit as naive about romance as Thea accused American Dan of being about life in London. But what she'd experienced hadn't solely been naivety. It was hope. Love. It had been a genuine shock to realise that the person who claimed to love her most had been lying. She wondered if Dan could have done the same to anyone, barely letting the thought take purchase before shaking her head. No. Absolutely not.

Mallory patted her hand and said, 'You look like you're thinking some deep thoughts.'

Ellie gave her head a shake. 'Sorry, I was away with the fairies.'

'Anything to do with that handsome man of yours?'

'He's just a friend,' Ellie said, a prickle of heat tickling her cheeks.

Mallory clocked her blush. 'But you'd like him to be something more?'

'He has a girlfriend,' Ellie said briskly and rose from the table. 'I should let you get back to your evening.' She stopped herself, not wanting to end their lovely chat so curtly. 'Thank you for looking after Gus the way you do. I couldn't have him without you.' She pressed her hands to her heart. 'I owe you a debt I can never repay.'

Mallory rose and locked eyes with Ellie. 'The feeling's mutual.' They shared a smile that told Ellie everything she needed to know. Mallory loved Gus every bit as much as she did. Both of their lives were better because of him. An idea occurred. She took out the money Dan had given her and offered it to Mallory. She refused it. Ellie insisted. 'In case of emergencies. Keep it in a drawer or whatever, but, if you decide you need it, it's not just for Gus. It's for you too. Okay?' She left the money on the kitchen table, certain Dan would've done the same thing.

As they hugged goodbye – their first – Ellie felt as though they were exchanging something unspoken but important. A shared respect. An acknowledgment that, as little as they knew about one another, they understood each other and, for now at least, that was enough.

◆　◆　◆

'Hi, love! It's Mum here. I'm wondering if you could try to ring a bit earlier on Sunday? Aurora and Chris are coming over for lunch and I thought it'd be nice to do a family Skype. Maybe Seb will be around for it too? Love you, darling. Bye now. Bye.'

Chapter Seventeen

WhatsApp Softer Landings Msg Group

Cuntificent Stephanopoulos:

ELLIE! Where are you? Simone and I are waaaaaiiiiiiting!

Ellie Shaw:

Sorry! Sorry. I meant to ring. Gus picked up some sort of tummy bug and, judging by the number of times he's thrown up in the past two hours, I think we'd better stay here. If I forward you the requests, would you and Simon mind having a look? We can sort out responses during our scheduled Monday meet????

Cuntificent Stephanopoulos:

OMG!!!!?!?!!?!? So gross. Are you picking up his puke? Don't answer that. Won't come near you with a barge pole!

◆ ◆ ◆

Simon Slippery Nipples Temple:

Can we bring you guys anything? Don't listen to Thea. She has a thing about germs and NO MANNERS.

◆ ◆ ◆

Cuntificent Stephanopoulos:

SOZ. Simone says I'm heartless. No surprise there, then. But seriously, Ellz, are you sick too? Did you ACTUALLY suggest that Simone and I sort the clients without your wise and empathetic counsel? I thought that was a hell freezes over kind of thing. Kidding! #NotKidding. Are you sure you're okay, babes? And also, GUUUUUUUUUUUS! Sending love to the Golden Furball. If you need us to call him an ambulance or whatever, just say. Or you. My sister brings her Shih Tzu to this amazing out of hours vet's, but it's in Holland Park. Can you get there? If he's pooping like a fire hydrant, maybe not. GUUUUUUUUUS!

◆ ◆ ◆

From: EShaw1995@gmail.com
To: TheaTheaBoBea@gmail.com,
NotSoSimpleSimon@gmail.com
RE: Client Submissions

FWD: SubLtr273, SubLtr274, SubLtr275

Here you go! As you know – I usually have a phone call with each client before deciding on the method of uncoupling. Each of them probably needs a one-to-one, but as you rightly pointed out, we've done this long enough that you and Simon should be able to make the call. I have also attached a list of things to consider regarding mental health when you do the calls, and factors to consider regarding the dumpees. If you have any concerns, do not hesitate to call. In fact, call me on speaker after and we can discuss. Enjoy! E x

PS: I'm thinking possibly Simon should call the gentleman who is a fan of musicals to discuss options as his case is most pressing. Just a suggestion.

◆ ◆ ◆

From: TheaTheaBoBea@gmail.com
To: EShaw1995@gmail.com,
NotSoSimpleSimon@gmail.com
RE: Re: Client Submissions

I *knew* you weren't letting go of the reins, you saucy little control freak, you. Don't you worry your pretty little head about the clients. Focus on Gus. We'll check out the submissions and then spend the rest of the night talking about you behind your back. And by the way? Simon is totally offended that you think he should call the gay guy. He doesn't like being pigeon-holed like that.

Yours, politically correctly, Thea

From: TheaTheaBoBea@gmail.com
To: EShaw1995@gmail.com,
NotSoSimpleSimon@gmail.com
RE: Re: Re: Client Submissions

PSYCH! Kidding. Totally kidding. Ellie????? Don't be upset. Ellie? Is Gus okay? ELLIE!!!! Simon's going to ring the gay guy, I promise. I obviously have a heart of stone and will ring no one.

To: Ellie Shaw
From: Simon Temple

Ellz. Don't listen to anything Thea says. She's on one tonight. I've taken her phone away and we'll talk tommoz. Simon x

PS GUUUUUUUUUUUUUS! I prescribe plain white rice and steamed chicken. It always works for Diego.

◆ ◆ ◆

Ellie didn't bother looking at the incoming number before she spoke. 'If this is about the questionnaires, can it wait until tomorrow, when you're sober?' She tried to readjust her numb leg, which was being held hostage by Gus's chin. 'Hang on a sec . . . I just need to . . . Gus? Budge over, pal.' She tried to move his chin elsewhere. Gus took umbrage, his big, brown, mournful eyes sending her a baleful *I don't feel* good look. Well, she wasn't feeling particularly fabulous either, but . . .

He put his paw on her knee as if he was giving it a *thank you for loving me even though I'm gross* pat. Awww . . .

'It's alright, Gussy.' She glanced at the screen to triple-check that it was Thea. Her heart rate doubled as her voice shot up into a squeak. 'Hey! Hi. Is that Dan?'

'Yeah, sorry. I'm guessing you were expecting someone else. Unless – do you require all of your friends to fill out questionnaires?'

Her stomach clenched as her voice shot up another octave. 'No! Nope. Sorry. Work.'

'On the weekend? Sheesh. Although . . . it sounded like it involved alcohol, so I'm guessing that means you're missing out on a work do?'

'No. Just a—' *Don't go there, Ellie.* 'So, hey! Yeah. Thanks for getting back to me.'

'Sorry it took me so long. I only just got your message,' Dan said. 'Sadie and I were having a bite to eat before she started her shift and because our time together these days is so limited, I tend to turn my phone off during meals out, and then I forgot to turn it back on until I got home and realised I hadn't heard from my sister, who'd promised to call, which she hadn't, but obviously I didn't know that until I'd turned the phone on again.'

He was babbling. It was weird. Dan was not a babbler. Especially about himself.

'No worries,' she said, suddenly succumbing to a wave of self-pity that she didn't have anyone to babble to. She smelt like puke, didn't feel so hot herself, and was wishing like hell she knew some-one – *anyone* – who cared for her enough not to be put off by how revolting and cranky she was. She felt sad and lonely and wasn't sure she had it in her to clean up any more dog vomit. She wasn't sure she had it in her to do anything any more, let alone build a nation-wide franchisable business that cracked faulty relationships in two. She caught herself almost saying as much when she realised that Dan was covering for her lengthy silence by talking her through everything he and Sadie had eaten.

'— this incredible souvlaki. It was amazing. With these little green speckledy bits on it – a herb, I guess? Not one I've had, any-way. Sadie said it was a properly traditional Greek place, but I've never been to Greece, so, like a lot of things, I just had to take her word for it.'

It felt like a confession of sorts. One that embarrassed him. And just like that, her own frustrations dissipated. 'I haven't been either,' Ellie said. Then, feeling the admission hadn't really helped, tried to pull some congeniality out of the hat and asked, 'Did you break any plates?'

'No.'

Well, that was something, anyway. At least she knew they weren't getting married. As she began to consider the benefits of encouraging Dan to propose to Sadie and move far, far away, Gus began dry heaving, sending her a pained look before belching in her face.

A sudden, acute need to cry swept through her like an unwel-come downpour. She felt heavy and miserable, and knowing Dan was on the phone waiting for her to say something, anything, made it even worse. She opened her mouth to say she couldn't remember why she'd rung him when Dan said, 'Have you ever had that thing where you get the feeling your partner's trying to tell you something and you're meant to guess what it is but, for the life of you, you can't?'

No. Which went a long way towards explaining why she'd thought she'd had a boyfriend for seven years but actually hadn't. 'I'm not sure I know what you mean.'

'Sadie just seemed like she was in a bad mood. Kind of snappy, you know? I mean, the work she's doing is tough and she's pulling a lot of hours, so I don't blame her for taking it out on a loved one, but . . . it just didn't seem like her.'

Ellie could almost picture him doing his trademark neck rub. His fingers running through the soft curls beginning to form at the nape of his neck. The ones she'd almost grabbed on to when she'd nearly launched herself at him in Westminster Abbey.

'I shouldn't complain really,' Dan chided himself. 'It's got to be harder for her than me. I work in a fancy specialist hospital twenty hours a week for twice the pay she gets, so . . .' He released a big old despondent sigh. 'Nice to hear a friendly voice, anyway,' Dan said. 'So! Sorry. I've been all me, me, me. I should've asked about Gus straight off. Is he okay?'

'Actually, Gus has been through the mill today.' She gave his head a soft stroke, explaining how they'd gone for a long walk in the park earlier in the day, and then, on their way home he'd snarfled something on the pavement before she could stop him. About an hour later his stomach had started making strange gurgling noises and an hour after that he'd started projectile vomiting.

'Did you take him to the vet?'

She winced, thinking of the pile of money she'd left at Mallory's that she really could have done with about now. 'Not yet. I'm pretty

155

sure it's just a food-poisoning thing. Obviously, I'll take him if he takes a turn for the worse.'

'Maybe you should run him up there.'

In what? The taxi she couldn't afford to pay the cleaning bill for? She barely contained a self-pitying whimper. The out-of-hours weekend vet was horrendously expensive. She'd taken Gus there a few months back when one of the well-meaning children at school had shared his chocolate bar with a very willing Gus.

'Soda crystals,' the vet had said when she'd blanched after Gus had had his stomach pumped and he'd handed her the eye-watering bill. 'Soda crystals down the throat and he'll throw it all up.'

Gus had done all of today's throwing up without the aid of soda crystals. He'd looked perfectly fine one minute, apart from the tummy gurgles, and then – *brrrackkk*. The stench was so acrid she had the flat's solitary window as wide open as it would go and was definitely experiencing the beginnings of a chill. 'I've just given him some plain steamed rice. He's kept it down so far.' She gave his head another soft stroke, hesitating before she admitted the real reason she'd made the call. 'The thing is, I don't think he should go to school tomorrow if he's going to be yakking everywhere.'

'No. Absolutely not,' Dan agreed solidly and then, catching up with what she was trying to say, asked, 'You have work, right? Don't worry about it. I'll look after him. He's our boy, right?'

Her heart skipped a beat. And then another. 'Could you?'

'Absolutely. No problem. I only have a couple of consults tomorrow. He can snooze in my office while I do those. The floors are moppable, so if he barfs, it's not a problem.'

'Are you sure?'

'Positive. I can reschedule them if necessary. Don't worry, Ellie. I've got your back.'

She pictured him in a cape. Then added some form-fitting Lycra. Hair fluttering in the wind as he flew in a determined streak of light through the night sky above Regent's Park towards her tiny little flat. American Dan to the rescue!

'Ellie? You still there?'

'Yup! Sorry. Just thinking logistics. You live in Marylebone, right? We could walk across the park to you in the morning. My work's not far from there, so if there's any emergency or anything—'

Gus abruptly lurched off the sofa.

'Gussy, no! Over here, over here. Where the newspaper is – ohhhhh, Gus.'

She gave him his space as he evacuated the steamed rice and then, because he looked so heartbreakingly beleaguered, gave him a gentle cuddle. It was only after she'd cleaned up the mess and given Gus's muzzle a clean, and taken him for a short walk outside just in case there was more, that she realised she had completely forgotten that Dan had been on the phone. She thought about ringing him back then decided against it. It was late on a Sunday night. They'd already agreed she would take Gus over in the morning. She looked down at herself and despaired. She was repulsive. Even to herself.

Maybe she'd text Dan, instead. Say that she'd reconsidered and had taken a sick day. Thea and Simon would be annoyed, but they could Skype their meeting and most of her work could be done from home. That way, if she did have to take him to the vet's, she could decide which one. When she and Gus got back to the flat, she tapped out an officious little text, pulled on another jumper because the flat was properly freezing now and began taking clothes out of her microscopic cupboard to pile on to the bed because she didn't have an extra duvet and it was only going to get colder. If Gus wasn't too sick, she'd use him as a hot water bottle. 'Do not honk on these,' she warned Gus.

Just as she was about to help him climb up on to the bed, there was a knock on the door. Weird. Her neighbours were definitely not knock-on-the-door-and-check-she-was-alright types. In fact, sometimes she wondered if they even existed. Thea. Had to be. Drunk Thea.

'Go away,' she called through the door, but by the way Gus began thumping his tail, she instinctively knew she'd got it wrong.

'Ellie?'

She opened the door, and standing there, face wreathed in concern, was American Dan.

Chapter Eighteen

The pretty vet nurse who had been trying and, Ellie was a tiny bit pleased to see, failing to flirt with Dan for the past hour called him to the reception desk. Ellie followed because, hello, Gus was *her* dog, but she stayed a step or so behind him, the solo participant in *The Danmaid's Tale*.

'Your lovely doggie will be ready in about five minutes, yeah?' the nurse said, exclusively to Dan.

'Great!' Dan grinned and threw a bright smile back at Ellie. 'Awesome.' He did a double-take, frowned, then pulled Ellie up into a half-hug beside him as if he'd done it a thousand times before. 'See? I told you he'd be okay.'

Before she could process the comment or the hug, he dropped a kiss on top of her head and quietly whispered into her hair, 'I'm always here for you, alright?'

She looked up at him from under the safe crook of his arm. His blue eyes were so warm and kind it was impossible not to lean into him, feel the solidness of his chest, inhale the deliciousness of his man scent. Tonight he smelt of butter and crumpets, and it was inconceivable to her that his girlfriend had the audacity to be anything less than bone-achingly thankful that the timeline of world events had come together to create this beautiful man and then do her the additional courtesy of putting him in her path.

The nurse cleared her voice and, to Ellie's disappointment, Dan's arm slipped away from her shoulders, leaving a cold patch in its place.

'He was ever so poorly. Quite dehydrated, as you very accurately assessed, *Dr* Buchanan,' the nurse said in a victorious *so glad we've broken up the love fest and that the focus is back on me* voice. 'As such, we've given him some rehydration solution.'

'Intravenously?' Dan asked.

'Yeaas. Exactly right! And a jab to settle his stomach, yeah?'

'Cerenia?'

'Look at you.' She beamed at him, then flicked a careless glance in Ellie's direction. 'You've got yourself a real brain trust here.'

'Oh, we're not—' Ellie began, her protest instantly dying away as an exhausted-looking vet led a much chirpier-looking Gus out into the waiting room.

'Gussy!' She dropped to her knees and was instantly engulfed in his big golden ruff.

She vaguely heard the vet talking Dan through the details. They'd done a proper check-up on him while he was there. His stats were fine. X-ray didn't show anything caught in his stomach or his intestinal tract. He might be a bit tired tomorrow. With some plain food, he should be fit as fiddle in the next couple of days. As the vet spoke and Dan *mmhmm*ed and *okay*ed and *righty-o, will do*ed, Ellie felt an overwhelming combination of fatigue and relief wash through her.

Ever since her dad had died, she'd been the one people leant on. The reliable one. The girl they turned to when things began to crumble. Extra-efficient Ellie! Sure, it was a role she'd created more than fallen into, but how could she not have? Her mother had been so absent-minded, she'd needed Ellie. To remind her that the guests could see her wandering around in her dressing gown. To make sure the staff did their jobs. To look after Aurora who, at eight years old, sunk deep into her role as the family baby, incapable of solving any dilemma on her own. She needed help with the simplest of things. Getting to school on time. Pouring cereal. Pairing up socks. Neither of them would've made it as far as they had without Ellie leading the way through the tunnel of grief towards the light that would one day free her of her responsibilities as the eldest child. But she couldn't solely point the finger of blame at them. She had basked in the unacknowledged glow of how essential she'd been to them.

With Seb, she'd not only been efficient, she'd been efficient with sparkle. She'd made having a relationship with her the easiest thing in the world. Away at uni during the year, he'd not had a thing to worry about to keep her happy. She'd organised his summer breaks so that when he came back, his visits ran like a catered holiday for one, dipping in and out of his timetable as and when it suited him to have a girlfriend. She'd asked absolutely nothing of him and, in return, that was pretty much what he had given her. Except for maybe dreams of something more.

Dreams she'd never let herself pursue until the day when she'd fought with Aurora, left Jersey, discovered her boyfriend was a liar and that her family were completely capable of living their lives without her. Every single person she thought she'd been propping up had been perfectly fine all along.

Her mum had no problem keeping the hotel full (Ellie regularly checked Tripadvisor).

Her sister had gainful employment in a florist's and had changed enough to accept a marriage proposal from her childhood sweetheart instead of laughing him off the island.

The staff who had depended upon the hotel for jobs were all grand. The vendors reliant on payment never shorted. And the list went on.

All. Perfectly. Fine.

And it had made her feel absolutely pointless. Wonder why she'd even bothered.

Right up until that knock upon her door. Having someone look after you when you couldn't was *amazing*.

From the moment he'd arrived, American Dan had taken one look at the situation, assessed it, bundled her into a jacket, scooped Gus into his arms, and brought them here. He was the male form of her she hadn't known she'd needed. Still cuddling Gus, she watched Dan sign the paperwork, absorbed the steadiness of his voice as he sorted out the bill he'd insisted on paying, felt the solid support of his hand on her elbow as he helped her up so that they could go to the car he'd double-parked outside the surgery, giving her a complicit *needs must* look as he slipped his Medical Doctor sign in the front window. After settling Gus in the back, he opened the door for her, waiting until she was buckled in to close it. She felt her weight sink into the pre-heated soft leather seat. Her skin felt prickly and stingy, her head hot, her hands clammy. And then, as if each of Dan's kindnesses was opening her eyes to the reality of just how difficult and painful the last year had truly been, she began to cry.

◆ ◆ ◆

Ellie had been a lot of things over the past year. Humiliated. Ashamed. Belittled. She'd felt the anguish of rejection viscerally. Her mouth had gone dry countless times. Her heart had both jack-hammered and beaten so slowly she'd worried she could count out the final few before it simply stopped. She'd hyperventilated. Held her breath. Felt sick. Numb. Stupid. But the one thing she hadn't done after finding out she'd spent seven years loving someone who had never loved her back was cry.

Despite her numerous protests that she'd be fine at home, Dan was driving towards his place in Mary-le-bone. 'Honestly. The guest room is great. You must stay.' He'd noticed her tears, of course. It would've been impossible not to. It was like a tap had been opened in her – a fire hydrant's worth of sorrow. Not just those she'd never spilt over her bamboozled heart, but the ones she'd yet to release for her father, having to care for a mother so mired in grief and depression she barely noticed her children, and a thousand other things that girls who have time for feelings cry over.

And Dan didn't freak out at all. Surprise, surprise. He tucked her hair behind her ears when it stuck to her face. He magicked tissues from the glove box, assured her they had boxsets to cure all ailments and that Sadie had enough clothes to dress the whole of London so she wouldn't have to worry about that in the morning. Nor would she have to worry about Gus. What was the point in going back to hers when he was going to look after him in the morning? Especially when he had three new jokes he wanted to trial run on her before he tried them on his patients. One, he warned, was a little blue, but it featured a parrot, so . . .

'Why don't you tell them to Sadie?' Ellie protested. Feebly. 'You need to take the next right to Kentish Town.'

'She's not a jokes person.'

It wasn't much of a surprise, but for some reason the admission made Ellie unbelievably sad. Yes, she was overtired. Yes, it had been an emotional night. And yes, she would've bet a kidney Dan's jokes were the awful dad jokes that made even six-year-olds groan, but she could easily picture herself laughing as he told them, at the punchline and beyond. Not because they were funny, but because it made Dan so happy to tell them.

'Hey, Ellie.'

In a last-ditch attempt to get him to bring her home, she cut in. 'You should be turning right here? It's the fastest way back to mine.'

He turned left. 'Why did the cookie go to the hospital?'

'I don't know.'

'Because he felt crummy.'

And just like that, she became too hungry for the comfort he was offering to protest.

The flat was every bit as wonderful as he was. As tiny and shambolic as hers was, Sadie and Dan's was an oasis of calm. It smelt of beeswax, warm cotton and almond floor polish. It was a huge top-floor, three-bedroomed mansion flat that faced a small private park for the use of the residents who lived on the square. The floors were broad thick planks of golden oak, strewn with pleasingly worn Persian carpets. The kitchen had high ceilings and a million built-in cupboards. It even had the old bell system that called the servants and various other building attendants the portered block had employed back in the day. The bedrooms, each one larger than her entire flat, had an air of yesteryear comfort, as if they'd been outfitted by a loving grandmother who not only made her own quilts but who'd fluffed each pillow and swept a caring hand over the bedding before pronouncing herself satisfied.

It was all Sadie's family's, Dan explained, when she gawped in awe. Sadie's dad had bought it years back when he'd done a lot of business in the UK and kept it when Sadie and her siblings opted to go to uni here. Apparently her mum liked to do her Christmas shopping here too, so they were keeping it for now.

'Yeah, it's great.' He frowned, then smiled, saying he would've been content with four walls and a kick-ass shower. 'Water pressure's a bit of a let-down,' he said in a way that suggested he was saying something else altogether.

After Dan settled Gus on top of a duvet he'd spread on the corner of one of the sofas and tucked Ellie under another one next to him, he excused himself to put the kettle on.

She gently stroked Gus's back, trying and failing to use the alone time to pull herself together. Being here was a mistake. A tortuous reminder of everything she didn't have. It wasn't even the *stuff*. It was Dan himself that she ached for. He was literally everything she could have ever dreamt of. The nicer he was to her, the worse she felt. Each of his thoughtful gestures another drop of bittersweet poison. Here's something you'll never have. And another. And another. All of which made her cry even harder.

Gus, unhindered by the anguish of accepting someone else's boyfriend's kindnesses, was already snoring. As she pulled yet another tissue from the box she'd brought in from the car, Dan came back into the room bearing a tray with two steaming mugs and a small plate of chocolate chip cookies. 'My sister, Maggie.' He beamed proudly. 'She packs one helluva care package.'

He sat down on a comfortably worn armchair adjacent to the sofa she and Gus were monopolising, took a slurp of tea then a big bite of a cookie. He shut his eyes and smiled as he chewed. 'Mmm. Tastes like home.' He grinned at her as if it was perfectly normal to be sitting with a woman with tears pouring down her cheeks and eating biscuits. He'd grown up with sisters, so maybe he was one of those rare creatures who didn't feel a need to fix a woman overflowing with feelings. Knew that it was enough to simply be there. He finished his cookie then took another, encouraging her to take one too. 'What reminds you of home? Taste-wise?'

'Potatoes,' she sighed, grateful for the distraction. 'Steamed. Salt and pepper. Butter.'

He looked bemused as he put on a Dick Van Dyke accent and asked, 'The common tattie's yor fav'rit food, guv'nor?'

She feigned a gasp of horror. 'These are no common potatoes, you heathen! They are Jersey Royals.'

'Fancy.' Dan gave an appreciate whistle, rousing Gus from his slumber. Well, he lifted his head up, but his eyelids were still super-droopy. 'Sorry, bud.' Dan leant forward and gave Gus's fur a little ruffle then sat back in his chair. Voice lowered, he prompted, 'What else? Tell me all about this island of yours.'

To her surprise, talking about home was a soothing antidote to her tears. She told him how Jersey used to be attached to France eight thousand years ago and that, even though the island was now firmly under British rule, courtesy of William the Conqueror, some of the older people still spoke an ancient version of French known as Jèrriais. She told him about the occupation during World War II, the detritus from said occupation that still washed up on the beaches. The fields of daffodils that, up until recently, had covered the island every spring. And, of course, about the Jersey Royal potato.

'How many people live there?' Dan asked.

'Permanently? Just under a couple hundred thousand. I think the last count was something like a hundred and seventy-eight thousand?'

'You're like a Wikipedia page.' He laughed. 'My descriptions of home are more like, you can get the best milkshakes here, I broke my collarbone for the first time there, my sisters convinced me I was adopted in that park up on that hilltop.' He laughed at the differences. Her stomach clenched at them.

She gave a defensive sniff. 'I don't think it's weird to know the population of where you're from.'

He nodded, taking no offence at her tone. 'Nope. Not weird at all.' He shifted position, stretching one of his legs out as he did, giving it a strange, rigid shake as if his calf had cramped.

A wave of guilt swept through her at her snippy response. *He wasn't judging you, Ellie.*

'I grew up in a hotel,' she explained. 'When people ask me about Jersey I'm used to offering tourist information.' She cleared her throat and took a sip of tea. Talking about home was no longer the salve it had just been. They sat in contemplative silence for a moment. Each of them remembering the places neither of them lived any more until Dan readjusted himself and said, 'Well, Jersey sounds real interesting. I'd love to see it sometime.'

'You should.' She hoped her voice conveyed the apology she owed him. Gripped by panic that it wasn't enough, she blurted, 'We've even got a zoo.'

He brightened at this. 'Seriously? How cool is that?'

'Super-cool.' Ellie grinned, her chest fluttering with butterflies of delight that he seemed so cheered by the information. Seb had actively exhibited disinterest in the zoo. She'd told herself it was his way of protecting her. Keeping her safe from a place so full of painful memories. But maybe he was just an asshole. 'My dad used to work there. At the zoo.' It was out before she could stop herself.

'Dude!' Dan's laugh was genuine and warm. 'You're a zookeeper's daughter? I love that.'

Her heart pounded out a clutch of large thumps of pride, tangled, as ever, with a throb of pain.

'He doesn't work there any more?'

She shook her head, wondering how she'd gone from being The Girl Who Never Mentioned Her Father to The Girl Who Couldn't Stop Talking About Him. 'He died when I was little. Well, twelve. So not really little.'

'No, no. That's little.' Dan's voice went scratchy as his blue eyes met hers, those lovely hands of his simultaneously clapping over his heart. 'That's way too young to lose a parent. I'm sorry, Ellie. I can't even imagine.' His forehead crinkled in concern. 'Do you mind if I ask how you lost him?'

She tucked the duvet she was snuggling under tighter round her. It was kind of a weird way to go. Having learnt the hard way that people sometimes laughed when she told them, she wasn't exactly seasoned in telling this particular tale. But, as if the cookies

167

they'd been eating contained some sort of truth serum, she just came out and said it. 'One of the silverback gorillas attacked him when he was trying to get to a little kid who had fallen into the enclosure.'

There. She'd done it.

Explained the facts as if she'd been reading them from the newspaper.

'Oh shit,' Dan whispered, his expression tragic-stricken. 'So . . . your dad was a hero.'

If Ellie had thought she'd loved Dan Buchanan before, her feelings for him doubled in that instant.

Her dad had been called a lot of things – headstrong, foolish, idiotic, insane – but rarely a hero. The decision to go into the pen instead of shooting the gorilla, as protocol dictated, had been too controversial to openly deem his actions heroic. The child had been saved, but not her father or the gorilla, in the end. People had taken Koko's shooting as a given. Were openly enraged her father hadn't done it immediately. Of course, Koko should've been shot to save a *child*. What people didn't consider was that her father had loved Koko as one of his own. He'd looked after him for seventeen years. Had nursed him when he was found, injured, clinging to the corpse of his mother, who had been killed by machete-wielding poachers. Had cared for him longer than either of his own children. Taught him to be nurtured and then, when he became a father himself, to nurture. He'd been an absolute sweetheart. Right up until Ellie's father entered the pen at the moment the screams and handbags being thrown by the crowd made something in him snap. Ellie knew in her heart he'd been trying to save the gorilla every bit as much as he'd been trying to protect the child. A child whose parents had sued the zoo for emotional damages rather than send so much as a thank-you card for having a zookeeper who'd lost his life to save their flesh and blood. Not that she stalked him on the internet or anything, but the little boy was entering his second year at Cambridge, where he was studying law.

Her mother had seen her father's actions as a betrayal. Proof that he'd always loved the animals more than he'd loved her, his own family.

'Had that been his dream? To work with the silverbacks?' Dan asked.

Ellie nodded. It had. He was a farmer's son, but had bucked the trend of following in his father's footsteps and all but grown up at the zoo. At first as a visitor, then as a volunteer, then an intern. He'd studied and studied until he had the qualifications to go on a research trip to Africa, and then another and another. Ellie's mum used to joke she knew the back of him more than the front, but they all knew she'd always been there to meet him when he returned.

'That's what you do when you meet the love of your life,' she'd told Ellie and Aurora during one of his many absences when they were little. 'You wait. You love someone the way I love your father and you'll wait until the end of time if necessary. Even if you only get a handful of seconds before the clock stops. You wait.'

It was why waiting for Sebastian to finish uni, and then law school and then his trainee internship at the law firm, had never seemed weird to her. She loved him, or at least she thought she had, so she'd waited. It was what the Shaw women did. Well, her mum and her, anyway. Aurora didn't wait for anyone. Aurora never had.

Dan finished another cookie, a thoughtful expression on his face. 'I saw them once on a trip to the Smithsonian Zoo in DC. Astonishing animals. Sadie and I had planned to go see them when we were out in Africa, but—' He abruptly stopped himself with a wave, as if he was Control-Alt-Deleting himself. 'Didn't pan out. Anyway. I'm interrupting. Tell me more about your dad.'

She closed her eyes and pictured him. Tall, gangly, almost always in earth tones; Aurora and Ellie screaming with delight and fear as he piggy-backed one of them around the kitchen, chasing the other while their mother protested through her smiles. *No, Harry, no! Someone will end up getting hurt* – never once imagining that person would be her husband. He was the lifeforce of their family. They'd all thought he'd live forever.

'There's not much to tell,' Ellie finally said. 'He was great. Funny. Smart. Love of my mum's life. Worked in a zoo, so, a totally awesome dad. He was my hero. And here I am, at the ripe age of twenty-seven, missing him as much as I did at twelve. Pathetic, huh?'

'Not even!' Dan protested. 'I'm thirty-two and I can't imagine life without my parents—' He swiped his hand over his face and mumbled something that sounded either like swearing or praying. 'Nope.' He looked back up at her. 'Can't picture it. I'll have to reanimate them or something if they ever have the audacity to die.' A stricken expression crossed his face. 'Sorry. I didn't mean to imply that your dad was audacious.'

Ellie considered it for a moment, and then, as if he'd poured rainbows and a herd of dancing unicorns into her memory chest, laughed. 'He was pretty audacious.' She remembered some of the things he would do to encourage the primates to play. Somersaults. Headstands. Cartwheels. He'd been a proper nutter, her dad. In the best possible way. 'He used to do these magic tricks for the chimpanzees.'

'Not the gorillas?'

'Nah. They were more into the improvisational bongo sessions,' Ellie deadpanned.

'Seriously? Your dad played them bongos?'

Ellie giggled, suddenly elated to speak about her dad with a smile on her face. 'I'm afraid the bongos thing is a lie.'

Dan sat back in his chair with a good-natured groan. 'Ha ha. It's the "Fool the Gullible American" trick. Thea used to love doing that. Saying all of this crazy stuff then laughing her head off at what I'd fall for.'

'Thea was horrible for making you feel bad about yourself.'

'It was fine.' Dan swiped the memories away, his ability to take jibes clearly much more robust than her own.

Ellie protested. 'Making someone feel bad because of things they don't know, things that are completely out of their control is—' She stopped herself, unsure if she was still talking about Dan and Thea.

The silence amplified the sound of a key entering the lock at the front door. Sadie pushed it open, her features completely unchecked, a mix of weariness and anxiety. She hung her bag on the coat rack positioned to the right of the door then looked up and saw the two of them there, a bundle of duvets and mugs of tea and hands stuffed with home-made cookies. Ellie scrambled up as if they'd been caught snogging. Dan did the same.

And just like that, the atmosphere in the room grew charged. Taut and expectant, as if actual thunder and lightning were crackling above them.

'Oh!' Sadie popped on a smile, her eyes moving from Ellie to Dan. 'We have company.'

Chapter Nineteen

Dan strode across the living room and pulled Sadie into his arms for a *welcome home* hug. Instead of wrapping herself around him the way Ellie would have after a long day at work, she watched, increasingly wide-eyed, as Sadie did that thing people who don't really like to touch other people do, a kind of lean into a hug, but with their extremities staying exactly where they were, as if she was a flexible ruler being arced in the middle. It was weird and made Ellie feel squirmy but she couldn't look away. Like when you figure out your best friend's parents hate each other and, because it's 'just you', don't bother to lower their voices when they fight.

'Well, who have we here?' Sadie asked when Dan released her.

Dan looked confused. 'It's Ellie. You know, Ellie Shaw and Gus.'

Gus dutifully lifted his head above the back of the sofa to say hello. Sadie gave Gus a surprised little *oh, look at you* wave. Ellie received a raised forehead and a waiting-room smile. 'Hi, I'm Sadie Goodwin.'

Dan shot her a look. 'You two have already met, babe.'

Both Sadie and Ellie gave tiny reflexive jerks at the term of endearment.

Sadie gave her head a few gold-curled shakes as if trying to shift the memory up to the front of her mental screensaver.

'At the bar,' Dan prompted. 'Remember? On our first couple of days here?'

She studied him for a minute as if his face was a PowerPoint presentation and she was waiting for a slide change. It arrived. 'Oh! The night we met your ex.'

Interesting. She remembered Thea more than the girl who'd taken his dog. She tucked the information away. Dan gave Sadie a quick rundown of what had happened. How Gus had fallen ill. Ellie didn't have a car so he'd offered to give her a ride to the vet's. He'd insisted she stay the night so she and Gus had another set of hands to rely on. Ellie noticed that he slightly tweaked the truth, making the course of events sound much more like a mutually agreed upon plan rather than what had actually happened: a knight saving a damsel in distress.

Sadie gave his chest a pat, and, finally, permitted him a smile. 'You can't help yourself, can you?'

Now it was Dan's turn to look perplexed.

Sadie's smile stayed static. 'Picking up your waifs and strays.'

Ellie began to fold the duvet. 'Maybe it'd be best if Gus and I headed back home.'

'No.' Dan held out his hand in a stop position.

Ellie shook her head and, mostly to Sadie, said, 'No, really. You weren't expecting company and I imagine you could do with a quiet night.'

Sadie looked about to agree when Gus padded over to see what all of the excitement was and managed to knock Ellie's tote bag over. A ream of client questionnaires fell out. Ellie dropped to the floor to gather them up and stuff them back in her bag. Dan sort of half leant to help, protesting that Ellie was hardly a waif or a stray when Sadie dramatically succumbed to a yawn.

'Sorry. It's well past my bedtime. Ellie, please do stay.' She went up on tiptoe and gave Dan's cheek a kiss. 'Darling, do you mind if I push off and get to bed?'

'Not at all,' Dan said.

Ellie stood, her skin crawling with discomfort as Dan and Sadie slipped their arms around one another's waists and faced her the way a well-meaning couple might greet a friend of a friend's daughter who needed 'somewhere safe' to stay while waiting for a train that wouldn't leave until the next day.

Ellie really wished she could go home, but that would make this already awkward scenario even more suspect, so she faked her own yawn and said, 'Gus and I are normally tucked in hours before this. Especially on a school night.'

Sadie gave her a crinkly nosed *how cute* smile. A far cry from the warm and utterly charming Kate Humble version of Sadie she'd met a few weeks back.

'Your bedroom's—' Dan began as Sadie asked, 'Do you have everything you need?'

'Actually, Dan said I might be able to borrow an outfit for work tomorrow?'

'Did he?' She gave Dan a look. 'Well, yes. Of course you may.'

Ellie's stomach churned with discomfort. If Sadie didn't like hugging her own boyfriend, there was no chance she'd want a stranger's body inside her clothes.

Ellie submitted herself to the inevitable once-over. The vomit-stained leggings and hoodie elicited a frown and a brisk, 'My clothes are in the room next to yours. Just help yourself.'

Ellie almost curtsied. 'Thanks.'

'Pleasure.' Sadie tilted her head to the side and, unexpectedly, gave Ellie an actual, warm smile. The kind that caught you so off guard, you'd do anything to be the recipient of another one. 'Sorry if I'm a bit off. Tough night at the office.'

Ellie's tension eased a fraction. She got it. If she'd come home after a hard day's work to find a stranger gabbling away with her boyfriend who had not only been invited to spend the night but to wear her clothes she'd . . . she'd probably have gone and picked out the outfit for her. 'No problem. Sorry to spring myself on you.'

'Life's just full of surprises when you live with this one.' Sadie gave Dan's chest another pat, her fingertips never gaining purchase, then wished them goodnight and disappeared. There was the sound of water pipes rattling into action, drawers being opened and closed and, from the sounds of things, a brief rehearsal of a monologue on manners.

'Can I get you anything?' Dan asked, his face creased into an apologetic *I really don't know what's got into her* face.

'No, I'm good. I think I'll head off to bed too.' She flicked her thumb in what she hoped was the right direction.

'Oh!' Dan bopped his forehead with the heel of his palm. 'You'll need a t-shirt to sleep in. Let me get you one of mine.'

'Oh, please d—' But he was gone before she could protest. She wasn't surprised to hear a tight exchange of low voices. More drawers opening and closing. A door closing with a clonk. Dan was back a few seconds later, unfurling a soft, well-loved t-shirt in front of his chest. It had a bright red bird on the front.

'Nice bird.'

'*State* bird,' Dan corrected. 'The cardinal.' He beamed a grin at her. 'Represents friendship, so it's perfect for us.'

'Extra perfect!' *Kill me now!*

He turned the shirt round and held it in front of Ellie. 'It suits you.' His gaze met hers and just like that another more-than-friends jolt of connection held them in place.

'Okay. Yeah.' Dan broke the silence first, shifting his weight from one hip to the other as if warming up for a sprint round the flat. 'I guess that's goodnight then.'

They did a quick exchange of alarm times and Gus's morning pee and poop routine, crossed their fingers that the icy weather might abate, agreeing that takeaway coffee and croissants from the boulangerie down the street would do for breakfast before Ellie set off for work, even though Dan insisted he could run to the shops and get some 'breakfast fare'. She assured him there was no need for him to do more than he had. He was a perfect host.

'Babes?' Sadie appeared at their bedroom door in a pair of immaculately ironed floral pyjamas. 'You coming?'

'Yup.'

'Can you pull the blinds when you get in? You know how the street light affects me.'

He nodded. 'Sure thing.' When she clicked the door shut behind her he stage-whispered, 'She is, like, the lightest sleeper in the world. If I breathe wrong she wakes up.'

'I heard that!'

'Well, goodnight, friend.' Dan pulled her in for a hug.

'Night,' Ellie said into his chest, then, after a discreet inhalation of his man scent, gently extracted herself from the hug because, unlike Sadie, she could've stayed there forever.

Email: February 7th
To: Thea, mailto:Simon
From: Ellie.Shaw@softerlandings.co.uk
RE: Client Submissions FWD: SubLtr276

Hey guys,

I think this one can be solved pretty easily. A nice 'don't have the same shared interests' type of phone call? I'm happy to do a one-to-one Skype with her tomorrow night so we can start getting on top of the backlog.

E x
PLEASE SEE ATTACHED

◆ ◆ ◆

How Did You Meet?

Blind date through bestie.

How Long Have You Been Together?

Five exceedingly painful dates.

Reason There Was More Than One Date If There Was No Chemistry On First Date:

He's my best friend's cousin. She set us up because she knows I'm struggling with the 'ticking clock'. (I'm 35 and female. Nuf said.) Anyway, he just got back from a second tour in Syria. He's a sniper with the Special Forces. Army? Whatever. Anyway, I would rather freeze my eggs than have babies with this guy. He is properly effed UP! Sometimes he's really smart and funny and then all of the sudden he gets this weird twitch. Plus, I'm pretty sure he's racist. But how do you dump the guy who 'fought for my freedom'?

Reason for Softer Landing:

My best friend will kill me because the cousin's mental health is . . . ermm . . . super-dicey. He needs to not want to date me for this thing to end. Believe me. I have tried. I talk about babies A LOT.

Normally that sends a guy running for the hills. Not this dude. So I threw a lot of crafting into the mix. Talked about crochet conventions. Knitting clubs. He's still hanging in there! I think he's clinging to me because no one else will date him. PLEASE HELP ME. He bites my lips when we kiss. It's weird and it hurts. Nice penis, though. Shame about the human attached to it.

Break-up Style (Please Tick Preferred Option *):

☐ Text
☐ Email
☐ Scripted Phone Call
☑ One-to-one tutorial (Skype/Zoom/In-person session, price gradient applies)
☑ Bespoke Split (POA)

NOTES:

Can't do text, because he spent first date telling me he'd been dumped five times by text. Can't do email because I'm really scared he'll misinterpret what I'm saying and do something regrettable or maybe, like, take me hostage? That happens. I'm pretty sure I've heard of that happening. FUCKING BRAVE, THOUGH. The man's a hero. Seriously. But not my bag. I feel like such a dick. Can women feel like dicks? Awful. I feel awful. Oh god. Why am I doing this? Maybe I should just call a shrink. Am I the headcase or is he? That twitch!!! The biting!!!! I can't take much more. HELP!!!! I don't think my lips can take any more!

NB: Softer Landings requires a telephone or in-person interview prior to agreeing to Break-Up Style and reserves the right to refuse a split and/or to recommend an alternative method to that chosen by the client.

♦ ♦ ♦

February 8th
To: Thea, Simon
From: Ellie.Shaw@softerlandings.co.uk
RE: Client Submissions FWD: SubLtr276

Hey guys,

Previous client might be solved more easily than I thought. Will prepare a sample text. See attached questionnaire.

E x

SOFTER LANDINGS CLIENT QUESTIONNAIRE

How Did You Meet?

Blind date through cousin.

How Long Have You Been Together?

Five unbelievably painful dates.

Reason There Was More Than One Date If There Was No Chemistry On First Date:

My cousin set this up because she thinks I have a screw loose after doing a couple of tours in Syria and that I need someone 'to ground me', but I'm fine. They have shrinks for that shit. Girlfriends are supposed to be for fun, right?

Reason for Softer Landing:

This girl is far too into crafting for anyone's good. And she wants babies, like, yesterday. I'm doing everything I can to get her to dump me. I've pretended I have a twitch. I've done a weird nibbling/biting kissing thing that she seems to lap up. I've even called the people in the Middle East offensive names because she reads the *Guardian*, but nope! Can't shake her liberal, tree-hugging, crochet-needled ass. Nothing I do sends her running for the hills. Proper nutjob. Good in bed, though. Great tits.

Break-up Style (Please Tick Preferred Option*):

☑ Text
☐ Email
☐ Scripted Phone Call
☐ One-to-one tutorial (Skype/Zoom/In-person session, price gradient applies)
☐ Bespoke Split (POA)

NOTES:

Short and sweet and to the point, please. There is no way I can make it through a Valentine's dinner without wanting to scoop my own eyeballs out with a spoon. And I actually know how to do that, so . . . just saying.

NB: Softer Landings requires a telephone or in-person interview prior to agreeing to Break-Up Style and reserves the right to refuse a split and/or to recommend an alternative method to that chosen by the client.

Chapter Twenty

'Hello, darling. It's Mum here. I'm sorry we keep missing you. I thought maybe in the morning before work might be a good time, but it looks like London is keeping you one busy bee. Maybe we could set a time in all of our calendars? The plans for the wedding are coming along ever so nicely. It'd be great to have some of your input, though. You're always so good at turning a muddle into a system. Alright, love. Speak to you soon. Oh! And give our love to Seb. We saw his grandparents the other day. Poor loves, they are getting on. They'd probably love a visit as much as I would. They said he's getting on well at the new law firm. Why didn't you tell me he'd changed jobs? Ta ta for now.'

'Oh my god! Are you watching porn?'

Ellie slammed her phone down on her desk and gave Thea a prim 'No.'

Near enough, though. Ellie had risen early and left Dan and Sadie's before either of them had woken up. Dismayed not to have been given a chance to 'dazzle her with his ability to buy pastries', Dan had taken it upon himself to text Ellie 'Gupdates'. The

Gus-centric texts featured newsie notes about what he'd eaten (rice and scrambled egg), whether he had peed and pooped (yes to the first, not so much the second one, but hardly a shocker) and the unsurprising news that the vet nurse had texted him her number in case he had any questions. She'd just been staring at an insanely adorable selfie. At the forefront of the picture was Gus, tongue hanging out, grin on his face, and Dan's big old happy smile nestled among Gus's ear fluff.

Thea leant against the doorway to her office, coffee in one hand, chocolate croissant in the other and gave her the side-eye. 'When did we decide to change our personal style from meek office mouse to hipster?'

Ellie looked down at her outfit. It was very trendy. It also wasn't hers. The sixties-inspired skater dress was Sadie's. As were the knee-high boots. They'd been the only footwear among Sadie's impressive spread that had matched the dress and mustn't have fit Sadie properly because they'd never been worn. At least, that's what Ellie had told herself as she'd zipped up the stretchy black suede boots over her calves. The tights were hers. (Thank you, Superdrug.) And she was wearing her own pants (inside out, obvs), but, yes, the simple truth was that she looked good today because she had stolen someone else's aesthetics. Living the dream. If she was Villanelle. The actual plan had been to sneak out, go home and get her own clothes. Unfortunately, after endless hours of tossing and turning, she'd finally fallen asleep at four a.m., panic-woke at six, thrown herself into the clean clothes, given a bewildered-looking Gus a cuddle, then fled. She would've loved to announce that she felt more comfortable in her regular 'uniform'. Dark trousers or a skirt from Next, a solid-coloured blouse from Uniqlo and ballet flats from Primark. But, as she'd walked into work, she'd felt good. Pretty, even. One guy had whistled. She knew she wasn't meant to approve of that sort of thing, but she wasn't the type of girl men admired in that way and, given that he hadn't shouted, 'Take it off,' the whistle had given her a little boost.

'They're not my clothes,' Ellie finally admitted.

Thea hmphed. 'I should've guessed. Who's the lucky lady?'

'What?'

'Your girlfriend.'

'There's no girlfriend.'

'Hmm.' Thea looked disappointed. 'I was hoping to unravel the Secret Dating Mysteries of Ellie Shaw.'

'No mystery here,' Ellie said. 'No dates.'

'Really?' This seemed an inconceivable reality to Thea, which, in a weird way, made her feel good.

'Really.'

'Whose clothes are they, then? OMG!' Thea pretended to look wounded. 'Do you have . . . other friends?'

Ellie snorted. As if. 'You know how Gus was sick?'

Thea nodded.

'Well, American Dan picked us up and insisted we stay at his.'

Thea's tone changed. 'Oh, did he now?'

'*And* because I didn't have a chance to grab clothes, Sadie said I could borrow some of hers.'

'Those exact clothes?' Thea asked pointedly. 'If I were her, I would've put you in a potato sack so you looked like shit. You look hot.'

'She was asleep when I took them,' Ellie admitted through a grin at the unexpected compliment.

'Ah, the old dine and dash.' Thea went to the doorway and shouted, 'Simone! You must join this discussion. Immediately. Ellie's trying to steal American Dan away from Sadie.'

'I am not!'

Thea cackled. 'Awww. Look. She's blushing. Of course you're not. Unlike me, you're far too pure hearted for that sort of Machiavellian nonsense.'

Ellie gave a *that's exactly right* purse of her lips. 'I'll meet you two later for our afternoon meeting, okay?'

'No.' Thea plopped down into a beanbag stolen from the creation circle. 'I'm bored of hiring secretarial staff. Gimme some of those.' She reached for the client files. Ellie pulled them close.

'No. We're only supposed to meet for one hour out of your Media Angel's workday.'

'Know the rules, so you know when to break them,' Thea intoned. She always pulled Dalai Lama truisms into things when Ellie got prissy. *Little Miss My Way Or The Highway.*

'Fine.'

'I want some too.' Simon grabbed his own stack of questionnaires and pulled up a wheelie chair to the far side of Ellie's desk.

They all began reading and taking notes.

Later, Ellie's phone buzzed with a message. No. Three messages. How could she have missed three messages in the space of ten minutes while being in front of her phone?

'Put it on speaker,' Thea demanded.

'No.' If it was one of Dan's messages, she wanted to keep it to herself.

'Please.' Simon put on a sad-puppy face.

She reached for the phone but Thea got there first.

'Voice message from an unknown number.'

Oh. Not Dan. Thea pressed Play.

'Hello, Eleanor. Eleanor Shaw? This is Tony Kurchfeld. Your landlord. We've not spoken since you took the lease. Well, ever, really. That's what the agency is for. Anyway, I thought I should do this call personally. I'm afraid I'm going to be selling the building by auction and hope to do so at the end of the month. Lifestyle change. Wife wants to live by the sea, so . . . By law you'll find this notice gives you the time you are entitled to. Three weeks in total. I'll put the paperwork through your door tomorrow. We'll see about getting your deposit back to you, but I will have to hold it until we see if any extra cleaning is necessary. Hope this message finds you well.'

Ellie sat, frozen in her chair. Thea pressed the button to hear the next message for her.

'Ellie, love, it's Mallory here. Apologies for leaving a message. I'm a bit of a slave to the break times at school. Anyway, I wanted to let you know as soon as possible – I've finally been given an appointment for that hip replacement I was telling you about? I'm fairly certain I mentioned it. They've had a cancellation and can fit me in next week, so . . . it does make things a bit awkward with Gus. I know he's a gentle little bear, but a bear nonetheless, and I should hate for him to have to be on his guard while I'm in recovery. Six to eight weeks, they're saying. Anyway. If you could give me a ring, I'm sure we can find someone at the school to help us out. I know you're chocka with work, so . . . speak to you soon. Bye.'

They all stared at one another. Thea pressed play for the next message.

'Hi there. This is Dr – it's Sadie Goodwin. Dan's girlfriend?'

Ellie, Simon and Thea threw one another perplexed looks. Ellie's heart lodged in her throat. Thea reached across the desk and pressed Pause.

'She totally wants her clothes back,' Thea said. 'To be fair, if you'd taken my brand-new boots, I'd be fuming.'

Simon shushed her with a 'Don't be a bitch,' then, 'Press Play.'

Ellie's heart was pounding so hard she could barely hear. Thea pressed Play.

'I was hoping we could meet up in the next couple of days. Just you and me.'

Oh god. Ellie was going to be sick. Sadie was going to tear her to shreds. Insist she pay for a new set of clothes and demand that she give Gus to Dan immediately as penance.

'Can you give me a call so we can diarise?' Sadie left her number, twice, and then, as if she'd been asking Ellie to ping her an article on face soap, signed off with a breezy, 'Thanks! Byeeee.'

Thea and Simon both stared at Ellie.

Thea broke the silence. 'I would change before you meet.'

Chapter Twenty-One

Ellie met Sadie two nail-biting days later at a cafe in Fitzrovia. A *green tea latte and chia seed muffin* type of place Sadie had suggested as it was equidistant between her flat and Ellie's work.

Sadie was already there, looking much more business-chic than the Urgent Care fatigue she had when Ellie had stayed. She looked up when Ellie entered, waved a twinkly fingered little wave and pointed at the chair across from her.

'Hi.' Ellie held out a dry-cleaning bag. 'Here're your things. Thanks so much for letting me borrow them.'

Sadie glanced at the clothes as if she barely recognized them. 'Hi! Thanks for coming. Here, sit down. Should we order you something?' She waved at the server then turned back to Ellie with a smile and a head shake. 'I have to say, I would not have guessed you ran such an interesting business.'

Ellie tried not to frown. Was that an insult or a compliment? 'Oh?'

'Mm, yes. You seem too . . .' Sadie inspected her for a moment as if the perfect adjective was alluding her. Then she found it. 'Sweet. Like the way Dan is sweet.'

'How did you find out about it?' Ellie squeaked.

'I found your questionnaires,' Sadie said brightly as she reached into her tote and handed a small sheaf to Ellie. 'Nice website, by the way. You've got a lot of rave reviews.'

'Thanks?' She took the sheets, her cheeks colouring as she realised they were some of the questionnaires she'd dropped when Sadie had come home the other night.

The server appeared tableside. 'Can I get you anything?'

'The green tea lattes are really good,' Sadie said in an encouraging voice. 'I get mine with oat milk for the slow release of carbs.' Sadie gave her a kindly smile in the way a wealthy godmother might have when forced to come to the aid of her gormless goddaughter when brought to high tea for the first time at The Ritz.

'One of those, please,' Ellie said numbly.

Now that the niceties had been seen to, Sadie pushed a prepoured glass of tap water towards her, then tapped the papers, her expression shifting into something more pragmatic. As if she was about to ask Ellie for a urine sample or the last time she'd had her period before saying, 'The more I thought about it, the more I realised how perfect it was.'

'What?'

'Hiring you to break up with Dan for me.'

Ellie choked on some water. 'You what?'

'I want you to break up with Dan for me.'

Ellie gawped at her. This was a mind game, right? A hoax to force Ellie into admitting she had feelings for Dan. She forced herself to play along. 'Why do you feel a Softer Landing is appropriate for your situation?'

Sadie's smile shadowed. 'Let's just say I'd like as much of Dan's kind heart preserved as possible.'

'What? He adores you. You adore him,' she tacked on for good measure.

'Oh,' Sadie laughed and patted Ellie's hand as if she were explaining to a toddler that Mummy and Daddy didn't love one another any more, but that didn't mean they both didn't love her very, *very* much. 'That's sweet, but . . . no.' She popped on her trademark smile and said, 'Right. I'm a bit of a novice to this, so . . . I presume this is the part where you take over. I have an idea that's growing on me, but let's start with yours.'

In a bid to give her brain a chance to catch up, Ellie ran through a few questions by rote.

She didn't want it done by text. (Fine.)

Or email. (Fair enough.)

Or phone. (Okay.)

Nor did she 'take to' any of the multiple, successful scenarios where Ellie fed the dumper lines in a public or a private space to optimum effect for the dumpee – aka Dan. Ellie even offered to try to find him another job, not that she had the remotest clue how to find eye surgeon posts, but desperate times and all that. 'Wouldn't that suit? A transfer somewhere far away?'

'No.'

Alright. 'So, you said you had an idea?'

'Yes, that's right.' Sadie played with one of her curls then looked across at Ellie with the directness of a surgeon about to explain precisely how they were going to drill into a loved one's brain. 'I want Dan to fall in love with you.'

Wait. What?

'Oh, no-oh-ho-ho,' Ellie panic laughed. 'I *supervise* the break-ups. I don't participate.'

'Hmmm,' Sadie said. 'Well, that is a problem because I want to hire you.'

'Why?'

'Because you're exactly the type of woman who's perfect for him. He talks about you all the time. Thinks you're absolutely

189

wonderful. So, really, he's halfway there. All he needs is a little nudge in the right direction. And you break up with people for a living, so . . . win-win.'

For whom exactly? Certainly not Dan. And, more to the point, not Ellie.

Sadie kept talking as a dull roar of panic began to take over her brain. Ellie pleaded with the buzzing to allow some of the snippets she was catching to become fully formed sentences.

'. . . want Dan to feel loved . . .'

'. . . know what it's like to be adored . . .'

'. . . really fall hard . . .'

Seriously?

Was she even remotely up for this? Getting Dan to fall in love with her for work purposes would not only be crossing the *don't date your friend's ex* line, it also meant she would have to get him to dump her after, because that's how Softer Landings worked. And that would mean . . . oh god, it was painful to even think it . . . no more Dan. Ever.

If she agreed to this deeply *bonkers* proposal, Ellie's own heart would bear the bulk of the brutality of the arrangement. Cyrano without the poetry. But that's why she had started Softer Landings, wasn't it? To absorb other people's heartache. And of all the people on the planet who didn't deserve to be rejected yet again, it was Dan Buchanan. Oh my god. Was she actually *considering* this?

Ellie pushed her mug away. 'Can we back up here? Before making a plan I need to know where this is coming from.'

Sadie's lips disappeared inside her mouth for a moment before admitting, 'I'm not in love with him. Never have been. Moving here was a mistake. I should've known it before things got this far, but I let myself get too wrapped up in—' She stopped herself as if she had nearly gone one admission too far. She wove her fingers together and wrapped them around one of her knees. 'Look. Dan is one of the nicest humans in the world.'

At least there was something they could agree on.

'He's the most genuine version of himself I've ever known any adult male to be,' Sadie continued. 'And if I stay with him, I will crush all of that.'

'Why?'

Sadie was getting impatient now. 'I don't love him, alright? I'm bitchy to him. I'm short with him. I make him feel bad about himself and it's not fair on him.'

'Then why'd you get together with him in the first place?'

Sadie shifted in her seat, for once reacting like one of her normal clients – uncomfortably. 'Have you ever had a relationship with someone because they were the best of the bunch?'

Ellie was about to say she'd never thought such a thing, let alone done it when Sadie's question doubled back on her and cleaved her in two. That's what she'd been. The best of a limited pool of summer girlfriends.

Sadie, misreading Ellie's nod of understanding, continued, 'The simple truth is, we were meant to have our little affair, wrap things up in Africa, then get on with the rest of our lives.'

'What happened?'

A hardness gripped Sadie's features. She took a sip of water, her hand betraying a slight tremor, before saying, 'You've met him. He's . . . he's one of the kindest men in the world and I felt I owed it to him to see if things would work. They haven't. Aren't. Believe me,' she continued before Ellie could ask any more probing questions, 'I didn't make the decision to ring you lightly. I called you because I genuinely think this is the best course of action for Dan. This is one hundred per cent for Dan. If you prefer, I can do what I almost did last night.'

'Which was . . . ?'

'Tell him to pack his bags and get out.'

And just like that, the ball was in Ellie's court. Free Dan from a doomed relationship and crush her own heart in the process or let Sadie take the reins, knowing Dan would endure the pain of rejection for having committed the crime of believing he was loved.

Sadie started to say something else then stopped herself, her left hand rubbing her throat as if an actual knot of emotion had lodged there. For the first time since she'd walked into the café, Ellie felt genuine concern for her. This obviously wasn't easy. The terse tone and businesslike demeanour were all for show. Sadie cleared her throat, then, in a crisp tone that suppressed a volcano's worth of feelings, said, 'Dan needs to know what it feels like to be loved by someone who genuinely thinks he's wonderful. I presume that's something you can do?'

Ellie stared down at her green latte, well aware of just how easy it would be, but then, mercifully, her much more practical side kicked into gear. She couldn't just wander up to him with a swirl of Disney birds making heart shapes around her head and have him suddenly realise he loved her. And what was she supposed to do once she got him to fall in love with her? Keep him, like a raffle prize? Not a chance. If, by some miraculous turn of events, Dan Buchanan fell in love with her, she wanted it to be real. There was no way she could live the rest of her life carrying around the guilt of knowing their relationship had begun with a cash transaction and false pretences. The weight of her lies would destroy her. And frankly, there was only so much emotional carnage she could deal with.

Ellie spluttered, 'If we accept the job, which I would like to make explicitly clear I am *not* doing by asking this question, but if we do and we are successful . . . what am I supposed to do with him after?'

'Whatever you like,' Sadie said, taking a delicate sip of her drink.

'But—' Ellie stopped herself because even picturing herself running off into the sunset with American Dan was just plain wrong. She forced on her Softer Landings hat. They had done a few break-ups using a new object of affection as a lure. Never Ellie herself, but experience had proven that knowing someone found you lovable was their most effective way of softening the blow that someone else didn't.

She forced herself to meet Sadie's unblinking gaze. 'I get that you don't want to hurt him, but whatever you both were feeling was enough to get the two of you to move countries. Get jobs. He thinks you're setting up a *life* here. A future.'

The light caught Sadie's eyes and if Ellie wasn't mistaken, for just a moment, they blurred with tears. 'It's . . . it's complicated. A simple situation became very complicated and now we're here.' Sadie released her knee, then recrossed her legs, flicking a bit of lint off a crisp seam as she did. 'He speaks very kindly of you. Says you're absolutely brilliant. One of the nicest people he's ever met. *The* nicest, in fact.'

Ellie dropped her head into her hands. She was going to do it. Of course she was. Even if it meant destroying herself in the process. If she couldn't, what on earth was Softer Landings good for?

Taking the melodramatic gesture as a yes, Sadie pulled her phone out of her pocket. 'How much is it? I can do the transfer now.'

Ellie's stomach churned. She would've protected American Dan's heart for free, but her office rent was due soon. She was about to be homeless. Gus needed his flea and tick medicine, which cost a bomb, and she really, really needed to book tickets to Jersey, given that Aurora's wedding was only three months away, which would mean finding a sitter for Gus, which meant more money. Not to mention Thea and Simon's salary contributions . . . *Argh!*

She scrubbed her hands through her hair, praying for a better solution to present itself. Sadie wanted Dan to fall in love with a mirage . . . and then, one day, realise there was no palm tree, no oasis. Just a girl, standing in front of a boy, who'd accepted money to lure him away from his completely perfect girlfriend. Then again. If she did her job properly, Dan would never know. Which was the entire point of Softer Landings. To gently guide a person towards the future they should be leading. Even though in this case Ellie would be the lure and not the ultimate prize (*waaaah!*), she simply couldn't see him hurt again.

'How much?' Sadie prompted with an impatient glance at her watch.

Ellie imagined herself retorting in a haughty yesteryear news-reel voice, *You can keep your transfer, I'll not take your filthy lucre*, but knew any more posturing was pointless. To save him from a broken heart, she was going to have to fake date the living daylights out of Dan Buchanan.

'Ellie? Sorry, if you don't give me a price, I'm going to kick him out tonight.'

'Alright, alright.' Ellie frowned, trying to look as if Sadie had interrupted some very complicated mathematical equation. The truth was, they'd never really done a break-up like this so she didn't really have a clue. This would take time. And much more careful planning than any of their other splits.

She thought of the most expensive dating agency fee she knew of then halved it. Then halved it again. No! Screw that. This was American Dan they were talking about, and he was her friend. Manipulating his heart out of a relationship he thought would last forever shouldn't cost less than the fee structure of an overpopulated love algorithm. She named a figure, terrified Sadie might tell her to stuff it.

Sadie's face creased in concern. 'That doesn't sound right.' That's because it wasn't. She'd never charged more than two-fifty for a job, and that one had involved a lot of extras. Ellie shrugged out an *it is what it is* shoulder shift, adding a lofty, 'Plus expenses.'

Sadie didn't bat an eye. 'And roughly how much do you think they will be?'

Ellie began pointlessly rearranging the cutlery on the table, about two seconds away from shaking Sadie by the shoulders and screaming, *Are you seriously kidding me? Dan is perfect!* She threw out a similar, laughably large figure.

Sadie considered her for a moment, then tapped at her phone and looked up at Ellie with a smile. 'There you are. All done.'

Ellie barked out a disbelieving, '*Ha!*' Sadie had completed the transaction the same way she might've bought a packet of gum or a set of supermarket underpants.

'You really want out of this relationship, don't you?' Ellie asked.

Sadie nodded, her eyes latching on to Ellie's as if, at long last, she finally understood the turbulent journey she'd taken to get to this point. 'I do. And though he may not know it, Dan does too.'

For the first time since they'd sat down together, Sadie seemed just like anyone else on the planet. A woman in a chaotic world trying her best to wade through it all. Her relief was almost palpable. A weight of guilt eased. What on earth had happened to make her want out this so badly? Was it really as simple as not fancying him in London? What would've happened if he'd left a dog in Paris? Tokyo? Wichita?

She was just about to see if she could root out more information, but Sadie pushed her chair back, gave her phone the tell-tale *I'm running late* wiggle and said, 'Look, I'm really sorry, but I've got to dash. I have a meeting over on Harley Street. Thanks ever so much for doing this.'

'I—' About a hundred sentences jammed in Ellie's throat. She wasn't even sure she had technically agreed to this outrageous task. Mission? An alert from her bank bleeped on her phone to tell her there had been a deposit.

Gulp. This was for *Dan*, she told herself.

Sadie gave her arm a little squeeze, the way you might show gratitude to an assistant who'd volunteered to oversee the tedious business of the Christmas tombola. 'If you could wrap it up in maybe a month's time? Two months max?'

'And what about you?'

Sadie tipped her head to the side, her expression reading like a pat on the head. 'You let me worry about me.'

And then, before Ellie could say or do anything, like try one last time to convince Sadie that she really, really should be doing this herself but perhaps not so cruelly, she left, leaving Ellie with a sizeable bump in her bank account and an enormous dent in her moral code.

Chapter Twenty-Two

'The person you have called is not available right now. Please leave a message at the tone.'

'Hi! Sadie? This is Ellie Shaw. I'm presuming this is your private phone, but if it's not, could you please call me to discuss a personal matter? Urgently? Thank you.'

◆ ◆ ◆

'The person you have called is not available right now. Please leave a message after the tone.'

'Hello, Sadie? Not sure if you got my first couple of messages, but I'm freaking out a bit here. I don't think I can do this. I respect Dan too much to screw with him in this way, you know? I mean, not that you're screwy because obviously you are a good person and everything, but . . . wait a minute. Are you ghosting me? If that's the case, I am not breaking up with Dan for you. Okay? If you could ping over your bank account details, I'll transfer the money back and that will be that. I will not be bought! This is Ellie, by the way. Call me.'

◆ ◆ ◆

'The person you have called is not available right now. Please leave a—'

'Fuck! Fuckety fucking fucker fuckballs fucktopia and all of the fucking reindeer in the North Pole. Oh shit. Hello, Sadie? It's Ellie Shaw here. Sunday now. Could you ring me, please? We really need to talk. If you plan on treating Dan like you're treating me, then I am definitely going to have to reconsider where I stand here. I'd really like your bank details so I can transfer the money back. Oh. And thanks for the boots, by the way. Dan dropped them off with Gus yesterday after his run. I'm sorry they don't fit you, but be assured that they will have a good home with me. Am I right in thinking suede needs a special brush? Call me back ASAP. Please.'

◆ ◆ ◆

'The person you have called is not available right now. Please leave a message after the tone.'

'Sadie? Ellie here. Fine. You win. I'll do it. But not because you asked me to. I'm doing this because, honestly? I am properly unimpressed by the way you treat people. I mean, the whole pulling double shifts at the hospital thing is nice, but I don't think you're doing it for them. I think you're doing it for you. I know from my admittedly online degree in psychology that you're not supposed to use accusatory language when discussing a delicate situation with a person, but you clearly have commitment problems. Helping all of those people who you'll never see again is an easier option than growing a spine and being honest with Dan about your feelings. And you know what? You must be blind

198

as a bat or a machachocist or whatever they call it. Dan is *the* best man I have ever met. He is honest, kind, gorgeous, genuine – unlike you. I mean, the man moved COUNTRIES for you. What more do you want from him? Actual blood? And why aren't you answering my bloody phone calls? Sorry. Sorrysorrysorry. Swearing's not nice. I'm just – I care for him. He's a good man. I think you know that so I'm praying you're being nice to him now even though it will make it really, *really* hard to get him to want to break up with you, but you know what? You don't deserve him. I do. And I don't even get the pleasure of keeping him at the end of it! Not that I deserve him. I already feel duplicitous and dirty and he deserves someone clean and pure even if I do actually love him. Unlike you. So the least you can do is ring me back so I can return your stupid blood money. You can't buy me love. Hey, Simon. What? No, thanks. I've had two glasses already. Could you get me a lime and soda, please? Gussypumpkinhead, comegivemummyahug. She's full of feelings. *Sugar.* Sadie? I said this was Ellie, right? Ellie Shaw? Call me, please. When you have a chance.'

To: Ellie Shaw
From: Dr Sadie Goodwin

Ellie, you're absolutely right. About everything.
I hope Dan sees in you what I do. Best regards,
Sadie

'The number you have called has not been recognised. If you believe you have reached this message in error, please check the number and dial again.'

'The number you have called has not been recognised. If you believe you have reached this message in error, please check the number and dial again.'

'The number you have called has not been recognised. If you believe you have reached this message in error, please check the number and dial again.'

'The number you have called has not been recognised. If you believe you have reached this message in error, please check the number and dial again.'

'The number you have called has not been recognised. If you believe you have reached this message in error, please check the number and dial again.'

SOFTER LANDINGS CLIENT QUESTIONNAIRE

How Did You Meet?

Underground – Northern Line, not that it matters, but . . . in case it does . . . Stockwell. So. South of the river.

How Long Have You Been Together?

Three months.

Reason There Was More Than One Date If There Was No Chemistry On First Date:

I hate doing Christmas on my own. We met after we'd both just come from our Christmas work dos. We were drunk. We fancied each other. We snogged on the tube and that was kind of that.

Reason for Softer Landing:

She was nice enough 'filler' but not really what I'm looking for in a long-term relationship. Makes me sound like a total arse, doesn't it? Maybe I should just do that. Tell her she isn't the woman I want having my children. Fuck. No. Seeing it in print is brutal. Can we just . . . dunno. Let's do the text thing, maybe? I could possibly do a phone call but I'd like to time it before a business trip or something, so that I can disappear after. An email suggests I want to engage and that is the total opposite of what I want. I'm going to Brussels for a few days next week. Would that work? A nice *see ya* text, then I get to disappear?

Break-up Style (Please Tick Preferred Option*):

☑ Text
☐ Email
☐ Scripted Phone Call
☐ One-to-one tutorial (Skype/Zoom/In-person session, price gradient applies)
☐ Bespoke Split (POA)

NOTES:

I don't really know what you want here. I'm a nice guy looking for love. Just not with a girl who snogs strangers on the Underground. It keeps reminding me of an old boss who'd always tell the lads, 'Put her down! You don't know where she's been.' And yeah, before you can say it, I know I'm a hypocrite.

*NB: Softer Landings requires a telephone or in-person interview prior to agreeing to Break-Up Style and reserves the right to refuse a split and/or to recommend an alternative method to that chosen by the client.

◆ ◆ ◆

Ellie was definitely not feeling herself today. A week of being ghosted by Sadie and actively avoiding Dan while ensuring he got to spend time with Gus was taking its toll. Her gaze sharpened on her prospective client.

'C'mon now, Alfie. Tell me truthfully why you want to end things with Leandra.' She ignored the heated WTF glares Simon and Thea were lasering in her direction. True, she'd never met Alfie Black before now, so determining whether or not he was being honest was possibly pushing it. But Alfie was getting on her tits.

'I – I thought I was.'

'No.' She gave his application a tap. 'You said Leandra was a Christmas filler. You did not say what made her inappropriate for the rest of the year. Or, more to the point, your life.'

'I'm pretty sure I did.' He reached out for the application, but Ellie snapped it away before he could get it.

'No. No cribbing. Tell me from here.' She pointed at her own heart. 'I want to know why you feel she's dispensable.'

'Hey.' Alfie faltered, his eyes sending pleading *help me* looks to Thea and Simon. 'That's not how I put it.'

Ellie clasped her hands together and leant forward. 'Basically, Alfie? You have. You are treating her like a single-use paper cup. Entirely dispensable. You saw her, knew you would never want to marry her, snogged her, then carried on dating her, knowing all along that we'd reach this point. The one with you trying not to pulverise her poor, misled heart into smithereens.'

Simon leant in and quietly corrected, 'Technically she wasn't single use, Ellie. They've been going out since early December.'

She shot him a death stare. 'As – and I quote yet again – "filler".' Ellie crisply slapped the form face down on the table and returned her gimlet gaze to Alfie. 'Let me paint a picture from my angle. You were riding home on the tube, a bit jolly, a bit worse for wear. It was almost Christmas. You were lonely. All of your friends had paired off and you wanted your own naughty elf to play with. So you thought, hey, why not take a pick from the Quality Street selection of booty calls right here on the tube? You began looking round at all the women, deciding whether or not you'd go for the pink one, the purple one, or – oooh – it's Christmas – the *red* one. You don't normally like the red one but thought, *what the hell? It's Christmas. When Veganuary rocks around, I'll throw her out with the rest of the box.*'

'No,' he protested. 'It wasn't like that at all.' He pointed at the application. 'I'm pretty sure I put that I fancied her on that.'

'Oh, that's right.' Ellie's tone was undeniably sarcastic now but she didn't care. She read from the application in a supercilious tone, '*We were drunk. We fancied each other. We snogged on the tube and that was kind of that.*'

'Who hasn't done that?' Thea snorted, then, remembering Ellie was in a mood unfit for joking, took an active interest in stirring her tea.

'It wasn't the end for Leandra, though, was it? It was the beginning. In fact, from what you've said, Leandra is perfectly happy with having chosen the blue Quality Street.' Ellie flicked her fore-finger at Alfie's periwinkle-blue puffa jacket, which was hanging limply on the back of the chair.

In fairness, he seemed perfectly nice. A thirty-something accountant in the building industry, Alfie Black was a footie-with-the-lads-on-the-weekend-and-Sunday-lunch-at-his-parents'-in-Pinner kind of guy. A good, solid bloke who knew how to match his socks and do his own laundry. He was no Bradley Cooper, but he was easy enough on the eye. And, begrudgingly, Ellie had to admit that he was trying to do the right thing by choosing a Softer Landing. But his word choice had riled her. Stuck in her craw like a sliver of apple skin and by jingo she wanted him to pay. Pay for making eyes at Leandra when he should have just gone home and had a wank. Pay for picking the poor girl up like she was a juicy red lollipop even though he knew from the get-go that red lollipops weren't his favourite, that he would never see it through, never finish it, leaving nothing but a half-licked, unloved, transparent lollipop in his wake. And no one likes a litter bug.

Alfie threw bewildered looks to Thea then Simon. 'We're just not a match. Going through the charade of Valentine's Day doesn't seem fair.'

'Fair!' Ellie hooted. 'Were you thinking about fair when you snogged her on the tube, knowing all along that the only thing you were after was a bit of mistletoe magic? A bit of rumpy-pumpy to see you through until the New Year?' She jabbed her finger against the table so forcefully everyone's tea spilt. 'You *knew* you didn't want to be with her forever, but you kissed her anyway. There are ramifications for that sort of behaviour, Alfred. Ramifications for taking something, or in this case, some*one*, even though you knew you didn't really want her.' She crossed her arms and in a move she'd seen Gillian Anderson use in a thriller once, softened her expression ever so slightly so as to give the impression that she really saw him.

Understood him even, and was doing her level best to help him even though they both knew it was within her rights to make an example of him. 'You strike me as the type of guy who considers himself "sensitive".'

He gave a wary nod.

'It's alright. Women like sensitive. But you see, Alfie, you aren't. You're a greedy little monkey who let things go too far and now you've found yourself too close to Valentine's for comfort because all along you've been hoping she would be the one to end it first.'

The flush on his cheeks made it clear she'd hit the nail on the head. Ellie was a nanosecond away from a triumphant fist pump when she noticed Thea and Simon were looking at her as if she'd been invaded by an evil monster designed purely for torture.

Her bravura faltered. Softer Landings had been designed for people just like Alfie. Men and women who'd taken things too far and who, realising their mistake, wanted to let their partners down gently. But was that good enough?

Her heart ached for poor Leandra Hallaway. A soon-to-be-singleton who thought she'd met her one and only at a chance meeting on the tube. That fate had put them on that carriage together. Jolted one against the other at just the right moment so that their eyes would meet and click and allow one thing to lead to another until *whoopdedoodle*! She'd fallen in love and now it was almost Valentine's Day. The icing on a cake Alfie had never once planned on giving her. But humiliating him because he reminded her of her own miserable past wasn't going to keep up their glowing Google reviews. Nor would it pay the bills.

'Right,' Ellie said brightly. 'How about we put together a nice little text making it clear Leandra is free to pursue other romantic interests?'

Chapter Twenty-Three

'Hi, Ellie. It's Dan here. I was wondering if you might have a few extra minutes for a coffee when you collect Gus today? I know you've been pretty busy lately. I had no idea media recruitment was such a twenty-four/seven thing. Anyway, look . . . I've had an idea I wanted to run by you. It was Sadie's, actually. I like it too, obviously, but – anyway. I'll see you around six-thirty? Four miles today. Gus is a champ. But you already knew that.'

◆　◆　◆

'Aren't you eating?' Simon, who had only ordered a black coffee, looked at Ellie in concern.

'Not hungry.' She pushed her untouched sandwich towards him. 'Want it?'

Simon shook his head no. He looked tired. Another rough night with Diego, no doubt. And, of course, The Great Unspoken: Ellie's disaster of a client meeting with poor Alfie Black. She'd given him a freebie and a coupon for another text or Skype session neither of which they expected him to use given his departing gambit had been, 'Fucking nutters, the lot of you.'

Thea noisily finished scraping out the remains of her vegan chilli, then slammed the recyclable container down on the table. 'C'mon, guys. Enough. So Alfie didn't love us. Whatever.' She tapped the pile of applications. 'Bring me to my happy place, Ellz.'

Simon fixed Ellie with the adoring gaze one might give a revered cult leader. 'Tell us, O wise one, what joy will we bring unto the world as we consciously uncouple these poor unsuspecting blighters?'

Ellie's chest tightened. She'd gone up and down the *am I doing the right thing* yo-yo so many times the past few days she hadn't realised how much she needed to hear this. Simon was right. They *were* helping. Of *course* it was the right thing to guide people seeking advice on a kinder, gentler way to end their relationship. Even Sadie.

Ellie squared off the startlingly large stack of break-up requests and tapped the questionnaire on the top of the pile. 'Okay. Let's do this. I was thinking a dine and ditch for this couple.'

She was about to start reading out the questionnaire when Thea thrust her hand into the centre of the table. 'Rock, paper, scissors?'

Simon and Ellie pulled faces at her.

'What?' Thea kept her hand out. 'There's loads and we're good enough at this now to do it rapid-fire.'

No. They weren't. This was a bespoke business where attention to detail was critical. But Thea did have a point. There were an awful lot of applications and they were rapidly approaching the maximum number of hours Vee had afforded them.

'Which one means which?' Simon asked after they'd exchanged *shall we* glances.

Thea thought for a moment then said, 'Instead of rock, paper, scissors, we say text, tutorial or face-to-face.'

'What about email?' Ellie asked.

Thea scoffed. 'Email break-ups are so last millennium.'

Simon's forehead tried to crinkle. 'You were, like, ten then. How would you know?'

Thea rolled her eyes. 'I have four big sisters, remember?'

She did? Ellie had known there was one, but . . . four? 'That's a lot of sisters.'

Simon made a sad-clown face. 'Our poor little Theadora here was meant to be a Theodore.'

'What?'

'I was supposed to be a boy.' Thea flicked an irritated glance at Simon, then, with her usual flair for dramatics, explained, 'I was my parents' last-ditch attempt to produce an heir for my father, the Greek patriarch, but—' She pointed at herself. 'Fail!'

Ellie frowned. 'I'm sure they don't feel that way.'

Thea grabbed at the pile of submissions. 'Believe me. They do.'

Ellie caught something in Thea's expression she hadn't seen before. A raw vulnerability peeking out from behind the bolshie loud-mouthed, nothing-can-hurt-me image she presented to the world. She was, in short, just like Ellie on the inside. Someone scrabbling to do the best she could in a world that didn't always play nice. Ellie was seized by an urgent need to let Thea know she was there for her. Just as quickly, her fear of being rejected as a friend overrode the instinct. If she lost Thea, she'd lose Simon too, and that was a whole other level of loss she couldn't cope with, so she swallowed down her offer of help and said, 'Okay, so, you think email's outdated. What do you think, Simon?'

He pushed his pillowy lips forward as he considered the matter. 'I think Thea's got a point.'

'Really? But there's so much more you can say in an email than a text.'

'Exactly,' said Simon. 'Who wants to know in detail why their partner doesn't love them?'

Ellie winced. 'Good point.'

'And also? They're not really personal.'

'And a text is?'

Simon shrugged. 'A text is how most of these relationships begin. And if it's nice . . . why not?'

It was a fair point. The bulk of their requests were from people who'd met someone on a dating app and wanted out in a kind way that meant they wouldn't have to change their number.

'I'll update the form,' Ellie conceded.

Thea punched the air then whacked her hand into a scissors shape. 'Awesome. Let's do this. Text, tutorial or face-to-face.'

Ellie's phone bleeped. Hoping against hope it was Sadie, she checked it. Her heart softened. A Gupdate from Dan. He and Gus were in front of a specialist running store wearing matching bright red headbands. Gus also had on wrist sweatbands. The message read, *Me and the Big G went shopping before our first five-miler. We'll pick you up after work if you like so I can drop you both at yours. Unless, of course, you've changed your mind and it's moving day.* 👟👟👟 *Dx*

Her heart rose and fell so rapidly it actually hurt.

'What?' Thea demanded as Ellie flipped the phone over. 'Are you watching porn again?'

'Look, she's blushing!' Simon looked as delighted as if he'd just hand-fed a baby deer. 'Is our Ellzybellzy getting dick pics from a suitor?'

'No!'

'Methinks the lady doth protest too much!' Simon clutched his heart and started humming a pop song about love.

Thea grabbed the phone before Ellie could stop her. When she'd read the messages, because of course just the one hadn't been enough, she looked Cruella de Vil happy.

'While the cat's double-shifting, the mouse will play, eh?'

'No!' Ellie tried to grab the phone back. 'It's not like that.'

'Oh no?' Thea teased, holding the phone up out of reach. 'What is it like?'

Ellie tried to put words in a row. Words explaining how her eviction notice and Mallory's hip operation and Vee's Succeed or Leave ultimatum had pushed her to the edge of a precipice. And then, after her meeting with Sadie, when she'd teetered on the edge, arms flailing, Dan had been there. Gorgeous, kind-hearted, oblivious Dan. Picking up Gus from school, dropping off bags of kibble, and delivering messages from his girlfriend who didn't want him any more that, if Ellie wanted, she was welcome to move into the spare room in the Marylebone flat. When she'd called him back last night, that had been what he wanted to talk to her about. Moving in. She'd not given him an answer yet, even though it would be a genuine lifesaver. Nor had she told Thea and Simon about Sadie's bank deposit.

'We're just friends,' she finally managed.

'Friends who fuck their actual friends' cast-offs?' Thea teased, her triumphant gaze flicking over to Simon for approval.

Thea's words eviscerated her. Surely she knew Ellie better than that. 'I wouldn't – I couldn't— Wait.' Her eyebrows shot up to her hairline. 'You want to be friends with me?'

'What are you, eight?' Thea pointed at Ellie's phone. 'And that's an *uh-uh* if this is the way you do loyal.'

Simon, to both of their surprise, snapped, 'Stop it, Thea. You're being horrid.' Then, to Ellie, said, 'Of course we're friends, you idiot.'

Thea gave an angry shrug. 'It's not like I actually care if you're riding Dan's little pony. I'm curious is all.' She began a rendition of Ellie and Daniel sitting in a tree.

'I'm not doing anything with him,' Ellie protested as Simon overlapped her with a pointed, 'They share a dog, stupid.'

Simon and Thea play-fought until Simon somehow wrested the mobile from her and returned it to Ellie. She prayed the teasing had finished but no. Thea was a dog with a bone.

'If you're just friends, why did you blush?'

'She blushes at everything,' Simon protectively answered for her.

'At a picture of a dog and a guy wearing sweatbands?'

'He's— Dan just needs a friend, okay?'

'Oh, does he now?' Thea intoned. 'And does he need a friend because you're finally admitting you are crushing hard on the man or is it because he's finally cottoned on that his girlfriend is shagging someone else?'

'Neither,' Ellie shot back. And then her brain caught up with what Thea had just said. 'She's what?'

Simon was watching them as if they were re-enacting a break point at Wimbledon.

'Thea? Did you just say Sadie is cheating on Dan?'

'I know, right?'

Simon's eyes pinged between them, trying to read the table.

'At least I wasn't that bad,' Thea said.

Ellie felt as if she'd been submerged in ice water. Was that what this whole thing had been about? Sadie had someone else. 'How could she be cheating on him? She's in Nigeria helping traumatised schoolgirls.'

'Is that what she told you?' Thea barked a laugh and then sobered. 'Oh. You're serious.'

She was. Dan had told her the other night when he'd brought Gus back. Unaware Ellie had met Sadie that same day, he'd plopped down on her sofa with an 'I didn't see that coming.'

When she'd asked what he was talking about, he said Sadie had blindsided him. Announced she'd signed up for an emergency charity medical trip helping schoolgirls recently released from a

Nigerian warlord's prison camp. She'd flown out a couple of days ago, turned off her UK phone and was now only reachable via a Nigerian mobile with sketchy signal.

Thea pulled a face, then drained her kombucha. 'This is why not sleeping with people you ultimately dump pays dividends. No guilt. No need to pay penance.'

Ellie and Simon gave her matching *what are you talking about* looks.

'Oh, c'mon.' Thea scratched at a streak of red creeping up her neck. 'You guys didn't think I actually *slept* with Dudley Do-Right, did you?'

Yes. They both had.

Thea tried to affect nonchalance but something about the confession stung through to a truer version of her. One who corroded when touched by air. 'So . . . what?' Thea scoffed. 'Has she hired you to dump Dan while she's away?'

Ellie felt the blood drain from her face.

'Oh shit.' Thea looked genuinely horrified and then shrugged it off. 'She was such a fake.' She put on a falsetto. '"I'm so amazing. I help poor people."' Thea made a guttural sound. 'She doesn't deserve American Dan. No one does.'

Ellie could barely speak. 'Thea? What did Sadie say? Exactly. That she's in love with someone else and wanted out?'

'Pretty much,' Thea said, and then, more shadily, 'Not really. Just that the whole thing with Dan was up in the air. And something about a boyfriend back home.'

Ellie's ears began to buzz. 'But she moved here. With Dan. As a couple. Who does that?'

'Easy there, tiger cub. Remember, we're talking about a guy who got a dog to prove he was committed to seeing things through with me because I wouldn't sleep with him and then left the country when you dumped him for me. So, this isn't exactly an issue-free zone.'

Okay. That was true as well. But . . . love made people do weird things, right? Even American Dan.

'He abandoned GUS, Ellie,' Thea said. 'GUS.'

Ellie tried to reorder the facts. She knew she was more forgiving of Dan's abandonment of Gus than she would've been if someone else had done it, but . . . Sadie had *moved countries* to be with Dan when she already had a boyfriend back home and was now dodging both of them? It was the kind of thing that made headlines in the *Mail*: *One Woman, Two Relationships, The Pact to End It All.*

Thea held her hands up. 'Okay, okay. She wasn't very specific, but it was clear she thought she'd made the wrong choice on the boyfriend front.'

'When did she say all of this?'

'When you two were down in the loos on margarita night when they first came back.'

'Why would she tell you all of that?'

Thea shrugged. 'I'd made some joke about you two disappearing at the same time for a secret snog and she said maybe it wouldn't be such a bad thing if you were.'

'Why would you make a joke like that?'

'Why wouldn't I, Ellie? He showed up at the office for you.'

'For Gus,' she corrected.

'And has he asked for the dog back?' Thea crossed her arms over her chest, waiting. 'Yeah. I thought not. Anyway, how did she know about Softer Landings?'

Ellie's lungs burnt, scalded afresh by her stupid mistake. 'I accidentally dropped some of the submissions when I spent the night at theirs and she found them.'

'Holy fuck.' Thea glanced at Simon, then back at Ellie. 'That's why you're being weird. She hired you before she left and you didn't want us to know you're breaking up with him for her.'

The atmosphere round the table grew dark and thunderous. Each of them throwing one another wary looks, unsure who would go first.

Simon broke the silence. 'Well, that's a bit shit for him, isn't it? Twice in one year?' He leant back in his chair. 'I'm guessing you're not doing it by email?'

Ellie pointlessly shook her head. She felt sick. For herself. For Dan. Even for Simon and Thea, who, by rights, should have been told about Sadie's request. They'd gone into this together and she'd gone rogue. 'I didn't know she was cheating. I would've made her do a face-to-face if that was the case. You know the rules.'

They did. Cheaters had to look into the eyes of their partner when they ended it.

'What's she got you doing, Ellz?' Thea asked.

'She wants me—' The words jammed in her throat.

'She wants you to what?' Simon asked gently.

'She wants me to get him to fall in love with me and then make it so that he dumps me after.'

'What? That's weird,' Simon said.

'Not that weird. We do it all the time,' Thea reminded him, and then added, 'But usually not with one of us.'

'Yeah. And also, we've only done it for short-term relationships where the couples haven't yet fallen in love. That's more . . . lust distraction. Showing someone the grass is actually greener.'

Simon tapped his chin for a moment. 'What made you take the job, Ellz? I would've thought it was an immediate *no, thank you, please grow a spine and do it yourself.*'

It was true. Normally, she would've sent the person packing. But this was American Dan they were talking about. She owed it to their friendship – no, she owed it to the very foundation of what she wanted Softer Landings to stand for – to take this job. Just because she might have at some point allowed herself to believe she was head over heels in love with the client's future ex was no reason to allow his heart to be savaged. Then, rather crucially, she realised she would not be able to do this alone. So she told Simon and Thea everything. From the beginning. If they were going to work with someone who dumped people they were in love with for a living, they would have to know where it all came from. She told them about her dad's death, her mum's depression, her sister's inability to break up with a boy herself, how she'd had to become unbelievably *useful*, how she'd met Seb, and then, of course, been dumped by Seb. How she'd been tortured by Thea's blithe treatment of Dan in the wake of having experienced a similar pain and so had had no choice but to stage the intervention, changing the course of not only her life but Dan's in the process. And now, here she was, being forced to face the consequences of meddling in someone else's affairs. Literally.

When she paused for breath, Ellie looked at her sandwich, and then, suddenly, felt insatiably hungry. In between ungainly bites she told them how the offer to take Gus had been impulsive. She hadn't really expected him to say yes, but when he had? She'd seen it as a sign that somehow her and Dan's futures would be intertwined. She just didn't know how. Friends, maybe?

Thea made bowm-chica-chica-bowm-bowm noises then started circling her hands round singing *With Sexy Benefits*. Simon told her to can it. Ellie plunged forward. Told them how she thought she might have a crush on Dan but was confused about it because maybe having her heart broken by Seb meant it was easier to have feelings for someone she knew she couldn't have. And then when he'd come back with Sadie she'd convinced herself they were just friends and mostly because of Gus. Ellie finished off her monologue with a sigh. 'I got the Gus part right, anyway. He's my friend.'

'You have us too.' Simon gave her knee a gentle nudge.

'I know, but, back then? You two had each other, really. And Diego. Not me.'

Simon tipped his head in silent acknowledgement. It was true.

She explained about Dan's jolly emails, the money he'd sent towards Gus's care and then how both had abruptly stopped.

'Why didn't you tell us?' Thea demanded.

'Because she was humiliated, you idiot.'

Ellie nodded. Yes. She had been. She continued. When Dan had reappeared and then sought her out at the cocktail bar she'd got the sense that something big had happened to him. Something bad. But her fear of losing Gus had made her too nervous to press for details.

When Sadie had rung her, Ellie had felt cornered into accepting the job but then had felt so awful about accepting it she'd rung her over and over to refuse it, hoping to give the money back. 'But she stopped her phone when she went to Nigeria. The last thing I heard from her was via Dan.'

'Which was?'

'Sadie suggested I move in while she's away.'

Thea barked with laughter and gave a too loud clap of her hands. 'Of course she fucking well did. What did you say?'

'That I needed to think about it.'

'So . . . you're playing coy to get his interest?'

'No. I'm trying to decide whether I have the ability to do this or not!'

And there it was. Out in the open. The question she'd been asking herself on a loop ever since she'd met Sadie. Was she brave enough to give her heart to Dan in order to set his free?

Simon bashed the table with his fist. 'Goddammit, Ellie Shaw! We are going to do this job and we are going to do it together!'

'Yeah!' shouted Thea when she realised Simon was glaring at her for back-up affirmation. 'Fuck yeah!'

'Really?' Ellie asked.

'Really,' Simon assured her as Thea started chanting, 'In it to win it.'

Okay. Good. She had back-up. She wouldn't be doing this alone. 'And if I turn into a melted puddle of sorrow and despair at the end of it?'

Thea made a *hel-looo* gesture. 'We'll scoop you into a lovely soup bowl and put you in the microwave until you're all warm and fuzzy inside. Or explode into smithereens.'

For some reason, it was exactly the reassurance Ellie needed. She felt bits of her old self pour back into place – the useful ones – and elements of a new version fill out the rest. She picked up a pen and turned her notebook to a clean page. 'Right then. Tell me everything you know about Sadie's bit on the side.'

Thea drummed her chin with her fingers. 'I didn't get much, but apparently, before she went on the mission thing with Dan, she'd been with someone back in Cape Town for, like, three years? They'd had a big old ding-dong about children. She wanted them, he didn't. She wanted to buy a house together. He didn't. Not yet, anyway. She stropped off on the mission to Ethiopia and, long story short, Cape Town guy was the person she was cheating on. Not Dan.'

Ellie shuddered. 'Dan would never knowingly have an affair with someone.'

'No,' Thea agreed. 'He wouldn't.'

'So, she obviously lied to Dan, but what we don't know is why she didn't end it with him when their volunteer thing finished.'

'Dan-Dan the Baby-Maker Man?' Thea's phone bleeped at her. 'Shite. It's almost two.' They began to push themselves up from the table when Simon suddenly stopped.

'I know we've got to get back to the office, but . . . should we have a group hug?'

Wow. Simon never voluntarily hugged.

'What? I feel like we've been through something big. We should hug it out, yeah?'

They exchanged uncertain looks, then agreed a fist bump would be fine. As they bundled out of the cafe, Thea began thumbing through her messages. Once she was properly engrossed, Simon leant towards Ellie.

'Don't worry, petal. We'll make sure Dan falls for you and hard. You both deserve some happiness.'

Chapter Twenty-Four

A couple of days later, Thea sidled into the office kitchen and hip-bumped Ellie. 'Hey, you.'

'Hey.'

'I want to do more Softer Landings.'

Ellie wanted long, curly hair, doughnuts to be fat free and for the world to be a place where ending relationships wasn't a marketable commodity, but that wasn't how the cookie crumbled, was it? She gave Thea an apologetic grimace-smile, holding back a sigh as she explained, once again, 'It's one hour per day until May, when we prove to Vee this a going concern.'

'But it's not just that, is it, Ellz?' Thea pressed. 'Vee's rules.'

'What do you mean?' She filled the kettle up and when she settled it into the charging platform, Thea reached across and flicked it off.

'What are you doing?'

'What are *you* doing?'

'I— What are we talking about, Thea?'

'We're talking about why you won't let me do any of the one-to-one calls.'

Oh. That.

The truth was, she still didn't trust Thea to toe the Softer Landings line. Even though she knew she had room for improvement herself, Thea was too impulsive, too fiery to give advice. Besides, Ellie had to pay her own salary with Softer Landings. Vee still paid Thea's, so even though it was Thea's questionable dating habits that had birthed Softer Landings, Ellie was the one who did the dirty work. As such? She got to pick.

Ellie turned the kettle back on. 'I'm just really aware of how close an eye Vee is keeping on things.'

'Control freak.'

'Am not.'

'Are too.' Thea made an exasperated noise and scrubbed her hands through her hair. 'Look, Ellie. Based on what Sadie alone is paying us? Your full-time job right now should be winning American Dan's heart. Without it, and the precedent it sets? We are F-C-U-K'd.'

Ellie twisted her mouth to the side. It was true. Out of principle she hadn't touched Sadie's money, but the truth was, upping their game meant increasing their prices and Ellie hadn't quite yet had the heart to do it. But Thea was right. It wasn't just the volume of clients they needed to increase, it was the fees. And using Sadie's willingness to pony up the cash as a marker, there was a much-needed income stream just waiting to be tapped.

Thea abruptly changed tack. 'How was your date last night with the Big Dan-o-rama?'

Ellie scrunched her nose and admitted, 'Not a date.'

'Oh? Even with the new dress?'

She and Thea had gone shopping yesterday and Thea had helped her pick out a few 'segue outfits' that were midway between Ellie's style and Sadie's. Then she'd met Dan for a Nando's after work and a walk back to his with Gus.

Ellie nodded. 'He said he liked it, but most of the walk was him trying and failing to take a call from Sadie.'

'Oh.' Thea pulled a *bad smell* face. 'That bites.'

'Agreed.'

'Did he ask about whether or not you would be moving in?'

'No.' He'd gone strangely silent on that front. Disconcerting considering the clock was rapidly ticking on her non-negotiable departure from her flat.

'What's the next move?'

'Not sure.'

'Go to St Paul's. You can climb up to the Whispering Gallery and send some sweet nothings his way.'

'Yeah, right.'

'Seriously! Tell him you think he's gorgeous and then pretend it wasn't you if he just says, "Hey, buddy".'

Ellie frowned. Maybe she should suck it up and ask Dan point blank about his and Sadie's relationship. See if Dan was aware of any fault lines beyond what he'd already mentioned.

Thea was studying her. 'You should wear your hair in that plait-thing you do. Like the girl from *Frozen*. It's cute that way.'

They fell silent as the kettle brought the water to a boil. This was about as close as they'd ever been to a girlie-girl talk. 'So . . .' Thea leant against the counter, crossing one ankle over the other. 'I know you're resistant, but . . . I've got an idea about the Skype one-to-ones.'

Ellie lifted her eyebrows. Hadn't they just been through this?

'They're our most lucrative options, right? So . . . the more we do, the sooner I get to do Softer Landings full-time. I think I can do a couple at lunch and then at least five each night.' Before Ellie could protest she said, 'Watch me do one. If you think I'm shit at it, I'll leave you in peace. But if I'm good at it –' she waved her jazz hands – 'then think about all of that free time you'll have to bobby dazzle American Dan.'

Her gut instinct said no, but Thea was right. She was being a control freak and the only way she could begin to consider franchising the business was to trust in her employees. 'Okay. Let's do it.'

Thea whooped. 'Where? Your office?'

Ellie shook her head. 'Vee will see, and we are definitely over the hours limit this week.'

'Disabled loos, then.'

'Good idea.' Fern had 'revisioned' it with an enchanted woodland wall mural, so if they angled the laptop so that the toilet and the emergency pull string wasn't visible . . . She pulled two chunky mugs out of the cupboard that had somehow survived Fern's clutter-clearing. 'Who do you want to start with?'

Thea beamed and pulled a rolled-up sheaf of papers out of the back of her waistband. 'I'm so glad you asked . . .'

◆ ◆ ◆

'You ready for this?' Ellie asked.

'I am ready to roll!' Thea crowed.

Ellie wasn't. She felt sick. But if she was going to devote all of her energies to Dan, she'd need to release her grip on the clients and allow her colleagues to project manage. Thea sat cross-legged on the toilet, balanced the laptop on her knees, then clicked on the little telephone icon before Ellie could stop her.

Ellie steeled herself, barely managing to lurch out of view as the plinky ringtone began and was answered.

A thirty-something African-Caribbean man with a south London accent, hipster beard and impressive man bun held with a hot pink hairband answered. 'Hey! Hi. This is Thea, right?'

Thea gave him a salute. 'The one and only. You ready for this, fam?'

Ellie's jaw dropped. Wasn't that against cultural appropriation rules? Or did Thea's Greek heritage make her eligible for blurring the lines of ethnic slang?

The guy didn't seem to care. 'Yup.' He pointed at himself. 'Chester. Look. I've got fifteen minutes max. I'm in the disabled loos at work, so . . .'

Thea cackled. 'Snap!'

'Whaaaat?' Chester grinned a huge, toothy smile at her then cracked his fingernails together. 'Snap, snap, little dragon. Nice wall mural.'

Thea snorted. 'Thanks. Hey, can I keep Little Dragon as my dojo name?'

He gave a sexy shrug, a hot glint of flirtation flaring in his eyes. ''S'all yours. But I think in this scenario, you're like the sensei, right?

Thea gave a smirky little bow then stroked her chin as if it had a long, wizened beard. 'So! You want to dump someone.'

Ellie glared at Thea. This was not how she spoke to clients. An image of Alfie popped into her head. Well, most of the time.

'That's about the long and short of it, yeah.' Chester was still smiling.

Thea held up his submission. 'Five dates. Smart, funny, successful and she fancies you, but she reminds you of your mum.'

'Got it in one, Little D.'

Ellie folded her arms over her chest. How had Thea managed to get not one, but two nicknames in less than thirty seconds?

Thea made Vs out of her fingers then used them to frame her heavily kohled eyes. 'You wanted to do a face-to-face break-up because why? There aren't any notes on this.'

'There's a notes section? Soz. Ummm . . .' He gave his beard a thoughtful stroke. 'She's nice. Doesn't deserve the flick, but I get the feeling she's expecting something I don't have to give.'

'Like . . . ?'

'Dunno. Presents. Weekends away. Future stuff. Like . . . plans, you know? I'd feel like a dick if I just ghosted her, but taking her out when I plan on dumping her seems worse, so . . . I was hoping you could help me out with some choice phrases and things so that I could let her go softly but . . . completely.'

Ellie wasn't getting a good feeling from this. Not because of Thea, she was doing fine, it was more . . . him. As nice as he was to look at, he made her feel icky.

'Is she still on Tinder?' Thea asked. 'That's how you met, right?'

He shrugged. 'Don't know. I'm not looking any more.'

Thea sat up straighter. 'Why?'

'I've just started my new micro-distillery. I'm bartending during the week so I can pay the rent. Money's tight. There's the herb garden. Making spice mixes for the small batch rum. It's just . . .' He put his hands in a prayer position under his chin, then tipped them towards Thea. 'I'm not in the zone with her, know what I mean?'

Thea nodded. 'I do. Loud and clear.' She gave him a bright smile. 'Okay. The good news is, this will be easy. On you and on her. You're going out tonight, right?'

'Yup.'

'Take her somewhere medium-priced. Can you afford that?'

He huffed out a laugh. 'Depends upon if you think Pret A Manger is medium-priced compared to the Aldi reduced-goods shelf.'

'There's some massive bargains, there, bruv!' They shared a laugh.

The banter continued. Subtle fact finding. Discreet emotional excavations. All swaddled in a trendy puffa jacket of slang, hipster gestures and references Ellie could barely translate. She was feeling super-beige. They settled on Chipotle for the break-up. There were seats, veggie options for her and, just as important, a fast turnover. As they built up to the *how do I actually do this* moment, Ellie had to admit she was impressed. Thea was a plummy-accented Whole Foods girl. She lived in a huge garden flat in Islington her parents had bought for her and her sisters, two of whom had already moved out to live with families of their own. And yet, here on the phone with this guy who had a council-house upbringing, was first in his famalam to go to uni, first to have a job that required a suit, and first to jack it all in to chase the dream, Thea was a kindred spirit. A natural at relating to someone whose life was completely different from her own.

'Repeat after me,' Thea coached. 'You deserve more time than I have to give.'

He repeated it then asked, 'What if she says she's busy too and that doesn't matter?'

'Say it matters to you, but don't make yourself sound awesome with it.'

'What? I don't understand that.'

'You know. If you come across as too sensitive, she'll want to wait. You do not want your baby mama to think waiting is a good thing.'

He screeched. 'Don't you go putting pictures in my head that don't belong there.' They shared another laugh.

Thea continued the tutorial. 'Tell her you thought you were in a better place than you were when you first went out, but that things with the business have changed. Paint a picture for her. A bleak one where you are not a shining star.'

'And how am I supposed to do that, huh? Being the entrepreneurial wunderkind that I am?' He winked and gave a self-effacing laugh. 'Chicks fancy guys who are twenty k in the hole, right?'

'Take all of your biggest fears and make them your future,' Thea advised. 'Tell her you're looking at bankruptcy. At a decade of scraping pennies out of the corner of your partially paid for DFS sofa. That you can't afford Sky or Netflix, and Chipotle is as close to Michelin-starred as she's gonna get. But most of all? Make it clear she's going to bear the brunt of your bad moods when breaking into the micro-distillery world turns out to be a fuckload harder than you'd thought.'

He let out a low whistle. 'You're a proper little ray of sunshine, aren't you, Little D?' He rubbed the top of his head, winced, then pulled his hair out of the pink elastic band and began to twirl it in his fingers.

'You could also tell her that you're cheating on your actual baby mama.'

He went very still, apart from his eyes, which bored directly into hers.

'How'd you know that?'

Her tone reminded bright. 'That's either your little girl's hairband or your partner's, right?'

'Right.'

Without judgement, Thea continued, 'Grab your phone. Text the bit on the side. Chipotle. After work.'

He didn't move.

'Go on!' Thea nudged with a whirl of her index finger.

'What? Right now, right now?'

'Yup! Type it up and show me the screen before you ping it to her.'

He did as he was told, then with Thea's approval pressed Send.

She got him to virtually fist bump her and promise not to be a lying, cheating bastard any more. He had a little girl to think of and he probably wouldn't like it if someone did that to her in ten years' time. He choked up and could barely speak to say goodbye. Ellie almost cried herself.

When the call finished, Thea closed her laptop with a satisfied grin. 'Now can I do some on my own, please, Mummy?'

Chapter Twenty-Five

'Repeat after me,' Thea instructed, her face yawning into the mascara maw that inevitably formed when applying eye make-up. 'Dan?'

'Dan?' Ellie repeated obediently.

'Will you marry me?'

'Will you—' She glowered at Thea, who received a smack on the arm from Simon.

'Stop it. This about moving in, not getting hitched. Stick to the script.'

'It's not my fault she didn't say yes to moving in when they went to Nando's last week.'

'I couldn't!' Ellie protested.

'Why not? It's an open invitation and apart from the fact you're meant to be busy getting him to fall in love with you, you only have a few more days until you have to move out!'

'I know, but—'

'But nothing, babycakes. Stay still for a minute,' Thea instructed, applying a few more licks of mascara to Ellie's lashes. 'Anyway, it's probably good that you at least look like you're playing hard to get, even if it's just you being all namby-pamby. Dan obviously likes a challenge.'

Before Ellie could protest, Simon cut in. 'I know. Text him and say, *Dan? I've been talking it over with Gus and he's agreed to move in.*'

'So what? Blame it on Gus?'

'No, not blame, just let him . . .' Simon smiled, clearly delighted with himself. '. . . let Gus's desire to live with Dan offer *you* a Softer Landing.'

It was a good idea. And yet . . .

'You don't look convinced.'

'No,' agreed Thea. 'She doesn't.'

They all stared at Ellie's reflection. Nope. She definitely wasn't there yet. She didn't even look like her. The make-up. The on-trend outfits. The so-kitsch-they're-cool tourist outings. She'd never even been in a school play and suddenly it felt as if she'd been handed a lead role in the West End. She was a helper. A server. A behind-the-scenes operator who made sure other people's lives ran smoothly and happily, but never her own. Which was, she supposed, exactly the point Thea and Simon were trying to make. This wasn't about her. It was about Dan.

'So . . . If you're not going to meet before, when *are* you going to ask him?' Thea leant in with her mascara wand.

'Not too much,' Ellie said. 'I don't know. When we meet?'

'I think you should wait until you get to the top of the O2.'

Ellie frowned. 'What if he says no?'

'Why would he say no? He's the one who asked you to move in.'

'No,' Ellie corrected, 'Sadie's the one who had the idea. Dan asked, but he hasn't mentioned it for a week.'

'That's because he knows it's creepy for a guy who has a girlfriend to push another woman into living with him.' Thea leant back to examine her handiwork. 'Horrendous. I can only do myself. Simone. Take over, please.'

Simon turned Ellie away from the mirror, pinched a make-up wipe out of the packet and started to prepare 'a clean palette'.

Thea leant against the edge of the sink and huffed. 'You're letting yourself get mired in details.'

'But the details are important!'

'Like the details about booking a sunset climb on the O2 in March when it's sub-zero and you could both fall off and die?'

'Can you stop talking for a minute?' Simon closed his eyes and exhaled slowly. 'Eyeliner requires serenity of spirit.'

Ellie held still, silently admitting that Thea had a point. This was not *the* most romantic date on offer, but at this point it didn't pay to be obvious. And also the tickets had been on special. Which, now that she thought about it, made sense.

Anyway, when she'd told Dan about the bargain basement tickets, he'd seemed enthusiastic.

'I think we should come along as a support team,' Thea suggested, not so casually, for the tenth time.

'Don't you think that'd be a bit obvious?'

'Not if we came incognito.' Thea hummed the *Mission: Impossible* theme and feigned trying to climb up the wall. 'He'd never know we were there. Simon and I could get matching trench coats.' Her eyes brightened. 'I bet we could get some delivered today from ASOS. They would totally be a legitimate business expense, right?'

'No,' Ellie said as Simon said, 'Only Burberry goes on this back.'

'Spoilsports,' she groused good-naturedly. A week ago it would've been a groan. Now that Ellie was giving her freer rein with the clients, Thea's mood was decidedly improved.

Simon turned Ellie round so that she was facing the mirror again. 'What do you think?'

Ellie blinked at her image. She looked . . . Gosh. She looked pretty. She *never* thought she looked pretty. 'Simon, you're really good at this.'

He shrugged. 'I know.'

Ellie grinned, then gave her reflection an *I can do this* nod. It was sink or swim time. If she pulled this off, she could end any relationship. She wasn't so naive as to believe Softer Landings would bring an end to heartbreak worldwide, but what she genuinely hoped was that it would bring an end to unnecessary cruelty. A service like . . . erm . . . recycling, say, that made people feel better about themselves. *Did you end it with Softer Landings? Yeah. So good. So good. I feel like I've had a soul enema.* Something like that, anyway.

Simon added a couple dabs of something glowy to Ellie's cheeks then dubbed her a True Love Paratrooper. It felt an apt description. As if she were literally putting herself in the midst of love's blazing flames to save a man who had no idea he was in peril. Simon handed Ellie her tote. 'You ready for this?'

She nodded.

'And you're sure you don't want me to come?' Thea asked.

Ellie gave a tight nod. The truth of the matter was, she was scared shitless. Proactively letting Dan see all of the feelings she'd been trying to hide from herself was one of the most vulnerable and possibly stupidest things she'd ever done. Not to mention the fact that it might not work. He wasn't a complete numpty. With her non-existent acting skills, he could easily figure the whole thing out, hate her and Sadie forever and, rightfully, demand full custody of Gus, at which point she'd have to throw in the towel and go and join a convent somewhere. If they still existed. But it was too late to change her mind. The prospect of being homeless and contributing to a heartbroken Dan was all the motivation she needed.

'Remember. This is work. You are doing this for the greater good,' Simon said, uncharacteristically pulling her in for a fierce, tight hug. 'I'm so proud of you,' he whispered before releasing her. 'So proud.'

'You guys do know I'm not going to get him to fall in love with me today, right?'

'Course,' they echoed one after the other in a way that made it very clear that they were both hoping she did exactly that.

Half an hour later, when Dan climbed out of his Uber and saw her leaning on a lamp post – and, as suggested, looking wistfully off towards the horizon – she knew her efforts had been worth it. He lit up, then whistled. Ellie blushed and instantly forgot all of the pre-scripted greetings Thea and Simon had suggested, her mind emptying of anything but the here and now. Dan Buchanan had a way of single-handedly obliterating everything false about her, reducing her to whatever was left. And somehow, in the process, making her feel as if that was more than enough.

'Look at you, all ready to climb a big old building.' He faked taking her picture like a fashion photographer and when he dropped his hands she caught a glimpse of a bit of toilet paper stuck to a nick beneath his chin. A very unprofessional shiver of delight rippled down her spine. He'd shaved to come out. Not that a bit of stubble was a deal breaker. She'd seen him unshaven a couple of times and she definitely wouldn't have minded having her cheeks exfoliated by the mix of gold and red hairs. But the fact that he'd made an effort was making her stupidly giddy. 'Your outfit really suits you,' he said. 'You look like you have a superhero costume on under that . . . what do you call that?'

'A jumpsuit,' she said, more coquettishly than she'd ever said anything in her entire life. She twisted back and forth like a child who'd worn her favourite princess outfit to the supermarket only to have one of the check-out staff exclaim over the perfection of her tiara. One part ridiculously proud to three parts *this old thing?* In this case, her 'princess outfit' was a brand-new cargo jumpsuit Thea had helped her select. Dan gave his chin a scrub and, finding the toilet paper, snorted. 'I'm afraid I'm lacking your panache.'

'Oh, I don't know,' she teased. 'Biodegradable neckwear is all the rage these days.'

'I think you'll find the lack of style is pretty much head to toe.' He laughed then opened up his 'non-biodegradable parka' to show off a navy-blue fleece and a pair of worn-in Levi's that looked as if he'd sat in the tub for days until they'd hugged his thighs with form-fitting perfection.

She shrugged and managed not to go super high pitched as she said, 'You'll do.'

He guffawed and pulled her into a hello hug. He was freshly showered and had that citrus smell she loved on him, but no baked-goods scent. Today he smelt more . . . virile. Like a hot Viking woodcutter with access to a power shower. He abruptly pulled his hands away and took a step back. 'Sorry. I'm a hugger. That seems to freak out a lot of Brits. Does it bug you?'

Rather than tell him she'd happily die in one of his hugs, she channelled Thea and said, 'I'm down with a bit of hugging.' When Dan gave her a weird look suggesting he wasn't entirely sure why that sentence had come out of her mouth, she said, 'How's Gussy?'

'We did five miles today,' he said proudly. 'I left him on the sofa, snoring away like a trooper.' He gave a proud papa grin then glanced at his watch. 'I told the sitter we'd be back by ten.'

'Sitter?'

'She lives in the flat below mine. She's maybe fourteen? Fifteen? The awkward teens.'

'Aren't they all?'

Dan tipped his head back and forth as if trying to reconcile the comment with his reality. From the looks of things, his had been great. 'Anyway, the few times Heloise—'

'That's her name?'

'Yup. They're French, I think. They moved here a couple of years ago. The few times she's met Gus she's gone all gooey over him. I thought giving the two of them some proper hang-out time would be cool. And we have Disney Plus, which her parents "don't believe in" so . . . win-win.'

Ellie snorted. 'Until you come home and find a party raging in your flat.' It was the type of thing Aurora would've done if left in charge of the hotel during the off-season, despite the ream of times Ellie reminded her not to do so.

A twinge tugged at her conscience. Would Aurora have behaved the same way if Ellie had shown more faith in her? The same way Thea was now stepping up after Ellie had 'stopped breathing down her neck like a hoary old micromanager'? Dan wouldn't have micromanaged Heloise. She could easily imagine the scene. Dan opening up his home, handing over the remote and pointing to the fridge, saying, 'Have at it, Heloise. *Mi casa es su casa.*' Ellie would've had a ten-page, double-sided instruction manual to the ready.

'I don't think parties are Heloise's jam,' Dan said. 'She said she's got homework and could do with the quiet space.' He sucked on his teeth as if debating whether or not to continue. He looked down then back up at her, his blue eyes darkening a shade. 'I get the feeling her parents are building up to a divorce.'

'Oh crumbs. Why do you think that?'

'They fight on the roof terrace. For some reason they think no one can hear them there. It's all in French, so for all I know they could be arguing the finer points of sentence structure. Weeeeth great passion,' he added in a cheesy French accent, then tacked on a few stabby-knife gestures along with the scary-movie music.

Ellie pulled a face. 'That stinks for her.' She glanced at her phone to check the time. 'Well, if anyone can cheer her up, it's Gus.'

He held out his hand to guide the way towards the ticket office. 'Definitely. When mine split it was pretty heinous.'

Ellie started. 'Your parents aren't together? I thought you said they were coming over.'

'They are.' His tone was bright but serious. In the way a doctor might confirm a surgery was going to be pretty invasive, but that it had to be done if survival was the goal. 'With their new spouses. Well, not *new* new, but—'

'Oh! I—' Ellie had no experience with step-parents. Her mum had been devoted to her father and, after he'd died, that had been that. A widow for life. 'Will that be weird?'

He shook his head. 'Nah. I went through the whole figuring-out-my-parents-were-human thing a while back.' He gave a self-effacing laugh. 'Not to say I dealt with their divorce very maturely.'

'You were a kid. How could you?'

He shook his head and through a swatch of hair threw her a sheepish look. 'I was twenty-one.'

'That's hardly geriatric,' she said in his defence, although . . . She'd pretty much been running the hotel at eighteen after yet another one of her mum's substantial 'turns'. It had taken years more before her mother had finally agreed to take the 'dreaded' happy pills that had, to her surprise, made her life much more liveable.

They reached the ticket office and were curtly informed they were late. Tickets in hand, they jogged to the meeting point. Dan turned his hand into a yapping mouth and gave Ellie a complicit smile. 'That told us, then.'

Her stomach released a flight of butterflies. As if sharing a complicit waywardness was on a par with a bare hand tracing the curves of her stomach. Not that she'd thought about Dan doing that apart from just the once. Well, twice now.

Once assembled, they and a small group of couply couples were given a welcome lecture by Garret, a fifty-something man who looked to be ex-military. Grey buzz cut, not an ounce of fat on a body that looked combat ready, he was friendly but briskly efficient, intent on reminding them that they'd all signed a waiver relieving the O2 of any responsibility if they did anything other than precisely what he told them to do.

'Winging it up there' – he pointed above them – 'on *that* roof –' he gave them all a narrow-eyed scan – 'means death. Are we clear?'

A couple of the men shouted cheery 'Sir, yes, sir!'s and were promptly hushed by their wives.

Ellie bit her lip and gave a wide-eyed look at Dan who, unusually, looked lost in thought. After the safety briefing, they were handed windproof coveralls to go over their 'fancies'. Everyone sat down on the long wooden benches where they'd gathered, took off their shoes and pulled on their coveralls, apart from Dan, who excused himself, saying he had to visit the gents and returned all kitted up.

The climb was well outside Ellie's normal activity base, and much more fun than she'd anticipated. Dan was quiet as they made the ascent, diligently adhering to Garrett's barked instructions as if he was being filmed for the safety video. It was, she decided, the surgeon side of him. Going through things step by step, with extreme care, because any mistakes he might make would change a person's life forever. Once they reached the top, everyone began pulling out their mobiles, taking snaps and chatting. There, Dan became a bit more like the guy who'd worn a Hawaiian shirt to Westminster Abbey in the middle of winter. Everyone's ray of sunshine. In a shockingly swift amount of time, he managed to extract the life stories out of the three forty-something couples who, it turned out, all knew one another from the 'cookie cutter' housing estate where they all lived. (A nice one, they were assured, by the wives. Posher than you'd think.) They'd bought the 'sunset experience' on Groupon, thinking it was going to be on Valentine's Day, realising too late it very much was not.

'There's nothing wrong with extending the romance out over the year, is there, sugarplum?' Dan asked Ellie, as if their lives were one romantic cartwheel into the next.

She just stared at him, forgetting, yet again, that this was all a charade.

The wives all hooted and, with pointed looks in Ellie's direction, said they wished they'd married Dan as he obviously knew how to properly woo a woman.

'Well, she wouldn't really know as this is our first date.' He dropped a wink. 'All the good stuff is yet to come.'

Ellie blushed, but not for the reasons they were thinking. The wives all laughed, and the men groaned a practised, near choral moan of despair. Ellie's eyes crept to Dan's, only to discover his gaze was still on her, his mouth soft with a quiet smile that suggested, if things were different, he just might have meant what he'd said.

Her heart swooped around her body like a lovestruck robin, making her feel as light as a helium balloon. Thank goodness she was clipped on to a belay line on top of a windswept stadium.

As the teasing continued, she smiled and did her best to play along. Gamely took on board all of the wives' relationship advice while the men joshed with Dan, told him to plug his ears, that he was in for a lifetime of pain if Ellie listened to anything their wives had to say about relationships. Garrett broke in to say that the sunset was at its apex, so if they wanted any pictures they'd better take them now.

Dan and Ellie took pictures of the couples, who then insisted on taking photos of them – the brilliant streaks of orange and red sky outlining their heads as Dan tugged her close to him and they gave toothy grins for the cameras. For just the briefest of moments he looked down at her when she was looking up at him, which was when, of course, the wives went wild and took a thousand photos and demanded a kiss. Ellie's body vibrated with panic. As nice as it was to be tucked under Dan's arm, inhaling his gorgeous citrusy Viking scent, she didn't know just how far she was meant to go on a physical level. Was he prepared to have a staged kiss for a staged first date? She stared at him, frozen, as the calls for a kiss morphed into a chant. 'Kiss! Kiss! Kiss!'

To her relief Dan waved them off. 'She's not getting her first Dan Buchanan kiss with a crowd.'

Garrett mercifully brought the egging to a halt by organising everyone back into formation for the descent.

When they got to the ground, had unclipped, and Dan and Ellie had a moment to themselves, Dan said he'd airdrop the photos on to her phone.

'I don't know how to do that,' she winced.

'Here.' Dan took her phone and, upon discovering she still had the factory-setting screensaver, changed it to the photo of the two of them. His eyes met hers as he handed it back. 'So you'll never forget me.'

As if that would ever happen. Their eyes held; something nearing expectation glinted in his.

'Right, you two lovebirds, let's get you out of the windproofs, yeah?' Garrett pointed them towards the changing area.

Too late, Ellie realised Dan had been giving her an opportunity to say she'd move in. It defied logic that she could be so brilliant at breaking up all of the other couples who had come to them for help and a complete dunderhead when it came to Dan. No wonder she was still single.

At Dan's suggestion, they all ended up sharing a minivan to Charing Cross with the Valentine's couples who had also

Grouponed dinner for four at a Cajun restaurant in Soho, and then, after an unusually quiet tube ride home, they went up to the flat. Heloise was sound asleep on the sofa, spooning with Gus. She bolted up, her face creased with pillow marks, her embarrassment gently soothed away by Dan, who said nap time was the best with Gus. After discreetly slipping her a few crisp notes she left with promises of more work.

'And you, young lady,' he said to Ellie as he tapped a couple of things out on his phone, 'have an Uber waiting for you downstairs.'

For the second time that night her heart sunk. She'd thought she'd take the opportunity to talk about moving in, but with an Uber downstairs and a *you can go now* look on his face, it would be impossible to do as much tonight.

She could already hear Thea's pronouncement when she reported back to them in the morning. 'Epic failure.'

He took her by the shoulders and held her out at arm's length. His eyes scanning her face, her hair, her lips in a way that felt tactile. A way that made her forget he was still someone else's boyfriend. His lips parted. A rush of energy swept through her, convinced he was on the brink of saying something big, like, *Who needs the rest of the world when I've got you?*

'You're a great tourist, Ellie.'

Not quite the line she'd been hoping for, but . . .

'You too. Even without the Hawaiian shirt.' Then she play-punched him on the arm, took Gus's lead and went home to contemplate where it had all gone wrong.

Chapter Twenty-Six

How Did You Meet?

Plenty of Fish

How Long Have You Been Together?

Four dates? Five if you count the first coffee meet. Six if you count last night, which I would very much like not to. *shudders*

What special sauce did you/your partner bring to the relationship?

I'm fun, not got many hang ups, pretty easy-going. He seemed the same. Just a couple of late thirty-somethings who haven't yet met their special someones.

What do you like about them?

He really seemed to have his act together. Job. Flat. Cool group of friends (we've met 'the gang' twice for bottomless brunch). We like a lot of the same extra curriculars. Or so I thought.

What do you dislike about them?

I found a sex doll in his cupboard that has his ex's face on it.

Reason you have chosen a Softer Landing:

I am afraid. Very afraid. And he knows where I live so ghosting is not an option.

Break-up Style (Please Tick Preferred Option*):

☐ Text
☐ Email
☐ Scripted Phone Call
☑ One-to-one tutorial (Skype/Zoom/In-person session, price gradient applies)
☑ Bespoke Split (POA)

NOTES:

I don't get paid until the end of the month, but is there any way I can do a payment-plan type thing??? My parents are coming over from Indonesia soon, so I need this guy OUTSKI. He loves contemporary 'art' and I think it's complete and utter wank. He wants our next date to be at a gallery opening. Maybe you can help me throw some paint on a Rothko or something? Draw smiley faces? Or maybe I could do my own 'installation' with his creepy sex doll. That wouldn't weird anyone out.

NB: Softer Landings requires a telephone or in-person interview prior to agreeing to Break-Up Style and reserves the right to refuse a split and/or to recommend an alternative method to that chosen by the client.

To: Thea
From: <u>Ellie.Shaw@SofterLandings.co.uk</u>

Hey Thea,

I was just looking through some new submissions and saw that the client form had been changed. While I admire the more contemporary style, I feel we should stick with the more neutral template as we are hoping to cater to all ages. Please do feel free to pop in and chat about it during your Softer Landings hour.

To: Ellie
From: <u>Thea.Stephanoplis@MediaAngels.co.uk</u>

Okay, Mother. *hangs head in shame* Was just trying to yank everything into the modern era. And you didn't have to lock the files to keep me out. The email telling me to back off worked just fiiiiiine. Byyyiiieeeeeeeee.

PS Simon's not coming to our meeting today. Diego had to go into hospital for tests or something. Couldn't get the deets so it must be bad. Txx

Ellie was in the throes of finding a church her client could bring her future ex to on the premise of getting him a sexual deviancy exorcism when Vee walked in, put some papers on to her desk and gave them a tap.

'It looks like things are going in the right direction . . .' Ellie got the feeling there was a *but* lingering in Vee's nasal passage. 'But . . .'

Ha! If she ever got her counselling credentials she'd be great. *Le sigh*, as they say in France.

'Mind if I sit?' Vee folded herself into a chair without waiting for an answer. 'I'm just wondering how much you're thinking outside the box here.'

Ellie templed her hands and put them under her chin because she'd seen it in a movie, hoping it made her look thoughtful rather than freaked. 'In what way?'

'Well . . .' Vee did a hand model-esque swoop over Ellie's tray of active submissions. 'What are we looking at here? Predominantly twenty-somethings? Thirty-year-olds?'

'Yes. Mostly.'

'Not huge income earners then.'

Ellie began nervous doodling. 'There are reports that suggest their levels of disposable income are increasing—'

'Not substantially, though, is it? A lot of these kiddos are still bunking with Mum and Dad to make ends meet.' Vee had obviously read the same reports.

'Well, yes, but . . .' Ellie toyed with the idea of telling Vee about Sadie's five grand sitting in her account, but announcing she was also planning on giving it back afterwards probably didn't sit within the realm of business models Vee was trying to steer her towards.

'The thing is, Ellie' – Vee templed her own hands, instantly capturing an air of worldliness – 'I think you're missing a trick here.'

'We don't end marriages,' Ellie said quickly. Definitely outside her skill base.

'No, no. I'm not talking about that. I'm talking about two big groups you're ignoring. The forty-somethings who have had enough of being trendy and single, and the silver foxes and vixens who've been married once or twice and are looking for that special someone to spend their golden years with. These demographics are more willing to invest in a romantic future—'

'Yes, but we don't really do future things.'

'In a way you do,' Vee corrected her. 'And this is where I think perhaps your thinking gets a bit . . .' Vee spun her hands round one another as if she was trying to give Ellie's brain a jog. '. . . limited. You rely too heavily on empirically validated approaches. You don't end things, you clear a path towards a Happily Ever After your customers still believe in. Think smarter. Aim higher. Separate yourself from the *emotional* outcomes and arrow in on the *financial* outcome.'

Ellie glanced out to the office. Had Simon or Thea told her about the five grand?

She looked back at Vee, who was, as ever, waiting patiently for Ellie to come up to speed. The whole point of Softer Landings *was* the emotional outcome. Right? Rather than disappoint Vee with her lack of cut-throat business acumen, she said, 'Absolutely. I'll take that under advisement.' And then muttered something along the lines of 'Silver vixens. Promising.' She rifled through a few papers as a distraction technique. 'You know, I got an interesting application today from a woman who wrote in for her sister. Maybe we could start exploring relationship interventions? Call them "reconsiderations" or something.'

'Okay,' Vee said, as if that wasn't quite what she'd meant but wouldn't mow down any green shoots before she knew how much cash she could squeeze out of them. 'Worth exploring. And how do you see things panning out for Thea and Simon?'

'Good! Great.' She meant it too. 'Thea's got a real flair for the one-to-ones? And Simon's got this incredible ability to stage manage the bigger set-ups that we do?'

Why was she answering everything like a question?

'Are you finding that you're needing to use Media Angels resources much?'

This was another one of those trick questions, wasn't it?

'No?'

'Interesting. Hmm. I thought it might be useful to spotlight the fact that Thea's monthly figures are not up to her usual standard. On the Media Angels side, of course. I'm not entirely clear on what her contribution is with your team.'

Ellie swallowed. Crap. So that's why Vee was here. 'I did not know this. Ummm – did you want me to reprimand her?'

'No, no.' Vee crinkled her nose. 'That's my department.'

'Of course. Definitely. Boundaries are important, right? Perimeters.'

'Parameters,' Vee corrected. 'Very much so.' She stood up and smiled. 'I'll leave you with those thoughts to reflect on and if we could circle back on this towards the end of the week . . . close the loop, as it were?'

'Yes. Very much so. Thank you. Good, deep-diving debrief. A customer's journey is the most important journey, right?' Ellie put her fingertips to her head and pretended she was getting an electricity volt. 'Lots of action going to take place up here today.'

'Good,' Vee said lightly. She gave Ellie a final, impenetrable gaze, then left, stopping in at first Simon and then Thea's desks for a brief whispered word before returning to her own.

To: Ellie, Simon
From: Thea@mediaangels.co.uk

Wot did Vee want and have you told Big D you are moving
into his underpants yet?

'Hi, darling. Mum here. Thank you so much for the offer to help
with catering suggestions for the wedding. I think Aurora and Chris
have everything pretty much in hand. Your only job will be to show
up! Talk soon, love. Sorry I missed you. Kiss, kiss. Bye!'

To: Simon, Ellie
From: Thea

Simone – you must talk some sense into Ellz. Just because
the boy hasn't asked a second time doesn't mean he
doesn't want her to move in and also MONEY. Tick FUCKING
Tock! The longer she draws this out, the fewer jobs we can
do and the longer I will be enduring the hellaciousness
that is Media Angels. Oh how I long to tell Vee to jack her
job in. Why can't Ellie just fuck him like a normal person?
Doing Dan = Freedom. Not exactly brain surgery. Wot's her
problem? At least I get to do the one-to-ones now. SUCH a
control freak.

To: Thea, Simon
From: Ellie

Thea, you do know I'm on this message group, right?

To: Ellie, Simon
From: Thea

Soz, babes. Love ya. Truth hurts. Light. A. Fire. Under. Your.
Cutsie. Pie. Bum.

'How many?' Dan gave his quads a quick rub. Like Ellie, he'd clearly thought there'd be a lift.

'I'm not sure.' Ellie looked down the massive nave of St Paul's Cathedral, half expecting a large set of celestial neon lights detailing how many stairs led to the Whispering Gallery. 'Two hundred?' She flipped through the small pamphlet she'd bought. 'Here it is. Two hundred fifty-nine.' Which would be more than enough time to talk to him about moving in.

After a few minutes of working their way to the front of the nave, they realised the large clumps of people ahead of them were actually huge tour groups waiting to ascend the stairs up to the various levels of the cathedral.

'What do you think?' She put on her best happy-tourist smile. 'Want to wait ninety minutes to climb some stairs and whisper something to me?'

Dan's expression shadowed briefly then brightened into his *let's go for it* smile. 'Lead the way, *mon capitán*. Just make sure I don't lose you in this crowd.'

Ellie gave him a look disguising her relief that he wasn't backing out. 'I think you'd be hard pressed to lose me in this outfit.'

The forecast had been for – and delivered – lots of rain, so she had switched from glasses to contacts, pulled on her trusty sou'wester and a shin-height pair of red polka-dot city wellies.

Dan eyed her. 'Oh I don't know. It's pretty subtle.' He smirked.

She blushed. When their eyes met something flashed between them that felt physical. Instead of looking away as she normally would have done, she forced herself to bite the bullet and hold his gaze. A kinetic energy hummed between them. A thrill swept through her. So this was what it felt like to be Aurora. To be any woman who had confidence in her power to attract. To lure. It was like being a *soothsayer*! She knew. She *knew* what Dan Buchanan was going to do next! He was going to lean in and whisper something intimate to her and she'd move in and boss the whole falling in love with her thing, and Sadie would be happy and Dan would be happy and Vee would be happy and Thea and Simon and everyone in the world, including Gus, would be happy, except for her, because she'd be living a lie, but that was fine, because she would have just aced boss-level businesswoman.

She glanced ahead at the long queue. 'Do you think it'll be worth the ninety-minute wait?'

He gave her a sexy, considered look. Gave his chin a thoughtful Clark Kent-style stroke. 'Dunno. What were you going to whisper to me?'

'That depends,' she said in a voice that had never once come out of her before. 'What were you going to whisper to me?'

His lips quirked into a smile. Her body went stupidly buzzy in anticipation. Dan leant in close, his lips accidentally – on purpose?

– brushing against her ear. Her skin rippled with goosebumps. 'Ellie?' he whispered.

If she turned towards him, their lips would brush and she would definitely kiss him or, worse, dedicate her somersaulting ovaries to him until the end of time. 'Yes?' she whispered back.

'I could murder a burger about now. You?'

Disappointed plunged through her.

'No?' He considered her weak smile as if she were a painting he hadn't quite perfected. 'Not even with cheese and bacon? I'm going to take that expression as a no.' Dan gave his quads another rub then held on to a column, giving one of his legs a proper runner's stretch. She stared at his thigh straining against the twill trousers he was wearing. A consolation prize for losing out to a Big Mac. Reminding herself this was work and she needed to salvage things, she asked, 'Was yesterday's run tough? You're really getting up there in the mileage, aren't you?'

He nodded, but didn't elaborate, then looked up ahead at the stairs, back down at his leg. He looked uncomfortable. As if yesterday's run, his third or fourth properly long one, had taken its toll. Maybe going up two hundred and fifty stairs when his hamstrings needed a day of rest was a bad idea. But not doing it meant yet another delay in addressing the moving-in issue.

'So . . . A burger, you say?' she said, just as he asked her, 'Do you remember that couple we met at Westminster?'

A tangled 'Yes' – 'No' – 'You go' – 'No' – 'You go,' culminated in Dan saying, 'You'd be cool with that?' He looked insanely relieved. 'A burger?'

'Well, it's not exactly as if St Paul's is going anywhere, is it?'

'Good point.'

They headed for the exit, both of their steps decidedly brighter.

Courtesy of the rain, all of the venues close by were crammed. After huddling in a doorway and unsuccessfully scrolling through their phones for a better option, she said, 'I think this might be a bust.' She pointed up at the sky. 'Time for a rain check?'

Dan shook his head. 'No. No. Let's figure something out. I wanted to talk to you about something important.'

Her stomach churned as the truth dawned. He knew. He'd been pretending to be nice all day and now the ruse was up. He was going to call her out for being the charlatan that she was.

Dan dipped his head to catch her eye. 'I think the way I've been with you lately might have been coming across as mixed signals.'

Yup! He definitely knew. She'd been playing him, so he'd started playing her, hoping for a confession. He'd obviously tired of waiting for her to spill her guts so now he was going to call her out.

Fighting the urge to cut and run, she gave a pathetic *yeah, maybe you have been a bit weird* nod instead of pointing the finger at her own bonkers *I'm dumping you again and this time for money* behaviour.

Dan continued, 'But somehow along the way I think the signals between us, you and me, grew a little . . . I don't know . . . I know you Brits don't like to presume anything and that you'd rather push stuff under the carpet than talk about it, so forgive me if I am completely torturing you, but I thought I'd go full-blooded American on this one.' He dropped to one knee.

Ellie gasped. Oh boy, how she had read this one so wrong?

'Ellie Shaw?'

No way was he going to propose.

He took her hands in his. Holy cow. He was going to propose!

'I've been thinking about this day and night for weeks now.'

He was proposing! He was proposing! Dan Buchanan was proposing!

'Yes!' she said at the exact same time he asked, 'Would you and Gus do me the honour of being my flatmates while Sadie's away?'

And just like that, the myriad of feelings she'd thought she'd tidily tucked away in order to do this job – the instant attraction she'd felt the very first moment she'd seen him, the heartache of waving goodbye so he could pursue his dream in Africa, the gut-wrenching disappointment when he'd returned with a near-perfect girlfriend, the bone-crushing anguish she felt knowing he loved someone who didn't love him – spilled into her bloodstream, polluting it with the one single truth she had known in her heart all along. She was in love with Dan Buchanan. And in a thousand more ways than she thought she ever could be. Telling herself otherwise was pointless. She wasn't his friend. Or his pal. Or his bud. She wasn't doing this for the greater good of mankind or Sadie or Thea or Vee or anyone, really. She was doing this because she loved him and she simply would not stand for him feeling the pain of rejection one more time.

'Great!' Dan beamed, then made a show of being a rickety-runner past his sell-by-date as he got up.

She felt it wise to pretend she had lost the power of speech.

He peered out at the rain, checked his phone clock then said, 'Should we forget about the restaurant? Go and get your stuff? We can get your things in, snuggle up with Gus on the couch and order a pizza? I hear *Encanto* is the bomb.'

Chapter Twenty-Seven

If Dan had been holding a ring, she would've ripped that thing out of the box and jammed it on her finger so fast it would've given him whiplash. They would be on the way to A&E now, laughing and cringing about their *funny later* engagement story, instead of in a taxi on the way to her flat to pick up what passed for her earthly possessions.

Dan was all chatty and whistling and so full of incredibly uncomplicated happiness Ellie forced herself to play along. She'd begged for this particular bed, and now she was going to have to lie in it. By herself. With only a wall between her and the life she so desperately wanted to live.

After they'd arrived at the Marylebone flat with her two duffel bags and Gus's food and water bowls, the atmosphere between them took on a decidedly awkward hue. Despite his efforts to make her feel at home – *Want a bath?* Nope! *Shower?* No, thank you. *To change into jimjams?* Nothing that involves being naked, thank you – Ellie took matters into her own hands and pretended Gus had pawed at the door, desperate for a walk. Insisting Dan rest up his legs, she took Gus for a spin round the new neighbourhood (super lush) and the private garden (loads of animal-shaped topiary), all the while giving herself a stern talking to. This was work. Not play. Matters of her heart were not a factor.

Sadie's instructions kept coming back to her. *I want Dan to know what it feels like to be truly loved. Adored, even.*

She forced herself to imagine a world in which Dan had overheard the entire conversation she and Sadie had had at the café and before she'd even got to the *how much will it cost* part she had to shut the imaginary world down. Even a glimpse at his own reality would savage him. Purpose flooded her as it never had before. She simply would not stand for American Dan discovering the truth. He *did* need to know what it felt like to be genuinely adored. Understand what it felt like to have one person in the world who had his back no matter what. A person who made him glow from the inside out. Who turned his heart into a sun-softened butter pat just by being there. She knew she could definitely do that. Blindfolded. And that's when it hit her. Maybe that would be enough. A simpler, less painful way for him to see the light. Despite Sadie's instructions, he didn't *have* to fall in and then out of love with her. Maybe by showing him her love, he would see that his relationship with Sadie wasn't the be-all and end-all. And that would be the spur he needed to walk away. Same bird, no stones. And they could all live mostly happily ever after.

'What do you think, Gussy?' she asked as she dug out her new key in front of the flat door. 'Is tweaking Sadie's remit the worst idea ever?' Before she even got her key in the door, Dan pulled it open, smile bright as can be, holding up a fistful of fanned-out takeaway menus. 'Hi, honey! Ready to clog your arteries and watch some sing-along Disney?'

'Why you bet I am, sweetie love poppet!'

He frowned.

Too much?

His forehead lifted and the brightness returned to his eyes. 'I've never been called a poppet before. This is great!'

High off her first successful step into Operation Show Dan What True Love Looks Like, Ellie took off her Paddington Bear raincoat and hung it on the rack right on top of Sadie's sleek Burberry trench coat. 'Bring it on!'

Dan looked over his shoulder at the TV. 'You want to watch *Bring It On?*'

'No.' Ellie did a cheeky little shimmy, thrilled with herself for jumping right in at the deep end. 'I want *you* to bring it on.'

He looked confused. Crumbs. Definitely a step too far. 'Disney's great. Anything's great.' Maybe there was time to run and find a YouTube video on successful flirtation techniques. 'Rom-com?' She crossed her fingers behind her back, hoping he'd pick *Hitch, How to Lose a Guy in 10 Days* or *The Wedding Planner*.

He tapped his finger on his lips, nodding along. '*When Harry Met Sally?*'

A bit too close to the bone for that. 'Indiana Jones,' she countered.

'Not exactly romantic,' he parried.

'*Frozen?*' They could sing along to 'Love is an Open Door' and he could swing her round and round and with any luck he'd become overwhelmed with a passionate desire to kiss her, be too noble to do as much, then call Sadie and break up with her.

'Nah,' Dan said, then, to her surprise added, 'Elsa reminds me too much of Sadie.'

Interesting. '*Brief Encounter?*' she tried.

'Amazing.' He thwacked his hand over his heart. 'I genuinely thought I could never do another crossword puzzle again after *Brief Encounter.*'

It was one of her favourite films too. And also a tiny bit like their lives were going to be over the next couple of months. Minus the *planning to run away together then returning to their spouses at the end of it*, but other than that very similar. 'It's definitely rom,' she said, 'but maybe not so much com?'

'No,' Dan agreed. 'But it is . . .' He shook his head, unable to put words to what he thought it was.

'A glimpse into what true love is supposed to feel like?' Ellie chanced.

'Yes,' Dan breathed. 'Exactly that.'

Their eyes caught, glinting with the joy of shared understanding, to the point they either needed to start snogging or pretend the moment hadn't happened.

Dan lifted his palm and said, 'High five, bud.'

Oh god. This was going to be the longest two months in the world.

They decided on *Love, Actually* and a curry in the end. (Sadie hated curry and, because of that, Ellie made a show of craving it like oxygen.)

When the film finished, Dan gave a happy sigh.

'I know, right?' Ellie swept away a few happy tears. 'That's my favourite part.'

'What? The airport part?'

She hiccoughed. 'Yup. I just— It reminds me of going to pick up my dad after his research trips when we were little.'

His smile was warm with heartfelt sympathy. 'I'm going to guess you were the one who launched yourself at him.'

'We all were.' She drifted away for a moment, remembering how she and Aurora got balanced, one on each of his hips, her mum hugging all three of them, laughing and crying, whatever sign they'd made for him getting crushed in the melee. They'd never cared. Not now that they were all back together. They'd all been so happy. It had seemed the easiest thing in the world, achieving that sort of joy. Little did they know.

'I thought women always liked the sign-guy bit the most.' Dan pointed at the rolling credits, then spooned the remains of his Netflix and Chill'd ice cream out of the tub.

Ellie pulled a face. 'I never liked that bit.'

'Why? It's a grand gesture.'

'A grand gesture that puts her in a really complicated position.'

His forehead crinkled. 'What do you mean?'

'He's telling her he loves her, but she's just got married, right?' Ellie warmed to the topic, despite warnings from her brain that she should shut up. But she couldn't help herself. In her heart of hearts she wanted Dan to figure this whole mess out by himself. Not be manipulated into feeling things by design. 'I genuinely feel sorry for Keira. I mean, how's she supposed to know what to do now that he's revealed his innermost feelings to her?'

Dan looked confused. 'I thought women liked knowing what a man felt.'

'Not like that! Not when it puts her in an impossible position!'

Gus lifted his head and looked at her. She gave him a grateful pat. She was getting a bit too riled for someone discussing fictional people declaring fictional love. She forced herself to calm down enough to explain. 'He loves her. That's fine. But he also knows she loves his *best friend*, to whom she has just publicly vowed eternal love and devotion. So from my perspective? He should've kept it to himself.' It was advice she had been giving herself on a minute-by-minute basis from the day she'd met him. Every time a touch or a look unleashed the butterflies, she could taste the words in her mouth: *I love you, Dan Buchanan.* And they tasted good. Like butterscotch. But she didn't say them because she also knew if he didn't say it back she'd want to shrivel up and die. And that was not an option. There was Gus to think about.

Dan considered her for a moment then asked, 'Do you mind if I ask how things ended with your ex?'

'He cheated on me.'

'Oh. Shit.'

'For several years.'

'What? That's fucked up.'

'Yes, it was.'

'And you didn't know?'

She shook her head. 'To be honest, I don't know if I was oblivious or playing the ostrich.'

'How do you mean? You don't blame yourself, do you?'

Maybe? Sometimes. 'He didn't live on the island, and in a weird way, that made things easier.'

'Explain.'

The story tumbled out of her. Ever since her dad had died, her mum had struggled with depression. Aurora needed a lot of attention. Ellie had lurched from school, to running the hotel, to making sure her sister didn't leave too many savaged hearts in her wake, to late nights in her bedroom trying to finish her online degree, but there was so much else in the way it took actual years longer than she thought it would. Having Sebastian appear every summer and, later, at the occasional weekend or Easter break, was like having a minor celebrity in their lives. A little breather from reality.

'When he shone his light on you?' She flickered her palms into jazz hands. 'It was amazing.'

'And when he was gone?' Dan asked.

'I got on with real life.'

Dan's mood turned reflective, as if he was absorbing her story into his cell structure. 'What made you finally come over here? To London. Could you sense something was off?'

'No. But my sister did.' Ellie sucked in a big breath and blew it out slowly. 'We had a huge fight and I packed my bags and left.'

He gave a big ol' nod, as if he could've predicted as much. 'My sisters fight. It's brutal. They lash out at one another and I think,

257

"Woah, man. They're never going to talk again." And then, lo and behold, the next time I see them they're all huggin' and kissin' and best-friending all over each other.'

Ellie ran her fingers through Gus's fluffy ear fur. 'We've never really been those kind of sisters.'

'Sounds like you had to be more like a mom than a sister.'

Yes. She had. And it had been exhausting. 'Turns out I needn't have bothered.' Her voice sounded brittle rather than the bright she'd been aiming for. 'She and Mum have been perfectly fine without me.'

'What? No. They wouldn't have said anything like that.'

'They didn't have to.' Ellie scrubbed her fingernails into her scalp. 'They've been great, actually. No cries for help. No *please come back it's all falling to pieces*. Aurora's even getting married. Sounds like they're having a gay old time getting it organised.' She heard the note of pain in her voice and prayed that Dan hadn't.

He frowned. Crap. He'd heard it.

'Did you want them to need you?'

'No. Yes.' She threw her hands up, then let them flop down on her lap. 'I don't really know.'

'You guys must talk about it when you go back for visits.'

'I haven't been back.'

His eyes widened. 'Seriously? In what . . . you said it's been a year that you've lived here?'

'I have a dog to look after, don't I?' Her voice sounded more embittered than it was meant to. 'I didn't mean—'

'I know. Look, Ellie. If you want to go—'

Ellie cut him off. 'I have to go in a couple of months. For Aurora's wedding.'

'Cool. Good. Well, I'll obviously look after Gus—' He stopped himself mid-flow, as if he'd been on the brink of adding a condition but had thought better of it. 'I will look after Gus.'

Ellie scrunched her face tight, then confessed something she had yet to tell anyone. 'I haven't told them about Seb yet. That we're not together.'

'What?' Dan was genuinely shocked. 'Why not?'

'Usual reasons, I guess. Shame. Humiliation.'

'He cheated on you, Ellie. You have nothing to be ashamed about.'

'Yeah, but if I'd actually been worth loving, he wouldn't have cheated, would he?'

Finally. After a year's worth of plundering the emotional thesaurus, she realised it all came down to this: she hadn't been enough.

'That's it.' Dan got up from his chair. 'Scooch over. I'm going to hug some self-love into you.'

'No.' She put her hands out like a barricade.

He stopped halfway to the sofa.

'You sure? You know I give good hugging.'

Oh, she knew alright. What he didn't know was that if he sat down and started hugging her, she would literally try to unzip him and crawl inside in a last-ditch effort to spend the rest of her life in a Dan Buchanan cocoon. Even she didn't need a YouTube video to tell her that her raw, desperate hunger for someone who thought they were in love with someone else might be off-putting. 'I'm sure.'

Reluctantly, he sat back down. 'For what it's worth, I think Sebastian's an idiot. You're a real catch and I don't like hearing you put yourself down that way. You're a great woman, Ell. Seriously.'

She shook her head, grateful for the chance to respond honestly. 'I'm not so sure about that. I mean, I want to be a relationship therapist. It doesn't really speak to my powers of understanding human nature when I can't even tell anyone my own boyfriend cheated on me for seven years, does it? And then responding to it all by keeping it a secret from my family, who I refuse to visit?' She made a weird squawky noise and balled up an invisible piece of paper. 'That was an online degree well worth getting.'

'*Hey!*' Dan was properly concerned now. 'We see what we want to see sometimes. Do what we need to do to get through tough times, and it doesn't sound like it was easy back home. Sometimes—' He stopped himself and gave his jaw a scrub.

Sometimes what? Sometimes we move to London with girl-friends we should've left behind in Africa? Sometimes we wish we didn't have a past so this very moment could be the beginning of everything? She scraped her teeth along her lips as she waited for him to answer.

Gus propped his chin on her knee. His version of saying, *I'm here for you.* She held her breath until Dan finally said, 'We all do out-of-character things sometimes. It's how we learn. How we grow.' He huffed out a laugh. 'Which, I suppose, means I should be incredibly mature now that I've gone through the *buy a dog to try to make something that wasn't meant to be happen* phase.'

'I, for one, am immensely grateful to you for being that imma-ture.' She smiled at him, then gave Gus's head a ruffle. He burped in her face. 'Thanks, Gus.'

The burp pulled Dan out of his funk. He grinned at her, then Gus. 'I'm glad I was too.'

'And it meant we got to meet,' she added.

'Yeah.' Dan's smile softened further as his eyes lifted to meet hers. 'It did, didn't it? Silver linings everywhere.' He gazed at her for a moment then, unusually, was the first to look away.

Ellie tried to recapture the moment. 'Was going out to Ethiopia another notch to your maturity belt?'

His expression changed. Closed down almost. Which wasn't the facial expression she'd thought she'd get. 'It was . . .' He looked at her, sky-blue eyes blinking in and out of sight as he visibly wrestled for a way to put his experience into words. 'Illuminating,' he finally settled on.

'And rewarding?'

He reached out to give his knee a scrub, as if the question registered on a physical level. An uncomfortable one. Ellie's heart squeezed tight. She wasn't sure why, but she'd never truly allowed for the possibility that his time out there might have been less than golden. Dan Buchanan and his Midas touch. 'Sure.' He began nodding with a fierce intensity, as if convincing himself that what he was saying was true. 'Absolutely!' As more positive words popped out of his mouth – great, super, tip-top – glimpses of the Dan she'd sat with all those months ago came in and out of focus. The one who'd bought a dog in the hope that he'd finally found his happily ever after. The one who'd just been informed he hadn't. The one who'd reached out for and latched on to another dream and run with it. The one who didn't know the woman he thought he loved now didn't want him any more.

'It was a once-in-a-lifetime experience,' Dan concluded, as if that explained everything. And then, with a loud clearing of the throat, pushed himself up to standing. 'Well, that was all a bit deep and heavy.' He did a big, dramatic yawn. 'Bedtime for me!'

Ellie stayed where she was, still wrestling with what had just happened. 'Sweet dreams,' she said, instead of what she really wanted to say, which was, 'I'm here for you, Dan Buchanan. In any way you need. I'm here for you.'

'You too, buttercup.' He gave Gus a little scrub on the head and then, to break the tension, did the same to Ellie. 'You, too.'

Chapter Twenty-Eight

SOFTER LANDINGS CLIENT QUESTIONNAIRE

How Did You Meet?

It's not me. I'm writing in for my sister and her mahoosive arse-wipe of a boyf. IT MUST END and she won't listen to me. Or anyone else for that matter. Believe me. We've all tried and she's all lalalalalala can't hear you!

How Long Have You Been Together?

They've been together about eight months and I've seen a massive change in her personality. She used to be all bubbly and happy and free-spirited and now she's pretty much a cross between a Stepford wife and a handmaiden.

What special sauce did you/your partner bring to the relationship?

I think he's rich. (Drug dealer? Dunno. Arsehole.) They go to a lot of nice places and have had some well swish holidays, but honestly? No amount of money would make me put up with an arse of his epic proportions.

What do you like about them?

Nothing.

What do you dislike about them?

Everything. He belittles her in front of her family and friends. He's put her on a diet despite the fact she is unbelievably gorgeous. She now freaks if you suggest going out without him because that's 'naughty'. He's fucking weird. Total control freak. I don't know what kind of voodoo he did on my sister but she needs some serious extraction. HELP PLEASE. DROWNING NOT WAVING!!!!!

Reason you have chosen a Softer Landing:

She's not listening to us and a friend of mine told me about a set-up you did for her where you made the guy getting dumped think he was dumping her or something? It was all a bit vague, but they're both happy with other people now and I just want my sister back and her guy would need some serious restraining-order crap if the whole split thing doesn't come from him, so . . . anything you could suggest will be happily received.

Break-up Style (Please Tick Preferred Option*):

☐ Text
☐ Email
☐ Scripted Phone Call
☑ One-to-one tutorial (Skype/Zoom/In-person session, price gradient applies)
☑ Bespoke Split (POA)

NOTES:

He owns a boxing gym, so just be aware that he's a big guy with big friends.

◆ ◆ ◆

Thea plopped into a beanbag and began peeling an orange. 'How's it going with lover boy?'

'Fine.'

'Ellie . . .' Her voice had a warning note in it.

'What? It's going fine. I moved in, like you wanted—'

Thea tutted. 'Like the *client* wanted. Hey! Don't purse your lips at me.'

'I'm not.'

'Are too. Simone – look.' She nudged a beanbag towards him. 'Tell Ellie to stop it.'

'Stop what?' Simon wearily lowered himself on to the beanbag and semi-curled into a foetal position.

'Behaving as if she doesn't owe it to us to make some progress with American Dan.'

Simon heaved out a world-weary sigh. 'Ellz. You will make your life so much easier if you either do what she says or find a way of lying about it. Voice of experience here.'

Ellie bit her tongue. She was 'making progress'. And it was driving her insane. Living with Dan was about as perfect as perfect could be. Okay, there were a few little things that made him mortal. He burnt toast. Made awful tea. Thought hummus was a food group. He would get strangely private sometimes, say he had to do something innocuous then disappear into his room and close the door. He never wandered around the flat half-dressed, so no accidentally catching him out in his boxers or anything. Which,

264

in some ways, was a bit of a let-down, in others a very wise safety precaution on his part.

It did make her feel as though she couldn't slob around in her jimjams, though. Not exactly a tragic problem, but . . . she and Gus had a routine too. Evening walk, jimjams, a bit of telly cuddled up together on the sofa and then bedtime. He had tried to follow Dan into his bedroom a couple of times but, finding the door closed, made his way to hers. Ellie had tried to keep him out the first couple of nights, aware of how fancy the place was, and then thought, *Screw it.* What they don't know won't hurt them. Dan was fastidiously tidy about his things, always kept his personal belongings in his room, tucked out of sight, but maybe that had been something that had come from Sadie. It was, after all, her flat. Her parents', anyway. The couple of times she'd asked if he'd managed to get hold of Sadie, he'd given vague answers about reception not being great out there and something even vaguer about goalposts changing.

Beyond that, it was perfect. They enjoyed cooking together. Laughter came easily. They'd already lost hours of their lives to the most ridiculous things. Thumbs wars. Counting one another's nose freckles (he had forty-two, she had a sparse seventeen). Taking portraits of Gus in human clothes (the best outfit was the one Dan had worn to Westminster). Dan had immediately gifted the outfit to Gus and then they'd both fallen silent because it had felt like acknowledging that this would all come to an end one day. Which, of course, it would. They each pulled their weight in the household chores department. He vacuumed. She dusted. He washed. She dried. Gus adored them equally. A match made in heaven, really. And it felt like dying inside.

'So . . .' Ellie tapped the client form on her desk. 'I think we should probably talk about last night.'

'Woot woot!' Thea gave a wicked laugh. 'Did you guys finally have sex?'

'No,' Ellie intoned. Nothing of the sort. She had merely spent a disproportionate amount of her evening wondering what Dan looked like in the shower. All slippery with soap and steamy and maybe a little bit hairy, but not too much. Just enough to make the tips of her fingers tingle with anticipation of—

'So . . . you masturbated to him?' Thea asked.

'I wanted to talk to you about the gallery,' Ellie snipped to cover the fact that she had never masturbated before and she certainly wasn't going to start in front of Gus.

'Ellie?' Thea began in the voice of a sex-ed teacher. 'You know masturbation is perfectly natural, right?'

Ellie turned bright pink everywhere. The furthest she'd ever got in an attempt to masturbate was to sort of skid her hand across her boobs.

Instead of laughing, Thea looked sympathetic. 'Look, babes. If you want me to take you to Ann Summers and get you a Rampant Rabbit, that is not a problem. Soho's full of dildos and only a short walk away.'

'No! Thank you,' she added.

'Oh my god, Thea!' Simon groaned. 'Can we *please* stop talking about your obsession with double-As for the va-jay-jay?'

Thea sunk back into her beanbag and began peeling off the skin of each orange segment with her teeth, then teasing apart individual bits of the pulp with her ebony-painted nails. 'It's more fun than talking about What Happened at The Gallery.'

'Yes,' admitted Ellie. 'But I'm afraid if we want this to be a going concern, we need to make sure that type of thing never happens again.'

'It's my bad.' Simon's muffled voice came up from the beanbag. 'I was in a bad mood, but it got the job done in the end, so can we just draw a line under it and move on?'

'Not really.'

'Why not?' Simon was irritated now.

Ellie struggled to find a tactful way to put this. She suspected the pressure Simon was under at home was crippling. She'd asked him, multiple times, if he'd wanted to sit this one out, but he'd insisted he was fine. 'It's just that . . . Well. Let's start with the positives. You two were definitely in the right to steer me away from the exorcism. I can see that now. The art gallery plan, in theory, was a good one. But it's not really customary to scream "Grow a pair" at the client.'

Simon pushed himself into a sloping position that looked relaxed but exuded hostility. 'Nor is it customary to pay someone money to break up with your partner, is it? So, frankly? As long as it got the job done – which it did – I would say . . . topic – closed.' He clapped his hands together as if shutting a book.

'Just to play the devil's advocate here.' Ellie had on her diplomat's voice. 'The whole point of Softer Landings is to ensure the person getting rejected feels as though the break-up is a good thing.'

'Not any more, it isn't.'

Ellie's hackles flew up. 'Yes, it is.'

'No. It isn't. Take off the blinders, Ellz. The whole point is to make money. When Vee's involved, that's always the goal, and don't pretend it's anything other than a game of spreadsheets at this point.'

Simon was right, but she wasn't going to admit as much. She was way too deep into this to let it fail now. It was franchise or bust, and franchising without hard and fast rules – like the way they always made French fries at McDonald's the same no matter where in the world you were – was critical. 'We have plans for a reason, Simon.'

'And sometimes plans need to be changed, *Ellie*.'

Thea threw some orange peel at him. '*Simone*.'

He batted it away. 'Don't call me that.'

'What the fuck?'

Simon half rolled, half lurched out the beanbag. 'I don't have time for this bullshit.'

'If you need some time off—' Ellie began.

'I don't need time off. I need everyone to start being honest with themselves.' He pointed at Thea. 'You need to admit you're only doing this because you don't have the guts to tell Vee you hate it here and you want to do something else but you don't know what it is.'

'That's not true!'

'It is. You've got your little schadenfreude thing going on with Softer Landings, but you don't know what you want to do. You never have. And you' – he wheeled on Ellie – 'you need to stop pansy-footing around, tell Dan you love him, that Sadie's not interested, and then get to work making babies or whatever it is you want from life. Time. Is. Precious. End of.' He swept out of the circle, dramatically took his place at his desk and pulled on his headset – the Simon Hudson sign for Back the Fuck Off I'm In A Mood.

Thea leapt out of her beanbag, and with surprising ferocity shouted, 'Oh yeah? Well, maybe you need to look in the mirror, Simone!'

He ripped off his headphones, shouting, 'And what exactly do you expect me to see, Little Miss Shitbag?'

'That Diego's dying and you're the only one who's not there for him.'

Simon turned ashen. The entire office went silent. He rose, visibly shaking with rage. 'Fuck you. Fuck the horse you rode in on. And never, ever speak to me again.' He grabbed his coat and left.

'Well, that told us, then,' Thea said sulkily.

'I think—' Ellie began.

'I don't care what you think,' Thea snapped, then grabbed a handful of client questionnaires before she, too, grabbed her jacket and disappeared out the front door.

◆ ◆ ◆

Ellie readjusted the bouquet of peonies, double-checked that the bow around Gus's collar wasn't wonky, then dinged Mallory's doorbell.

The visit was a welcome respite from the chaos at the office today. After Simon and Thea had stormed out, Vee had popped in for another 'little catch-up'. Ellie had done her best to stay professional but had admitted to 'certain unexpected challenges' presenting themselves.

'They always do,' Vee had said with a mysterious smile before adding, 'Riding out the storm often pays dividends.'

An hour later Dan texted to say he had a last-minute appointment at the hospital and would she be able to pick Gus up from school. She'd pounced on the opportunity. Sitting in her office after Thea and Simon had swept out with operatic *Sturm und Drang*, she'd felt like a horrific window display – one the rest of the Media Angels staff kept walking past, glancing in, then averting their eyes, as if Ellie's failure to keep Thea and Simon happy had morphed her into something physically repugnant. Once she'd collected Gus and those big brown eyes of his assured her he was still very much her best friend in the world, she'd not felt quite ready to head home, so she'd texted Mallory, who, mercifully, was more than happy to have visitors. With any luck, the sensible librarian might be able to help her put things back into perspective.

'You seem to be getting around well,' Ellie said, after Mallory had led them into the kitchen, where Ellie had insisted she sit down and let her get the tea things together.

269

'Everything takes a lot longer,' Mallory admitted as she eased herself into a chair. 'But I'm not complaining. A new hip is far better than lying in bed waiting to die.'

Ellie winced.

'Sorry, love. Did I say something to upset you?'

'No, not at all.' Ellie debated whether to tell Mallory about her day and then decided the melodrama might be a welcome respite from thinking about her ageing joints. Mallory listened and nodded and *mm*ed and *tsk*ed, going quite still when Ellie reached the part where everyone swept out of the office, ultimatums vibrating in their wake.

'Can you run me through what it is you do again? I thought you were an office manager.'

'I was.' Ellie bit her lip. She wasn't really in the habit of telling people what she did, but if it was a service that was going to go nationwide, maybe she should test new waters. See what Mallory thought. 'I'm working on a project – a business idea – that stems from an incident at work a while back.'

'Oh?'

'How much time do you have?'

Mallory smiled and pointed at the full pot of tea. 'We've got time.'

So Ellie went back to the beginning. Told her about Sebastian. About the betrayal. About Thea getting her the job at Media Angels. And, most importantly of all, she told her about American Dan. 'The same Dan who comes by with Gus?'

'Yes, exactly.'

If she wasn't mistaken, Mallory gave her the side eye. As if re-evaluating what she thought of her.

'Dan's the one who actually got Gus in the first place.' Ellie began panic-explaining, desperate to assure Mallory that the leap from A to B to Softer Landings had actually been a very pragmatic one. 'It was something that ended up helping everyone in the end.'

'And . . . is there an end?'

'Not exactly.' Ellie felt the Terms and Conditions of her agreement with Vee begin to press against her lungs. 'Ummm, Vee's actually repurposed my old job so that I can explore the growth potential with this new venture.' It was one way to put it. The positive way.

'So . . . you don't have a job any more.'

Or you could put it that way.

'Well . . . no . . . I mean . . . obviously, if Softer Landings can be made into something bigger, I'll have a job there. Being in charge of the franchises or, well . . . you know . . . making sure certain guidelines are adhered to . . .' Oh god. This was horrendous. If she couldn't form an actual sentence in front of Mallory about her ambitions for herself, let alone Softer Landings, how on earth could she convince other people to buy into the franchise? She was doomed. Doomed to be jobless, homeless and, if Dan ever found out what she'd agreed to, Gusless.

Mallory took a sip of tea, studying her, then set down her cup and said, 'I get the feeling the whole franchise aspect of it bothers you.'

Desperately trying to keep the building emotion at bay, Ellie admitted, 'It does. There's not a formula for doing it, you know? It's not a one-size-fits-all service.'

'And you feel responsible for them emotionally? The couples?'

Soooo very responsible.

'It's meant to be a helping service. The entire premise is to cushion people's heartbreak at the end of a relationship. Make moving forward easier. If the set-ups go poorly, it would be our fault. My fault.'

'It's a big responsibility, dabbling in other people's relationships.'

Mallory's tone was nice enough, but something about it added a lead weight to Ellie's stomach.

'But . . .' Mallory went on, 'people do have a way of tying themselves in knots about things that should be straightforward. With the right staff in place – trained relationship counsellors, maybe? – it sounds like you're providing people with the ability to do the right thing.'

Mallory was a genius! It hadn't even occurred to her to hire people who specialised in relationships. 'You really think it's a service that might take off?'

'Well . . .' Mallory sing-songed the word as her eyes took on a faraway look. 'If there'd been a service like yours back in my day, I might not be growing old alone.'

Ellie started. 'What do you mean?'

'It's nothing too thrilling,' Mallory preambled, before continuing in a tone she might've used to describe the precise way to make a perfect roast chicken. 'I was mistress to a gentleman I loved with all my heart for some twenty years.'

Ellie blinked her surprise but didn't say anything.

Mallory allowed herself a forlorn smile, then brightened it. 'I knew the set-up from the beginning. That he wouldn't leave and I wasn't to expect him to.' She took another sip of tea before continuing. 'He was a professor at the university where I worked as a librarian.' Her smile faltered as she placed a hand over her stomach. 'There was a spark from the start. Something deep inside here that just knew he was the man for me. He felt it too. Said as much, all the time. But he was married. Had children. Wasn't the sort to walk away from commitments because of feelings.'

'But . . .'

'But I let myself fall in love with him anyway. It was what my heart wanted and, at the beginning anyway, I thought he couldn't possibly stay. Not when we shared what we did. We made love as if

272

we'd been made for each other. Talked and talked. Soul-quenching conversations, the likes of which he said he could never have with his wife. Slowly, very slowly, I began to see that he had told me the truth. He wasn't going to leave. His life was perfect just the way it was.' Her smile was sad now, pierced through with an unbearable loss. 'Maybe if I'd known you, I could've found the strength to walk away.'

It was an impossible question to answer. 'Do you still see him now?'

Mallory pursed her lips and gave her head a tight little shake. 'He died.'

Ellie pressed her hands over her heart. 'I'm so sorry.'

'Don't be. I deserved it. Every last gory bit of it,' she explained. 'He had a heart attack while we were engaged in sexual congress.'

'Oh *crumbs*,' Ellie said as her hands flew to her mouth.

'I tend to use another turn of phrase,' Mallory said, 'but . . . that's about right.'

Gus got up and put his head on Mallory's knee, clearly sensing a need for some moral support. She gave his head a few distracted pats then looked Ellie in the eye and said, 'The point being, darlin', whoever said the road to hell is paved with good intentions was right. I learnt a crucial lesson the hard way: don't take what isn't yours until it's truly yours for the taking. Now, would you mind taking a look at this flower catalogue with me? I'm stuck between these two different types of dahlias and I'd really like to add some colour to the garden this spring.'

Ellie took to the task with possibly too much relish, but they both knew that the distraction was welcome. As much as she told herself she had taken Sadie's job to save Dan from unnecessary heartache? She felt seen. Very, very seen.

After a long walk across the park thinking about everything Mallory had told her, Ellie finally went home via the deli that made Gus drool, only to find Dan was in a similar mood to hers. Grumpy. Distracted. Rubbing his knee and losing track of their not particularly engaging chit-chat.

'How's the running going?' she asked.

'Good. Fine.' He grimaced as he stretched his leg out under the table.

'You sure about that?'

'Some days are better than others.' He didn't elaborate, his tone managing to convey what he wasn't saying: *I don't want to talk about it.*

'I've got a cream that's meant to be good for aches and pains.' She began to rise from her chair. 'Want me to grab it?'

'No,' he said curtly enough to make her sit down like a naughty schoolgirl. And then, clearly displeased with himself, added, 'Thank you.'

If she'd been his girlfriend, she would've pushed. Asked for more details. Demanded access to what was really troubling him, but with Mallory's words echoing in her head like a portent of doom, she didn't press. Which, to be fair, was probably what most boyfriends wished their girlfriends would do when they weren't in a good mood. Even so . . . she hated seeing him like this. She edged the plate of cupcakes she'd bought on the walk home towards him. 'We saw Mallory today.'

Dan left the cupcakes untouched but brightened. 'Oh good. That was kind. How is she?'

'She said something really interesting.'

'Oh?'

'Yes. She said you'd taken up the role of Gus's supervisor while she was off.'

The news, imparted when she and Gus had hugged Mallory goodbye and Mallory had asked how Dan was getting on at the school, had really caught Ellie off-guard, but going by Dan's expression, he clearly didn't think it was a big deal. In fact, quite the opposite, judging by the rapid withdrawal of tension from his features. 'Yeah, I have been. I thought I told you. It's been great. Seeing Gus in action. Those little kids are—' He clapped his hand to his chest. 'They get to you. I could spend the rest of my life listening to them read about Loraxes and Gruffalos.'

'What about your job?' she asked, far too testily for someone who'd just been told she was supposed to have been in the loop all along. 'Not much call for ophthalmologists in the eye hospital these days?'

He stiffened, visibly stung by her tone. She wished she could claw the words back. It wasn't her business. Dan wasn't hers to micromanage. Dan wasn't hers at all.

'Sorry. I thought I'd said.' He winced, gave his knee another rub. 'I've taken a bit of time off from there. With Mallory out of action and the run coming up and my parents flying over . . .' He left the sentence open-ended in a way that suggested there was something much more informational lying in wait.

She waited for him to fill the void. To explain what the heck was going on. This run that meant so much even though it was obviously taking a physical toll. The push-pull of affections. The tight hugs she'd seen him give Gus, knowing in her gut there was something more to them than the simple joy of a dog cuddle. 'Dan?' she tentatively asked. 'Is everything okay?'

When his eyes met hers she knew for sure it wasn't. There was something weighing on him.

'You can talk to me, you know.'

'Yeah! Course.' He laughed uncomfortably through the words. 'I just . . . you know . . .'

'No. I don't. That's why I'm asking.'

He gave her an out-of-character *I can't help you* shrug. As if it was all in her head.

Though she knew she had no right to feel hurt, she did. Like one wedge after the other was falling between them. Not that she had a leg to stand on in the *I tell you everything* department, but she'd never once felt as if Dan withheld information from her. Before she could say anything, he abruptly heaved himself up, almost tipping the thick wooden table in the process. 'I'm going to turn in early. Read. Get some shut-eye.' He stopped himself and, a bit guiltily, asked, 'Are you okay to give Gus his walkies tonight?'

'Of course.' He thanked her in his silent hand-over-heart gesture then they wished one another a good night, but, unlike most nights, there wasn't any warmth in it.

After his bedroom door clicked shut behind him, a swell of loneliness crashed into her. She slid down on to the kitchen floor with Gus, rearranging his languid body so that it was draped over her lap like a security blanket. Dan's pensive mood could be over anything, she told herself. Sometimes people were grumpy just because. Sometimes, like in Simon's case, there were unbelievably painful extenuating circumstances. Maybe the hospital hadn't been able to come up with the full-time job they'd promised Dan and he was trying to figure things out before he told anyone. Maybe he'd had a bad phone call with Sadie. Maybe he knew Ellie had been lying to him and that the people he'd thought had his back had been holding knives to it all along.

A core-deep ache began to tighten inside her. She had to tell Dan everything. Unburden herself of all the things he didn't know. 'What do you think, Gus? Will he judge me if I tell him?'

Gus looked up, gave her hand a nudge indicating he would like his ears scratched, please, and then, after she'd obliged him, left the room for his favourite spot on the couch.

◆ ◆ ◆

Ellie took a deep breath of the early spring-infused night air and pulled out her phone. She thumbed up the first number in her contacts and, heart already pounding, pressed the little green dial button. It barely made it through the first ring before it was answered.

'Ellz? Is that you?'

'Hey, Aurora. How's the bride to be?'

Chapter Twenty-Nine

'And you promise to keep your grubby mitts off the entire split?'

Ellie didn't want to, but if she really was going to expand the business, she had to loosen the apron strings at some point. Thea was looking at her with as much excitement as a little kid about to make her debut as the Grinch in the school play. Three parts giddy with delight to one part terrified to disappoint.

'You're in charge. If we're going to do Softer Landings properly, we have to trust each other, right?'

She and Aurora had discussed this exact thing last night, after Ellie's first call had led to a second and a third. A week later, they'd lost count and now both felt comfortable enough to talk about dresses and bouquet ideas without Ellie offering suggestions and Aurora hanging up in a strop.

'Let me learn from my own mistakes!' Aurora had play-screamed. A far, far more pleasant way to be told to back off than the way they used to speak to one another. Baby steps, her mother would call them, but they felt like great strides forward and she was hoping she could let this new-found ability to own her mistakes help guide her forward.

'You'll be great. I know you will,' Ellie said.

Thea shrugged, but her cheeks went a nice happy pink.

'Ellz?' Thea swirled a figure eight into the mini-Japanese seren-ity garden one of their clients had gifted Ellie after extracting her from a *now I see why he's single* dad at her daughter's school. 'Do you think anything Simon said had merit?'

Ellie thought carefully before she replied. 'Some of the things.'

Thea winced.

'Not just you. I have to take a lot on board as well.' She bright-ened. 'He was definitely wrong about the horse you rode in on. Everyone knows cruelty to animals is wrong.'

Thea managed a half-hearted snort. As pathetic as it was, the snort felt like a win. Thea never laughed at Ellie's jokes, but . . . Dramatic Exit Day had changed the way they treated one another. There was less snark from Thea and more trust from Ellie. There was also the shared pain that they'd each, somehow, contributed to Simon's departure.

After a week's silence, Simon had, through Vee, informed them he wouldn't be working for Softer Landings any more. He was also taking an indefinite compassionate leave of absence from Media Angels.

'He's where he should be,' Vee had told them both earlier that morning, and she was right. He was. Even if it was a harsh way for the right thing to happen.

Ellie ducked her head to get Thea's attention. 'What you said finally got him to face some hard truths. You were right. He would completely and totally regret not being with Diego when he— He—'

'When he dies,' Thea reluctantly finished for her. 'Yeah, I know, it's just a bit shit that I'm not there for him as back-up. I mean, it's not like it's going to be easy.'

'You two are best friends,' Ellie reminded her. 'You'll make up.'

'You think?'

'I know.' If she and Aurora could talk after a year's silence, anything was possible. All it had taken was a massive swallow of pride to admit to everything that had happened over the past year. It wasn't like freezing her sister out had helped anything. As painful as it had initially felt, admitting to so many things going wrong, Aurora had not judged her once. A very good first step towards believing going home might not be as horrible as she'd feared. Ellie pointed at the door. 'Now go out there and slice and dice some relationships for us.'

Thea snorted. 'That sounds so wrong coming from you.'

Ellie tried again. 'Try not to break any hearts today?'

'Better.' Thea gave her arm a play-punch. 'And you go out there and dazzle Dan the Man's parents.' She pre-empted Ellie's inevitable provisos with a heartfelt 'Because you're a nice person and that's what nice people do. Regardless of if they're secretly in love with their son.'

Ellie turned beetroot red. 'I am not!'

'Are too.'

Ellie began to protest again and Thea stopped her with a *la-la-la can't hear you*, and then, to Ellie's surprise, she stopped teasing and said, 'Look. It's okay. Feelings are what they are and, whatever happens, I'll be here for you.'

Ellie's eyes widened in disbelief.

'What?' Thea looked over her shoulder, then back at Ellie, concern etched into her features. 'I'm your friend, aren't I?'

'I'd really like that.'

'Good,' Thea said, openly pleased. 'Now, tell your bezzie Thee Thee . . . have you wanked to him yet?'

How did she *know* these things?

'Yes!' Thea punched a hand into the air. 'I knew it!' She pulled her chair up close to Ellie's desk, popped her chin on her hand and said, 'Tell me everything.'

'No, it wasn't really—'

'Rampant Rabbit? Big black cock? Butt plug? What'd you go for?'

This was humiliating. She began to fastidiously staple random pieces of paper to one another, too mortified to explain how, the other night when she'd been brushing her teeth and Dan was right there on the other side of the wall in his bedroom, possibly shirtless, possibly wearing nothing at all, she'd looked at the electric toothbrush vibrating away in her hand and thought, why not? Just as she'd put it . . . down there . . . Dan had rat-a-tat-tatted on the door and asked if he could borrow some toothpaste. The toothbrush had fallen on the floor, she'd conked her head trying to retrieve it, and Dan had burst in thinking she was having a stroke. Really good first experience, all in all.

Thea was staring at her as if trying to divine the truth and then sat back with a satisfied smile. 'I know – you went *au naturel*, didn't you?'

Ellie made a vague head movement.

'Don't be shy, country mouse.' Thea raised her index and middle fingers. 'These two fingers are a girl's best friend.' Then she patted Ellie's hand with them. 'Well, then!' Thea pushed herself up and out of her chair. 'If you'll excuse me, I'm off to crush some hearts while you're busy winning one.' She put her hand out for a fist-bump and Ellie met it gratefully.

In all honesty, she was cacking herself. She was scheduled to be at the London Eye at six. Dan would be there, of course. And Richard, Dan's dad, and his wife, Sherry. Also meeting them were Marlene and her husband, Yves.

There were dinner reservations after, but everyone agreed it would be a nice idea to take a spin round and get the bird's-eye view of London 'for Sherry's sake', then walk across the river to supper at the Portrait Gallery restaurant where they had all been before but would go again as the night-time views of London were lovely and more than worth a revisit, 'for Sherry's sake'.

The more Dan told her, the more she realised quite a few things were being done 'for Sherry's sake' and, for reasons Ellie couldn't define, her heart went out to the woman. Sherry was Dan's step-mother. A born-and-bred Carolina girl, she had barely been outside of her state, let alone the country – unlike Richard, Marlene and Yves, who was Marlene's third husband (Ellie was informed that there'd been a second one a few years back but he, apparently, wasn't discussed).

As Ellie made her way across the Hungerford Bridge towards the Eye, she reminded herself that if or, more likely, *when* it got too awkward, she could use Gus as an excuse to duck out early. She felt a bit guilty about it but had already discussed an exit plan with Heloise, who would ring in about seven-thirty to check in. If Ellie told her the sunset was lovely, Heloise would know she'd be needed until eleven. If Ellie said nothing about sunset, Heloise was to tell her she thought Gus wasn't feeling well.

Not that she was panicked Dan's parents would instantly know she was in love with him and spend the night torturing the whole truth and nothing but the truth out of her or anything.

Ha! Of course she was.

◆ ◆ ◆

Riding on the London Eye with Dan was something Ellie had imagined a hundred times. There would've been some silence at the beginning as they enjoyed the view. Then some joking. Lots of talking. One hand brushing against the other as they pointed out landmarks to one another. And, eventually, because by that point it would be so clear they were pre-destined for one another, there would be kissing. An endless, seamless, array of kisses to float them back to earth.

Being trapped in a glass bubble with Dan and both sets of his parents was quite a different scenario.

In their late fifties, his mum and dad were very much of the *opposites who attracted* variety.

Dan's mother, Marlene, was a petite, intense woman whose leanness came across as intimidating, as if it had been crafted from a gruelling regime of eight-mile runs (uphill) to work, followed by ten hours of uninterrupted ground-breaking surgery, wrapped up by another long run home (also uphill) and a meal of unpronounce-able ancient grains and micro-vegetables. His father, Richard, was the complete opposite and, Ellie noted, a glimpse into the type of man Dan might, one day, become. He had the congenial air of a paediatrician but was, like his ex-wife and now his son, an oph-thalmologist. He was tall, easily carried a lightly padded version of Dan's athletic physique, hair more salt than pepper and had a pair of warm hazel eyes that instantly put Ellie at ease. Dan's bright blue eyes were entirely his mother's but backlit by his father's warmth. From the way the oxygen felt sucked out of the capsule from the moment they'd been sealed inside, it was evident that divorce and time hadn't turned them into lifelong friends. All of which made for a slightly uncomfortable environment as they rotated oh so slowly up and around the London skyline. There was a bit of awkward jok-ing, but very little catch-up talk considering they hadn't seen one another for ages. It was as if all of the parents – biological and step – were in a conversational holding pattern, circling round Dan, waiting for his approval on which topics could be pursued and which couldn't. Which was weird because the Dan Ellie knew was a pretty relaxed guy and was happy to talk about anything. Neither of them had brought up their shared grump night, which, in the end,

Ellie had written off as a universal day of bad moods. Since then, he'd been exactly like the Dan she knew and unrequitedly loved.

'Well, this is a lot less interesting than I thought it might be,' Marlene groused.

'I heard they had scaffolding up there on the Big Ben for a while,' Dan's father cut in, annoyed because his wife, Sherry, had just said, 'Isn't this fun?!'

It was clear travelling as a foursome wasn't a dream for any of them, but somehow, beneath the tension, it was equally clear that they were all thrilled to see Dan. Their maypole.

'I'm just psyched you all could make it.' Dan spread his arms wide and tucked his mum and Sherry under each of them so that they peeked out from under his coat sleeves like little freshly hatched chicks. Dan started pointing out landmarks to Sherry and offering little nuggets of historical information to his mum. Yves, who had been born in France and done some work experience over here in London 'way back when the Eurostar was shiny and new', also pointed out areas of London he remembered.

'We should go to Paris,' he said, eyes suddenly bright. 'For lunch.'

'You can do that?' Sherry was astonished. 'Just whizz over to Paris for *lunch*?'

'Any meal you like,' Yves said, then tipped his head down to whisper something in French to Marlene who snorted.

Conversation stop-started for the rest of the ride. Ellie was largely quiet, as she didn't feel she could properly engage in a conversation about the New York Mets or the disappointments over that year's Super Bowl. Plane food as a topic turned out to be quite the leveller. No one, they all agreed, liked soggy pastry. Also occupying Ellie's thoughts amid the awkward smiles, the *well would you look at that*s, and the *now how old is that building then* type questions, was the way Dan had introduced her. He'd said, 'Meet

Ellie, my tourist bud.' The moniker meant no one was entirely sure how to treat her or how openly they could speak to their son. Was she a brand-new friend? Someone trying to elbow Sadie out of the way? A paid tour guide? The truth, of course, would be impossible to reveal.

When they were finally released from the capsule and began a startlingly brisk walk towards Trafalgar Square (Marlene had set the pace), Heloise rang. Ellie was more than prepared to fake a Gus illness. Dan caught a glimpse of her phone screen, bent down and whispered, 'If this is Heloise acting as your wingman and you think you are ducking out of here, I will fire you as my best friend.'

She managed to smirk instead of swoon into his warm gingerbread-man scent and refused the call. Since when had she been upgraded from tourist bud to best friend? Had *the parents in a capsule* thing been a test that she'd unwittingly passed?

He gave her hand a squeeze and somehow, magically, as they continued walking across the bridge towards the restaurant, their little fingers stayed hooked together. Ellie's entire body buzzed with endorphins.

Later, in the restaurant, wine loosened up the flow of conversation.

'*Goodness.*' Sherry gave the menu a wide-eyed look, head shaking back and forth. 'These prices sure are steep. Worse than New York even, and you would've thought I'd've gotten used to them after— '

'Now, don't you worry about that, Sherry.' Richard's voice was low. 'We don't treat ourselves as much as we should, so . . .'

'Well, how could we with all of the toing and froing—' Her eyes flicked to Dan and then, as if someone had flicked a switch, she began reading the list of desserts out loud, saying she always liked to work backwards from dessert to make sure she got the pairing right. Most people started at the beginning, but how were you supposed to know what you were aiming for if you didn't start with the grand finale?

Ellie smiled. It was a variation on how she approached each of her break-ups. Endgame? Happiness. But how you got there was always different.

'Dan tells us you're in the recruitment business, Ellie,' Marlene pointedly broke in.

'Yes! Yes. That's right.' For some reason her pulse quickened. What else had Dan told them about her?

'Which sector?'

'Media. Film and television mostly.'

'*Fantastique!*' Yves kissed his fingers. 'I am so in love with a quality film. None of this CGI, franchise stuff that dominates now.' He began to tell her about a producer friend of his who was involved in the arthouse film scene in Paris. 'Do you do any work with him?'

'No, I'm just the office manager,' she lied, 'but my colleague Simon might. He works with a lot of producers.'

'Oh, so you don't actually *do* any recruitment,' Marlene clarified for everyone at the table. 'You're just office support.'

'Well, office *manager*,' she doubled down on the lie. It had been true. Once. She began to study her own menu in earnest, wondering if they were all holding her credentials up to Sadie's and, finding her wanting, positioning their menus so that they could share complicit looks that said, *she's not really up to the Sadie Standard, is she?* Sadie would've passed a Marlene grilling with bells on. Or – Ellie allowed herself the possibility – maybe she wouldn't. Relocating Marlene's son to London instead of North Carolina only to abandon him a few weeks later? It didn't look great, even if you left in the part about the traumatised schoolgirls.

'And you have no plans to push yourself?' Marlene tapped Ellie's plate with the edge of her menu. 'Aim a little higher than the status quo? What are you? Pushing thirty?'

'Mom! Ellie's doing just great as she is.' Dan gave her a *can it* look, then said to no one in particular, 'Maybe we should pick some starters, yeah? Who's for starters and a main?' Dan shot Ellie an apologetic smile and gave her knee a rub. Her skin tingled under his touch, instantly feeling the loss of it when he removed his hand, but the warmth of his protective *Mom!* remained.

Shelley started reading the starters out loud.

Ellie felt a sudden, deep kinship with Shelley. What was wrong with toeing the line? Not everyone could be a renowned eye surgeon. The world couldn't function if they were. Who would collect the rubbish bins from the hospital? Prepare the takeaway sushi or power smoothies Marlene very likely had for lunch? Who would unclog the printers jammed up by hospital executives who'd not bothered to read the laminated How To Make A Photocopy form Blu-tacked to the wall? Anyone? Anyone at all? Why did people like Marlene even question why someone would do something 'ordinary'?

Someone had to.

Someone had to unblock the toilets, paint over the graffiti, drive lorries from one part of the country to the other delivering supplies to banks and shops and hospitals where yet more low-paid, underappreciated people got those things on to shelves and into theatre so that people like Marlene could operate on the windows to the soul without a care in the world!

She opened her mouth to say as much, but nothing came out. Feeling humiliated for doing the right thing had a way of doing that to a girl's vocal cords.

Mercifully, no one noticed, as starters had finally gained traction as a conversation topic. As the seconds ticked by, the humiliation shifted to indignation. Doing the right thing by someone was, after all, the reason she'd decided to become a therapist. Her mum, a former fountain of youth, had looked so unbelievably tired after her dad had died, even with the countless hours of sleep she had each night. Ellie had been desperate to know what to say. To be able to phrase things so that her mum might be able to see the world a bit differently. To help. The only thing she'd known how to do was the hotel. Not even that, really. She knew how to start the coffee, fill in the reservation forms, pile the laundry bags outside the door on Tuesday night rather than Wednesday morning because the guy who picked them up periodically freelanced as a fisherman so would sometimes collect the linens in the middle of the night. These and countless other small, seemingly insignificant tasks that, like a Lego set, all came together in the form of a fully functioning family-run hotel. She'd made it her mission to do these things so that, no matter what, her mum would never, ever have to worry about the roof over their heads. Ten years on, she'd done little more than alphabetise, make tea and change ink cartridges for a living. So what? It helped people. Just like Softer Landings did. It was a grubby job, but if she didn't do it, who would? Marlene? Unlikely. But she bet Shelley would.

Over dessert and coffees, the conversation turned to West End shows.

'It'd be fun to see *Hamilton* with the authentic accents,' Shelley said.

Marlene shook her head, barely containing an eye roll. 'The only one who would have a proper English accent is King George.'

'I think a lot of the original colonists would've had English accents,' Ellie said with what she hoped was an air of authority.

'Well,' Shelley sniffed, 'that's obviously what I meant.'

Dan laughed, and his blue eyes twinkled with mischief when they met hers. 'I always thought it'd be funny to take you to see *Jersey Boys*.'

She giggled. 'That would be funny.' *Always?*

'Why would that be funny?' Marlene asked.

'Because Ellie's originally from Jersey.' Dan quickly explained about it being an island off the coast of France.

'I still don't get it why that's funny?' asked Marlene. '*Jersey Boys* is about singers from New Jersey.'

'Yeah, I know, Mom, that's the point—'

'Lovely seafood,' interrupted Yves.

'Don't forget about the potatoes.' Ellie smiled at him.

'Oh! *Well*. Speaking of potatoes.' Shelley clasped her hands together at her sternum. 'Daniel, do you remember that potato dish we all tried last autumn at that little restaurant in the Italian district? When was it? Near to Thanksgiving, I think. I know we were up there with you then. Those restaurant meals all kind of rolled into one, but – anyway – I was absolutely desperate for the recipe.' Completely oblivious to the fact the rest of the table had fallen deathly silent, she turned to Ellie, 'We were in New York near the hospital and took Daniel here out for a meal. You know, a proper one, because he hadn't had one in ages—'

Dan started clearing his throat and pushed back from the table. His dad cut in. 'It was a lovely meal, Shelley, you're right. So, Daniel. Son. Before we turn in for the night, how about this race tomorrow? What time did you want us all there?'

Shelley threw Richard a hurt look. Dan began rattling through all of the details for the run as Marlene pointedly made a show of waving her hand at the waiter for the bill. Yves, who'd had his eye on the digestif menu, placed it back in the card holder, clearly resigned that the eighteen-year-old cognac he'd been hoping to try would be nineteen by the time he got round to it.

What on earth had happened just then?

And then it hit her. Dan had been home. Shelley was talking about New York. And a hospital. Marlene and Yves lived in New York, where Marlene still practised, so . . . maybe he'd been visiting them with Sadie? A break from the rigours of Ethiopia. Or maybe something had happened to one of his sisters and he'd had to fly home for moral support. The tension was so thick around the table Ellie didn't dare ask for an explanation. The bill arrived. Richard and Yves had a fake little tug of war over it until Marlene handed the waiter her platinum card and asked him to just get on with it, could he, it had been a long day and she didn't know about everyone else but the jet lag was beginning to take its toll.

Dan called three Ubers and, to her surprise, climbed in one with his dad and Shelley, saying he'd catch up with Ellie back at the flat. When he got home she was in the kitchen giving Gus his goodnight treat. Dan shouted out from the hallway that he was going to hit the hay, it was going to be a big day tomorrow, and went straight to his room.

Chapter Thirty

Dan was up and out of the flat before Ellie had returned from her morning walk with Gus. She'd assumed she'd see him this morning so she could wish him well, but guessed that he was nervous so had set off early. That, or he was proactively avoiding her. Which would be weird, but last night had been weird too. Best friends? Hand holding? Well, little-finger holding, but still. Everyone knew little-finger holding was like a promise. Then again, he'd ridden home with his parents instead of her . . .

A thought struck. Were Dan's feelings beginning to shift from Sadie to her?

A raft of complicated emotions tied themselves in a knot in her belly, them morphed into tiny little swords soaring up past her vital organs and pricking at her conscience. Even though she was doing exactly what the client wanted, it felt wrong.

Instead of allowing herself to examine the situation further, she began to clean the kitchen as if her life depended upon it, then poured her creative energies into making a *Go, Dan, Go!* sign, and dressed Gus in his red sweatband and legwarmers before setting off at a Marlene-style pace until, sweating, she arrived at the spot along the route that Dan had suggested was a good one because, even though they'd missed the first few miles, he would be passing by three times for the last part of the race, which was a series of loops around Hyde Park.

Dan's parents were already there, coffees in hand. Sherry and Yves also had sugar-dusted almond croissants. None of them were particularly chatty, apart from Shelley, who was revelling in just how old their hotel was and wasn't it funny how London was so full of modern things, like the robot lawnmower she'd spotted during an early morning walk past the Tower of London, and yet their hotel plumbing was still as old as Queen Victoria herself. Yves suggested she visit Paris. Napoleon, he claimed, may not have been the nicest of men, but he knew how to build a city. Marlene stoically kept her eyes trained on the cordoned-off running track, and Richard, who'd given Ellie a warm, but distracted hug when she'd arrived, was doing the same.

They took up posts along the areas demarcated for onlookers, Ellie making sure Gus had a good view. Conversation remained stilted, apart from Sherry's endless observations. It would have been a perfect time to quiz them about Dan, find out more about the man who had held her imagination captive for this past year, but something about plundering their knowledge of him felt invasive. As if she hadn't quite earnt their trust enough to ask anything beyond their excitement about being here. Her tummy fluttered as she remembered him bending close to whisper into her ear . . . *my best friend* . . . and wondered for the millionth time where the comment had come from. Their lives did seem as though they'd been destined to collide, but the reason why remained elusive. Was it really as simple as each of them needing a companionable tourist bud? A pizza pal? A flatmate?

This was, after all, a man whose merest glance could send her entire nervous system into overdrive. Maybe *that* was it. In the same way she was trying to show Dan what it was like to feel loved, perhaps he was showing her the type of man she should be loving. Only he was doing it for free. And it wasn't supposed to be him.

Or . . . maybe Dan wasn't who'd been written into her stars at all. Perhaps it was *Gus* she'd been destined to meet and Dan's only role was to play the gorgeously distracting middleman. A role that he was fulfilling with Oscar-worthy panache.

Shelley leant in and said, 'I always find this little app-doodad helps calm the nerves.' She directed Ellie to the app, then gave her Dan's number so she could track him on her phone, saying it was what they normally did when they followed him in a race. As Ellie plugged the number into the app, she allowed a thought that had been niggling at her some air. Wasn't it a little weird that his parents had flown across the ocean to see him run if he'd done it dozens of times before? She glanced across at them and they, like her, all looked a little bit anxious.

According to her phone, Dan was already about three miles into the race. They were at the six-mile mark. Racers had been streaming past for a while now. Long gone were the types Ellie had seen winning marathons on television. Lean, sinewy runners with eyes on nothing but the road in front of them. Next came the earnest whippet-like runners who might not run professionally, but wished they did. The Marlenes. Now, the flow of runners was growing thicker. Their expressions were focussed, but not exhausted. Still half a race to go and the energy to finish it. She was surprised not to see Dan among them. He'd put in so much training she was certain he would've been in this group. Then again, he did keep rubbing that knee of his. Maybe it was giving him trouble. She hoped not.

Next came a sea of t-shirted runners – the proper amateurs – all running for charities. Large cheers erupted from boisterous clusters of volunteers stationed along the paths, all in support of the runners raising funds for every charity under the sky. Cancer. Mental health. Bereaved children. Dozens more. Watching all of the people run past wearing shirts with names and pictures of loved ones lost or present was a lot more moving than Ellie had anticipated. Tears kept tickling at the back of her throat. So many people working through so much pain, and almost all of them with a smile of triumph on their faces that they'd made it this far into their journey.

'It gets to you, doesn't it?' Richard leant in and asked.

'Yeah.' Ellie blew her nose. 'It's such a big event, I thought it would feel impersonal, but when you break it down like this and realise that each person is doing this for something so personal . . .'

She couldn't finish the sentence.

'I know. I know.' Richard gave her a shoulder squeeze highly reminiscent of the ones his son gave. For just a moment, she allowed herself to lean into it, wondering if her life would be the way it was now if her dad was still alive.

A woman ran past them holding on to a thick elastic band with another woman. Ellie caught the backs of their t-shirts. They were running for the Guide Dogs charity. A blind woman and a sighted guide. Ellie cheered. 'That's the human form of you, Gussy!' She turned, beaming, and asked Richard, 'Is that who Dan's running for? He's been so secretive about this.'

'No, dear. I don't think that's it.' There was a catch in Richard's voice that caught Shelley's attention.

'Would you put the poor girl out of her misery?'

Ellie's eyebrows dove together. 'Sorry?'

'*Shelley!*' Richard whisper-growled. 'Would you please leave it? Daniel wanted her to find out this way.'

Find out what? Shelley and Richard continued to glare at each other. A swell of nausea sloshed through her. This was it. The moment she discovered Dan was running for a little-known charity called Fuck You, Ellie Shaw – Don't Go Breaking My Heart. Her own heart felt as if it was impaling itself on her ribs and her breath was coming in weird, hitched gulps.

Yves began to shout. 'There he is. There's Daniel.'

A charity group across the route from them started cheering and waving their signs. They were all wearing purple shirts reading *Finding Your Feet*. It wasn't a charity Ellie knew. She turned and saw Dan, his handsome face glowing with sweat, his expression strained, but smiling as he saw the group. He turned when his mother called out, 'Keep up the pace, Daniel. That's right, son.' He, too, was wearing a purple shirt. It, too, said, *Finding Your Feet*. Its hem grazed the top of a pair of black shorts. She'd never seen him in shorts. She was midway through her cheer, 'Dan! Dan! Run as fast as you can—' when she realised he had a blade for one foot. Dan was an amputee. And then, before she could fully process it, he was running past them, quickly absorbed into the crowd as if it was the most perfectly normal way in the world to let his newly knighted best friend know that he didn't have a leg below his knee. Not one he'd grown himself, anyway.

She realised Dan's father had his arm around her and she leant into the support of it as she faltered on her own two, perfectly serviceable, feet. She looked at him, lost for words.

'I don't know why,' Dan's father began, 'but he didn't want us to tell you until you saw him.'

The awkwardness of yesterday's get-together suddenly made sense. They'd all been keeping this secret. 'New York . . .' she managed.

'Yes. That's where they flew him after the accident.'

So it had happened in Ethiopia. Her brain buzzed with confusion and disbelief. Trying and failing to piece together everything she knew about Before-Africa Dan and After-Africa Dan.

'I had no idea. I feel so stupid. I could've been helping—'

'Oh no. Don't you do that. Daniel's one stubborn sonofabitch when he wants to be and right now he wants to be. He said you did right by him a while back and that of all the people in the world, yours was the one dose of pity he did not want.'

'What?' Ellie recoiled at the thought. Among the countless things she had felt for him over the past year, pity had never been one of them. He was too strong a soul for that. She felt another blast of admiration for him detonate in her chest. Even when he'd endured an impossible-to-imagine tragedy, his main interest had been protecting her. How Sadie had the ability to walk away from this man was beyond her. She wobbled again. Richard took her sign and handed it to Shelley, suggesting he find Ellie a park bench somewhere in the shade.

'This is ridiculous,' Ellie protested.

'What is?'

'That I'm the one who needs to sit down.'

'Don't you worry, honey,' Richard said. 'We all needed to sit down when we heard.' He told everyone they'd be back soon. Shelley gave Richard a kiss on the cheek, suddenly exuding the aura of a much more capable woman than she'd been a few minutes ago, as if keeping the secret had somehow hobbled her own inner strength. She pulled Ellie into a hug and whispered, 'I know, baby. I know. It's a shock, but look at him now. So strong and determined. He's a fighter, our Daniel.'

Ellie leant into her. It was like hugging a human sugar cookie. Reassuring. Warm.

After a few moments, Shelley held her out at arm's length and, wiping away some of Ellie's tears, said 'He's a keeper. You hear me? That boy's a keeper.'

'But . . . he's not mine to keep.'

Shelley screwed her face up as if the whole thing with Sadie was much of a muchness. 'Good things come to those who wait, honey. Trust me on this.' She threw a look at Richard that told a story.

As Richard guided her away from the runners, Marlene reached out and gave Ellie's arm a squeeze, as if she too was trying to absorb some of the blow Ellie had just endured. Not that anything had happened to her. This was about Dan.

When they were a few metres away from the crowd, Ellie asked, 'Why didn't he want me to know?'

'At first he didn't want anyone to know. Apart from Sadie, of course, who'd been there. She's the one who reached out to us, helped us find the best hospital for him to be evacuated to.' Richard pointed to a bench under a tree. 'There was a lot of emotional trauma to absorb on top of the physical trauma.'

'What happened?'

Richard wove his fingers together and cupped one of his knees in them, twisting his own, fully fleshed human ankle round and round. His eyes were on the crowd, but his energy was here with Ellie, on the bench. 'Of course Daniel will tell you about it all later, but the long and short of it is that armed bandits came to the camp where he and Sadie and the rest of the medical types were set up. Sadie tried to run away to phone for help and they opened up fire – with machine guns. Daniel threw himself on her to get them through a nearby doorway but, unfortunately, his ankle caught the brunt of the gunfire. Completely shattered it and some of the fibula. The tibula wasn't much better, so, in the end, they decided it all had to come off. Thank god his knee was alright.'

'So . . .'

'He has a below-the-knee amputation. Worked his butt clean off at rehab to get to this phase.' Richard cleared his throat and pulled a handkerchief out of his pocket to blow his nose. 'I'm damn proud of that boy,' he said through gritted teeth. 'Damn proud.'

Ellie felt shell-shocked and then, as she absorbed the facts and married them with the little behaviourisms she'd taken as privacy and pernicketiness over how tidy the flat was, she realised it was all to do with his foot. 'Does he have several prostheses?'

'Yes.' Richard smiled and turned to her, his body language more congenial now. More familiar. He clapped a hand on her knee. 'Did you know they can 3D print those things? All based on Daniel's actual calf and his actual foot.'

'That's amazing.'

'It is.' Richard lost himself in thought for a few moments, his hand still resting paternally on Ellie's knee as if he'd been doing it for years. Eventually, he turned to her. 'I owe you a thank you. We all do.'

'What? Me? I didn't do anything. I didn't even know.'

'You and Gus gave him something to aim for. He couldn't stop talking about you. This kind woman who'd pointed him in the right direction during a dark time. Helped him fix a foolish mistake.'

'Is that what he told you?'

It wasn't how she would've painted what had happened. Broke up his relationship, took his dog and sent him out into the world without so much as a flak jacket would've been her angle. The enormity of the role she'd played in this crashed into her like a tonne of bricks. This was all on her. 'If I hadn't helped him back then' – she stumbled over the word 'helped' because it felt like the wrong one – 'this wouldn't have happened. I interfered where I shouldn't have.' A raw pain scorched her heart. 'This is my fault.'

'Hey. No.' Richard was deadly serious. 'Do not say that. Do not think that. Daniel is a doctor. And a pragmatist. He is well aware of what can and can't happen in the world. He sees it on a daily basis. He will forever be grateful to you, and that is it. Do not take on a burden of guilt that is not yours to bear.'

'But if I hadn't suggested he follow up on his dreams—'

'Uh-uh!' Richard cut her off again. 'His dreams. *His*. Not yours. I didn't hear anything about you filling out forms for him or pushing him to jump on a plane to go help those poor folk out.'

It was true. But still. She felt a need to confess everything. As if speaking the truth would purge her of the guilt corroding her lungs, her gut, her heart. The words converged in her throat, sharp edged and painful. 'I—' she began.

Richard held up a hand. 'We all have a past. We are also all blessed with a future. Make the most of it. This is not on you. Daniel's healthy and happy so far as I can tell, and most of the reason for the happy part is because of you. Now.' He gave her knee another pat as if they'd made an agreement and everything was all settled. He rose and aimed his hand in the direction they'd come from. 'Daniel will be coming round again soon. Let's make sure we're back out there cheering for him when he is.'

When Dan came round the second time, Ellie could see the tight grip both fatigue and the desire to not give up had on him. This was hard. Excruciating mind-over-matter territory. She cheered and whooped as if her own life depended upon it. When his eyes met hers she saw fear at first, and then, to her joy, relief. He surged past them and once again disappeared into the crowd of runners.

The third time he was definitely flagging. Only one more mile to go. Each step looked painful. Ellie wanted to run to him. Tuck her shoulders under his arm or hold hands or sing all of the songs from *Jersey Boys* she just might have memorised last night in bed, wondering if he was doing the same. But it was obvious that finishing the run on his own was something he needed to do. She glanced around him. The charity volunteers were jogging along the cordoned-off section, waving giant foam fingers and blowing kazoos and calling out his name. There were a couple of other runners nearby who were keeping an eye on him, visibly preparing themselves to jump in if he needed help. It was comforting, but still didn't feel enough.

Gus took matters into his own paws. Before Ellie could register what was happening, he'd slipped under the barrier and took up his steady, reliable pace alongside Dan as if they'd been running together all along. The crowd loved it. The cheers and applause buoyed both man and dog, and once they'd turned the final corner towards the finish line, Ellie and Dan's parents made their way there too.

There was, of course, a tremendous fuss as Dan and Gus crossed the finish line together. The newspaper photographers ate it up. A photo of them with their medals along with #DansBestFriend quickly went viral. He had run for two and a half solid hours. Ellie was in awe of him.

'What do you need, son? Shall I get a wheelchair for this bit? It's quite a walk.' Richard and Marlene were in full-on doctor mode now. Despite his protests, they insisted he go to the medical tent for a once-over. Ellie hesitated, unsure if he would want her there, but when they arrived, Dan tipped his head towards the interior and with a sheepish smile asked, 'Hold my hand?'

She would've held all of him. Submerged herself in one of the ice baths and cradled him for hours if he'd asked. 'Of course.'

He held out his hand and, fingers safely woven together, they entered the tent.

After a few minutes of back and forth with the paramedics and one another that they only had Dan's best interests at heart, Yves suggested all of the 'oldies' head off and find some cool drinks. They'd all meet later at Marlene and Yves' hotel for a meal despite Shelley's suggestion that they find somewhere that didn't require anyone to remortgage their home.

'So . . .' Dan said when they were finally alone.

'Yeah.' Ellie was still holding his hand so tightly it felt as if the warm support of their intertwined fingers was for her, not Dan. 'So . . .'

'There's a lot I probably should've told you a while back.'

Ellie shook her head. 'You had your reasons.'

He tipped his forehead to hers. 'It's all pretty messed up.'

'What is?'

He placed his index finger just above her sternum and then moved it to his own. He sat back and inspected her as if seeing her through a different lens.

'What?' she asked again.

'I have feelings for you.'

Her heart flew into her throat. This was it. The moment she'd been waiting for. She forced the gaggle of other people who were also waiting for this moment – Sadie and Thea and Simon and Vee and probably Gus – out of her mind and let the rest of the world fade away, just for these few precious minutes before it all, inevitably, came crashing down around her. 'I have feelings for you too.'

'And you don't mind about—' He waved in the direction of his leg, now relieved of its blade prosthesis. Shelley, unbeknownst to Ellie, had been carrying around a second leg in her enormous shoulder tote so that Dan would find the journey home more comfortable. They'd also made arrangements for him to use crutches or a wheelchair if it came to it, but Dan had insisted he wanted to walk. To a taxi. They'd all laughed at that. They'd all laughed a lot once he'd finished the run. That epic, epic feat.

'I don't mind in the slightest, but . . .' She bit her lower lip.

'Yeah.' He tucked a few stray strands of her hair behind her ear and, meeting her eyes with his kaleidoscope blues, said what she didn't have the courage to. 'Sadie.'

Ellie nodded, absorbing the new reality as her heart began pounding out large, life-affirming thumps, building and growing in speed until there was no start or finish to them. She needed to speak to Sadie before Dan did. Give her back the money. Remind her that she had never wanted to do this in the first place.

And that's when the elusive truth behind Sadie's request finally hit her. Sadie hadn't wanted out of her relationship because she thought Dan was broken or less of a man. Nor was he too nice to dump. He was *impossible* to dump. He'd risked his life and lost an actual limb to save Sadie's life. She hadn't come to Softer Landings to be cruel. She'd done it because she was generous. Kind. She knew she didn't love Dan. Not the way he deserved to be loved. She'd been loyal to him, according to Richard, who'd become a real chatterbox through the rest of the race. She'd stuck with him through rehab. Had fought like hell to try to get a visa to the US so Dan could be close to his family. And, when that had failed, and Dan had insisted upon staying together, had agreed to move to London, promising both sets of his parents that she would look after him to the best of her ability. And this, Ellie realised, was the best of Sadie's ability. Outsourcing.

She'd read Ellie like a book. Saw the lovelorn looks in her eyes. The devotion. All of the things she wished she felt for Dan but, for whatever reason, didn't. And with that revelation, Ellie felt a massive surge of compassion for her. How on earth did you break up with the guy who'd not only saved your life, but had had his changed forever in doing so?

'I'll tell her. Soon,' Dan said. 'But no pressure. We have time to explore whatever this is.'

'What about the hospital? I thought you'd taken time off from there.'

'I did, but not because they didn't want me. It's because they *do* want me. Full-time. I was all knotted up in here.' He splayed his

302

hand out on his chest and, for the first time ever, Ellie didn't resist the urge to put her hand on top of his. 'We'll talk it all out later, but . . . long story short, I knew things weren't right with Sadie shortly after we arrived here in London.'

'Really? How?'

'I saw you.'

Oh, Dan Buchanan. You're breaking my heart.

The moment should've made her feel whole. Shot her into the stratosphere. Instead she felt her insides crust with uneasiness. She ached to tell him everything. Let him know exactly who he was falling for, but she knew deep in her gut he'd be as disgusted with her 'work' as she was with herself right now. She thought of his dad's words to her. *We all have a past. We are also blessed with a future.*

Was a clean slate really a thing?

And then, as if to show her what the future could have in store, Dan loosely cupped his hands around her cheeks, drew her to him and kissed her.

Chapter Thirty-One

Ellie had never imagined a solitary kiss could change her life, but this one did. It was a proper game changer.

Soft. Inquisitive. Ignited intricate sequences of fireworks across even the finest threads of her nervous system, short-circuiting just about everything she knew about the world except for the here and now. Until Gus broke in on the kiss, concerned he was missing out on a group-hug opportunity.

They laughed and cooed over him. Told him that they loved him, then shyly looked away when their eyes met with such strength, such clarity of purpose, it was impossible to deny their love for one another, but . . . #ItsComplicated.

So they did what any normal, newly in love couple did when one was still in a relationship and the other was being paid a packet to end it: they pretended none of the bad stuff existed. Instead, they lost themselves in a whirlwind of tourist hot spots with his parents, physio appointments for Dan, dinners, dog walks and, of course, lots of yearning looks and little-finger holding. They even got a picture with a Beefeater.

When Ellie went to work she felt as if she was slipping from one reality to an entirely different one. Softer Landings came with a harder edge now. Thea had yet to speak with Simon and, as such, her enthusiasm for life in general was sub-zero. She'd all but taken up residence in one of the beanbags in the Softer Landings office, not even bothering to be snarky to Ellie. It was worrying.

'Have you tried ringing him?' Ellie eventually asked when Thea's sighs of despair had become too loud to ignore.

Thea looked at her in horror. 'Are you joking with me?'

Ellie gulped. 'Text? Maybe that'd be a gentler way to ease in.'

Thea gave a careless shrug, its slight hitch betraying how much she actually cared. 'I liked something he put on Twitter.'

'That's good. A start, anyway.'

'Yeah, but he never really checks who likes what.' She fuzzed her lips. 'He's posting pictures of kittens.' She stopped Ellie mid-*awww*. 'Kitten gifs mean things are very, very bad.'

Ellie winced.

'I can't even imagine.'

She couldn't either. The way she'd lost her dad had been so short and sharp there'd hardly been any time to absorb what had happened until it was over. She did a quick scroll through some gifs. 'You know . . . when I need Gus . . . I *need* Gus, in the same way that one tub of Ben & Jerry's won't do. What about sending him a bouquet of kittens?'

Thea made a derisive noise. 'Yeah. I'll just call the RSPCA on that. "One bouquet of grief kittens, please."'

'No. I meant gifs. Here. Look. Here's one of kittens hugging.'

Thea looked at it. 'No way.'

She crawled over to Ellie's desk, grabbed the tiny rake from the mini-serenity garden, then began to rake and rake and rake the sand before abruptly throwing it down so hard it bounced off the desk and into the bin. She didn't pick it out. 'C'mon.' She flopped back into the beanbag. 'We've got to make a plan for Julia and her Fifty Shades of Shitty boyfriend.'

◆ ◆ ◆

A few hours later Ellie was feeling as if the two carefully segmented parts of her life had each grabbed an arm and blown the start whistle on a brutal game of tug-of-war.

Was she a woman who ended relationships? Or one who began them? Was there any way to be both? Not when the Dan in question still had a girlfriend there wasn't.

Less than twenty minutes ago she'd been hiring an actor to play Thea's faux-busive boyfriend for this week's set-up. Now she was sitting cross-legged on the floor of Gus's school library at parents' evening about to die of a cuteness overload. Watching Dan fold his long-legged body into one of the tiny reading chairs was a level of adorable she could hardly bear. Little kids leant on him the way they leant on Gus when they read aloud. His big arm looped around their small, little-kid shoulders as their parents watched on, breath held, tears glittering in their eyes as they dealt with a heady cocktail of joy, pride and disbelief. It was slaying her.

Dan Buchanan was born to be a dad. It was making her ovaries ache. Mallory was here too. With spring in full bloom, she'd arrived at the library saying she always loved parents' evening, but something told Ellie that even though the topic remained unmentioned, Mallory had really come for an update on the Dan and Ellie situation. Current status? Confusing. After that soul-quenching kiss of theirs, they'd agreed that nothing romantic could happen between them until Dan spoke with Sadie. Something he'd failed to do all week. He wasn't prevaricating or putting off the inevitable. Her phone was just never on. As such, they were living a sort of costume drama courtship, minus the haberdashery. They flirted. They blushed. The merest proximity or touch sent them both into paroxysms of response. She'd tried the toothbrush thing again and it had worked, like, really fast. It was awesome.

And it was all a form of torture she wasn't sure she had the strength to endure. Because the truth was, at some point, this would all have to come to an end. Dan would know what being loved felt like, she'd have to do something to bring it to an end because that's what Softer Landings did. He'd move on and Ellie would be left a husk of the woman she'd finally realised she could be. On the plus side, Dan had finally got so tired of trying to have a private talk with Sadie he now left his notebook with her number in it out on the kitchen table, which meant Ellie could surreptitiously try too. No luck thus far.

'He's got those kids eating out of the palm of his hands,' Mallory leant over and whispered. 'He should've been a teacher.'

Mallory was right. Dan was nailing it. After another few moments of open ogling, Mallory propped her chin on the backs of her fingers. 'I think he's one of those rare breeds who's good at anything he sets his mind to apart from seeing what's in front of his face.' She gave Ellie a knowing look.

Okay. That was a pointed comment. When Ellie spoke, her voice was high. Nervous. 'I actually think he's a bit more aware of things than some people give him credit for.'

'Okay,' said Mallory.

'He's calling Sadie.'

'Alright,' said Mallory.

'And I'm going to tell him all about Softer Landings and, you know, everything.'

'Oh?'

Okay, so maybe she wasn't going to tell him, like, *everything* everything.

'You do what you think is best, honey,' said Mallory. 'Just make sure you're listening to this and to this.' She pointed to Ellie's heart and head.

Before she could think of anything to say, Ellie's attention was snagged to the front of the room where Dan had turned into a human climbing frame. Three six-year-olds were clambering all over him, fighting to get hold of the book he was holding above them. She smiled, felt her heart soften, then heard herself commit to the dream she hadn't let herself believe again until now.

'Do you think I should start with telling him I'm going to get my masters in relationship counselling? You know . . . to make Softer Landings sound more legitimate?'

Mallory sounded out a neutral-ish *mmhmmm* and left it there.

'I am,' she whispered. Hotly.

'Okay,' said Mallory.

'I am!'

A few parents turned to stare.

Ellie blustered, 'I am . . . PROUD . . . of all of you.' She swooped her arm around the room in a grand gesture, then started a round of applause for the children, slowly taken up by the confused-looking parents. 'And how about some applause for the amazing Gus!'

Everyone complied. One of the children who had been getting very excited by the book-grabbing took advantage of the distraction and threw herself on to Dan's knee. His foot slipped out from its position and cracked against the other foot. He gave a cry of pain. There was a strange hissing noise. When all of the kids withdrew, one of the parents gasped and two of the children began to cry while one went gape-mouthed and pointed.

Dan's foot had fallen off. His recovery was faster than anyone else's.

'Oops,' he said, his smile mischievous. Then, 'Surprise! It's International Prosthetic Day!'

The children fell about laughing. The parents, not so much, but Dan's relaxed demeanour eased everyone back into the mood they had all just been in: positive and good-humoured.

Mallory was shaking her head back and forth.

'What?' Ellie asked, mortified her outburst had led to this.

'That boy is something else.' She fixed Ellie with a stern gaze. 'You better do right by him.'

Ellie felt the words ricochet around her insides. She knew. He was an extraordinary man who deserved to be loved by someone unencumbered by secret professions that involved holding thousands of his girlfriend's pounds in exchange for winning his heart. If she had to call the president of Nigeria himself to send out a search party and make Sadie turn on her damn phone, she would do it. This wasn't a question of life or death. True love was at stake. And nothing trumped true love. Not on her watch.

Two hours later Dan still had the giggles. 'Did you see their faces? It was like watching a swarm of Macaulay Culkins doing the *Home Alone* scream. Hilarious.' He happy-sighed, then beckoned to Ellie to join him on the couch. 'C'mere. Snuggle with me.'

She drew back. 'I thought we agreed that was dangerous.'

'We did, but . . . I have some grown-up talking to do with you, young lady.'

He did? Oh lord. 'Sure. I can be grown-up.' She silly-walked to the sofa. 'What's up?'

He waited until she had curled up on to the couch with him, his arm tucked around her shoulders, a soft kiss dropped on top of her head. He took her hand in his and played with it, his fingers slipping up and down each of hers as if he was confirming that she was a living, breathing being.

'I wanted to thank you,' he finally said.

'For what?' She twisted round so she was facing him. His hand slipped to her knee. His expression grew earnest, a picture postcard American Dan face. If he were a portrait it would be called *The Sum of Things* or *Rumination*.

He looked up at her, their eyes catching – as they so often did – with a physical reverberation. 'Thank you for accepting me how I am. Faults and all.'

'What? Don't be daft.'

'Well . . .' He began picking at a tiny thread on the seam of his jeans. 'You've seen me go through a few things. The leg's the most obvious, of course. It will have knock-on effects to some things in my life, but . . . it's more the emotional side of things I've been thinking about.'

'How do you mean?'

He teased at the thread some more then left it so he could look her straight in the eye. 'You've seen me date two people who were very unlike the type of person I'd actually like to end up with.'

Really?

'Well . . . I'm not exactly in a place to cast aspersions in that department.'

He gave her a look that suggested he thought she was talking rubbish. If only he knew.

'I just . . . I hope you know that I'm not exactly proud of what went down with Sadie.'

'What do you mean?'

He heaved out a sad sigh. 'She had a relationship back in Cape Town. One I knew she wanted to continue, but they were "on a break" after a disagreement about children.'

Her stomach clenched. He'd known all along. Dan continued, 'She wanted a fling. I was at loose ends. We both figured why the hell not? They were on a break, right? No one would be any the wiser, so no one would get hurt. And then . . .' He put his fingertips together, bounced them apart and mouthed *kaboom*.

Ellie felt the explosion in her gut.

He looked away, regained his interest in the thread on his jeans, teasing and teasing it until finally, with a yank, he tugged it free. 'It's just . . . Sadie was amazing. She stuck by me, did all the rehab stuff. Told her guy back home it was over, even though I knew in here it wasn't.' He poked himself in the chest.

Ellie voiced a hunch that bordered on questionable. 'Do you think she's really in Nigeria?'

'Yeah,' he said. 'I do. I think she's paying penance.'

'How do you mean?'

'I think she's torturing herself because she doesn't want to be with me but she wants to do the right thing by me.'

'Which is . . . ?'

'Show her gratitude for saving her life by staying with me. Which makes me feel like a proper asshole, you know? First, because I didn't pull the plug before she left. I mean, Nigeria can be dangerous. And now, dumping her by phone to say thanks but no thanks I've found what I really want? It doesn't really show much gratitude for what she's sacrificed.'

'Oh, I don't think—'

'Ellie,' he cut her off. 'She ended her relationship with a man I know she loved for me. But when I saw you again – I knew it wouldn't work.'

As amazing as that was to hear, Ellie became very, very scared. Swallowing against a huge lump of I'm-not-entirely-sure-I-want-to-hear-the-answer, she asked 'Why didn't you tell her how you felt before she left?'

He doofed himself on the forehead. 'I was all muddled up. It took me a while to realise what I was feeling for you was a lot stronger than what I was feeling for her. Loyalty and love are different beasts, and when we first got back I wasn't able to separate the two. She saw it, though.'

'You think?' Oh god. She was definitely going to burn in hell for playing the fool.

'It took me a few weeks, but . . . I think Sadie saw the writing on the wall straight away. Saw it, moved a few chess pieces around, put you right under my nose so I'd finally see what I was meant to. I bet you any amount of money that's what she did. Organised this whole thing.'

A snip at five thousand pounds. If he wanted actual figures.

His features shadowed as he began to berate himself for not stopping her. For not insisting she go home to South Africa and her ex instead of doing the mission in Nigeria.

Tears floated in his eyes when he asked, 'Do you think less of me? For what I did?'

'No.' She really didn't. 'They say it takes two to tango, so . . .'

Dan shook his head. 'It takes one to stand up and call a spade a spade.'

Ellie's stomach churned. This was a thousand times more awful than she'd imagined it would be. Like being filled with tar and acid. Maybe . . . as they were in confessional mode . . . maybe this would be the best time to explain . . .

Dan took both of her hands in his and gave the backs of each of them a kiss. 'Anyway . . . the way things have been between us lately, since the race . . . It's been a game changer. I'm not asking for promises or guarantees because I know life doesn't work like that, but, knowing that you care about me, despite everything, the secrets I've kept, it's . . . I like that being with you is making me a better man. And that I might be lucky enough to have a woman in my life who cares more about what happens in here' – he pointed to his heart – 'than down there.' He pointed at his foot, which was, for the first time in their shared life, sitting apart from him, now that Gus had learnt that it wasn't a chew toy.

'Oh, well . . . I'm sure Sadie didn't mind—'

'She did,' Dan quickly disabused her. 'Not necessarily because of the actual physical loss, but all the memories that came with it. Look, I know there's a long road ahead, but I feel I've come on actual emotional miles since you've become part of my life. Without knowing you, I wouldn't have had the strength to deal with the kids the way I did today when my foot fell off. It was so rewarding, you know? Not the screaming part,' he added with a snort, 'but seeing them laugh and hold the prosthetic and look at it and then forget about it . . . It was cool. A reminder that what's physically broken in me isn't what's important. This is.' He pointed at his heart, then hers. He looked ear-to-ear happy. 'I am strongly considering chopping off all of the right legs on my trousers as a public declaration of my gratitude to you, Ellie Shaw.'

Ellie laughed, privileged and awed to be part of this moment. To have played even the tiniest role in it. And equally horrified at how they'd arrived here. She swiftly rammed the feelings into a cupboard and kicked the door shut as Dan pulled her into a hug and, despite a vow not to, kissed her.

To avoid the increasing awkwardness of saying goodnight to one another without accidentally on purpose diving into bed together, when Dan succumbed to a yawn, she suggested he head to bed and she'd take Gus out for a final perambulation.

His smile softened. 'Say perambulation again.'

She did.

'Say caterpillar.'

She did.

He smiled, then let it fade. 'Do you think this is right? What's happening between us?'

'I hope so.'

'Me too, buttercup.' He grabbed his crutches, they rose, and when neither of them moved, he ran his finger along her jawline. 'Me too.' He kissed the top of her head and pulled her in close. *Mmnn.* Crumpets and strawberries tonight. 'I'll keep on trying.' He didn't need to explain. They both knew he meant settling things with Sadie.

'Maybe you should wait until she gets back,' Ellie said into his chest.

'Maybe,' he said into her hair, then pulled back, his hands resting loosely on her hips. 'It's probably super-dickish to break up with someone on the phone. God. Could you imagine if I texted her. Who even does that?'

Ohhhh boy.

Chapter Thirty-Two

Ellie scanned the outdoor eating area at the Regent's Park cafe one more time. They'd got the tables they wanted. The actor, Callum, was here. Thea was here. They'd already had a little run-through of the scene. Despite Ellie telling Callum this genuinely wasn't an audition for something bigger (he'd been put forward by Flicka Bright, who was now enjoying a much higher profile after her character came out on a live episode), he insisted upon going method. He sat them down and ran them through a panoply of accents and character choices. Thea, already bored after the first one, said she didn't give a flying fuck. Ellie said they all seemed pretty good to her but thought that the Reggie Kray accent was, possibly, a bit too full on. In the end they flipped a coin and got the Estuary English boyfriend whose simmering rage was inspired by the 'inherent and near untameable but perpetually undermined masculinity of the classic *TOWIE* male'. Whatever that was. All they needed now was for Amy Starling (their client) and her sister, Alexandra (their unsuspecting client), to arrive.

After a final check that Callum's earpiece was working, he excused himself for a short walk to 'get in character' before the Starling sisters arrived. Before turning her phone off for the duration of the set-up as they normally would, Thea wiggled her screen in front of Ellie. 'Look.'

Ellie's heart softened. 'Awww. Hugging kittens. You never post kittens.'

'I know, right?' Thea scrunched her nose, like she was fighting off tears.

Ellie, who knew better than to acknowledge the unusual show of emotion, took the phone and scrutinised the post. 'Hey!' She beamed. 'Simon liked it.'

'He did?' Thea grabbed the phone and stared at it as the tears she'd been trying to keep at bay trickled down her cheeks.

'Have you thought about calling him?' Ellie asked.

'Nah.' Thea swiped at her cheeks and, after thumbing through a few gifs turned the phone to Ellie. 'I was thinking of sending this one later.'

It featured a kitten trying to catch some goldfish on an iPad screen. Ellie laughed. 'I bet he'll love it.'

Thea shrugged her *doesn't matter* shrug again. It did, of course. It mattered a lot. Thea frowned and gave a distracted nod. 'What about Dan?' She was still thumbing through kitten gifs.

'What about him?'

Thea gave her a look. 'Has he dumped Sadie yet?'

'Not strictly speaking.'

Before Ellie could explain, Thea said, 'That's so fucked up about his leg.'

'I know. I don't know how I would've coped in the same circumstances.'

'Have you touched it? The stump?'

Ellie gave Thea her version of a look.

'Gawd, just asking. I totally would've touched it right away.' She gave her hair a scrub. 'I have to admit, I was surprised Sadie told him about the other guy. I underestimated her.'

316

Ellie agreed, then gave herself a little wriggle and shook her hands out. 'Okay. Right. Dan's actually going to meet me here in an hour with Gus, so hopefully they'll show—' She suddenly pointed to the patio doorway, where the Starling sisters had just appeared. Amy, the one who'd got in touch with them, was looking round. 'Heads up. Here we go.' Thea scuttled off to her seat so that Amy would know which table to pick. They'd never done a scenario like this before. Alexandra was in a relationship her sister and family felt was toxic. Their pleas for her to end the relationship had fallen on deaf ears. 'She can excuse every single thing he says, and some of the stuff is proper vile,' Amy had said.

After a couple of Skype sessions, they'd decided having outsiders interfere would only make it worse. So instead, they were going to try to shine a light on her boyfriend's behaviour by having Thea and Callum re-enact some of the interchanges Amy and her family had witnessed with Alexandra. Maybe then, they reasoned, she'd be able to see what was happening in her own relationship. Judging by their body language, Amy and Alexandra were very close. Thanks to Thea's microphone, Ellie could hear them talking about their days at work, how their parents were, whether or not Alexandra had worn that top they'd bought down at Primark.

'Nico wasn't much of a fan.' Alexandra fiddled with her teaspoon.

'What? You looked well cute in it when we tried it on.'

'Maybe I'll wear it when he's away. He's got a business trip next week.'

'Are you actually telling me—' Amy stopped herself. 'That's cool. Weather's meant to be better anyway.'

You could tell Amy wanted to protest, but they'd recommended she dial back her frustrations and let Thea and Callum's role play do the work for her. Alexandra needed to know her family would be there for her because she was going to need them when and if they successfully 'showed her the light'.

Callum entered in a much more grandiose style than they'd discussed. The patio area was surrounded by a waist-height wrought-iron fence. He hurdled it like a parkour guy and slid himself into the chair across from Thea. It made him look very, very cool. She leant in for a kiss. He half leant in then pulled back.

'What are you even wearing?' He flicked his hand at Thea. 'Fuck's sake. You could see that bloody cardigan of yours a mile off.'

She meekly looked up at him, said sorry, and began peeling off the brightly coloured cardigan.

They began to talk about his day. It had been alright, but it would've been better if she hadn't kept interrupting his work with her endless stream of texts.

'I only texted you once.'

'Yeah, well, that was one too many times, wasn't it?' he said with a bang of his fist on the table. They had Amy and Alexandra's attention now.

Thea and Callum sat back in their chairs as the server approached and slid a tray of baked goods on to the table.

He was kind and polite to the server, jokey even. When she'd gone, his voice got low and aggressive. 'What the hell is this?'

'It's tea time,' Thea said. 'I thought you might like some.'

'First of all, you better not be planning on eating any of it, because we discussed your weight situation already, yeah?'

Amy shot Alexandra a look. Alexandra, now openly watching, winced. 'And second of all, is this your version of a joke? Because if it is, it ain't funny.'

'No. I seriously thought you'd want some cake.'

Ellie shivered. She felt as if she had wandered on to the set of a domestic violence film. There were quite a few other people around, all of whom were now openly earwigging. Ellie was genuinely shocked that no one was interfering. Which did beg the question, would she have if she wasn't the puppet master?

Callum was on a roll now. He arrowed his index fingers at the food. 'It's full of car–bo–hy–drates, innit? You know I'm on the keto.'

Thea mumbled an apology. She obviously hadn't thought.

'No, you didn't, didja?'

'Why don't I order something else? I think they have protein balls or something. Fruit. You can eat fruit, right?'

Ellie squirmed. She was getting properly sucked in by Thea's performance.

Callum scowled and blew out a nasty 'Puh-lease.' As if Thea's offer of help disgusted him. 'You do you, boo. I'll do me.' He picked up the tray, walked over to the rubbish bin and dumped the entire contents of the tray inside. Plates and all. Amy and Alexandra looked horrified, but, like everyone else in the café, they said nothing. Ellie watched, catching a glimpse of a golden retriever off in the distance. She smiled, thinking she must have a sixth sense for the breed. There were quite a few people on the path so she couldn't quite make out who was walking the dog.

'What shall I order you?' Thea was asking. 'C'mon, babes. My treat, yeah?'

'I'll do it myself, arright?'

Ellie's attention was shifting between Thea and the dog. There was something extra-familiar about the gait of . . . Oh . . . no. Time took on a different, ethereal quality. But not the dreamy kind. The nightmare kind. As gripping as it was, Thea and Callum's performance blurred into white noise as the feet and their now very recognisable gait pulled into focus alongside Gus. She couldn't look up. She couldn't do anything.

'Ellie?'

She looked up. *Oh shit.* It was, of course, none other than Dan. Gus bounded over and demanded cuddles. They were early. Far too early.

'Hey!' Dan gave her a peck on the cheek, then pulled out the chair across from her and sat down. 'I didn't think you'd be here this early.'

'Hey! No, me either.'

Despite telling herself not to, she threw a panicked glance in Thea's direction just as Callum was grabbing her wrist. Callum was properly in character now. In a much louder voice than Ellie would've hoped, he growled, 'Put that ridiculous cardigan back on. You look like a proper slag, dressed like that.'

Alexandra looked horrified.

So, unfortunately, did Dan. He was up and out of his chair before Ellie could stop him. 'Hey, bud. Let go of her,' he commanded, and then he realised who it was. 'Thea? What's going on here? Is this your boyfriend?'

Callum, confused, shot Ellie a look. She was too shocked to say anything. Callum, clearly taking her silence as a cue that Dan had been sent in to riff off for the scene, kept hold of Thea's wrist and, emanating rage, gravelled, 'This is a private matter, *bud*, and I would kindly ask you to step aside.'

'Take your hands off her, pal.'

'I'm not your pal.'

Dan pulled out his phone. His energy was concentrated and powerful. Heroic. Alexandra was cowering in her seat, her eyes glued to Dan. 'I'm calling the police. Let go of her. Now.'

Callum didn't.

Dan started dialling.

Ellie screamed, 'No!'

Dan looked at her, completely confused and also horrified. 'What do you mean, no? This jackass is being physically abusive to your friend. How could you not have seen her? Thea? Why didn't you ask Ellie for help?'

Alexandra looked very confused. Amy dropped her face into her hands.

Callum released Thea's wrist with an apology, his voice low as he put his hand on Dan's shoulder. Dan brusquely shifted it off.

'Hey.' Callum raised his hands. 'Easy there, mate. I think you've blown it now that you've dropped the fourth wall.' He tipped his head towards Amy and Alexandra, who were gathering up their things to go. 'Apologies, ladies. Hope that did the trick.'

'What are you even talking about?' Dan asked.

'It's a set-up, isn't it?' Callum said, in his normal voice. He shifted back to his *TOWIE* accent. 'We wuz play-acting, innit? Thea?'

She was speaking to Amy and Alexandra, apologising over and over for upsetting their coffee date. Offering to pay for it. Everything. Even the fee.

Amy's eyes bulged.

'What fee?' Alexandra asked. 'Amy? What is going on here?'

Thea blanched and threw a 'help' look at Ellie.

Ellie was frozen to the spot. This was the most horrific day ever.

'Will one of you please tell me what's going on?' Dan demanded. Gus left Ellie's side and went and sat by Dan.

Amy shuttled Alexandra out of the café, hissing a very pointed, 'Fanks for nuffink,' over her shoulder as they left.

Callum looked confused. 'Do you think that was a comment on my accent? Did it lack authenticity?'

No one was really paying attention to Callum.

'Ellie,' Dan asked again, his voice level, but in a scary way, 'could you please explain to me what the fuck is going on?'

Thea jumped in. 'It was something for me, actually . . .'

'Am I still going to get paid?' Callum asked.

Dan's eyes bored into Ellie's. 'Why is this joker expecting payment?' He flicked his thumb at Callum, who decided now would be a pretty good time to leave.

'I'll just . . .' He jumped over the fence the same way he'd entered and started running.

'Dan, it's not—' Ellie began.

'She's helping people,' Thea interjected.

'Really? Because from where I was standing, it was looking an awful lot like you were getting hurt.'

'No,' Thea persisted. 'We do this. For work. We set things up so couples who are struggling can see a better path. This one was really different to what we normally do.'

'Oh?' said Dan, eyes widening. 'And what's "normal" in the recruitment business?'

Thea swallowed and took a step backwards.

Ellie sunk into her chair. 'I think you'd better sit down.'

Thea, bless her, stayed on as Ellie's 'emotional support human' as Gus had chosen Team Dan. In the larger scheme of things, she understood Gus's call. Dan was the one who was being dealt the biggest blow here, but Ellie already knew she'd be the one who hurt the most when it was over.

She forced herself to look him in the eye and told him about Softer Landings.

'So . . . people pay you to end their relationships,' Dan said after a very long and very painful silence.

'Yes.'

'And this all came about after you broke up with me for Thea.'

'And my super-slutty period of rebounding. My bad.' Thea pointed at herself. 'If you want to blame anyone, you should blame me.'

'But Ellie's the mastermind,' Dan said. It wasn't a question.

'Well . . .' Thea struggled with this one. 'She is the most skilled at it.'

'I used to break up with my sister's boyfriends for her,' Ellie said in a rush. 'Ever since junior school.'

'Oh!' Dan said. 'I see. Well, that makes it alright, then. Because you're a seasoned hand at it. Got it.' He tapped the side of his nose, his face twisting into a withering *are you fucking kidding me* look.

'No. That's not what I'm saying. It's more . . . I didn't like seeing them tortured – seeing *you* tortured – by someone who clearly didn't want to be in a relationship with you. Sorry, Thea.'

'No offence taken.'

Ellie shot her a grateful smile.

Thea started explaining how they'd set things up, create an artificial proximity or scenario so that they could highlight how a relationship wasn't working for the potential dumpee so that they could leave the relationship without feeling like a complete and utter jackass.

Dan thought for a moment, then gave a scary, humourless laugh. 'Everything you've explained sounds exactly like what's been happening between me, Sadie and Ellie.'

Ellie felt the colour drain from her face.

'Oh my god.' Dan's expression was wreathed in disbelief. 'Is that what this has been, Ellie? A set-up?'

She said nothing.

Thea looked like she was going to be sick.

Dan cocked his head to the side, as if the different view of her would help him get the facts straight. 'You know Sadie rang today?'

She shook her head, her lungs straining against the pain of not breathing. But she couldn't. She didn't deserve oxygen. She didn't deserve anything at all.

'She's on her way back. Wants to talk. I was this close to telling her about you and me.' He held up a pinch of air. 'This fucking close, Eleanor.'

She shuddered at the name change.

'Dan,' Thea cut in. 'Ellie loves you. She didn't want to do this. She's tried to give Sadie back her money half a dozen times. More!'

Dan laughed again, clapped his hands together. 'This is rich. Wow.' He tipped his face into his hands, swept them through his hair then looked directly into Ellie's eyes. 'You are the last person in the world I would've thought could do something like this.'

She said nothing. He was right. She was a horrible, horrible person.

'Ellz!' Thea gave her hand a squeeze. 'Defend yourself, mate. Softer Landings is legit. So are your feelings for Dan.'

The tears she had so far kept at bay began to surface. She really didn't want to cry in front of him. When it became clear Ellie wasn't going to defend herself, Thea reeled on Dan. 'You listen to me, Dan Buchanan. This woman here loves you. It may not seem that way right now, but I have never in my life met anyone more loyal or true than Ellie Shaw. And what she's done? It might seem bad right now, but I think a careful look at any rom-com filmography will make it clear that this sort of thing is not new.' She put her fists up between them then started lifting fingers as she rattled off film titles. '*Cyrano, While You Were Sleeping, Guys and Dolls, The Philadelphia Story* – you love *The Philadelphia Story*.'

They paused to wait for a response from Dan.

No response.

Thea continued. '*It Happened One Night, When Harry met Sally*, like, five times in *When Harry Met Sally*. *Twelfth Night*. William fucking Shakespeare, Dan! If Shakespeare did it, Ellie can do it because her heart is in the right place, just like bloody Viola when she's head over heels for Orsino. Olivia and Orsino weren't a good match. *We* weren't a good match. Just like you know you're not meant to be with Sadie. You should be with Ellie. End of.' She dropped a mic.

Again, they waited for a response.

Nothing.

He just sat there, blankly staring at them. Ellie had no concept if it had been one minute or twenty. It felt like a lifetime. And then, as if he'd made a decision, Dan shifted Gus's lead from one hand to the other, got up and left.

Chapter Thirty-Three

Ellie spent the night at Thea's in the end. She arrived in a stupor, barely capable of speech. She and Dan hadn't exchanged a word as she'd packed up her duffel bags, dropped to the floor to silently sob into Gus's ruff as she bade him farewell, finally forcing herself to slip out of the flat after placing her key on the hallway table. Leaving Gus behind had been like ripping part of her own body off, but she guessed she deserved as much, seeing as Dan would be living with that exact, very real pain for the rest of his life. All of it, everything, was her fault.

Thea was a surprisingly good post-break-up buddy. No pressing questions. No cries of dismay when Ellie sobbed about not knowing if she wanted to franchise Softer Landings or keep the London branch open any more. She didn't know anything. Just that everything hurt. Thea kept her in tissues and supplied mounds of discounted profiteroles from Waitrose that they ate like peanuts. One after the other until she felt sicker than she already had.

Vee, to whom she told the truth, the whole truth and nothing but the truth, was understanding when Ellie asked if she could shutter the business for a bit to regroup. After twisting the blinds closed on the windows of her office, Vee slid a huge mug of 'plain old builder's tea' in front of Ellie along with a packet of caramel

Hobnobs she'd pulled from her desk drawer. 'The only cure for a proper shock, darls. Don't you think?'

After taking a half-moon bite out of her biscuit, Ellie said, 'You knew I'd faceplant, didn't you? Make a hash of the business.'

Vee gave a shrug indicating, yes, she had thought as much.

'Why? Why'd you let me give up something safe when you knew I'd fail?'

'You see this as failure?' Vee looked properly concerned.

'Yes?!' Ellie spluttered. Her business model had been blown to bits, Simon had quit, and Thea had begrudgingly admitted she'd seriously need to start looking for another job if Ellie wasn't going to give her a date to start things up again. If that wasn't failure . . .

Vee fixed Ellie with a look. 'Believe it or not, businesses do not always run smoothly. If I expected every idea I invested in to run like clockwork, I'd be a fool. Listen, dollface, you have yourself a great idea. Getting it up and running as a going concern always meant hitting some bumps in the road. But focus on the positive. You have created a proactive, dynamic approach to an age-old problem. One that's not just limited to relationships. Ending things is a classic HR problem, which, by the way, is an area you might want to consider if you decide to throw in the towel. Not here of course . . . burnt bridges and all that, but . . .' She held up her hand to say it wasn't necessary to worry about that now. 'What I think has tripped you *and* Simon *and* Thea up here was a failure to look at the bigger picture.'

'What do you mean?'

Vee's smile was kind. 'Simon was avoiding Diego's death by pouring himself into other people's problems. Thea is bored out of her skull and needs to figure out what it is she really wants to do with her life – something that gives her a sense of pride. Of passion. And you, my little chickadee . . .'

Ellie held her breath. This was going to be really, really bad.

'. . . you need to realise that you're enough. You're lovable just as you are. You don't need to sort out everyone else's problems in order to be valued as a good person because you already are a good person.'

Tears trickled down Ellie's cheeks. 'I don't feel like a good person.'

'I know.' Vee nudged a box of tissues towards her. 'But sometimes you have to go through a proper life-changing disaster to see what's left standing.'

'I guess I was an idiot to think being dumped by Sebastian was disaster enough.'

Vee gave a nod that read as a silent *amen to that*. 'If he'd really broken your heart, you wouldn't have come back fighting the way you did. My guess is you were more disappointed in yourself than in him.'

It was a valid point. One she'd definitely have to slot into place once she had some space between her and what had happened with Dan.

They talked a bit more, hugged and, after it was agreed that so far as Vee was concerned this was a temporary closure, Ellie walked back out into the streets of London with one question in her head: what next?

Decision made, she called in on Mallory, who, as if she'd been handed a baton, doled out tissues and biscuits as Ellie sobbed out her story again, this time including the part about how Dan would be Mallory's point of contact for Gus now because the one thing they had agreed on was that Gus had found his calling at the school. Mallory hugged her and wished her well and told her she was always welcome to visit Gus during school hours. A kind gesture that they both knew was too painful to accept right now. And, anyway, she was going back to Jersey for Aurora's wedding, so . . . visiting wasn't really an option.

When, at last, she packed her bag to go, Ellie felt as if she'd gone full circle. In a bad way. She was leaving London almost as she'd arrived: heartbroken, with nothing more than two duffel bags stuffed with a hodgepodge of clothes, no job and no idea what was next. As she waited on the platform at Paddington to catch the Heathrow Express, her phone rang. It was Thea. As much as she didn't want to talk to anyone right now, she owed it to Thea to answer it. She'd gone above and beyond these past few days.

'Diego's died.'

Everything turned into a blur.

Simon, Thea screeched, was losing the plot. 'I don't know what to do.' Thea was pretty near hysteria herself. 'He just keeps rocking back and forth, saying, "Get me out of here. Get me out of here."'

Ellie cancelled her flight and went straight to Simon's, where they mopped up tears, kept him hydrated and absorbed as much of his grief as they could, so that above all, the one thing he knew was that he was not alone.

A couple of days later, after coming to the conclusion that perhaps a change of scene would be a good thing for all of them, Thea, Simon and Ellie all checked into a flight to Jersey.

Once they'd got through security, Thea guided them straight to the bar, where they ordered drinks so that they could toast Diego. They did and, after a few moments' silent reflection, Thea asked, 'Are you sure your sister won't mind? Us crashing her wedding?' She took a huge glug of her margarita and clutched her hands to her head. 'Brain freeze.'

'Course she won't,' Simon said, flicking his fingers on Thea's forehead. 'Distraction technique,' he explained. 'Who doesn't want three misery guts at their wedding? Even if Aurora's day turns out to be shit – which it won't – she can be assured it will be better than ours, right?'

Ellie didn't have a clue what Aurora or her mother would say. She hadn't had the heart to tell them on the phone. And anyway, she'd arrive home, her failures plastered on her like travel stickers on a steamer trunk. It was time to show her family who she really was.

In the end, she needn't have worried. Her mother met them at the airport with open arms. She looked different somehow. Her hair was still pulled back into a loose French twist, but her sense of style was . . . not changed exactly . . . but more purposeful than it had been.

'My darling girl,' she said over and over as she pulled Ellie into her arms. 'My darling, darling, girl. At last you've come home.'

Later, after Thea and Simon had been shown how to work the remote for the new telly in the Presidential Suite – a pair of adjoining rooms Ellie was delighted to see had received a proper, modern makeover – she and her mother sat down for a long-overdue talk.

'How's it been?' they both asked. 'You first.' They both laughed.

'Please,' her mother managed before Ellie could insist again. 'Tell me. Let me be mum for once.'

The comment should have hurt. Instead, after all of these years of trying to keep the family together as best she could, it soothed. Words flowed along with the tears. She started at the beginning, of course. There was no other way to do it. Her mum nodded along in a way that almost made it seem as if she'd already heard the story when it suddenly occurred to Ellie that she had. 'Who told you?'

'Sebastian's grandparents. Well, Aurora really.' Her mother's smile was sad but proud. 'When we didn't hear from you after you went off to London, Aurora stormed down to their house and demanded they ring Sebastian and find out what had happened. He'd said he'd seen you after . . .' Her mum twirled her finger round.

'After I saw him with his girlfriend?' Ellie filled in.

'Yes. After that.' Her mother's features tightened. 'There'd always been something about that boy, something . . .'

'Vile?' Ellie suggested.

'Yes,' her mother agreed with a grimace. 'That's probably a good word to put a pin on.'

They smiled at one another, shyly, and then it shifted into understanding. Her mother reached out and held her daughter's hands, rubbing her thumb along the backs of them, over and over, as if smoothing away any rough edges the two of them might have encountered through the years, paving the way for a smoother future. Ellie felt a warming kinship with her mother she'd never experienced before. An equality. They had both loved and lost. Admittedly, in very different ways, but they'd each had hurdles to surmount before being able to move forward.

'Why didn't you call me out?' Ellie eventually asked. 'When I pretended we were still together.'

Her mother looked surprised. 'We love you, Ellie. We thought it was your way of processing.'

'But . . . I was outright lying to you.'

Her mother pulled her hands back, ran her finger along the rim of her teacup, a slight tremor shifting through it as she did. 'Aurora thought you needed space. From us.'

'What? Why?'

Her mum met her gaze head on. Ellie was startled to see how bright her eyes were. How alive. No longer dulled by medication or grief. 'Now don't be cross with her. I actually think she was right. You dedicated yourself to us, Ellie. For years of your life that you should have been out there dating and going to uni and whatever else young people do these days when they aren't looking after their depressed mother and wayward sister.'

Ellie went to protest. Her mother stopped her. 'We needed the space too. Aurora and I.'

A twist of shame squeezed in her gut. She really was a micro-managing control freak. Little wonder Aurora hadn't spoken to her until now. 'Not from your love. Or your care,' her mother quickly cut in. 'For that we were grateful. But we needed to see what life was like without you. I don't think either of us realised just how much you did to keep us running.'

'I shouldn't have left like that.'

'Well . . .' Her mum opened her hands up. 'At first we thought so too, but then, once we realised just how much you'd sacrificed to keep us afloat, we started looking at everything from a different angle. Your angle. And that's when we both had to plumb deep. Find out what was really going on in here.' She tapped her chest. 'It turns out Aurora and I had more resilience than we thought we had, but only because we both fell flat on our faces first.'

Ellie pressed her fingers to her eyes then peeked out from between them. 'I'm so sorry.'

'Don't be. We might have carried on in the same old patterns forever if you hadn't taken matters into your own hands.'

Ellie had never really looked at it like that. When she'd left, it had felt like running away. Maybe, like Vee had intimated, she'd known she'd needed a change and had, consciously or not, put herself in the most impossible situation to see how she fared. Not very well, from the looks of things. Then again, she was regaining her mum and, hopefully, her sister. But she had lost the most important man in her life and, of course, the most important dog. Tears welled up in her eyes again.

Her mum gave her hand a squeeze. 'Why don't you go rest up? You look exhausted. Rauri's got a few projects that need sorting before the wedding and I think you're just the person to help her.'

'Oh, I'm sure she doesn't want me butting in. She'd probably already got a maid of honour helping her?'

'Yes, she does.' Her mother rose and cupped Ellie's face in her hand. 'And her name is Eleanor Shaw.'

Aurora, it turned out, had lots of projects and required no in-depth conversations about what had passed between them apart from an assurance that Ellie would under no circumstances ever date any future divorce lawyers ever again.

'Don't worry,' Ellie assured her. 'That ship has long since sailed.' Her lower lip quivered.

Aurora noticed. She made a beckoning gesture. 'Out with it. Who do I need to beat up for my big sister?'

Ellie, humbled by her sister's open, non-judgemental love for her, told her everything about American Dan, including the way he smelt like a tropical gingerbread man and, sometimes, a wood-chopping Viking.

'Well, someone needs to jump on a plane and beg your forgiveness,' Aurora concluded.

'You think?' Ellie pulled a face. 'No. That's not going to happen.' She'd hurt Dan permanently. Far more deeply than Thea or Sadie ever had. And there was no undoing that sort of betrayal.

'He better give you your dog back.'

Ellie teared up for the thousandth time. 'I don't think that's going to happen either.'

Aurora pulled her into a hug and squeezed her tight. 'I'll get you a million puppies if that'll make it better.'

It was a nice offer, but . . . she'd been happy with that particular one. 'C'mon. Let's get to work.'

'So, what?' Thea looked around her, acres of flowers craning upwards towards the warm, late April sun. 'We just pick them?'

Ellie scanned the field. It was a sea of colour. Ranunculi and anemones. A rainbow of chrysanthemums and germini. Chris's family had moved well beyond the traditional daffodil of days gone by. This field, Chris's wedding gift to Aurora was literally filled with thousands of her favourite flowers. Dahlias. Peonies. Freesias – and dozens more Ellie couldn't name.

She held up her pair of secateurs they'd each been handed. 'You cut them low, apparently. So Aurora can arrange them into bouquets.'

'And these are going to be the *actual* bouquets for your sister's wedding?' Thea looked as if she'd just learnt that milk came from a real cow and not a carton with a picture of a cow on it.

'Yup!'

'Don't they have florists for that?'

Ellie laughed. 'Aurora *is* the florist.'

She was so proud of her. With Chris's help, she'd set up a little shop in a converted shepherd's hut placed by the road outside Chris's family's farm. Aurora's Blooms. If the queue outside the shop was anything to go by, it was doing a roaring trade.

Simon had opted to stay in bed and 'languish in his despair', but Ellie's mum had texted her while she and Thea were picking flowers to say he'd wandered down and nibbled at the breakfast bar, along with a few of the guests, and had asked for directions to find a chemist's. And no, Ellie wasn't to worry. She had called ahead to warn the chemist that Simon wasn't to be allowed to purchase anything that might be detrimental to his health if taken in bulk.

They needn't have worried in the end. He'd bought lip salve, eye cream and a green mud mask that he was already wearing when they found him wrapped in a thick terrycloth robe on the balcony, 'offering himself' to the sun.

Later, when it clouded over and began to rain, Simon insisted they let him go to the end of the quay to play *French Lieutenant's Woman*, a book neither Thea nor Ellie had read, but it sounded dramatic and Simon was clearly exorcising his grief the only way he knew how – theatrically. Thea and Ellie found window seats at a quayside café and, keeping half an eye on Simon, began to talk.

They talked about their job options (no idea), living options (Thea said Ellie could move into hers if she wanted, especially if she regained custody of Gus), and what they could do to keep Simon's spirits up both before and after the funeral (hip-hop dance classes; a make-up artist course; a chemical peel). When conversation inevitably came round to Dan, Thea rearranged herself a few times, avoided their eye contact and then, eventually, asked, 'Do you know why I didn't sleep with him?'

Oh god. Ellie didn't want to go there. 'Who? Simon?'

Thea pursed her lips. It was a pathetic dodge and they both knew it. 'American Dan.'

Ellie shook her head. She hadn't really wanted details on that front.

'I didn't sleep with Dan because I don't sleep with anyone these days. For the past couple of years anyway.'

'Oh! Umm . . .' Wow. Thea had always given the impression she enjoyed a healthy sexy life with a wide array of partners. By choice. 'Are you asexual?'

'Nooo . . . I am – I used to be,' she corrected, 'too sexual.'

Ellie arrowed her index fingers at herself. 'I did it with a toothbrush.'

'Did you? Good girl!' Thea beamed and then, quite plainly, announced, 'I have herpes.'

'Oh!' She hadn't seen that coming. 'I'm so sorry.'

'It's not your fault.'

'I'm guessing it isn't yours either.'

335

'Nope!' Thea bubbled her cheeks with air then popped them. 'Although I suppose I could've been more strident on the *let's use protection* front.'

Ellie thought for a minute. It wasn't her area of expertise, but she'd learnt a few things about STDs courtesy of Jersey's Summer of Syphilis – a rather tumultuous spell a few years back when Aurora had narrowly avoided being wooed and won by a particularly gorgeous French 'manny' who had made it his mission to enjoy as much 'local talent' as possible. 'Does it prevent you from having sex?'

'Sometimes. Well, you *can* have sex, but there are times when you shouldn't. If you respect your partner, that is.' Thea started picking up stray cookie crumbs with her finger pad and flicking them on to her saucer. 'If it's active, you can give it to your partner, so that's an obvious no-no time. Like, if you have a sore on your mouth you shouldn't snog anyone, but sometimes, you can't really tell what's going on down there, so it's a case of having to always tell everyone you have sex with what the situation is so that the choice is theirs in case you accidentally give it to them.'

Jeez. That sucked.

'And . . . you didn't think you could tell Dan?'

'No. The opposite. He was the first person I actually felt comfortable telling.'

Ellie could see that. Dan was a guy you could share anything with. Anything apart from the fact you'd been paid by his girlfriend to get him to fall in love with you. So, she guessed there were limits to his largesse after all. Even so . . . 'Being able to tell him is a good thing, right?'

'I thought so too, but it actually made me panic. He was so nice and so kind and accepting of it. Some guys are genuine arse-holes about it, so I thought – this is it. This is my guy.'

'Only he wasn't?'

Please say no, please say no.

Thea nodded. 'Only he wasn't. That's why I couldn't go there. It just felt wrong. Like defiling a Boy Scout.' She took a thoughtful sip of her coffee, eyes shifting to Simon. She started laughing. 'Holy mother of fuck. Would you look at that?'

Ellie followed her gaze. Simon was flinging his arms out, first left, then right, dipping down, popping up in a starburst shape. 'I bet you any money he's singing "Let It Go".'

Ellie started laughing too. It looked unbelievably freeing. 'I kind of want to join him.'

Thea was up and out of her chair in an instant. 'C'mon, then!'

Old Ellie would've said no. Old Ellie probably wouldn't have let Simon even go to the chemist's on his own, let alone stand at the end of a quay during a rainstorm. But she wasn't that Ellie any more. She'd weathered storms of her own. Had no idea which way her life would go now, but knew that somehow, some way, she would be alright. She was brave enough now to throw caution to the wind and endure the fallout. 'Let's do it.'

◆ ◆ ◆

Ellie popped her keys into her pocket and looked up at the arrivals board. She'd been shuttling people to and from the airport for three days now and this, allegedly, was the final run.

She was early. As ever. But after nearly a week of full-on Thea and Simon time, as well as maid-of-honour time with Aurora and catching up on all of her mum's hotel innovations, it was kind of nice, having this clutch of alone time. She found a stool at the edge of the coffee shop and let her mind wander as she watched the electronic doors open and close as streams of couples and singletons, business travellers and tourists arrived, eyes bright with expectation, whether or not there was anyone to meet them.

Sebastian saw Ellie before she saw him. By the time she realised who was making a beeline towards her it was too late to hide. She was surprised to discover, as he drew closer, that she didn't want to hide. For the first time ever, Sebastian Cabot looked . . . mortal.

'Ellie! Hi. Gosh.' He swept his hand through a flop of blond hair. 'What a surprise.'

'Yes.' It was, but also, weirdly, not. Something about this entire week had an otherworldly feel about it. As if the energies of the universe were colluding to give her closure on this one, crazy, tumultuous chapter in her life so that she could move, unburdened, to the next. 'What are you doing here?' she asked when he just stood there, a mystified smile on his face.

'Seeing my grandparents,' he explained. 'It's the last week Nicole can fly before—' He stopped, realising there was a whole lot to unpack there. He turned towards the exit, where the same woman she'd seen him holding hands with a year ago stood, hands pressed to her lower back, supporting the large bump protruding from her midriff.

'Wow! Congratulations.'

He began to nervously twist a ring on his wedding finger, noticed her noticing and held it up, his face turning red as he said, 'It was a really small event. Not a shotgun. It's for real—'

She surprised herself by laughing. 'Don't worry. You don't owe me explanations.'

His expression sobered. 'I do, actually. Apologies, anyway. A lot of them.' She shook her head no, but he stopped her. 'You might not know this, but you were my rock during my parents' divorce.'

He was right. She hadn't known that.

'I was such a jackass. If I could go back and change everything, change the way I treated you, I would.'

She chewed on her lip, giving genuine consideration to how her life would've been different if he had done the right thing and

338

split up with her years ago. She wouldn't have met Gus or Dan, Mallory, or Thea or Simon or Vee, for that matter. She wouldn't have had her heart broken twice, or lost the doggie love of her life either, but . . . at some point, all of that history had to become water under the bridge. Otherwise, how did a person move on? Look forward? Forgiveness, she supposed.

'It's okay,' she said. 'I think I came out a stronger person because of it.'

'That's incredibly generous of you,' he said.

'I know,' she chirped, enjoying the smile they shared that, at long last, put them on an even playing field.

They shook hands farewell, which somehow seemed more fitting than a hug, and when he crossed to his wife, Ellie heard her ask, 'Who was that?'

'A friend,' Sebastian said, turning to smile once more as he added, 'A really good friend.'

Once he'd gone she felt something lift in her. A weight she'd been vaguely aware of carrying for years, and now it was gone. What a difference an arrival-hall encounter can make.

She turned back and remembered to hold up her sign just as a pair of young men's eyes lit up and made a beeline for her. The cousins. Right then. Onwards and upwards.

◆ ◆ ◆

Aurora's wedding was, unsurprisingly, utterly incredible. Despite the entire outdoor setting having to be relocated into a not entirely beautiful village hall because of yet more unexpected downpours, Aurora's love for Chris glowed from her like sunshine. A glow he returned in spades. They were, Ellie realised, perfect for one another. Not despite their differences or multiple relationship hiccoughs, but because of what they'd gone through together. They were proof that weathering the storm reaped dividends. As individuals and as a couple. After they'd stuffed cake in one another's faces and had a frosting fight that lured most of the children in the wedding party into the fray, Ellie and Aurora escaped to the hall's lone toilet, where Ellie began the careful task of wiping the frosting off her without messing up Aurora's up-do and make-up any more than it had been.

Simon barged in, then recoiled, clearly horrified at Ellie's efforts. 'Oh god. Budge over. I've got this.'

Thea came in too, took one look at the situation and pulled an impressively large make-up bag from behind the toilet. 'What?' she asked when they all gawped at her. 'I wanted to be prepared in case, you know' – she tipped her head out to the lairy crowd – 'there were options.'

'And are there?' Aurora giggled. 'Was the guest list to your satisfaction?'

'Very much so,' Thea intoned. 'Not only are there a veritable plethora of cousins to plunder, there is a rather alluring supply of strapping young farmers to bewitch with my big-city ways.' She winked at Ellie. 'Now then.' She unzipped the make-up bag and held it open for Simon to inspect. 'Aurora first as she's the bride, but then me.'

Simon was more than happy to oblige, and Ellie, for once, was perfectly happy to sit back and watch the action unfold.

Chapter Thirty-Four

'You sure you're going to be okay without us?' Thea was already turning towards the departures lounge, so there really was only one answer here. The honest one.

'It's *stand on my own two feet* time,' Ellie insisted.

Thea threw Simon a look.

'I'll be fine! Honestly.'

'You're not going to stay out here "thinking on things" forever, are you?'

'Not at all. I need to apply for uni spots, see what kind of course I can get myself on and—' She wasn't quite sure what form Softer Landings would take from here on out but she was sure of one thing. 'I'll be back.'

Simon swiped at the air between them, aligning the wheels of his bag with the security zone. 'Just so you know, you can do all of those things in London. There's a room with your name on it at mine if you want one.'

'No, there's a room at *mine* with your name on it,' Thea said.

'She's mine,' Simon whined. 'I'm the one grieving.'

'She's mine!' Thea insisted. 'I'm the one trying to grow a soul.'

They began to play-fight. It was all wonderfully comforting.

They hugged goodbye, reiterating an earlier promise to fly back and physically drag her on to a plane if she didn't appear in London by the end of the month. After she'd waved them through security, she went round the building to the cargo area, where Aurora, now on her honeymoon, had asked her to collect a parcel for her. She hadn't said what it was, but Ellie assumed it was something to do with her flower business. But it wasn't.

It was Gus.

And it was Dan.

She froze, barely able to believe what she was seeing. What on earth were they doing here?

Could it—?

Were they—?

Should she—?

She knew she should be the first one to move, to react. But she couldn't. More than anything she wanted to freeze this moment in time and savour it as much as she could before the balloon popped, because there was no way Dan would've flown all this way *with Gus* to tell her they loved her. Right?

They were standing in an area filled with huge wooden crates and massive luggage trolleys, each wearing an expectant look on their faces. Gus wagged his tail enthusiastically when anyone approached, happy to receive the odd pat and comment on how handsome he was. Dan wore his trademark all-American smile, but it wasn't until his eyes finally lit on hers that she felt the warmth of it. And just like that her world felt complete again.

He was as gorgeous as ever. Tousle-haired, startlingly blue-eyed, a physique that would've looked perfectly at home using a phone booth as a changing room before flying off to save the world from certain destruction. He also looked tired, stressed and heart-achingly hopeful. He was holding some signs in his hands, the blank side to her. Gus – her gorgeous, fluffy, brown-eyed Gus – had one round his neck. It read, *I miss you.*

Her heart began pounding out huge, resounding, enthusiastic thumps of joy. Her stomach was beside itself – fizzing and tingling, with the odd triple-vault twist, just to show off.

Forced to dodge an incoming fork-lift moving towards them, Gus spotted her and broke away from Dan's loose grip on his lead, bounding towards her, his approach only interrupted by the bounces of joy, so exuberant they were practically vertical. Hugging him was like trying to embrace a fur-covered pogo stick. And it was bliss. When she looked up, Dan had flipped his signs over. Her heart lurched into her throat and when their eyes met, hers glassed, instantly, with tears. But she was still just about able to read the signs.

I know you hate Sign Guy . . .

(Flip.)

But I was panicked . . .

(Flip.)

I wouldn't be able to get this out . . .

(Flip.)

Without crying.

Ellie felt the first in a long queue of tears spill on to her cheek.

But the thought . . .

(Flip.)

Of never hearing you say caterpillar again . . .

(Flip.)

Nearly killed me.

She pressed her knuckles to her mouth to stem a sob. She swept some tears from her cheeks and somehow managed to say, 'Caterpillar.'

He pressed his hand to his chest. They both laughed, weird, watery laughs. She had so many questions. How could he still want to talk to her, let alone fly across an admittedly small portion of the ocean to be with her? The gesture was enormous. The biggest anyone had ever done for her. He'd not only bought a ticket and gone through all the kerfuffle of bringing Gus along, he'd made signs. Lots of them. And, more importantly, he didn't seem to hate her. He lifted the signs up again and this time she didn't even try to stem the flow of tears.

I have been a knucklehead.

(Flip.)

That's American for:

(Flip.)

I blew it.

That was the last card. Dan was staring at her, waiting for a reaction.

A knot of frustration exploded in her chest. This was why she freaking hated Sign Guy. What was she meant to do with that? She had a cute accent and he'd screwed it up by not believing her intentions had been founded in love, The End?

Ellie looked up. Dan's eyes were glassy with emotion. But not the kind that meant he was going to turn around and find himself in a piano bar where throat-scalding shots of regret were accompanied by minor chords and a not-so-happy ending. What was he trying to say to her but wasn't?

It suddenly occurred to her that this might be his way of hand-feeding her an opportunity to say thank you for the good times and walk away.

No. This was not her ending. Their ending. He was here for a reason and idiot Sign Guy was not going to ruin this for her.

He frowned at her, clearly confused by her reaction, then looked down at his empty hands, then back at her, then at the last card he'd just put on top of Gus's enormous crate. The hopeful expression he'd been wearing crumbled. A stream of surprisingly colourful language flew in an angry, self-admonishing whisper as he looked around the crate, in the crate and then, finally, groaned. 'Oh Gus.'

'What?' Ellie joked. 'Did you store them in there for the flight and he shredded the most important one?'

Dan's expression was utterly mournful. 'Yes.'

Her hand was rubbing Gus's ear like a child fretted at a corner of their favourite blankie. She gave Dan a shaky smile. 'What did it say?'

He bit his lip, clearly debating whether it worth saying it now that the taut emotional environment had changed into another, more disjointed one.

The energy zapping between them was painful. As if Cupid's arrows had been replaced by a volley of darts. She wondered if this was what being tasered felt like. Every nerve ending in your body feeling more breathtakingly alive than it ever had, but only because it was enduring excruciating pain.

She stared into those fathomless kaleidoscope eyes of his, the windows to the soul of this amazing, heroic man who had captured her heart. Apart from not being particularly organised in the grand-gestures department, he was still everything she'd adored from the instant she'd laid eyes on him. Kind, loving, more than happy to make a fool of himself if it meant making the one he loved happy. And that's when it hit her. What the final card's message must've been. It set her body ablaze with joy. But it frightened her too. If this mangled rom-com moment was all it took to make them crumble, how would they get through any of life's other hurdles together? Accepting her business for one. The truth of what she wanted bloomed from her toes all the way to the ends of her hair. She couldn't let Softer Landings go. She believed in what they did and, like any business, it wasn't perfect, but it had so much room to get better and she wanted to be the one to steer it towards that future. Like she'd learnt working with Thea and Simon, if she and Dan were going to work as a couple, they had to be a team. And the only way they could be a team was for him to know where he stood with her.

'I love you, Dan Buchanan,' she said.

'I love you too, Ellie Shaw.'

They stared at one another, delivering disbelieving, wide-eyed blinks at one another. It took another fork-lift intervention to get them to stop grinning at each other like lunatics.

'Can we kiss now?' he asked, not even waiting for her answer as he closed the space between them, cupped her face in his hands and lowered his lips on to hers as if this kiss alone had the power to change the world.

It had the power to change hers. She saw stars and rainbows and love hearts. She saw Dan Buchanan. His perfections. His imperfections. She let her fingers do what they'd ached to do for months, and run through his hair. It was as perfect as she'd hoped. She felt one of his hands slip to the small of her back and pull her in closer, nudging her into the nooks and crannies of his body so perfectly it was as if they'd been made for one another. As she'd dreamt, they fitted like Lego. And whatever way you put them together they made a whole. When they heard applause, they pulled apart. The airport cargo staff had collected in a semicircle round them and, despite having an appreciation for their loved-up moment, suggested now would be a good time to get a move on as they had to clear the area for the next flight.

As they walked, hand in hand, Gus merrily bimbling along beside her towards the car park, she asked, 'How did you even know I'd be here?'

He lifted up his phone. 'Thea. Who, apart from telling me I was the luckiest man alive for winning your heart, instantly formed a posse of helpers.'

'Aww.' Her heart bashed against her ribcage and she thought about how now, today, she would have absolutely no problem calling Thea one of her best friends. 'She's a softie at heart, isn't she?'

Dan agreed, she was a softie, swiftly adding, 'With a crème brûlée topping.' He went silent for a moment then said, 'She also explained a lot more about Softer Landings. Told me that woman you two were trying to help left an abusive boyfriend, even though I acted like such a caveman.'

Ellie shook her head and protested. 'Oh no. She liked that you acted like a caveman. The part where you stepped in to help Thea when no one else did. She said seeing that made her realise what she wanted in a relationship.'

'But what about after when I—' He scrubbed the back of his neck and pulled a face.

'She was gone by then,' Ellie explained. 'All she'd seen was you stepping in to help. So . . . technically, I owe you a fee.'

He gave her a *thanks but no thanks* grin, then rubbed his thumb along the back of her hand. 'I had a couple of long talks with Sadie as well.'

'Oh?'

'She thinks very highly of you.'

'Oh?' That was a surprise.

'Yup. She said I'd be the biggest idiot she knew if I didn't get over myself and get on a plane.' He looked down at Gus. 'It was my idea to bring along the support team.'

'Good call,' said Ellie, her nerves beginning to feel a bit less shredded than they had before.

Dan being here felt like a miracle, but they still had to talk about reality. His life, her business, Gus. How those three things would – if they could – work together.

'Fancy a bit of a drive?' she asked when they reached the car park.

'Your wish,' Dan said, 'my command.'

If only it were that simple. Ellie bleeped open her mum's sky-blue Mokka. As Dan put his bag in the boot, Gus took instant advantage of the space in the back seat to stretch out, and before the hatchback was closed, began snoring. Without a destination in mind, Ellie began driving, pointing things out, answering Dan's questions – most of which involved how old things were. She ended up driving to the west coast of the island, where there were ruins of an old castle. 'Super-old,' she said when Dan ogled the ruins. 'Fourteenth century.'

He clutched his hands to his heart. 'Can you imagine how many love stories this building has seen?'

She wondered if that's what he thought they were. A love story.

For the first time since he'd arrived, she allowed herself to believe in the possibility that this was a beginning. An entirely new one. They spread out an old picnic blanket they'd found in the back of the car and talked for ages. Dan said he'd been shell-shocked by all of the revelations at the park That Day, but, a couple of days later, Sadie had returned from Nigeria and knocked some sense into him. She'd told him everything. How Ellie had refused. Had left countless messages begging Sadie to reconsider. He'd even called Thea to get confirmation.

'Wow.' Ellie stared at the ground. 'You really didn't believe me, did you?'

'No, it wasn't that.' Dan crooked a finger under her chin so that he could look in her eyes. 'Well, it was partly that. I was taking it the wrong kind of personal.'

'How do you mean?'

'Being set up like that.' He held up his hands. 'Even though I know you did it with my best intentions at heart and that you hadn't been given the full story . . . When I thought everything I believed you felt for me had been an illusion . . . it killed me.'

Ellie grimaced.

'Being conned like that—' He stopped and rephrased. 'Being steered in a different direction without my knowledge highlighted all of my biggest fears after the accident. Shone a spotlight on all of the reasons I clung to Sadie even though I knew it wasn't right.' Dan shot her a grin that was sad, but self-effacing. 'I went through it all. How can anyone love me when I look like this? Maybe being with someone who was there is better than trying to get someone else to understand. And, of course, I asked myself over and over how anyone as perfect as Ellie Shaw could ever love a man who had a fling with someone he knew wasn't right for him, dumped his dog on her, disappeared, then came back into her life, hoping against hope she could love him, only to screw it up again when all she was trying to do was her best by him?'

If humans could melt into puddles of soppy love punch, Ellie would've done it. Right here beside him. But she didn't. She stayed whole and, to her surprise, felt stronger, better able to look forward towards a shared future. As long as . . .

'What do you think about Softer Landings now?'

Dan pulled a face. 'Well . . . I definitely hope to never, ever be one of the clients again.'

She laughed and then, more seriously, said, 'I believe in what we do there.'

Dan nodded. 'Are you still thinking of getting that degree in relationship counselling?'

'More than ever!' she said and, unable to stop herself, began telling him about how she'd had a couple of really great talks with Vee and Mallory. A lot of the observations they had made made sense. Getting seasoned relationship counsellors as staff members. More therapy dogs. Poets.

'Poets?'

'For the text dumps,' she explained. 'I mean, I think I'm pretty good at it and Thea has quite a flair for it, but if we go national? We're going to need to up our game. *Roses are red, violets are blue, you might be for me but I'm not for you* isn't exactly the best way to give someone a gentle shove, is it?'

Dan laughed and pulled her close to him. 'It should bug me that you want to break up people for a living, but that's not it really, is it?'

She pulled back and looked at him. 'No. It isn't.'

'Well . . . based on where my Softer Landing placed me . . .' He held his arm out and pulled Gus into a big old group hug. 'I would say you could consider me a very, very happy customer.'

'Would you leave a review?' Ellie asked, a cheeky smile teasing at her lips.

'How about this?' Dan murmured, closing the space between them and showing her, once again, just how life changing a solitary kiss could be.

Chapter Thirty-Five

Two Years Later

'Gus! Stay still.' Thea finally managed to secure the buttonhole to Gus's collar and then, with shaking fingers, the ring boxes.

She sat back on her heels, admired her handiwork, then threw her arms around him. 'You are so freaking gorgeous! If Ellie is too busy snogging her new husband later, I might steal you away tonight.'

Ellie gasped in horror. 'Never!'

'Stop moving,' Simon snipped. 'I'm doing the eyes. When you marry an ophthalmologist, it's very important he sees that your soul is smokin' hot.'

Ellie grinned. 'You are loving your new job, aren't you?'

'I'm pretty sure MAC owe the bulk of their profits to *moi* this year,' he said smugly. 'Selfridges may have to up their ante, though . . .' He pulled a face for her to mimic as he swept her lashes with mascara. 'A friend of a friend from the Media Angels days thinks they can get me a gig on a horror film.'

'No, Simone! I forbid it. You may never leave Selfridges,' Thea instructed firmly. 'I live for your free samples alone.'

Simon made an appreciative noise, but kept his eyes on Ellie's as he teased her bridal face into the land of make-up magic. 'A girl's gotta do . . .'

'Would they let you have a dog at work?' Ellie asked Thea.

Thea stood up and straightened her dress. 'I don't know. Maybe, if he was a PAT dog like Gussy. I suppose I could get a handbag one and smuggle it in. Call it an emotional-support guinea pig or something.' She wandered over to the chair where Ellie was sitting and sighed. 'So pretty.'

'Are you talking about me or Ellie?' Simon smirked.

'You, obviously. Faux-father of the bride.'

Simon grinned. 'Yes. Well, I just feel sorry for Ellie that she's going to be overshadowed by yours truly as we walk down the aisle.'

Ellie tried to turn and look, but Simon tutted and forbade her to until he was finished. 'Back to Thea . . . Do you think you actually need an emotional support dog?'

The question was a leading one and they all knew it. The day after they'd returned from Jersey, Thea had left Media Angels and asked Ellie for part-time-only work with Softer Landings. After dabbling in a few different posts, she'd finally taken a job as a call handler at an STD hotline. The pay was pants, the phone calls were all horrific, but she seemed to be thriving off it. 'I'm pretty good, actually.' She gave Gus's head a loving stroke. 'That's not to say having someone to cuddle at night would be a bad thing.'

Ellie took her hand and gave it a squeeze. She loved this version of Thea. She still looked like the same *don't touch me* hipster she'd first met, but there was something softer about her. Something more approachable. The *Thou Shalt Not Have Actual Feelings* force fields had been taken down and, at long last, her smile was that of a genuinely happy person.

Thea ohmigawded. 'I forgot to say, did you know that Mallory and Jasper are out there in the audience, or whatever you call it, and that they came . . .' She paused for dramatic effect. '. . . together?'

'Jasper from the Flower and Tun Jasper?' Simon asked and then, as he thought about it, smiled. 'Yeah. They'd make a nice couple.'

Aurora popped her head into the room. 'Dan's here!'

Ellie's heart rate accelerated. This was really happening.

'Are you ready to look?' Simon asked after a couple final tweaks.

Ellie turned around, a bit nervous because he had been working on her for quite some time. She needn't have worried. Knowing she wasn't one for a heavily made-up look, he'd somehow achieved completely natural perfection.

'One hundred per cent amazing,' Thea sighed as they all gazed at her.

When she rounded the corner, past the giraffes, beyond the penguins and now, just beyond the chimpanzee enclosure, rows and rows of guests turned to look at her as she made her grand entrance, with Simon shaking almost as much as she was. She beamed at everyone. Mallory and Jasper. Vee, Topaz, Lara and a host of others from the Media Angels gang. The newer staff who had joined her as Softer Landings grew and grew. Sadie and her guy – a dead ringer for Val Kilmer back in the day. Aurora and Chris and their new little bubba. Dan's parents – both sets, with Marlene swiping some invisible speck off Yves' immaculate suit, and Shelley, beaming at her as if she'd organised the whole thing herself. Ellie's mum and her new beau, a really lovely fishmonger called Harley. But mostly she had eyes for Dan. Her light. Her life. Her one true love who, even though it had been a bumpy ride, had been waiting for her all along. The End.

ACKNOWLEDGEMENTS

It may take a village to raise a child, but it takes just the perfect bubble to inspire a book during a global pandemic and I was lucky enough to be in such a bubble.

First and foremost, thanks go to Chantal, without whom I would never have led break-up coaching sessions. The fact you listened to this book chapter by chapter, dog walk by dog walk, and are still looking forward to reading it in hard copy thrills me to no end. Gratitude and thanks to the rest of the outdoor distanced yoga/brunch posse: Annie, Stormy, JP, Andy, James, Anne and Jeanne. You all brought your own bits of stardust to the weeks in which I was writing this book and beyond, and to you I send a glittery rainbow's worth of *om shantis*.

A huge thank-you to my editor, Victoria Pepe, whose tingly fingers led her to write an email to my agent asking if she could champion this book. (Yes! Yes! The answer is yes!) Another big juicy dollop of thanks to Salma Begum, whose editorial nous and cheerleading were most happily received. Ditto to Melissa and Sarah who literally ensured my i's were dotted and my t's were crossed. To my agent, Jo Bell, without whom Victoria would have never seen this book. Thank you for your encouragement and sage professional advice.

For the early reads and daily email vitamins, I thank you, Cressida McLaughlin. You're sunbeams and joy, and I'm so happy we are friends. Likewise to Pam Brooks, Christine Brookes, Alex Hutchinson and Nicolette Heaton. You were amazing for reading those rough drafts and lifting my spirits throughout. For being friends and cheerleaders, I would ride a mechanical bull with you anywhere, Michelle Kem, Lisa Martinez and Samia Staehle.

A very weird thank-you to all of the men who've dumped me. I've learnt something from each of you. Possibly unpleasant lessons (mostly unpleasant lessons) . . . but most of all you taught me what I didn't want from life and what I did (see last sentence).

A huge, fluffy thank-you goes to Harris the Wonderdog. He came to us one week before lockdown as a skinny little street dog and is now a big, fluffy beast who bears a remarkable resemblance to Gus.

From the very depths of my heart, a gigumbous thank you to Norman, without whom I don't know if I'd ever have finished a solitary book. You are the sunshine of my life and, even though you're Scottish, you're also my American Dan.

And, of course, a huge thank-you to you, the readers, without whom my husband would most likely go insane as I would be doing endless sock puppet shows for him instead of writing. Please do reach out. It'd be great to hear from you. Sx

ABOUT THE AUTHOR

Sheila McClure lives in the English countryside with her Scottish husband, their dogs, Harris and Skye, and a small herd of delightfully striped Belted Galloway cattle. Prior to rural life in the UK, she was a camerawoman and news producer for Associated Press. As she's originally from Seattle, she began her working life as a barista. She will never refuse a quality dill pickle.